THE
ENEMY
OF GOD

Midlothian Libraries

901154554   3

THE
ENEMY
OF GOD

ROBERT DALEY

AN OTTO PENZLER BOOK

Quercus

First published in Great Britain in 2006 by

Quercus
46 Dorset Street
London
W1U 7NB

Published by arrangement with Harcourt, Inc

A CIP catalogue record for this book is available
from the British Library
ISBN (HB) 1 905204 08 6
ISBN (TPB) 1 905204 09 4

Printed and bound in Great Britain

10 9 8 7 6 5 4 3 2 1

THE
ENEMY
OF GOD

THE INVESTIGATION

———

1

THE OFFICE OF THE CHIEF MEDICAL EXAMINER — the city's principal morgue — is at 520 First Avenue. After getting out of his car,
Chief Driscoll hesitates, unwilling to face what he knows is ahead
of him. He glances at his driver, at his car with its bristling aerials,
at traffic passing in the street. Finally he goes into the building.

The waiting room is distinguished from other waiting rooms he
knows, his dentist's for instance, principally by the boxes of Kleenex,
their tongues sticking out, that stand on all the end tables, the coffee tables too. There are people on one of the sofas even now, both
sniffling, an old woman and a younger one, perhaps her daughter.
He flashes his shield at the receptionist, whom he does not know,
goes past the snifflers and through the door at the end of the room.

Downstairs is the business level of this place. He knows where he
is going. He does not need a guide. His shoes ring cheerfully on the
steps, and the sound seems to him obscene. To his left now is a wall
of stainless steel doors to the refrigerated lockers, 126 doors, someone
told him once. It takes no great imagination to visualize what lies behind them: nudes on trays with tags on their toes. Men, women, children, white, black, brown — former people of all ages and kinds,
none of them personal to him. Against the opposite wall rise stacks
of the cheap wooden coffins most of them will eventually be nailed
into.

He tries to get his thoughts off himself, off his grief, off what he is here for. This place is like a store, he tells himself. The lockers contain the inventory, so to speak. The coffins are the eventual packaging. Above the lockers, as if attesting to the freshness of the goods, a digital thermometer monitors the refrigeration inside, its figures flickering between 33 and 35 degrees. The corpses are kept just above freezing. When their turn comes in the autopsy room no one wants them to blunt any knives.

Chief Driscoll is 53 years old, and if he were in uniform there would be three stars on his shoulders. In a 30,000-man department only one cop outranks him, plus the commissioner and his deputies, all of whom are civilians. Driscoll is stocky, baldish, heavier than he once was. He likes to smoke cigars. By the end of the day his clothes tend to smell of them. If a man's career is like a railroad line, then this morgue, for him, has been a regular stop for 30 years. He witnessed his first autopsy when still a patrolman. He has witnessed dozens, but the one coming up he never wanted to see.

He goes through the door into the autopsy lab. White tile walls, and a row of eight stainless steel dissection tables with naked stiffs stretched out on most of them, either waiting their turn or being actively worked on by men in white coats and rubber aprons.

The table he wants is the third one along. Two pathologists, one of whom he has met before, watch him approach.

"Gabe," says the man he knows, offering his hand, "we've been waiting for you, as your secretary requested."

Driscoll, who cannot remember the man's name, nods.

"Now that you're so high and mighty, we don't see you here anymore. Congratulations, by the way."

In New York the world of street detectives is delimited by corpses. Gabe Driscoll was a street detective for most of his career, meaning a student of death, and each unexplained corpse that he was obliged to investigate brought him to this room to watch the autopsy and to ask questions that the official report, when he received it later, possibly would not answer. But now, as commander of several of the department's most sensitive units, including Internal Affairs, he has risen to a level where he is no longer concerned with what happens on these tables. Until today.

"This is Dr. Paget."

Driscoll shakes hands with Paget.

The corpse on the table is scrupulously clean, but looking at it makes Driscoll wince. Jagged white bone protrudes from the no longer bloody thigh. The broken jaw gives the face a rather wry grin. A disarticulated shoulder lies six inches lower and at a different angle than it should be. The back of the skull is caved in, as are some ribs on the right side. The x-rays would most likely show other damage as well.

"He doesn't look too bad for a jumper," says the pathologist.

"Maybe it was a car crash," says Driscoll.

"You're kidding me."

Driscoll remembers that the man's name is Levin.

"A jumper," says Dr. Levin. "Can't be anything else. Fourth floor I would guess. Am I right?"

Driscoll has a detective's distaste for people who jump to conclusions before the evidence is in. Forced to reply, he says: "I don't know. I haven't seen the building yet. I came here first."

"A free-falling body accelerates at the rate of thirty-two feet per second per second, did you know that? You must have studied it in physics class."

Driscoll never studied it until he became a cop.

"Newton's Law," Dr. Levin says. "From the fourth floor your speed when you hit is not too bad. About thirty-five miles an hour."

Gabe Driscoll does not like the image this presents. The man on the table, alive, in the air, flailing.

"Any higher up he'd look much worse," says Dr. Paget.

"You better believe it," says Levin, who begins to expound on Newton's Law, and how it relates to jumpers.

"Not a bad way to go," says Paget. "Can't get much quicker in fact."

They are joking about it.

Pathologists working on corpses are almost always lighthearted, and sometimes funny. Presumably it is how they stay sane, and in the past, at this table or another, Driscoll himself has contributed a joke or two. But in the presence of this corpse here he cannot bear to listen to jocular comments. So he interrupts. "I'm in a bit of a hurry, Dr. Levin. I'd appreciate it if we could get started."

Levin seems to feel he has been rebuked. For a moment his fingers toy with his tools. He has a number of them laid out, scalpels, bone saws, loppers that could take the branch off a tree. Tools uglier than corpses, Driscoll thinks.

A microphone hangs over the table. Levin turns it on and begins to dictate what will be, once it is typed up, the official autopsy report: "Body is that of a well-developed white male about fifty years old—"

"Fifty-three."

"Oh," says Levin, switching off the mike, "you knew him."

Driscoll nods.

"And that's why you're here. How do you know him? What was he, a cop?"

"A priest. Father Redmond. Frank Redmond."

"Catholic priest?"

"What other kind is there?"

"Priests don't normally jump off roofs. It's against their religion."

"We don't know yet what happened."

"I don't think I've ever worked on one."

Driscoll says: "Can I ask you to look for signs indicating a struggle?"

"Foul play, you mean. Someone pushed him off, threw him off. Murder not suicide. External trauma compatible with a life-and-death struggle. That what you want me to find?"

"I want to know what happened."

"He was a friend?"

"Yes."

"Close friend?"

"Yes."

"I see."

Levin doesn't see at all. Grief is a private emotion. Driscoll can't share it with Levin, or with anyone.

The pathologist moves his tools around. "What did he land on?"

"Part of the stoop, the sidewalk."

"You want to know about lacerations, surface hematoma, something of that nature. It's difficult to tell. The landing would have covered it up, whatever it is."

"No stab wounds, bullet wounds? Nothing like that?"

"He's got three broken teeth on the left side. But the fall could have done that."

"You can't be sure?"

"No."

Dr. Paget hands Levin a scalpel. "Height six feet three inches tall," Levin says into the microphone. "Scale weight 202 pounds, obvious visible trauma include compound fracture right femur—" Again switching off, he says to Driscoll: "He was a big guy."

"Yes."

"Nice musculature."

"He worked out regularly."

"It shows."

"He was a priest. He was such a decent man."

Levin makes the Y-shaped incision into the abdominal cavity.

Driscoll says: "Any abnormalities you might find in there, I want to know about that too. Maybe he was dying of cancer, or some goddam thing. If he jumped, which I don't believe, maybe that's why."

Levin's scalpel moves up and down. He dictates. From time to time Paget hands him other tools. Bones crack.

"You all right, Gabe?"

"Just do your job."

"You don't look so good."

In Driscoll's earliest memory Frank Redmond had been as naked as this. Driscoll also. They were 14 years old and trying out for the Fordham Prep swimming team along with other boys their age. They had been ordered up onto adjacent blocks in the Fordham pool on the Rose Hill campus. The chamber was barely heated, the air felt frigid. The water, they knew, would be colder still, and it looked rough down there. Naked and shivering they waited for the coach, who was also their algebra teacher, to blow his whistle and send them plunging in to swim twenty laps. Swimming that year had been considered a minor sport. By the time Frank Redmond, Gabe Driscoll, and the others graduated they were the best in the city and the stars of the school.

Levin has begun to extract Frank's internal organs. Each is weighed and the weight read into the microphone. The liver weighs so much, the kidneys, the heart. Driscoll, who cannot bear to watch, stares at the floor.

"He seems to have been in pretty good shape internally as well," Levin comments, "near as I can tell. Liver is fine."

"He rarely drank."

"Of course we can't be sure until the lab work comes back."

Driscoll remembers, more or less, how Frankie's body looked that first day. Smooth hairless skin pulled taut over a boy's pointy bones: the clavicle, ribs, knees all prominent. Still almost a baby, he himself the same. Not a surgical mark on either of them.

And now this.

By the start of the following season, both having sprouted pubic hair, they had looked with disdain at younger boys waiting their turn to swim. "Look at those babies," Frankie had remarked one day. "If we could sell them a tonic that would grow hair on their balls we could make a fortune." There was always something raunchy about Frankie. He used to bring salacious poems to school. When he decided on the priesthood it greatly surprised Gabe Driscoll, who had never figured him for piety.

Nor for an end like this either.

Levin goes on cutting, weighing, dictating until the abdominal cavity is almost empty. "Not much blood left in him," he remarks.

"He was lying in a pool of it," Gabe manages to say.

"That makes sense." Levin goes in with a soup ladle and scoops out what there is.

Making an intermastoid incision across the scalp the pathologist peels the skin down over the face. Frankie's wry grin becomes a leer, then disappears. Again Driscoll stares at the floor. Levin picks up a Skilsaw. Driscoll hears him saw off the top of the ruined skull. Having removed what is left of Frankie's brain, he weighs it, and sets it aside.

"You sure you're all right, Gabe?"

"Fine." He feels Levin looking at him.

"You really don't look so good."

"I said I was fine."

"You could wait outside. I can bring the report to you outside."

"Just finish the goddam job."

"You didn't used to be as squeamish as this."

It didn't used to be Frankie on the table either.

When the autopsy ends Driscoll must stand out on the stoop for a time trying to catch his breath. He feels he is suffocating. He can't get enough air. His driver, standing beside the car, watches him curiously.

But Chief Driscoll's day is not over. An almost equally unpleasant job comes next. While being driven uptown he studies the checklist attached to his clipboard. He has already made many calls. Undertaker, cemetery, flowers, and headstone have all been crossed off the list, but not the funeral itself, which is still up in the air. Monsignor Malachy, Frank Redmond's pastor, has decided on his own authority that the dead priest was a suicide, and has refused to allow him a mass of Christian burial or to be buried from the church he served.

On the phone the pastor had sounded adamant. None of Gabe Driscoll's arguments changed his mind. In the first conversation the detective chief attempted to talk patiently. By the end of the second it was all he could do to keep from screaming.

Frank's church is St. Ambrose on 148th Street in Harlem, located about two blocks from the patch of sidewalk where he was loaded into a body bag. The parish is small in numbers of faithful for in Harlem there are many denominations, some operating out of storefronts. The St. Ambrose parochial school has been closed for some years. Lately there have been only the two priests, Frank and the pastor. There must have been more once.

A cleaning woman or housekeeper or whatever she is shows Gabe Driscoll into the parlor, where he waits staring out through dirty curtains to the street. Finally Monsignor Malachy enters, cassock swaying.

"I'm afraid you've wasted your time coming up here," the pastor begins. "That man is not going to be buried from my church."

He is short, a bit stout. His cassock does not look clean. Its red piping denotes his monsignorial rank. He looks to be about 60, and speaks with a faint Irish brogue. "Canon law is firm on the subject. According to doctrine, suicide is the one unforgivable sin. You're a Catholic, are you not?"

Chief Driscoll nods.

"So you already know that. You also know that the Catholic Church cannot condone suicide, or seem to condone it. Suicide is a sin against the Holy Ghost."

Driscoll remembers hearing these arguments at Fordham Prep and later, and at the time believed them himself. They are arguments that as a grown man he has come to scorn. Much of Catholic doctrine he has come to scorn, as well as priests like this one.

"Suicide is the worst of all sins because it denies God's final grace."

"We don't know yet whether it was suicide or murder," Driscoll interrupts.

"One of your detectives was here. He says suicide."

"I don't think he could have said that."

"Suicide seems clear to me, and it's what I must act on."

"There's no way my detective could know yet. The investigation is just starting."

"Suicide. Nothing could be more obvious."

"Or somebody pushed him or threw him off that roof. Killed him."

"Suicide," the pastor says. "The unforgivable sin."

"I've just come from the autopsy. He had three teeth knocked out. That's consistent with a terrific fight. Somebody hit him with something and threw him over."

The pastor shakes his head.

"Here is the preliminary autopsy report." Driscoll holds out the pages.

"I don't need to look at that, and I won't."

"This is a tough neighborhood you live in, Monsignor. Frank was out in the street at all hours, I'm told. Some people called him the missionary to the junkies. Any one of those people could have killed him."

"I'm not going to listen to any more nonsense on the subject. You're not going to change my mind."

"All right," says Driscoll. "Assume for a moment that suicide is what it is. In recent years the Church has become more reasonable, a bit more Christian, you might say." His words sound stilted to him. He is virtually making a speech, but it is one that has to be made.

"The Church now accepts the possibility that a man who has killed himself is so distraught as to be counted insane, unable to tell right from wrong. And therefore still entitled to a Catholic funeral."

The pastor is again decisively shaking his head.

Driscoll's voice rises. "Frank Redmond was a Catholic priest, for Christ's sake."

"Don't take the Lord's name in this house."

"A Catholic funeral is what he would have wanted. And I'm here to see that he gets it."

"He was a bad priest," the pastor says, and his voice too has begun to rise. "I could have predicted this is how he would end up."

"A bad priest?"

"He did not care about doctrine. Listening to him preach you were listening to heresies, one after the other. He condoned artificial contraception, for instance."

"Refused to preach the party line on birth control. What else?"

"Ignored the teaching of the Holy Father in Rome. He believed that a marriage sanctified before God could be dissolved by divorce. He condoned heinous sins."

Having turned away, Chief Driscoll has begun contemplating part of the wall.

"Man had other problems too. Of an amorous nature. Do I make myself clear? I couldn't control him. He couldn't control himself. Yes, he was out on the street at all hours, but not always on Church business. I asked the Chancery to remove him. They said they would, but it wasn't done. Not in time, it wasn't."

Driscoll's voice goes low, menacing: "I've arranged for a priest from Fordham, one of Frank's former teachers, one of mine as well, to come in here and say the mass. I also talked to the auxiliary bishop to whom you report." The detective chooses his words with exaggerated care. "Bishop Ahern, his name is. He is sending up an order that the funeral is to take place. He did not like the sound of

what you are doing, trying to do, with regard to the funeral, so perhaps there will be a letter of reprimand along with it. The funeral is
tomorrow at noon."

"Funerals in my church are at ten A.M."

"Noon, so as to give his parishioners a chance to get there. Now
are you going to make the arrangements, or do I go back to Bishop
Ahern?"

Driscoll heads for the door. He is amazed at the intensity of his
feeling. His mouth seems clogged with venom. At the door he turns
snarling. "It's because of men like you that people are leaving the
Church. I hope you know that."

In his car he draws a line through the word "funeral," after which
his grief comes down hard once again. He has only one more job
left to do.

TROY SITS IN A HOTEL ROOM IN WASHINGTON trying to write for tomorrow's paper. His column appears three times a week on the Op-
Ed page. Some days he writes it as fast as he can type. Other days
are like this one. So far he has managed only his byline:

By Andrew L. Troy

Since then an hour has gone by. He has sat studying his own
name, or paced the small room, or stared out the window smoking,
all the while waiting for something to happen in his head. But nothing has happened, the words are not there, do not come. He imagines he knows why. He is trying to write about the senior senator
from Texas whom he interviewed that morning and whose views he
despises. The man himself he despises, but he can't say so in print.
A columnist like Troy is in many ways a law unto himself. He can
lay his opinions out for all to read. It is thought by people who do
not know that he can write anything he pleases. But he can't. There
are rules even for columnists. The senior senator from Texas is an

elected official, and his office must be respected, if not the man himself.

Troy has spent his entire career on this paper, working his way up from copyboy to reporter to foreign correspondent—he reported from Vietnam during part of the war there, afterward living nine more years abroad, heading the paper's bureaus in Berlin, South Africa, and finally Moscow. Hating Moscow, his wife went back to America after the first winter, taking their two daughters with her. He stayed on alone, and won a Pulitzer Prize for his reports on Kremlin intrigue during the war in Afghanistan, which he also covered. He was named a columnist shortly after.

He lives now in New York, insofar as he lives anywhere. He travels the world, almost always alone, for his wife and daughters no longer wish to accompany him. Next week he expects to be in Lebanon, and from there will go to India, Thailand, and Hong Kong. He has come to Washington this week to arrange briefings from State Department contacts, chiefly the men manning the various foreign desks. When he gets to where he is going he needs to know who holds power and how much, and which problems preoccupy each country. He needs to know who to try to see, and which questions to ask.

He has, in addition, interviewed American politicians earlier this week, particularly congressmen and senators with seats on the two foreign relations committees. He has asked his questions while concealing his distaste for the men across the table from him. He sees them as smarmy, venal men, bland and arrogant at the same time. He sees politicians as men without principle, their only object to get reelected, and become rich. Every one of them will sell his vote to the highest bidder, and describe whatever comes in as a campaign contribution. They are men who pay for nothing and would be surprised if anyone asked them to. Lobbyists pay, or journalists, or rich constituents, or they charge it to their campaigns. They never consider themselves dishonorable men. Troy's own code, a remnant of his Jesuit upbringing, is strict. If he behaved like any one of them he would not be able to live with himself.

The typewriter on the desk is an Olivetti portable. There is something a bit staid about Troy. He tends to adhere to the old values. His paper went over to the new computers a year or so ago, but Troy himself did not. This typewriter is good enough for him, and his fingers know how to work it. He intends to hold out as long as he can.

Now he sits down and types out a lead paragraph, but after staring at it a moment, gets up and paces again. He takes his glasses off and rubs his eyes.

The telephone rings, and it is Gabe Driscoll.

"I've been trying to reach you. Don't you ever call in for messages?"

Most often the paper has only a vague idea where Troy is, and he keeps it that way. When on the road he works out of hotel rooms, not the paper's bureaus. He sees this as necessary to maintain his independence. Editors who can't find a man can't lean on him. His wife seldom knows where he is either, and in recent years has not seemed to care. The downside is that Troy lives a lonely, isolated life. He meets regularly with world leaders, so called, but in his free time has no one.

Troy says: "How's Barbara?"

Barbara is Driscoll's wife, who suffers from Parkinson's disease, and can no longer walk unaided. "About the same," Driscoll says.

"And the boys?"

"They're fine."

Troy waits to hear the purpose of the call. Even for a detective like Gabe Driscoll, running him down in Washington could not have been easy.

Driscoll says: "Are you coming to the funeral?"

"What funeral?"

"Frank Redmond."

"Frankie?"

"I left messages for you."

A stricken silence. "Frankie?"

"I've made most of the arrangements. I'd like you to be there. I need you there."

"Heart attack?"

"No, he went off a roof."

"A roof?"

"You're named as an executor in his will. So am I."

"Somebody killed him, pushed him off."

"Or he got tired of living and jumped."

"This is Frankie you're talking about."

"Yeah."

"It's impossible."

"When you've been a cop a long time what you learn is, nothing is impossible."

Troy says: "I hadn't seen him in a while."

"Funeral's tomorrow."

"I guess I haven't seen anyone in a while."

"You coming or not?"

"I have an interview with President Reagan tomorrow."

"You can't put it off?"

"Do you know how long I've been waiting for this interview?"

After what Troy senses is a disappointed silence, Driscoll says: "Reagan's senile, I heard."

"I'll let you know after tomorrow."

There is a second silence before Troy says gently: "The reason you go to funerals is not for the deceased. It's to show support for the grieving relatives. Frankie didn't have any relatives, and he himself won't know if I'm not there."

"The only grieving survivors are you and me."

"Yes, I suppose so."

"I was hoping you'd be there. It's been tough to go through alone."

"When and where is the funeral? I'll try to get there. I'll get to the cemetery at least. I'll try to get to both."

When he has hung up Troy phones his wife in New York, and tells her about the funeral. He asks her to attend.

"Where will you be?"

"I'm not sure I can get there in time. I have an interview with the president."

Troy wants the interview badly, for it will prove — again — both to his readers and his bosses that he is big enough to demand and be accorded an exclusive interview in the Oval Office. On the day the column appears his prestige, already high, will go higher. But he must get to Frankie's funeral too. In his head he has begun rearranging his schedule.

His wife says: "You should be at the funeral."

"I'll get there if I possibly can."

"Your place is at the funeral."

"I've been waiting weeks for this interview."

"Cancel it."

"I want you to go in case something goes wrong. As my representative."

"I'll be there. I'll be representing myself."

This causes silence at both ends of the phone.

"Your place is at the funeral," Maureen Troy says again.

"I'm almost sure I can get there. I'll see you there."

"I can't wait," says Maureen Troy.

After another silence, both hang up.

AT THE WHITE HOUSE THE NEXT MORNING Troy sits in an anteroom waiting for President Reagan, who is in the last year of his second term, to get around to seeing him. The journalist drums his fingers on his knee, swills coffee he doesn't want, and can't get his mind off

Frank Redmond. Frank's smile. How physically big he was. When Troy and his typewriter first got to Vietnam Frank was already there, a Marine Corps chaplain. They met whenever they could, and several times got shelled and shot at together. The world called Troy a world traveler, but when he got to Africa during the time of Apartheid Frank was there already too, a missionary living in a hut on the Zambezi River.

A press officer enters the anteroom. "The president will see you now," he announces.

Troy has waited 35 minutes past his scheduled appointment. He is furious. He may miss his plane and the funeral. He is reminded of still another reason he despises pols. They are never on time. It never occurs to them that other people might have pressing business apart from them.

The press aide escorts Troy into the Oval Office. The president gets up from the big desk and comes halfway across the room to shake hands, his greeting as effusive as if they are best friends. A White House steward in a white jacket materializes, and Troy is offered more coffee he doesn't want.

The three men sit down in armchairs, for the press aide is staying for the interview, it seems. Troy switches on his tape recorder and the press aide does likewise. This gives the president deniability if the interviewer, Troy in this case, should try something funny with the quotes.

As Troy brings forth his questions the president's actor's smile, the one the country seems to be in love with, is out in full force, and Troy, looking into it, imagines he might eventually describe it for a paragraph or two if, as is probable, the man says nothing newsworthy during the next half hour.

Sometimes government officials use an interview like this one to make an official announcement. A policy change of some kind. But not today. This president only wants to be friendly. Troy is so conscious of the minutes passing that he cannot concentrate on his questions.

Frank Redmond was worth ten of you, he thinks.

Abruptly he gets to his feet, cutting the interview short. He thanks the president for his courtesy and walks out.

He has a car waiting, but as he runs out from under the White House portico and yanks open its door a hard rain is falling. The traffic on the bridge is backed up solid. It takes 30 minutes to cross. At Washington National he finds all flights delayed. He drinks still more unwanted coffee while remembering Frank. When Troy's marriage started to go bad, Frank was the one he wanted to talk to. They sat in a bar for hours drinking beer while Troy poured out his aching heart. Frank didn't have any answers for him. He also did not offer pious inanities. He just listened. He was a beautiful listener. At the end he apologized that he had never been married, that maybe if he had been he could help, would know what to say. But in fact he had helped so much.

Troy's flight is delayed still again. This means he is not going to make it even to the cemetery. He pictures Gabe Driscoll standing more or less alone over an open grave with this same rain pelting down. There will be police photographers present, if he knows Gabe. They would have been at the funeral too. They will be standing some distance away, photographing every face. In terms of photographers Frank's farewell will resemble a Mafia don's, no different, for Gabe is an exact kind of guy, and afterward he will scrutinize the photos. If Frank was pushed or thrown off that roof, maybe whoever did it showed up to watch the ceremonies.

Will Barbara Driscoll be at Gabe's side? She moves about in a wheelchair now, would have to be pushed to the graveside over muddy ground, so he supposes not. Maureen Troy will probably be there, but not himself. There will be one or two of Frankie's fellow priests, probably. Frankie's Harlem parish is of course poor and few people have cars. So there won't be many parishioners.

Good-bye, Frankie, Troy thinks. I'm sorry, Gabe, he thinks. I wish I could have been there for you both.

THE NEXT MORNING TROY AND DRISCOLL meet on West 146th Street in Harlem, outside a four-story brownstone that, when built a hundred or so years ago, must have been the last word in elegance. Now it is a tenement. The steps of the stoop are half broken away, and one of the wrought-iron balustrades is missing.

Driscoll leads the way into the building and up the narrow staircase four flights to the door to the roof, where he pulls out a key.

"It was in his pocket," he explains.

They go out onto the roof.

The roof is flat, the surface tar paper, and it is taller by eight or ten feet than every other roof on the street. Except for that, one might walk from one corner to the next by stepping over low parapets.

"He used to write to me," Troy says, "particularly when I was in Moscow. He was always up on these rooftops apparently, looking for junkies he could help. Or else just sitting under the stars trying to feel close to God."

"Was that the way he put it?"

"Yes, trying to feel close to God. On the nights that it worked it was a sublime experience, apparently. So he said."

"I wonder what he really believed."

"Do you still go to mass, Gabe?"

"No. Not in years. And you?"

"No."

After a silence, Chief Driscoll says: "I don't think there were often junkies on this particular roof. It was kept locked, I'm told."

"That key of yours means nothing," Troy says. "Anybody could have had a key. Or could have got up here from one of the other buildings in the row, and lain in wait for him."

"Yes, it's possible."

They walk to the front of the roof where the parapet is no more than two feet high.

"Here's where he went over," Gabe Driscoll says, pointing.

"He could even have fallen off by accident, a parapet as low as that. I just don't believe he jumped."

"He used to give us—me, I mean—information on dangerous criminals in the precinct. Over the years it resulted in some good arrests, even once a promotion for me."

"You never told me."

"He didn't want me to. He was a modest guy. He didn't want to be considered a hero."

"That's your answer." Troy peers over the parapet. "One of those people threw him off."

"There was no sign of a struggle up here." Driscoll glances around as if looking for one.

"The guy surprised him. Someone he knew."

"Maybe."

Troy looks at him. "What about internal abnormalities?"

"No."

They hear doves or pigeons cooing. Walking back, they peer behind the door-housing at stacks of cages containing pigeons, ten or more cages stacked one on top of the other. Nearby is a ten-gallon can that, when Troy pries off the lid, turns out to be birdseed.

"Frankie's?" Troy inquires, pointing to the cages.

"I don't think so."

"I never heard of him being interested in birds."

"No."

"Somebody's been up here feeding them though. Who?"

"It's a kid, we think. Keershawn Brown. He's about seventeen. We're trying to find him."

"So he had a key too?"

"I guess so."

"He pushed Frankie off the roof. Or somebody did."

"Maybe."

"Nobody loved life more than Frank. It's inconceivable that he would do away with himself."

Driscoll says: "I'm trying to keep an open mind. But I'm like you. I can't really believe that Frank could do such a thing."

"But what?"

"Trouble is, there's no evidence to the contrary."

"Actually, there's no evidence either way, from what you tell me."

Downstairs on the sidewalk, they stand beside Chief Driscoll's department car.

"Another thing that idiot monsignor said—I wasn't going to tell you, but perhaps I should. He said Frank had trouble with women."

"Do you believe that?"

"I don't know."

"More probably," the journalist says, "he was like all these priests. They cozy up to any housewife who'll invite them to a home-cooked meal once in a while."

Driscoll laughs. "You're a cynical bastard, aren't you?"

Troy looks pensive. "What did the monsignor say exactly? How did he phrase it?"

"He said Frankie had problems of an amorous nature."

"He didn't mention women specifically?"

"Come to think of it, no."

"You know what that could mean?"

"Horseshit," says Gabe Driscoll, "absolutely not."

After a pause, Troy says: "How many detectives are working the case?"

"Two. And they're not shining lights either one of them. Furthermore, people clam up in front of detectives. Especially people in precincts like this one."

"Put more on."

"I can't. It doesn't demand more. I'd be severely criticized. There are no suspects, no evidence as yet. And it isn't my jurisdiction anyway. I'd have to ask colleagues to assign men, because detectives assigned to me work only against cops who have gone bad. They don't work murder cases."

Troy looks off down the street. It resembles many other New York residential streets except that the once-noble brownstones have become tenements, their stoops broken, their walls streaked with graffiti. And there are few white faces on the sidewalks, or going by in cars.

Driscoll says: "I'd like your help. You can ask questions detectives can't ask, or wouldn't think to ask. You can get close to people who won't talk to cops. I want you to find out what was going on in Frank's life. Why was he on that roof? Who might have been on it with him? If it's murder, why? If it's suicide, why?"

Troy gives a wry laugh.

"Did I say something funny?"

"I just realized I've seen almost nothing of him in the past several years. I don't know where to start."

"Lately I haven't seen much of him either," Gabe Driscoll says. "We talked on the phone occasionally. I saw him at John's funeral a few months ago." John is Mr. Small, their former swimming coach and algebra teacher.

"I didn't know John died."

"You live a pretty isolated life, don't you?"

Andy Troy shrugs.

"I'm not asking you for a police investigation. We'll handle that part."

"I've always thought that journalists and detectives are the same," Troy says. "The good ones even to the bravery."

"I'm not asking you to do anything dangerous. You come upon something dangerous you let us investigate it, is that clear?"

"I can give you two weeks," says Troy.

Driscoll looks up at the building, Troy too.

Troy says: "Part of our boyhood went off that roof with him."

"Most of what was left, yes."

"Once there were four of us." He is speaking of their relay team, which dominated the leagues in which they competed in high school and college both.

"Just you and me now."

They gaze at each other, then Driscoll opens the door to his car. "Can I drop you somewhere?"

CHAPTER ONE

FRANK REDMOND WAS THE SON of a beer salesman. He grew up on the fourth floor of a walk-up apartment on Marion Avenue in the Bronx, a predominantly Irish Catholic neighborhood not far from the Fordham campus. He played in the streets, which were safe at that time, with kids whose fathers were often cops or firemen. All four of Frank's grandparents had been born in Ireland before the turn of the century, had been brought to New York as children, and his two grandfathers, who were carpenters, kept their Irish brogues until they died.

At Our Lady of Mercy parochial school the girls were on one side of the building, the boys on the other, and rarely the twain did meet. On the boys' side the parish priests came into the classrooms regularly, proselytizing for the seminary. On the girls' side the nuns probably did the same. The priests nabbed a lot of boys early. Some went away right after grade school, 13 or 14 years old. Before they were out of their teens they had taken their vows. Not Frank. He was a good student, not great, and an eager though unskilled athlete in all sports, and a reliable altar boy. Even when assigned to serve at the earliest masses, he never overslept, and on the altar he never forgot or mangled the Latin responses. When up there serving, wearing the red cassock and white surplice, he always imagined that the congregation was glued to his every move. He felt like an actor, and they watched how well he played his part. He loved wearing the gaudy cassock. He loved the pomp and ceremony of all the church's services, even Benediction on Sunday nights, which most of the other altar boys tried to get out of serving. They considered it boring because there was little for them to do.

After graduation from parochial school, Frank was sent to Fordham Prep. This was a financial stretch for the beer salesman, but there were no free Catholic high schools, and what was important to Frank's parents—to all the parents in the parish—was that their children should continue to be educated in their faith. As he entered Fordham Prep and came under the sway of the Jesuits, Frank was 13 years old, small, skinny, no growth spurt yet, but with very big feet that he might or might not grow into. All his classmates were Catholic, most were of Irish extraction, and most of the rest were the sons of immigrants from Sicily or Calabria.

He had read a great many novels about boys his age, written by Catholic authors whenever possible, and he wanted a high school career such as the ones depicted for these boys. He wanted to be like the heroes of the books. Accordingly, he went out for all the extracurricular activities, including the band, though he knew nothing about music, even the dramatic society, though he had never seen or read a play. He tried out two years in a row, but did not last long with either group either time. He also went out for all the teams, aiming particularly at football and basketball, whose players he considered the real stars of the school. Again he tried two years in a row, but even in sophomore year he wasn't very big, about five feet eight, weight under 125 pounds, and because of his big feet he could not run very fast. His feet made him a bit clumsy as well, and so to his despair he kept getting cut, often only a day or two after tryouts began.

Finally he decided to go out for swimming.

Frankie liked swimming well enough, though at Fordham Prep it was a minor sport, nobody cared about it, no glory there, no maroon and gold uniforms, no uniforms at all.

He had learned to swim at Orchard Beach on Long Island Sound, which is out Fordham Road past the Bronx Zoo and was reachable at that time by trolley car. A number of neighborhood kids would gather nearly every morning in summer, and go out together, either bringing a picnic lunch or buying hot dogs at the concession stands, and would stay all day. The trolley ride cost a nickel, the hot dogs fifteen cents. The water was calm, the sand hot. They would sometimes listen to the voices—Mel Allen from Yankee Stadium, Russ Hodges from the Polo Grounds—calling the afternoon ball games on the radio, and they would not come back until dark. A public beach is not the best place to learn to swim properly, to hone a smooth fast stroke, but it seemed to work for Frank.

At the Prep the swimming season ran from December to March, coinciding with basketball. But basketball games drew crowds of students. A swim meet drew nobody, and at season's end you won only a minor letter to sew on your sweater.

The pool was a barely heated chamber in the basement of the gym, dank, low-ceilinged, cold. In winter the air in there was frigid. The swimmers were naked, and as they waited their turns, Frank among them, they were shivering. The water seemed icy each time they plunged into it, and also rough from the backwash of the five boys who had just climbed out, and from their own racing dives, so that it was impossible to swim very far without swallowing a mouthful.

After a few days the coach and algebra teacher, Mr. Small, seemed pleased with Frankie, and told him, to his relief, that he could stay. He had made the team. He began to practice religiously every day. He swam more laps than the other boys, and he swam them harder. If he couldn't play on the football or basketball teams, at least he would be the best of the swimmers. He had that long, smooth stroke no one had ever taught him, and his specialty became the 220-yard freestyle. For a boy his age, given what little was then known of high-powered training methods, the 220 counted as an endurance race. Frankie could not quite sprint all eight, almost nine, laps, but it turned out that no other kid could either. He could sprint most of them, seven laps, some days more, and his rivals could not stay with him.

Now a strange thing happened. The football team that fall had lost all but one game, and the basketball team too started a losing streak. The swimmers, meanwhile, had begun to win dual meets. Frankie Redmond was unbeaten in the 220. And then at the end of the season the team won the biggest meet of all, the New York Catholic High Schools Championship, the first time ever for Fordham Prep. Suddenly the swimmers were the toast of the school. The headmaster, Father O'Connell, praised them from the stage during an assembly, the prefect of athletics, Father Dolan, ruled that they had earned major letters, not the dinky minor ones of the past, and the trophies they had won went into the glass case opposite the bulletin board where, shiny and new, they stood beside trophies won by the glorious football and basketball teams of the past, though not by the inglorious present ones.

The first friend Frankie made on the team was Gabe Driscoll, who swam backstroke. Gabe was in his class but not his section and they had not really known each other previously. Gabe lived in Manhattan down on East 90th Street opposite the Ruppert Brewery and almost under the Third Avenue El, which he rode up to the Bronx to school every day. His father was a retired patrolman who had taken a bullet in the groin in a shoot-out and now didn't do much of anything except drink. Gabe didn't think highly of his father or of the police department. He always said that when he grew up he would become something else, would never become a cop in his turn, though eventually that's exactly what he did.

In the way of teenage boys Frankie considered Gabe his best friend, and they were together constantly, most days leaving the campus together after practice and stopping for ice-cream sodas in a drugstore out on Fordham Road before parting almost reluctantly, as Gabe went up the stairs to the El to go home.

But Frankie was almost equally close to two other boys, Andy Troy, who swam the 50-yard freestyle and who was in Gabe's classroom section, and Earl Finley, the diver, who was in his own. Troy came from Good Shepherd parish at the northern end of Manhattan. He lived in a third-floor apartment on Cooper Street in the Inwood section. This was about two blocks from the end of the line of the 207th Street crosstown trolley, which was how he got to school each day. It took him about half an hour each way. His father was a well-known radio announcer, which probably helped Andy land his first newspaper job later, though he became the famous syndicated columnist on his own.

The diver, Earl Finley, had no father at all. Nobody was sure who paid his school bills, including Earl. His mother had been divorced three times, and she moved about the world with a succession of "companions," leaving the boy behind to fend for himself. Many nights he slept on the floor in Andy's bedroom, or Frankie's or Gabe's. His mother's conduct was considered highly immoral at the time, not to mention damaging to her son, and Finley, who later became the best-known—some said the most notorious—prosecutor in the city, was deeply ashamed of her. He was a blond, blue-eyed boy with extravagantly bowed legs. When he stood up straight there was an eight- or ten-inch gap between his knees. This should have cost him points in a diving competition scored according to elegance and beauty, but his deformity was so awkward and so pronounced that judges seemed to make allowances for it and for him. He had learned the rudiments of diving from a gymnastics instructor at the

YMCA next door to the apartment in which he lived with his mother when she was around, alone when she was not. He was a fierce competitor and a nerveless inventor of new dives. He learned to do a cutaway two-and-a-half somersault, tuck position, off the low board—for a boy, incredible. Also dangerous. He learned to do a full twisting one-and-a-half—at his age, equally incredible. He did these dives precisely, smoothly, no jerking, with a smooth entry despite his bowed legs, and his results would be multiplied each time by the high degree of difficulty accorded such dives, which no other boy could do at all.

The final event on each program was always the 200-yard freestyle relay, which was weighted to give more points than the individual events, and was therefore the important climax—and these four boys, Frankie, Andy, Gabe, and Earl, constituted the Prep's relay team. Andy Troy led off, followed by Earl, then Gabe, with Frankie swimming the anchor leg. They depended on each other, and together they won race after race. They were too strong for everybody.

The radio announcer, who apparently made good money, owned a summer cottage on a lake north of the city, which was where Andy had spent his summers for years. Now, as soon as school let out, Earl Finley and Gabe Driscoll pitched a tent in the woods in back of the cottage and there they lived through July, through August, Gabe wanting to get away from his abusive father, Earl because his mother was summering in Europe somewhere, and he didn't want to be alone in New York. Together with Andy, the boys helped Mr. Troy with chores when he was there, and otherwise passed the days swimming, fishing, and paddling around in the Troys' canoe. Mrs. Troy fed them all without complaint, two extra teenage boys at her table every night eating like wolves, although occasionally Gabe and Earl became embarrassed and told her they weren't hungry, on which nights they would dine in front of their tent on Campbell's soups out of the can. Frankie Redmond had a job that summer selling peanuts

at the Polo Grounds and Yankee Stadium, but would come up by
train whenever there was an open date.

School started again, the football team was as bad as the year before, and Frank Redmond and his pals waited impatiently for the
swimming season to begin. On the first day of practice Coach Small
clocked Frankie in the 220, and to the astonishment of everybody the
stopwatch showed him eight seconds faster than the year before. The
explanation must be, Frankie thought, that his form had improved
over the summer. This seemed to him mysterious, for he had spent
most of his time at the ballparks and hadn't even swum very much.
The true explanation would not occur to him until years later: that
he had simply grown. In the previous few months he had added four
inches in height and gained twelve pounds.

That season he won all his races easily, at times by half the length
of the pool.

Having added to his repertoire new and even more difficult dives,
Earl Finley won by margins just as large. Much of the time Gabe
Driscoll and Andy Troy won their races also, and in the freestyle relay
the four boys were untouchable. Other teammates always scored
points here and there as well, and after winning twelve straight dual
meets, the team competed in the championships of the three leagues
to which Fordham Prep belonged — the Jesuit High Schools, the Private High Schools, and the Catholic High Schools — and won the
team titles in them all.

But this year there was to be something new, the National
Catholic Interscholastic Championships in Philadelphia, which Fordham Prep had never entered before, an event that would mark all of
them more than they knew, not only that year but for a long time to
come.

There were ten boys on the team. Mr. Small called them all together and announced not only that he had decided to enter them
in the Nationals, but that he thought they could win not only a

number of individual events but the team championship as well. He was rubbing his hands together, and on his face he wore a quiet, confident smile.

So at the end of this winning season there was to be a different climax. The climax of climaxes in fact. The Nationals. It was both unexpected, and daunting. Only Mr. Small looked happy. He had brought them this far and now they would crown his coaching career. They were the ones, however, who would have to win the races.

They practiced hard all week. In class Frankie hardly heard a word for he was busy trying to think up the strongest possible lineup for the Nationals. Latin class. Religion class. He heard nothing. Instead he made lists of the various events. He kept writing names in beside each event, and then erasing them and writing in others. At recess he would run out into the hall with his latest lineup and find Mr. Small.

"What do you think of this, Mr. Small?" Small, who had nine children of his own, was a bald, fat man about 45. He would take the sheet of paper from Frankie's eager hands, shove it into his pocket without looking at it, tousle the boy's hair, and send him back to class.

Early Saturday morning they met at Penn Station, ten boys and an algebra teacher. Outside it had begun to snow. Mr. Small had money from the headmaster to buy the tickets. They boarded the train. For 90 miles Frankie looked out the window, watched the falling snow, and worried about the meet. This was the Nationals. If every boy swam his best they might win it. Could they possibly win it? Possibly become national champions?

The meet was to be held at the Pennsylvania University pool, which had bleachers for many spectators, none of whom, Frankie worried, would be rooting for them. Eighteen schools were entered. They came from as far away as Chicago and St. Louis, he learned. How good were the teams from out there? Probably very good. Only the best would have bothered to make the trip.

All afternoon there were heats. Frankie went on worrying. Gabe won his heat in the backstroke, but was only third fastest overall. Andy Troy was the sixth and last qualifier in the fifty. After the compulsory dives Earl Finley was ten points behind a boy from St. Mary's of Pittsburgh. The judges didn't know Earl and perhaps had been surprised by his bowed legs. Perhaps they had focused on that instead of how well he dived. In the 220 Frankie won his heat easily, and when the other clockings were posted saw that no one was within four seconds of him. In the 200-yard freestyle relay they swam their fastest time ever but qualified only second. North Catholic High of Philadelphia was faster.

They all got dressed. Outside, everything was white, snow was still coming down, and on the sidewalk was ankle deep. They trudged several blocks to the University cafeteria. Inside they stomped their shoes, shook the snow off their coats, and sat down to dinner. But no one was hungry. They were too worried. Mr. Small railed at them that they had to eat, and finally most of them forced food down. The conversation was entirely about the meet. They kept counting up their own possible points and then the possible points of the two or three other strongest teams, one of them North Catholic. North Catholic seemed the team to beat.

They went back inside the hothouse that was the pool, where they stood around in their tank suits and beach robes waiting, worrying. The bleachers filled up. There was more noise than in any pool in which they had ever swum. The place had become an arena, and it scared them.

The finals began. As feared, North Catholic began to pile up points, winning the medley relay, the fifty, the hundred, 22 points already. Gabe got second in the backstroke, and in the fifty Andy Troy fought his way up from sixth place to third. Other Prep swimmers chipped in with a point here, two points there. Frankie won the 220 with ease but was not impressed with himself. He had known all day he would win. He had always been a modest, selfless boy, which was probably what led him toward the priesthood later. His own triumph was not important to him. It was the team victory that counted. He had just won not a gold medal, but a trophy, the first he had ever won, and it would look swell on his dresser in his room, but it was no good unless all his teammates shared in it. He wanted them to be able to call themselves national champions.

The series of optional dives began. Slowly Earl Finley cut into the big lead of the boy from Pittsburgh. Between dives Earl sat beside the boy and worked on him. The other boy's signature dive was the cut-away two-and-a-half. A dangerous dive, Earl told him. Such a dangerous dive. How had he learned it, had he ever hurt himself? Earl would never dare try such a dangerous dive himself, he said, for he had known boys who had tried it. One of them had struck his face on the board on the way down. It had mashed his entire nose into his head. The reconstructive facial surgery had lasted nine months, the boy still didn't look the same, and of course he could no longer dive.

The two-and-a-half cutaway by the boy from Pittsburgh was announced. He stepped to the end of the board, spun around to face the way he had come, steadied himself, and then flung himself far enough backward to be sure of missing the board. He flung himself too far, so that he was unable to complete the two-and-a-half somersaults in time. As he struck the water he was still partially tucked, so that he threw up a tremendous splash. His scores were all fours and fives, and he dropped to fourth place. Now leading the event, Earl had only to complete an easy dive to win. Instead he announced his own two-and-a-half cutaway, and stepped up onto the board and stood poised at the end of it, feet together, bowed knees as far apart as ever. The crowd was hushed. He launched himself into the dive. One somersault, two, and then the half. He entered the water cleanly, almost no splash at all. He had performed a nearly perfect dive and was rewarded by the judges with eights and nines.

In team points Fordham Prep and North Catholic were now tied, 22 points each.

The freestyle relay, the final event on the program, was announced. This one race would decide which school had won the national championship. The four Prep boys trooped to the end of the pool where they stripped off their robes, tightened the strings of their silk tank suits, then clasped their hands together and prayed. When the prayer was finished, they blessed themselves, and Andy Troy stepped up onto the starting block, where he stood shaking out his arms, trying to become loose. The other three boys were talking to him, encouraging him, reaching out to touch him, pat him. At this point in his life, the future Pulitzer Prize winner was already six feet tall but weighed only about 135 pounds. Nice long length, girth to come later.

The starter raised his pistol. "Swimmers, take your marks."

Toes clenched on the edge of the block, Andy leaned out over the pool. To either side of him, the five other boys who would race the first leg had done likewise.

The gun went off.

Andy flailed his way down the pool. Beside him, separated only by the floating lane marker, was the North Catholic boy who had won the hundred earlier, but Andy stayed with him, made a clean flip turn at the wall, and came back, gaining a bit, finishing half a yard in front, even as Earl Finley sailed out over his head. Earl was the slowest of the four boys, but nerveless, heart beating no faster than normal, knowing at each moment exactly what point he had reached in the pool. Nor did the weight of the occasion, the national championship in the balance, affect him in the slightest. The diving champion hit his turn squarely, his second lap was as fast as his first — he held the slight advantage all the way to the wall — and when his hand smacked the tiles and he looked up Gabe Driscoll was long since in the air out over the pool.

Gabe was a nervous boy, perhaps because when he went home each day he never knew what he would find. Sometimes he found his father in a chair contemplating the ex-service revolver in his lap, as if any minute he planned to put it in his mouth and pull the trigger. This was frightening enough. Other times Gabe found his mother in tears with new bruises showing on her arms and face, compliments of the ex-cop. In the past often enough his father had hit Gabe too, though the boy was getting too big now, and could fend him off if he tried anything.

Gabe knew how important it was for him to give Frankie a decent lead, two or three feet at least, for North Catholic's anchorman had already won the fifty, was obviously the fastest sprinter in the meet and maybe the country, and Frankie was a 220 man. Frankie couldn't expect to outsprint him. He needed at least three feet if he hoped to beat him home on the final leg.

As a result of these worries Gabe was stroking too fast, and too shallow, almost thrashing. His timing had become disorganized, and then he did not see the far wall coming, did not get ready for it in time, and his head crashed into it. For a moment he floundered, half stunned, then managed a turn and raced back the other way, but now the North Catholic boy was ahead by almost a body length. Gabe fought him the length of the pool but gained back no more than half of what he had lost.

Poised on the starting block, Frankie watched, his entire being focused on this swimming pool, on the humid heat, the slap of the water, the supercharged chlorinated air, on the two boys, arms flashing, coming closer, the North Catholic boy ahead by too much.

Frankie crouched, he curled and uncurled his toes over the mat. He had the best racing dive on the team. All the other boys were envious of it. Nobody could dive as flat and shallow as Frankie. It was nothing anybody ever taught him, he simply did it one day, and then every day thereafter. Now as Gabe touched the wall he launched himself straight out from the block, not cupping his body as some boys did or entering the water at an angle, but reaching far out, then dropping his head between his arms and landing flat with a smack so hard it could be heard in the last row of the grandstand. His body barely broke the plane of the water before he had resurfaced and was stroking fast, not even lifting his head to breathe, pulling with every ounce of strength, his legs beating as fast as a drumroll. He was behind, too far behind, but hoped he might have gained half a second on his racing dive, and could perhaps gain another on the flip turn when he came to the wall, for he had practiced these turns for over a year. He could still win, it was possible, it was all up to him.

He saw the wall coming, his hand grazed it and instantly he flung himself into his turn, a kind of underwater somersault, got his legs folded into position behind him, and gave himself a terrific push off the wall. He risked a glance at the other boy. The water was rough, they themselves had made it rough, he couldn't see much, had to lift his head higher than he wanted — saw he had reached the boy's shoulder with two-thirds of the pool still ahead.

From there to the finish he matched him stroke for stroke, but was able to gain only inches, no more. Some people said afterward that if the race had lasted a few more yards, Frankie would have pulled ahead. But there weren't a few more yards, there weren't any. The two boys struck the wall almost together, but it was clear who had won, no question.

In the locker room Gabe said it was his fault, he was the one who had lost the race, the trophy, the national championship. He had lost for everyone. They kept telling him this wasn't so. They embraced him, until tears came to the eyes of the future tough cop, and then he was weeping. Frankie and Andy were weeping too, but not Earl, who had no home, not much of a mother, and was tougher than they were. Earl had learned most times to get by without help from anyone.

On the midnight train going back to New York the four boys sat in facing seats. Earl and Frankie had their trophies in paper bags on their laps, but neither wanted to take them out and look at them. For tonight at least their own victories meant nothing to them. Mr. Small came by and told them how well they had done, which only caused their chins to quiver again—this time Earl's too—and their eyes once more to fill with tears.

They didn't realize it then, or for many years to come, but losing had bonded them together more firmly than any victory could have done.

Troy wrote an article about the meet for the school paper. He was not a famous journalist yet, he was a 16-year-old boy, so it began exactly as one would expect: "Down in Philadelphia on Saturday, March 26, the gamest, greatest bunch of guys I ever met almost won a national championship."

It went on that way to the end. Not very subtle, not artistic. Somehow, however, Troy conveyed the love he and his teammates had one for the other, which is not easy to do, as well as the cost to them all, the pain of losing, which is not easy to do either.

When the article appeared—"By Andrew L. Troy," for the first time—everyone came by to tell him how good it was, even the teachers. He cut out the clipping, folded it up small, and carried it around in his billfold for months, taking it out from time to time to read it again. From then on he never wanted to be anything except the newspaper reporter he eventually became.

All four of the boys went on to Fordham College. So did Mr. Small, who, based on his success at the Prep, had now been named to coach the college team as well.

But college swimming wasn't the same. For one thing, freshmen could not compete in varsity events, and there were no freshmen events, meaning that the first year was wasted. A whole year of training, of plowing endless times up and down the pool, of mindless,

face-in-the-water laps without any races or competitions to get ready
for. Their next year was wasted for another reason. In New York,
sophomore year coincided with a terrible drought. There was so
little water in the city's reservoirs that the mayor ordered all swimming pools closed. This was silly as the pools, the Fordham pool and
all the others, were already full and the water in them was recircu-
lated. Nonetheless the season was canceled.

With two years of college remaining the former Prep swimmers
went back into training. But the excitement was gone, for the lives
of all four had taken different, more serious turns. They still saw
each other constantly, took certain classes together, met often for
lunch in the cafeteria. But after school they had different priorities.
To pay their tuition bills Gabe Driscoll and Earl Finley had had to
take nearly full-time jobs, Gabe because one day his father had indeed put the revolver in his mouth—Gabe had come home and
found him on the living room floor, his brains on the wall, and had
had to help clean up—and Earl because his mother had married
again. She and her fourth husband had settled down in Monte
Carlo, and she had informed Earl by mail that she could send him
no more money.

Now almost 20 years old, Andy Troy and Frank Redmond no
longer cared for swimming very much either, certainly not in the
same old way. When not in class, Andy spent most of his junior and
senior years writing articles for the college paper. Frank Redmond,
meanwhile, had met a girl. The future priest was in love. He did not
want to spend his afternoons facedown in a swimming pool, he
wanted to be with the girl. He wanted to be with her all the time.

THE INVESTIGATION

2

ANDY TROY IS THIN, SIX FEET FIVE INCHES TALL, with wide shoulders but not much chest, and he carries himself in a bit of a stoop, as if embarrassed by his great height. His face is angular, with a strong push of jaw. He has enormous feet, size 14, and hands to match. He still has all his hair but it is gray. He wears horn-rimmed eyeglasses, the lenses now thicker than they once were.

As he starts his half of the investigation he is troubled. He must work the way he always works, the way most journalists work: He will entertain various suspicions, then follow them as far as they will go.

The word "amorous" is what troubles him. Could Frank Redmond have kept a woman on the side? Knowing Frank, it would be the deepest secret any man ever kept, so how is Troy to find her? A married woman? With a homicidal husband? Or the jealous woman herself? In college, Troy remembers, Frank was not particularly pious, and never talked of becoming a priest. Instead he liked girls, got serious about a certain girl, and said he wanted to marry her. But that ended abruptly, he would never tell his friends why, and he went into the seminary instead. Swore off sex forever at the age of 21. Troy shakes his head at this idea. That anyone would make such a vow at that age. That anyone could stick to it for over 30 years.

The possibility of a male lover must also be examined. This would greatly surprise Troy, but it must be checked out. If Frank had turned gay they were perhaps dealing with a homosexual killing. Frank going to bathhouses, to gay bars? Troy's stomach goes queasy. He can't believe this of Frank, but—

In the course of his career Andy Troy has looked into as many dark corners as Gabe Driscoll or any other cop, and in more countries, met just as many strange people, has often enough watched the inconceivable become commonplace. So anything is possible, Troy tells himself, and who can understand what 32 years of enforced celibacy might do to a man. At bottom, who ever really understands the soul of another? He himself has thrown off the Catholic teaching, and has come to believe that all priests are sexually repressed or perverts or both. Could Frank Redmond have been that much different from his colleagues of the cloth? Until now Troy has never had such thoughts about his childhood pal, has considered him in a separate category among priests, among men. But he realizes he has spent so little time with him in recent years that he can't be sure what he might have become. In prisons, after years of being penned up, pent up, hardened convicts turn to contacts with each other. Some do. Maybe most do. Troy knows this from articles he has researched and written. The sex drive in men is that strong. Priests too are penned up, in a way. They too must get pent up. Then what?

As a newsman Troy is paid to be cynical—in this respect he does not differ much from cops like Gabe Driscoll. Unfortunately, cynicism has become the dominant quality in Troy's life, and in his head. Everyone has something to hide, he believes. Everything must be checked out. He will check this notion out too, and go on from there.

Did the priest still swim? That was the place to start.

The nearest pool to Frank's church is the YMCA on 135th Street, but as Troy goes inside and glances critically around he decides he will find nothing here. The Frank Redmond he has known since childhood was too fastidious a man to be comfortable in a place like this one. Troy spends 20 minutes in the halls and locker room, and talks to a number of people. They know about the dead neighborhood priest, but none has seen him use the pool here, that they remember, has ever seen him at all.

At Troy's second stop, the Columbia University pool, he does better, and is annoyed with himself for not coming here first. The Columbia pool is not only close, only a few blocks away, but it is a place that once meant a good deal to Frank and would have attracted him immediately. For it was here at age 15 that he won his first city championship. Troy remembers the day, and Frankie's face when he climbed out of the water after the race. His principal emotion was astonishment that he had won. He had never dreamed he was that good.

Of course this pool is where he would have come.

Troy stands on the tiles and watches boys swimming laps. He listens to the muffled slaps of the water, he breathes in the moist, chlorinated air. For him it is the odor of many pools, many yesterdays. It evokes more memories than he can sort out, and a barefoot man in a gray sweat suit, with a whistle around his neck, comes over to him, smiles, and says: "Can I help you?"

The swimming coach, obviously.

Troy introduces himself.

"Jim Cronin," says the coach, and they shake hands. Troy remarks that he used to race in this pool years and years ago, and so had his friend Father Redmond, who has recently died.

"I know about Father Redmond," Cronin says. "So sad."

"Frank and I swam on the same relay team. I swam the first leg and he was the anchorman. Nobody could beat us. We won the Citys two years in a row in this pool."

Cronin blows his whistle. After ordering several boys out of the pool, and several others in, he comes back.

"You must have seen Frank every day, if he came in here as regularly as I think he did," Troy says, and watches for a reaction.

"Nearly every day. That's how I knew him. Came in about ten A.M. most days. Before practice started. He'd do his thirty or forty laps, whatever, then go into the weight room and do a program of lifting. Then he'd take a shower, comb his hair, and leave."

"You never talked to him?"

"Oh, we'd gab from time to time."

"How did he seem to you?"

"He had a smooth, pretty stroke. What was he, about fifty? Half my kids he could have beaten even now."

"No, I mean apart from swimming. Did he seem troubled?"

"He seemed healthy, cheerful. What can I say?" And then, after a pause: "Why did the—the thing that happened—happen?"

"That's what I'm trying to find out."

They watch the swimmers for a time. "I need to know who his friends were," Troy says. "Did you ever see him with anyone?"

"No. He was always alone. I have the feeling he was a lonely man."

Troy asks the next question because it seems to him it must be asked. "Could he have been gay?"

The coach's eyebrows go up. "If he was I'd be surprised. After so many years here I can pick the gays out pretty quick. Nothing against them, you understand. I certainly never saw any of that in Father Redmond."

When the coach leaves him, Troy sits down in the bleachers and broods, while sleek teenage boys churn the lanes to froth, and he is conscious again of the noise they make, and of the moist chlorine odor, and for a time he remembers when he and Frankie were that young, and among them, and life seemed more vivid than now.

CHAPTER TWO

FRANK HAD SCARCELY KNOWN ANY GIRLS BEFORE, which was not surprising. Because he had never gone to school with girls there was no selection to choose from, and he had no ease with the few he did meet and felt himself drawn to. After nerving himself up to make the necessary telephone call, he had managed to invite several of these to the movies, or a school dance. Twice he had developed crushes that were not, however, returned. These romances had never got beyond good-night kisses — which in the early '50s was not so rare. He had certainly never been in love.

Her name was Roxanne Harley, and she seemed to him, as is the case at that age, perhaps at all ages, perfection. She was a year younger, meaning very young when it started, not much older when it ended. She had a sweet face. On the first day he saw her, and on the days immediately following as well, she wore only a black swimsuit, or else a white one. Though not bikinis they clung to her, especially when wet, and would have entranced almost any teenage boy, not just Frank, who was aware from the beginning not only of her looks and personality, but also of her body as showcased in those swimsuits. When finally he saw her at night wearing a dress and high heels, he was surprised.

She was called Rocky, which seemed to him inappropriate. Such a harsh name for such a delicious girl. Gabe, Andy, and Earl came to know her well, for he took her to a barbecue early on so they could meet her, and once school started up again he took her to the Fall Fling and, later, to the Senior Prom. At both dances the four boys and their dates had a table.

Because Frank talked about her a good deal, the other boys were able to follow the romance every step of the way. Almost every step of the way.

He met her at the Glen Garry Country Club in Larchmont, a rich man's club in one of the rich suburbs north of the city. He had gone there to apply for a summer job as one of the lifeguards at the club pool.

Actually, he first met her father, a tall, thin, austere man, who interviewed him for the job at ten o'clock in the morning in the empty club dining room while other boys waited their turn outside.

The dining room looked huge to Frank. The tables were already set, so that the sun bouncing off so much whiteness, so much silverware, seemed blinding. A ski slope of tablecloths. Mr. Harley offered no handshake or greeting. He was neither friendly nor unfriendly. He invited Frank to sit down in that explosion of light which, to the boy, was an explosion of luxury as well.

It was a Saturday morning. Nonetheless, Mr. Harley wore a formal business suit, his collar looked starched, and the tie at his throat was somber. He had gray hair that was formally combed, and the formality with which the interview started did not change that day or ever. He was, Frank learned later, president of Korvette's, a department store chain whose headquarters were in New York, and which would go bankrupt some years later, forcing him into personal bankruptcy too. As one of the directors of the club, it was his job this day to interview prospective lifeguards. Frank was intimidated by Harley from the first, and remained so during all the months that the romance with his daughter lasted.

The interview endured about ten minutes, during which Mr.

Harley displayed no warmth or humor, and never smiled, though at the end he did hire him.

The Harleys lived in a big English Tudor house on Glen Garry Lane overlooking the golf course. A mansion to Frank, when he first saw it. Steep slate roofs, leaded windows, impeccable garden. He was in this house often enough in the next months, having come to fetch Rocky. Usually he was left in the entrance hall to wait for her to come downstairs. He never saw much of the house from the inside, beyond what showed of the living and dining rooms to either side. He was never invited to dinner, never invited even to sit down while he waited. The girl's mother was pleasant enough to him, but Harley usually just nodded, then went through into another part of the house.

Another detail Frank learned later, and it would prove important. The Harleys were a churchgoing family, and Harley himself was an elder of the local Presbyterian church. He attended services regularly, and made his family—there was a younger son in addition to Rocky—do likewise.

After surviving the interview with Harley, Frank wanted to see the pool. He could have walked around the building, but the direct route was through the men's locker room. He had been in many locker rooms but this one surprised him, for it seemed luxurious beyond any other. Instead of an open shower room there were individual glass stalls. Opposite was a row of sinks, and on the shelf above them stood a dozen or more combs and brushes, plus bottles of every hair tonic he had ever heard of, and some he hadn't. In the corners were piles and piles of fresh towels, and he came upon two attendants working on members' golf shoes, one cleaning the dirt out of spikes, the other buffing the uppers to a shine.

He nodded to the two men, as if to prove he had a right to be there at all, then went past them and out to the pool, and it was there he saw Rocky for the first time.

It was late May, the pool was not yet officially open, she was the only one in it, and he watched her swim to the ladder and as she climbed up and out he watched the water sluice off her. It seemed to caress her body. A black bathing cap hid her hair but framed her face. She had the face, he thought, of a Madonna. Dripping, she mounted the diving board, took three brisk forward steps, bounced into the air, and performed a forward one-and-a-half somersault, pike position, coming out of it and slicing into the water well in time. Frank, who of course knew dives and diving, was extremely impressed.

The scene, the scenery, then repeated itself. She did the same dive again, and then again. A serious practice session, he realized. She wasn't just playing at fancy dives.

As she began a series of back one-and-a-halfs he moved forward a bit, close enough for her to become aware of him, which seemed like permission to move closer still, so he did.

Once more she climbed out of the pool, and picked up her towel, but now he was standing nearby, waiting for the opportunity to speak — when the towel came away from her face, perhaps. He thought that if he praised her diving this would be a good way to start, but when she unexpectedly smiled at him, he botched his lines.

"You're a beautiful diver," he said. "I mean the dives are beautiful, not you. I mean you're beautiful too, of course you are, but the dives —"

Already she was disturbing him in profound ways.

"My father won't be happy unless I get into the Olympics, which is crazy. I'm not nearly good enough."

"You could be. I mean, if you keep at it." What a stupid thing to say, he thought, and frowned. Got any more inane comments like that one, he asked himself.

"Yeah, if I practice ten hours a day. That's what my father wants me to do, and that's what it would take, practically. And even then —"

She peeled the bathing cap off and shook out her hair. It was wet anyway—he found he wanted to wring the water out of it for her. Amid the freckles on the flat of her upper chest sparkled beads of wet—he wanted to lick them off. He was amazed at the intensity of his feelings. Worse, he was in danger of becoming speechless. Knowing he must say something, he offered: "I'm one of the new lifeguards. This man Mr. Harley just hired me."

"That's my father," she said.

"Oh." The silence that followed seemed to call for another inane comment, so Frank made it. "He seemed like a nice guy."

"You don't know him."

She sat down on one end of a bench, so he took the other, not too close, about a foot away. The right distance, he judged.

It took a moment for the conversation to start up again. When it did, they told each other their names. She had been diving since she was ten, she said. Her father's idea. He paid for the lessons, drove her to lessons two winters in a row, entered her in competitions in which she rarely did her best and rarely won, which made her father furious.

"Some people are good in competition." She laughed. "They have nerves of steel. I guess I have nerves of spaghetti."

She was twisting her towel, not looking at him, whereas his eyes were fixed on the girl herself, on her face, on the rather fleshy lips that all this new information was coming from. The sun was drying her skin. Only a few drops glittered still on her arms.

The conversation continued. Where they went to college and what they were studying. She was already home for the summer, having completed sophomore year, whereas he still had finals to take.

That they were attracted to each other would have been obvious to anyone watching. They were aware of it themselves, or thought they were, though by no means certain as yet that the other was experiencing anything similar. In each other's presence both felt suddenly, physically different. Felt some precious tingling of all the surfaces of the skin. Nature makes this happen, and makes it known to the participants as well. For these two love was perhaps in the air, but could not be grasped as yet, and so neither dared make any forward step. Love, if it was to occur, was important, was rare every time at whatever age. But to reach it a good many banalities had to be got through first. She said she attended Beale College for women, which, though he was to visit her there several times, he had never heard of. She told him where it was—in Aurora, New York, up in the Finger Lakes region, near Cornell. The town overlooked Lake Cayuga. The Cornell guys came up from Ithaca on weekends and hazed them. What a bunch of jerks.

She said: "Fordham is Catholic, isn't it?"

"Yes."

"Are you Catholic?"

"Yes. Are you?"

"Presbyterian."

The warning bells went off in his head. Any of his Jesuit teachers would have warned him now not to get involved with a non-Catholic girl. Often enough in classrooms in the past, he had been so warned, had he not? An eventual mixed marriage, although tolerated by the Church under certain circumstances, barely tolerated, was a terrible idea and was to be avoided at almost any cost. One risked losing one's faith. And except as a step toward marriage, there was no point to seeing a girl regularly, especially a Protestant girl, at all.

So he heard the warning bells clearly, but he had not done anything yet, and did not want to listen.

He looked at the surface of the pool, which was now smooth and flat, not a ripple on it.

She said: "I know a boy from your school, Ray Rooney."

Rooney was the No. 2 backstroker behind Gabe Driscoll. "Ray's the reason I'm here," said Frank. "He's the one told me you were hiring lifeguards."

"I've dated him a few times."

For Frank this remark set off a second set of warning bells. The word "date" did not at that time have the sexual connotations it came to have later, nor did the word "girlfriend." But in Frank's circles they were serious words. If she was Rooney's girlfriend, then he himself had to step back. He could not betray his teammate Rooney.

The voice behind Frank was loud, curt, and piercing. "Rocky," it said, "I thought you were supposed to be practicing." Frank turned and saw Mr. Harley. Still in his suit and starched shirt, he had come out of the locker room as far as the far end of the pool.

"Yes, Daddy."

To Frank, she said: "I have to practice." She tugged her bathing cap back on, moved quickly to the diving board, and sprang up onto it.

"Young man," called Harley, "I suggest you let her concentrate on her diving."

"Yes sir."

After nodding at the girl, who gave him back a half smile, Frank went through the opening in the fence and crossed the grass in front of the golf shop. He looked back only once, saw her do only one dive. A few minutes later he left the club.

HE STARTED WORK ON MEMORIAL DAY WEEKEND, which was one of the hottest on record, the pool crowded all day, many grown-ups but hundreds of kids. Small ones who swam uncertainly, rambunctious bigger ones running up and down the pool apron, wrestling each other in on top of swimmers. He had to watch closely. He had to blow his whistle a lot. He wore a kind of undershirt with LIFEGUARD written on it, and sunglasses, and a New York Giants baseball cap — the Giants did not depart for San Francisco for two more years.

Late in the day he ran into Ray Rooney in the locker room. Frank was still wearing his LIFEGUARD shirt. Rooney had come in from a round of golf. Frank thanked him for getting him the job, then brought the conversation around to Rocky. He had seen her diving. She was a fine diver.

"She's a great girl," Rooney said. "We're going steady."

Well, thought Frank, that ends that. For him she was definitely off limits.

A week later Rooney threw a house party, to which he invited Frank, saying, "Bring someone, if you like."

But Frank had no girl to bring. He went anyway.

The Rooney family lived in a big house with no other houses too close. There were flower beds, lawns, a pool — the usual setup thereabouts. It looked sumptuous to Frank, who had not yet seen the Harley house, which was even more so.

The party spilled out onto a flagstone terrace. About 20 young people had been invited, all friends from the country club except Frank. He knew no one present beyond Ray and Rocky. There were stacks of sandwiches on a table, a cooler of beer and soda, and music from records that kept dropping onto the turntable.

At first there was aimless movement and equally aimless conversation. Boys and girls flitted here and there. Sandwiches were handed around. It was still light out. Nobody knew very well what to do. Later the night got quite dark. By then the dancing had started. Frank danced several times with Rocky while Rooney, who sat in a wrought-iron chair nursing a beer, glowered at him. He tried to steer Rocky in Ray's direction, planning to hand her over, but she resisted. So he held her in his arms a bit longer, her cheek against his. Such proximity to her, he knew, was temporary. It was a torment to him as well. Such sweet torment.

For a while he watched Ray dance with her.

But that record ended, and in the time it took another to drop she came toward him. As the next song began she came into his arms already swaying to the beat.

"Ray tells everybody I'm going steady with him."

"Is it true?"

He was aware of his sweaty hand holding her dry one, of his other hand on her back. He could feel her breath on his ear. He was no longer aware of the music, or of anything else.

"I'm not going steady with anyone."

"Oh."

"He did ask me the other day."

He held her, remembered to move her this way and that.

"What did you tell him?"

She smiled. "I told him no thank you, that he was getting much too serious."

Frank thought he would have to mull this over. What were his obligations now?

All this time Rooney's parents were present in the house, apparently, but discreetly out of sight until about eleven P.M., when Mr. Rooney's head appeared in an upstairs window and he called out: "Turn the music down a bit, kids." By then most of the beer was gone, several boys looked drunk, and several couples were missing, had disappeared into dark corners of the garden. A little after that somebody pushed one of the girls into the swimming pool. When they had fished her out her ruined dress hung as shapelessly as her hair and she was crying.

Frank thought he should leave. He said good night to one or two people he had talked to during the evening. He thanked Ray for the party, and said good night to Rocky.

"Do you have to go?" said Rocky.

"Yes, it's late."

It was time to go back to the Bronx. He went out through the garden. He couldn't see much, but it smelled of flowers, of fresh-cut grass, and of the night. His car was parked in front. He had recently become the owner of a ten-year-old Oldsmobile with a hole in the muffler, and more than 100,000 miles on the clock. He thought he would have it paid off by the end of the summer. He looked up at the Rooneys' dark, looming house, then got into the car. The engine started right away—it didn't always—and he drove back to where he had come from.

HE SAW ROCKY NEARLY EVERY DAY, but the pool was so crowded he did not have much time to talk to her. Then in the evenings, the light beginning to fail, she would come to the pool again, usually accompanied by her father, for a practice session that would last half an hour, sometimes longer. If she was alone he would stay to watch. If her father was there he would leave, for it was clear Mr. Harley did not want him there. Her father knew nothing about diving, Frank decided. He could not give her tips. All he could do was make her practice.

As part of Glen Garry's Fourth of July festivities, Earl came to the club. He had worked up an act that summer and was taking it from one club to another to earn tuition money. It was Frank who had recommended him to Mr. Harley and others. To preserve Earl's amateur status, the checks were always made out to Fordham, not to himself; otherwise the Amateur Athletic Union would have banned him from any future competition. Scheduled that day were a barbecue, fireworks, and then a dance, all following Earl's exhibition off the high board. The first part of his act was pure comedy; he wore funny costumes, he played roles. At one moment he was a drunk who in his drunkenness climbs up onto the high board imagining himself a diver. Next he became a blind man with a stick tapping his way off the board into the void. He would sometimes strike the water pedaling, or in a belly flop. Other times he would convert the awkward, frantic fall into a perfect dive. He made an excellent clown. The second part of his act was classical diving. The crowd loved him, especially the children.

Frank introduced him to Rocky, making him the first of his friends to meet her. From then on, whenever he wanted to talk about her, or sing her praises, he sought out Earl. He told Earl everything she said, everything they did together. Almost everything. Later that summer, together with whatever girl Earl was interested in at the time, they went on many double dates together. Earl obviously liked Rocky, but he showed no romantic interest in her. Not then.

That first night, following the conclusion of Earl's diving exhibition, when the people had left the pool area, when most were waiting outside the dining room for the barbecue to begin, most of them swilling gin and tonics, some of them getting drunk, Earl dived with her, gave her tips on how to speed up her somersaults, her twists. She picked up the new tricks very quickly, but was not comfortable with them. Earl seemed much taken by her, but saw at once, he told Frank, that she did not really love diving as he did, she only did it because, having learned it, she was supposed to.

At the barbecue a band played, and an entire lamb turned roasting on a spit. The three of them sat together on wrought-iron chairs at a big wrought-iron table. But soon they were joined by Ray Rooney, and then by some others. When the dancing started Rocky danced with Frank and with Earl but not with Ray, who did not ask her but only sat drinking cans of beer while staring at her in sullen silence.

Presently there were five empty cans in front of Ray, who abruptly stood up from the table. "Come on, Rocky, I'll drive you home."

It was by then quite late. "Frank's taking me home," she said, "aren't you, Frank?"

He required a moment to reply. He glanced from Ray to Rocky and back again. Rocky smiled at him; Ray's face was hard. This

annoyed him, and the last of his scruples disappeared. "I'd be glad
to take you home," he said.

"Have it your way," snarled Ray, and strode off.

Frank and Rocky left shortly after. She got into his car and slid
across the seat until she was close to him. He pushed the starter button hoping the car would start. It did, and they left the club parking
lot and soon were parked in front of Rocky's big house.

The garden lights were on, shining upward into the trees, illumi-
nating also the path to the front door. The small amount of light that
fell into the car fell on the planes of her young face. She was beautiful to him, and they began kissing.

The kissing lasted 30 minutes, perhaps more. It was interrupted
each time a car went by in the lane. They would feel the approaching headlights on the backs of their heads and would split apart. As
soon as darkness reclaimed the lane they would start again.

Many nights that summer ended similarly, and some of the days.
They went to movies together, to an outdoor concert, to parties at
friends' houses. One evening, when most of the foursomes had completed their rounds, they went for a walk on the golf course. Frank
had known nothing about golf courses and he found this one, seen
for the first time in the company of this girl, unimaginably beautiful. Unimaginably luxurious too, the sculptured greens, the great
trees standing guard over the fairways. Frank wanted to be successful enough in life to belong to this club, to learn golf and play 18
holes every weekend out here on this course. When they were far
out with no one in sight, he hugged Rocky tight and kissed her, and
one kiss led to another.

All this was kissing only, called necking at the time. Kid stuff, so far.
It would not stay kid stuff long. In a later age, when morality had
changed, or rather people's idea of morality, the kid stuff might have
ended already. But at that time, temporarily at least, they had reached
the limit of what both of them considered permissible, though certain

adults imagined, or feared, they were doing more. Once when they were parked outside her house in the night a Larchmont cop whose habit it was to prey on young couples in such situations sneaked up on the car from behind, and from one second to the next came the beam of a powerful flashlight. They were bathed in it. The light disclosed no disarranged clothing, nothing. The cop must have been disappointed. They themselves were scared, particularly Rocky, who imagined such a man might have a relationship with her father, and might tell on her.

Another night they were kissing each other good night in the hallway just inside her front door. This always required several kisses, in the middle of which came the voice of her father from the top of the stairs:

"Rocky!"

"Yes, Daddy."

Frank was out the door in an instant, proof again that nothing untoward had been interrupted.

One night he told her he loved her. He had never said this to a girl before. Tears came to her eyes, why he never knew. She told him the same. That night or the next they began talking of marriage. Of course they would have to wait until both had finished college. Another two years, because Rocky was a year behind him. And until Frank had a job. What he would really like to become, he said, was a teacher, and help people and do good in the world. But teachers got paid very little, he knew, so the idea wasn't practical. Therefore he thought he might try for the advertising business, he told her. Plenty of money there, and he would need enough to support a family, namely her and their children. He thought he'd like to have about six kids. Rocky laughed and said two would be fine with her. She was thinking of becoming a nurse, she said. She could work as a nurse before her children came, and again after they had left home.

Neither had much of an idea of what life was, much less what marriage was, so talk like this was kid stuff also, but soon it had an edge to it, as Frank began urging her to take instruction in the Catholic Church. She said she didn't think so. He said he wanted them to be together in all things, especially in important things like religion. She was happy being a Presbyterian, she said. And — and —

"And what?"

She laughed. "My father would have a hemorrhage."

"No he wouldn't."

She shook her head. "It would kill him."

She was religious too, in her way. But her way was different from his way. He felt the need to convert her. He was at this time a normal young Catholic bigot. It was what he had been taught to be, and it was what he was. If he could convert her their marriage would surely work. They would live happily ever after.

HE GREW EVER MORE ENAMORED. He loved everything he had found out about her. There was hardly anything about her ideals and background that he did not know. She worked hard in school and got good grades, as he did. She knew much he didn't know, particularly about music and art. She had passed every inspection, so to speak. A disciplined, conscientious, loving young woman. Every time he saw her she looked better, felt better in his arms, tasted better. Being with her was torture of the most exquisite kind. After their dates he felt limp, bedraggled. He told himself that he truly loved her, that this was no summer infatuation. At night, thinking himself calm at last, he would lie in his bed experiencing what he imagined to be clear-headed rationality, and he would imagine them married, and it seemed to him certain that it was what would happen.

He had known her only a summer. In a way he was ashamed of himself for caring so much so quickly, as if it argued for some unstable quality of character. As if it argued that because it was quick it must necessarily be false. This too had been taught to him by the priests at Fordham.

Often the subject of religion arose between them. As summer waned, religion began with increasing regularity to spill over their lives. In their conversations Rocky seemed to worry about it a good deal more than Frank. Every time she opened her lovely mouth he leaped in with the penny catechism and the ready answer, somewhat desperately trying to reassure her that it would all work out with her becoming a Catholic and the two of them happy together for the next 50 years. But she doubted she ever would become a Catholic, she said, and though he could present a confident facade when with her, he began to doubt it too. He saw her as totally sincere, totally honest with herself and with him. To her, religion was a gulf between them, and she worried already about the unhappiness it could cause them. One night she told him that because of "this religion business" she was afraid to really let herself go with him. He was afraid too, he said. But they were in each other's arms at the time and it was clear that both were irrevocably gone.

Their love was no less real because they were the ages they were.

Summer ended. He drove her back to college, a distance of about 250 miles, worrying all the way that his car might not make it, though it did. Most of the interstates were still works in progress, there were few places where roads were open enough to permit speeding, so the trip took more than eight hours each way. Because his own classes started the next day he could only drop her off and turn around and drive back. He didn't mind. He would do anything for her.

Now he knew the way, and it was a trip he would make several times over the next school year.

After that he wouldn't see her for months, supposedly. Unable to wait until she came home at Thanksgiving, he drove up to see her in mid-October. He saw her again at Thanksgiving, of course, and then at Christmas. They wrote to each other every day, x's at the end of each letter to signify kisses, the stamps on the envelopes upside down to signify love, Rocky's letters sometimes sealed with a lipsticked kiss—all these were the conventions of the day. Again, kid stuff. At Christmastime he bought her a silver bracelet with his name engraved on it. In effect she was now wearing his brand. This too was a convention of the day. As her present to him she had knitted a pair of striped woolen socks in maroon and white, the Fordham colors.

At Beale College she was making friendships with new girls, and fending off Cornell boys on weekends, she told him. She was majoring in art history, with a minor in home economics. He didn't know what home economics was and never thought to ask. How to run a house, he supposed. A useful subject for a girl to learn and a woman to know, for at that time relatively few careers were open to women. The best that most of them could look forward to, even the educated ones, was raising children and running a house, while their husbands ran companies, ran after other women.

On a curriculum level Rocky and Frank did not have much to talk about. At Fordham, freshmen and sophomores had no electives. All subjects, including Latin, including religion, were compulsory. As juniors and seniors religion was still compulsory, and so was scholastic philosophy, also called Thomistic Philosophy, the official philosophy of the Catholic Church, invented by St. Thomas Aquinas in Paris around the year 1250, and unchanged since. After that a student could fill out his course hours with two choices of his own. Frank, who had decided to focus on English Literature, selected, without really knowing why, Seventeenth-Century Poetry, and the Victorian Novel. Even so, he spent more course hours in philosophy and religion classes than in his so-called major.

Thomistic Philosophy as taught at Fordham by Jesuit professors was divided into separate subjects. In junior year he had studied cosmology, which dealt with the origin and structure of the universe (created by God according to the divine plan); ontology, which dealt with being; and logic, in which the students were introduced not only to orderly thought, but also to syllogistic reasoning—the construction of arguments so ironclad that any man, whatever his ignorance or passion, could only accept them as proven.

Now in senior year the subjects were ethics and theology.

Until the swimming season started Frank played touch football on the quadrangle most afternoons, and did his reading and studying at night. He also had a part-time job opening the doors to his parish church every morning at six A.M., and locking them every night at nine. For this work he had been given his own set of big keys. The job paid well enough, considering that it took so little time, and he was saving most of what he earned so that, two years from now, he would have enough set aside on which to get married. He wasn't seeing any other girls. He wasn't interested in any girl but Rocky.

In midwinter he drove up again though the weather forecast warned of snow and icy roads. It was snowing hard by the time he got there. He lodged with a middle-aged woman in a frame house in the town. In all her rooms were boys like himself who had driven a long way to spend the weekend with their girlfriends.

That afternoon he and Rocky parked beside the road and watched the snow come down. In 15 minutes it had blanketed all the windows. No one could look in or out. It was the most private, most silent time they had ever had together. Snow enveloped the car. He could hear her breathing. He told her again he loved her. She said she loved him too. There was much passionate kissing. He unbuttoned her coat and put his hand on the front of her angora sweater. How soft it was, the sweater and her. He had never dreamed it would be so soft. She held his hand there. He had heard of girls who would permit more than this, but he hadn't met any yet. Sluts would, of course. But he didn't know any sluts.

It began to be cold in the car.

"We better go back," she said.

He put the windshield wipers on and when the glass cleared drove her back to her residence hall to get ready for the dance that night.

At Easter while she was home a crisis came upon them. Her father, she explained tearfully in the car, had forbidden her to see him. Her father had told her to stay away from Catholic boys, and to disentangle herself at once from this one. He had claimed to be speaking for her own good. Marry a Catholic and she would be pregnant every year, have ten or fifteen children, was that what she wanted? Look at the McCormicks down the street if she doubted him, nine children, the oldest of them not 13 yet.

"He told me that if I would break up with you, he'd buy me a car."

"A car?"

"I told him I don't want a car."

"But you do. You said you did. You do, don't you?"

"Maybe."

"So what did you tell him?"

"I told him I'd think about it."

"Oh."

She took his hand. "Silly. I told him he was asking me too high a price."

During the week she was home they managed to see each other a few times, not enough. She would take the bus into the village and they would meet inside the darkened movie theater. Or they would arrange to meet at a girlfriend's house.

There was no question of him driving her up to college this time. Her father put her on the train himself.

THIS MUCH OF THE STORY BECAME KNOWN because he told Earl, and also Gabe. He was in love, but there was a problem. He had to talk to someone or go crazy, he said. He was very upset. He didn't know what to do. He talked to them separately and also together, usually in the cafeteria over lunch. He did not talk to Andy Troy, whom he saw less often these days and who seemed to be writing half the college paper each week, and had grown somewhat aloof. To his other two friends he described his feelings for Rocky, and also his various dealings with her father, leaving out almost no detail. But neither Earl nor Gabe could help him very much. They didn't know what he should do either.

The rest he never told anybody, and it did not come to light until Rocky spoke of it to Andy Troy's wife many years later.

FOR TWO WEEKS IMPASSIONED LETTERS passed back and forth between Frank and Rocky. Then the future priest drove up to her college still again. When he met her outside her residence building they were extremely glad to see each other. They kissed and hugged, and then both began talking at once.

But Rocky quickly got quiet.

This time she had had to reserve him a room in a motel, she said. The motel was in Union Springs, which is two towns away. Nothing else was available, she assured him, which he doubted, since today was not the start of a big college weekend, just the evening of an ordinary Friday. As they drove to the motel together—so she could show him the way, she said—she sat not close to him, as she usually did, but against the opposite door. He saw how nervous she was, and began to be nervous himself. Union Springs, he realized, was outside the college orbit. Outside her orbit, outside his as well. It was unlikely that anyone she knew—they knew—would see them there, no one who might note their comings and goings.

The motel was a collection of pseudo–log cabins at the edge of a woods, a bigger cabin that was the office, and a row of smaller ones dribbling off into the trees. He rolled in over the gravel, stopped, and got out. Rocky said she would stay in the car. He went into the big cabin and signed in.

"I put the heat on in there about an hour ago," the woman told him. He thanked her.

"You're going to stay two nights?"

"Yes."

"Checkout time is noon on Sunday."

He was given a key attached by a string to a slab of wood with a number burned into it.

"Cabin number six," he told Rocky as he got back in the car.

He drove along the gravel and parked in front. He got his bag out and slammed the trunk down. He unlocked the door to the cabin and pushed it open. They both went in. It was evening and with the door still open the cold air followed them inside.

Rocky turned around and closed it, which darkened the room considerably.

Frank moved to turn on the light.

"No, don't," she said. "Leave the light off."

There was a double bed. Both had glanced in that direction, but neither moved toward it.

At this time what they meant to do, if in fact they meant to do it, if in fact they went through with it, was not spoken of in the company that either of them kept.

In the darkened room, they stood apart from each other, a yard of air and his suitcase between them. In a sense they were still playing at being adults. But playtime was almost over.

He had been driving for altogether nine hours, and was dressed for the road: khaki pants, a wool polo shirt, a cardigan sweater. She wore penny loafers, a plaid skirt, navy blue twinset sweaters with the sleeves pushed up on her forearms. She wore pearl earrings, and a rope of pearls at her throat.

They fell on the bed fully dressed and began kissing. It was the same type of kissing they had engaged in previously although, given that it occurred for the first time on a bed, and in a place in which they would not be interrupted, it soon became more torrid.

After a time Rocky stood up and drew him to his feet where, after another kiss or two, she began to undo the buttons of his cardigan. Seeing how scared she was, he embraced her, squashing her fingers against his chest.

"You don't have to," he said into her hair.

"I want to."

"No you don't."

"I want you to be mine."

"I am yours."

"In every way. I want to make it so that nothing can keep us apart, not my father, not your religion."

This was what he wanted too, though the doing of it would be a great sin. He had been taught by his teachers that passion was to be avoided at all costs, for it blurred the mind and led men astray. But he was in such a state that he did not see this clearly, did not see anything clearly. Was this only passion, or a love so profound that he was powerless against it?

The first part was awkward. Belts and buttons are awkward for fingers working on someone else in a direction opposite to what one is used to. Stepping out of clothing is awkward. What do you do with it, just leave it on the floor? One could trip over it, and it would be in no shape to put back on later. But such thoughts as this were fleeting. Presently they contemplated all of each other. She covered her breasts with her hands. He was embarrassed, afraid she would find him repugnant. But after a moment her hands dropped, and her gaze came up, as if daring him not to admire her.

"Do you think I'm pretty?"

"Pretty? I think you're gorgeous." He said this with so much fervor, and they were both so tense, that both of them laughed briefly.

Taking her by the wrist, he led her toward their joint future. Together they drew back the counterpane, the bedclothes.

The sheets were rough and so icy cold that they pulled the blankets up and under them huddled together for warmth. They talked to each other almost normally, as if nothing unusual was taking place, was about to take place.

"Where did that woman get such rough sheets?"

"She seemed like a nice woman."

"I think she froze them as well."

Her body against his felt red hot, her breath on his shoulder as well.

He said: "What time do you have to sign in?"

"Eleven o'clock."

"We have time, then."

"Time for what?"

"Well, for the bed to warm up."

"Oh, is that what you meant?"

"Time for everything."

"What's everything?"

"You know, everything."

After a time the bed was warm. Warm enough, anyway. He could not wait any longer, had waited too many years already. And so he started.

She said: "I don't know how to do this."

"I don't either."

"We'll teach each other."

"It can't be too hard. Everybody does it."

At a later date when they remembered this remark it would make them smile, or even laugh. Not then.

It took them most of an hour to accomplish what they had set out to accomplish. Success was signaled on both sides by a sudden intake of breath. Innocence was over. Real life had begun. They were filled with surprise, and a kind of wonder.

True rapture occurred only later, for they kept on for another several hours. Frank would have called it ecstasy, and perhaps Rocky would have too. It became very sweaty, very noisy. If anyone had told them that in the course of marriage this act would be performed thousands of times, and more often in friendship than in passion, they would have been astonished. But it was something they would learn, if they went on.

The sheets were in disarray, the blankets on the floor, Rocky still writhing about and moaning. She still wore earrings and pearls, Frank only his wristwatch, at which he now glanced.

"My God, it's past ten thirty."

And so they stopped at last. They rolled off the bed and began hurriedly to dress.

In the bathroom he watched Rocky primp.

"My face is all red," she said. "That's your doing." From a small compact out of her handbag she tried to tone it down with powder. "It'll be late when we get back to the college," she said, "maybe the old witch won't notice."

She took one last look at herself in the mirror. "Do you still think I'm pretty?"

"More than ever."

"You can tell me the truth this time. Flattering me now will get you nowhere."

"Gorgeous." Again he had spoken with what might have been considered too much fervor. Again both laughed. But the fear, the passion, the other strong emotions were over for the day. They were able to laugh again normally at last.

They started back to the college, Frank driving too fast to get her there in time. Both were famished, for they had forgotten to eat.

Now they would have to go without supper, for there was no time to stop. Nor did there seem to be anything open, not up here in the boondocks, not in the villages they passed through.

At the college Rocky gave him a quick kiss, and jumped out running for the door. He watched her go inside, and waited until she appeared in the window of her room and gave him a brief wave.

He drove back toward his motel. He could not remember being this hungry ever, and briefly considered driving as far as Auburn, which is a good-sized town. Surely there would be something open there. But what he really wanted to do was return to his room and lie between sheets that still smelled of her, bury his nose in the pillow where her head had lain.

In the morning he met her early and they drove to a diner in the town where they ate tremendous breakfasts, first pancakes, then eggs and bacon and toast, plus several cups of coffee each.

"We haven't talked about your father."

"Well, we've been very busy."

"What were we so busy doing? I can't remember."

"I'm sore in certain places. Maybe that has something to do with it."

It was nice to talk casually about yesterday. About the secret world they had entered that they alone shared, that the rest of the world was excluded from, and knew nothing about.

"We should talk about him."

She reached across the table and took his hand. "It will work out."

"Maybe we should just run off and get married."

But both knew this was not a solution.

Afterward they went sightseeing along Lake Cayuga, which is about 30 miles long but in some places as narrow as a river. They had lunch in another diner in a town called Geneva.

But in time they became bored with driving aimlessly around.

"What do you feel like doing?" Frank asked her.

"I don't know, what do you feel like doing?"

Without a further word Frank drove to his motel.

They spent the rest of the day there, until finally Rocky stopped him, saying: "I'm so sore."

So they went out and ate a late supper, and Rocky laughed and joked. Did she seem to him to be limping? When she went back to the campus tonight, if she was limping, everybody would guess what she—what they—had been doing all day.

"If there was any justice in the world," she told him, "you'd be sore too."

"I am, a little."

"I didn't see where it slowed you down any."

"I was like a football player. The good ones go on playing even when hurt."

He thought it thrilling to be able to talk like this, to joke about something as intimate, as secret, as momentous as what they had shared since yesterday.

But later, when he had got back to the motel, he began to brood about morality and how it related to his own recent conduct. During the past two days he had experienced certain periods of rationality. Not too many, always brief, and only when Rocky wasn't there, as now. In her presence he could not keep his eyes and his hands off her, much less his thoughts.

In his room, as he remade the bed, it seemed to him she was still there, he could feel her all around him. But she wasn't, he couldn't, so he brushed his teeth, put on his pajamas, got into bed in the dark, and, lying there alone, tried to examine his conscience. But he was as physically tired as if he had been climbing mountains for two days, he too ached in many places, and he soon fell asleep.

There was a Catholic church in Aurora. He had been to it before when up here for one of their big weekends. The next morning,

Sunday, he drove back to the campus, picked up Rocky outside her building, and after breakfast in a diner he asked her to come to the ten o'clock mass with him.

"I don't know."

"Please."

After hesitating a moment longer she agreed.

Inside he knelt amid the congregation, the girl he loved kneeling beside him, or sitting or standing, politely following along with whatever the rest of the congregation did, finding the service curious, no doubt. He didn't really know how she found it. He did know how he himself found it. He felt himself both a wrongdoer and a hypocrite. He was outside his Church now, cut off from it, for he had committed one of the gravest of sins. So had said his teachers at Fordham and before. These were the same men who had taught him everything else he knew, so how could he doubt them now? And although the experience with Rocky had seemed to him the opposite of what they had led him to expect, not ugly, not degenerate, not even sinful, but somehow pure and beautiful, even holy, still he thought he must be wrong. He and Rocky had committed what was surely a great evil—he more than she since he had known he was doing wrong but had done it anyway, had reveled in it. For her he had been willing to challenge damnation. Whereas she could be in the clear, he hoped she was, if she truly believed that what they had done together was good—this was the type of dichotomy he had been taught in Ethics class, and by considering ethical value according to the principles taught him in Logic class he saw that his reasoning was correct. It made perfect sense. But he was confused. He was trying to equate his Thomistic Philosophy courses to two days of the most intense love he had ever known, but the two did not seem to fit. He wondered if perhaps ethical principles could not be applied logically to human acts after all. Or perhaps not all acts, or not always. Perhaps only not this time.

He was struggling to understand what had happened to him, to them, on a purely intellectual level because that was what he had been taught to do, but it was impossible, he couldn't.

On an emotional level it could not be understood either. It was too gloriously unexpected, and he was too filled with wonder.

After mass they drove back to the college, where they stood beside his car. She had homework to do and he faced the long drive home, but both were reluctant to say good-bye. To part was hard, and as the minutes passed it got no easier.

"They taught us that if you let a boy have you he will think you cheap," Rocky said. "But it isn't true, is it?"

"No."

"That he would have contempt for you." She grinned at him. "But that isn't quite the way you feel about me, is it?"

"No," said Frank.

She was laughing at him. "In fact, you love me more than ever."

"More than ever."

"You love me more than anything."

"Well," he said, "not as much as hamburgers."

"More than anything."

"More than anything."

She laughed happily. "And nothing can come between us now?"

"No."

"Not ever."

"I adore you," he said. And then after a pause: "And you? Do you love me?"

"You know I do."

He kissed her good-bye, then got into the car and started the engine. For several paces she walked beside the window holding his hand, then stopped and he went on alone. In the mirror she stood waving until he had turned the corner and she was gone.

The drive home was long. Leaning over the steering wheel he

brooded all the way, but never managed to see very much very clearly. He did realize that when he got back to New York he would have to go to confession. Even though what he had done did not feel wrong he believed it was wrong. He must seek absolution. There was however a problem. For the absolution to take effect he would have to promise—and mean it—that what had happened would not happen again. Convince himself. Convince, in a manner of speaking, God. A firm purpose of amendment, it was called. Even though he knew that the minute he saw Rocky he would want it to happen again, and if they could find a place and a moment alone together, it would happen again, he would not be able to help himself.

He was in love with a particular sin, then. But this notion he refused to accept. He was in love with a girl, and she was in love with him. What happened had happened, and would again, for that's what love was.

So what could he do to regain the serenity he had known such a short time ago?

The future priest had an ideal of goodness and it was implanted deep in his being. It was not his own ideal. Somebody else had implanted it there. Nonetheless he was its prisoner. He wanted always to do the right thing. But being so confused made it impossible for him to recognize what the right thing was.

THAT WAS MAY 1. Rocky came home for the summer four weeks later, but he did not see her right away. She had written that she might get off the train in Albany and spend a few days with her grandmother, who lived there. As the days passed he did not know for sure where she was, and felt he could not call her house to find out. He would have to wait until she called him. And so he fretted, but the telephone did not ring.

Finally he drove up to the country club. He thought someone

there might have news of her. Or perhaps he might ask one of her girlfriends to phone the house for him.

Instead he found Rocky herself sitting in a deck chair beside the pool. She was wearing a sundress and reading a magazine. She smiled up at him, and when he bent down allowed him to kiss her on the cheek.

"How long have you been home?"

"About a week."

"A week?"

Since there were people nearby she got up and they walked out to a bench that overlooked the first fairway.

"You know the car we talked about? My father bought it for me."

For the moment he let this statement pass. "I was waiting for you to call me."

"I didn't feel up to it just yet."

"I don't understand." But perhaps he did. His heart had fallen a long way.

"I haven't been feeling very well."

"You look fine."

"I haven't been sleeping well, and—other things."

There were golfers halfway down the fairway, and others on the distant green.

"You've just been studying too hard."

"Maybe."

His stomach was churning, his head. He wanted to kiss her eyes, her lips, her neck, but she seemed more distant to him than the first day he ever saw her. He wanted to hold her tight, but couldn't. He didn't know what to do, what to say.

"I have a doctor's appointment tomorrow."

"I'll take you there."

"You don't need to do that."

"I want to."

"I have my own car now. I can go by myself."

"Let me meet you there, then."

"What for?"

"To be sure you're all right."

"They're only going to do tests. I won't know anything for a few days." She took his hand. "Just let me get this doctor thing behind me."

"All right."

Golfers came out onto the first tee. He bit down on his lip and watched them tee off.

"Do you want to see my new car?" she said brightly.

She walked him past the clubhouse and into the parking lot. Rows of cars were parked in slots and baking in the sun. About halfway along they came to a red Triumph sports car.

"Is that it?"

"What do you think of it?"

"Very nice."

"You don't like it?"

"What did you promise your father?"

"I didn't promise him anything."

Frank looked back toward the golf course.

"Do you want to go for a ride in it?"

"No."

"You can drive."

He shook his head.

She had displayed pride and pleasure in her new car. His reaction seemed to have deprived her of both.

"It's just a car," she said.

"It's a nice car. I told you that already."

"My dad didn't ask me to promise him anything. And I didn't."

He looked along the row at his own car, the now eleven-year-old Oldsmobile.

"Do you want to have a drink in the clubhouse? It's so hot today. Iced tea or something?"

"No, thank you."

He had no intention of riding in the car her father had bought her, nor of having a drink in the clubhouse where only members could sign the chit; Rocky would sign, and her father would pay for that too.

He said: "I have finals this week. I guess I should get home and study."

She walked him toward his car, but his steps got slower. He wanted to tell her he had a job lined up. The training program of a major ad agency. He planned to save all his money. He wanted to tell her that as soon as she graduated they could be married. But he couldn't do it.

They came to his car. He wanted her to beg him to stay with her another hour at least. It was a nice afternoon, they could go for a walk—anything. But she didn't.

He got into his car. "Call me after the doctor," he said through the open window.

"All right."

"Promise."

She nodded.

She stayed to watch him leave the parking lot, he noted. When he looked back she waved. He was looking for signals she might give that would prove she loved him still, and he chose to interpret the wave in this way. Maybe that's what it meant. But he couldn't be sure.

When he got home his mother was out. The apartment was empty. In his room he got his textbooks out, and his classroom notes, and tried to study, but the words meant nothing to him. He went and stood by the window and looked out at the Bronx street.

Most of the next day he sat by the phone, and the day after as well, but it did not ring.

On the fourth day it was ringing as he came into the apartment. He had just completed a three-hour Ethics exam. Graduation was now two days off. He grabbed the phone and it was Rocky.

"How was today's exam?" she said.

"It was easy." But he knew this wasn't why she called. "What about the doctor?" he said.

"He says I'm not going to die."

"What else?"

"I'll tell you when I see you. When will I see you?"

It made him wary. "When do you want to?"

"Are you busy? How about right now?"

An hour later they sat on the same bench overlooking the first fairway.

"Can I ask a favor of you?" Rocky said.

"Of course."

"I have to go back to the college for a day or two. Would you drive up there with me? I don't want to go alone. We could take my car. Or yours, if you prefer."

"What's wrong, Rocky?"

"Nothing's wrong."

"The school year's over for you."

"That's right, it is."

"So why do you have to go up there?"

"Well, you see, well, I'm pregnant."

This stunned him, the word itself, and also what it meant to both their lives.

"Pregnant?" For the past four days, though refusing to admit it to himself, this was what he had feared.

"And so I have to get an abortion."

"Oh, Rocky."

"It won't be one of these back-alley jobs. There's a doctor up there who does them. A real doctor. In a town with a college full of girls it must happen rather a lot."

"We'll get married."

"I called a girl I know, a senior. She's set it up for me."

"We'll get married right away."

"And I'll have ten kids by the time I'm thirty and weigh 300 pounds. No, we won't get married."

"It's the thing to do and it's what we both want."

"I'm too young to get married, and I'm too young to have a child. I'm nineteen years old. I'm still a child myself."

"We've talked about getting married for months."

"I want a life first. Is that so wrong?"

"Abortion is out of the question. It's killing the unborn. It's a terrible thing even to think about."

The legalization of abortion was years and years in the future.

"It's also a crime," Frank said. "Get caught and you go to jail."

"I've thought it all out. God, I haven't been able to think of anything else. And that's what I'm going to do."

Frank's head felt as if stuffed full of wadded paper. He could read nothing of what was in there, none of the ideas, arguments, explanations he needed. He decided to fight for time. He would have to change her mind, but it would take time. For the moment, he told himself, let her think I agree. Try to slow her down. Concentrate on details. He said: "How much will it cost?"

"Five hundred dollars."

"I don't have that kind of money," he said, "but I can get it." But where? "Give me a day, two days."

"Never mind the money. I've already got the money."

He was immediately suspicious. "Where did you get it?"

"I borrowed it from my grandmother, if you must know."

"No, I'll pay for it. I did it, and I'll pay for it."

"You didn't do it. We both did it."

In his agitation Frank got up and paced in front of the bench.

"Sit down," Rocky said, "you're disturbing the golfers."

He sat back down.

"You haven't even thought about my father. If I married you now he'd cut me off without a penny. If he knew I was pregnant he'd throw me out of the house. It would kill him, but he'd do it."

"This is not about your father, it's about you and me."

"It's about me, mostly, I think."

If he refused to help her he would lose her, and there would be no getting her back. "When do you want to go?"

"I've started to throw up all over the place, so as soon as possible, please. Before everybody knows. My father—it would hurt him so much."

He saw that tears had come to her eyes, but when he tried to embrace her she shrugged him off.

"I don't know how this happened," he said. "I was so careful, Rocky, honest I was."

"Not careful enough, I guess."

Birth control pills did not yet exist, and slot machines selling condoms were even further off than that. In drugstores condoms were kept out of sight under the counter. One had to stand amid patrons who waited for prescriptions, and ask for them aloud. Frank could not have imagined himself doing this. Besides which, it seemed to him, the use of condoms would have debased both Rocky and the love they had for each other. So he had used the other alternative. He had been, as he said, "careful."

He was silent for the time it took four golfers to tee off, pick up their tees, and start down the fairway. Then he said: "I'll stand by you, Rocky. I'll be there for you. I'll never leave you."

How stupid these words sounded to him. Why was he unable to think of better ones?

When he took her hand she let him hold it, and there they sat, gazing after the departed golfers. Frank did not know what to say next, and supposed she didn't either.

"We'll go tomorrow," he said.

"When's your graduation?"

"In two days."

"You can't skip your graduation. You can't do that to your parents."

"The day after, then."

In a small, wistful voice, not looking at him, she said: "All right."

THE CEREMONY TOOK PLACE ON THE QUADRANGLE, where rows and rows of folding chairs had been set up in front of a temporary dais wrapped in the Fordham colors. In a rented robe and mortarboard, the tassel hanging down over his ear, Frank listened to the speeches, two by classmates, one by Father Curran, the university president, and the fourth by a Broadway comedian imported for the occasion. The two classmates were earnest and boring, but the comedian was quite funny. Father Curran in his turn encouraged the graduates to go out into life and manifest their precious faith to a largely unbelieving world.

When his name was called Frank climbed the steps to the dais, was handed his diploma, shook hands with Father Curran, with the dean of the college, and with the comedian. Then he went down the steps and back to his seat. The ceremony ended soon after.

Then for a while the graduates milled around accepting congratulations from parents, relatives, and friends. The rows of chairs were soon in disarray. People stumbled into them, knocked them over, and here and there someone went down among them. Frank told his friends and parents that Rocky was sick, and that's why she couldn't be there.

The next morning he met her in the country club parking lot. She had a small suitcase. So did he. She was wearing a pale blue linen suit, and looked dressed as if to start out on her honeymoon. Instead of going in his car, she suggested, if he wouldn't mind, that they take her new car, which was parked nearby. They had a mild argument over this. It was really important that they get there on time, she said, and his car wasn't in such great shape. There was a chance it could break down, whereas the new one wouldn't.

"It's never let us down yet," he said.

"But there have been times it wouldn't start. You said so yourself."

"Never when you were in the car."

"That's true. Still—"

He had just turned 21, and he wasn't the wisest 21-year-old in the world, but he saw the strain she was under. He wanted to comfort her, but did not dare. All he could do was say: "All right, we'll take your car."

"Will you drive?" she said, holding out the keys.

And so they started out. It was parkway as far as the Bear Mountain Bridge where they crossed the Hudson. After that they drove all day on small roads across southern New York State, passing through the Catskills, and into the farm country beyond. It was June, the leaves were full out, and in the open car the sun was hot on their bare heads. In places the land was sparsely settled, and they might go half an hour between towns with, to either side of the road, good-sized farms, and fields of grazing cows.

At first Frank had tried to make bright conversation, had tried to amuse her, perhaps even make her laugh. But she didn't laugh, and the conversation went flat, and then faded out. It became a long, silent ride, during which Rocky gazed for the most part straight ahead or else at her hands in her lap. She looked closed in on herself, and soon he was too. He was appalled to find himself engaged in an errand of this kind. He could not stop thinking about what he was doing. His conscience nagged at him, and he was afraid to examine it closely. All he knew was that he loved this girl, was terrified at the idea of losing her, would do anything for her, even help her to commit what was to him an unpardonable evil.

They stopped for lunch in a town called Cannonsville, and as Rocky walked from the car toward the restaurant he examined the line of her stomach, which was still flat, despite the miracle that was in it. She saw where his eyes were fixed, and snapped at him: "Stop that. Nothing shows yet. What's in there is no bigger than a bug."

He could not keep himself from saying: "It would grow into our son, or daughter."

"If you want a child so much, go have it with someone else."

Inside they took a booth, and when the waitress came they ordered.

"I'm sorry," Rocky said. "Just because I'm upset is no reason to take it out on you."

He gave her a half smile of gratitude.

"You didn't do anything wrong," she said, "any more than I did. We just weren't lucky."

Presently the food was put down before them.

But Frank found he could not eat it and she had to coax him. "We have another four or five hours to drive. You have to eat something."

She picked up his fork and began to feed him. This seemed so suddenly silly that they grinned at each other, and for a moment felt close again.

By the time they reached the foot of Lake Cayuga the sun was going down.

"The doctor is where?" Frank asked.

"Union Springs."

"I know a good motel in Union Springs." It was a way of alluding to the intimacy they had known. He had meant it as a bit of a joke, but it only sounded hollow.

"It's as good a place as any."

A little later he drove in over the gravel and stopped in front of the office.

"Ask for two rooms," Rocky said. Then, having seen the way his face fell, she added: "I'm not rejecting you, Frank. I'm up half the night with cramps and I'm retching for the first hour in the morning. I'd keep you awake. You'll be much better off alone."

He found he wanted to be kept awake, to share even the cramps and the retching with her, as much as he could, but he said nothing, and while she stayed in the car he checked in for both of them.

He came back with two slabs of wood attached to keys by string, and he drove down along the line of cabins and parked in front of number six. "Our honeymoon cottage," he said with a smile. "Who gets it, you or me?" An amusing remark, he hoped, that with luck might make her laugh, or at least smile. But it wasn't, and didn't. "You can have it all to yourself," he said. "I'm in the one next door."

But, after giving him a look, she took key number five and went in and closed the door. After a moment he entered number six, and put his bag down. He felt not like a young man returning to the scene of his honeymoon, but like a criminal returning to the scene of his crime.

He woke in the dark about three A.M., did not know where he was, then remembered. He lay there awhile, fully alert, troubled, unable to sleep. Finally he got up, put his shoes on, and stepped outside. The crickets were buzzing. He could smell the forest. Overhead rode a sliver of moon, and clouds that impaled themselves on its points. Rocky's cabin was dark. He listened at her window but could hear nothing. Finally he tried her door, and it opened. He stepped inside and looked down at her sleeping. He had never seen her asleep before. A bit of light shone through the window and slashed across her cheek.

What he wanted to do was get into the bed beside her, and, when she awakened, hold her tight and beg her to reconsider. They could be married, he would tell her, she could have the baby. Young as they were, he didn't want a baby any more than she did, but what happened had happened. They could start a life together, and have this baby, and probably others later.

Instead he backed noiselessly away from the bed, and outside into the night, pulling the door closed behind him.

In the morning he knocked on her door and she invited him in. She was sitting on the edge of the bed looking gray. She said she had been retching for an hour. She wore a loose-fitting nightgown. When she leaned forward he could see her breasts. Well, he had already seen her breasts. Seeing them again didn't change anything.

They had breakfast in a diner. She wanted only dry toast and a glass of milk.

As he drove her to the doctor's office, he suggested once more that they get married, and in the parking lot said it again. That they have the baby. But her mouth got hard. "It's my decision," she said, "and I've made it."

They went inside. The doctor's receptionist took down Rocky's name, handed her a questionnaire, then said: "What seems to be the problem?"

"I've talked to the doctor on the phone. He knows about it."

The woman told her to fill out the form. Allergies. Past illnesses. This she did while leaning over the desk. The woman told them to take chairs. Frank thumbed through a *Time* magazine six weeks old. Rocky still wore the linen suit. Sitting with her handbag in her lap she only stared at her hands.

Two patients already waited, older women, neither afflicted, obviously, with Rocky's problem. The first was sent into the inner office, to come out a few minutes later clutching a prescription.

The doctor, who stood in the doorway, seemed to study Rocky

for a moment, before addressing the second woman by name, and inviting her inside. He was a short, stooped man, about 50 years old, bald, wearing a white coat. He stepped back into his office and closed the door.

The second woman was in there 30 minutes, perhaps more. By the time she came out two more patients had entered the waiting room. The doctor took both of them, out of turn, before Rocky.

Frank, who had begun to pace, was furious. "What's going on here?" he demanded of the receptionist. "We were here first."

"The doctor will see you when he can," the receptionist said.

She left for lunch a bit later. Frank and Rocky were the only ones left.

The final patient came out, the doctor behind him. "You can come in now, Miss," he said to Rocky.

Still angry, Frank stepped forward as well.

"Are you the husband?" the doctor said.

"No. I'm the father."

"Wait outside," said the doctor. "This way, Miss."

The door closed on Frank.

Having sat down behind his desk, the doctor said: "You have the money?"

Rocky reached into her handbag, drew out the five folded, hundred-dollar bills, handed them over, and the doctor slipped them into a drawer and closed it.

Next he studied Rocky's questionnaire. "No allergies," he said. "No previous illnesses. You're not currently on any medication. Is that correct?"

Rocky nodded. At this point, she told Frank later, she was so scared she was unable to speak.

"You're nineteen years old," the doctor said, "and there's only the one thing wrong with you. Get undressed."

"Here?" Rocky said, glancing around. His desk had pens and prescription pads on it, she noted. There was a glass cabinet containing instruments, and an examination table fitted with stirrups. She looked for a changing room but there was none. She waited to be offered a hospital gown to wrap herself in, perhaps a sheet. But this did not happen.

"Here?" she said again.

"Let's not be prudish," the doctor said. "You couldn't have been too prudish when you got yourself in this condition."

She took off her skirt, folding it, placing it on a chair.

"When you are ready sit down on the table."

Rocky took off her panties. Naked from the waist down, she lifted herself onto the edge of the table, where she sat with her legs tight together. She had begun to cry.

"The rest of your clothes too," the doctor said.

She stripped down to her bra. He took her blood pressure. "Blood pressure's good," he said, noting the figures down.

"That too," he said, indicating her bra.

Behind her back her fingers fumbled with the catch.

"Let me help you." He undid the catch, pulled the bra down her arms, and began to palpate her breasts.

Rocky sat weeping.

"Lie down," he said. "Put your feet up."

She did so. He pulled on surgical gloves, smeared a lubricant on his forefinger, and rammed the forefinger into her. This almost lifted her off the table. His finger slid around in there. "I need to be sure," he said. "Relax. It will go easier if you do."

She lay with her knees wide apart, eyes screwed shut, weeping.

She saw nothing that happened after that. She felt the ice-cold speculum go into her, widen her. She felt another instrument go in deep, heard it scraping inside. Then she felt the blood seeping out, not a flood but a flow, like having a particularly heavy period, the blood sliding down the crease of her buttocks.

The instruments were removed from her. The doctor pressed a Kotex between her legs.

"Get dressed," he said.

He sat down behind his desk and wrote something in his book.

Rocky was weak, dizzy, and half blinded by tears. She had trouble getting her clothes on. The doctor did not help her. When she was finished she looked at him but he said only: "You may leave," so she staggered out into the waiting room, where the anxious Frank grabbed her to keep her from falling down.

"Let's go," she said.

They got into the car and started home. Rocky again began weeping. When she told him what it had been like Frank's reaction was fury. He wanted to go back and beat up the doctor.

"No," sobbed Rocky, "let's just go home."

They stopped at the first drugstore to buy a box of Kotex. After that they had to stop frequently so she could go into a ladies' room and change the blood-soaked pad. At each stop he made her drink copiously, telling her she had to replenish the blood she was losing.

As he drove he tried to put in order a number of heavy ideas. Basic among them was his vision of right and wrong. He felt himself guilty of a terrible crime, not knowing that Rocky beside him felt guilty of the same crime, perhaps more guilty. He was not old enough to divine her mood at all. In any case, it seemed to keep shifting. He glanced across at her from time to time but she would not look at him. Instead she gazed out the window at the fields and cows. Sometimes he sensed she was weeping, but her face was always averted, and he could not be sure. Sometimes he tried to talk to her, but her answers were brief, when she answered at all, and her voice so low he could barely hear her. He became surly in his turn, and then depressed, struggling with notions of dating non-Catholic girls, which led to pre-marital sex, both of which he believed to be wrong, because this was what he had been taught, even though loving Rocky and making love to Rocky had felt so right. But what this love had led to was definitely evil, there was no defending it.

He said: "I'm like the man driving the getaway car. According to law I'm as guilty as the guy who actually pulled the job." An accurate description of what he felt, but not what he should have said to this girl at this time.

She looked at him then, and when she spoke he heard her clearly. "You didn't suffer a thing. You get away with nothing."

"I didn't mean that the way it sounded."

"My body's been violated, my life's been violated."

"I shouldn't have said it. I'm sorry."

"You love your religion more than you love me. You always have and I always knew it."

"I said I'm sorry."

To both of them the road seemed endless. As night fell they stopped for dinner, but she refused to eat. He ordered soup and tea for her, and made her drink them.

Next door was a motel where Frank told her they should spend the night. She couldn't go home looking and feeling the way she did, he said. Was she grateful for his concern? If so, it didn't show. He checked in. The motel was very expensive, so he took only one room. In bed in the dark she lay on the far edge, as far from him as she could get. When he sensed that she was weeping again he slid closer and tried to comfort her but she shook him off.

"Leave me alone."

Later he moved close once more, and put his arm over her. This time she let him stay, or perhaps she was already asleep. And that was how they spent the night. Perhaps it could be said they slept in each other's arms, but Frank feared that it was both the first time and the last. That what they had had together had been lost.

The next morning she was stronger, even made a weak joke about being over the morning sickness. Otherwise she was silent. They had breakfast, got into the car, and started out. She rarely spoke. She did not tell him how she felt, principally because she didn't know how she felt. Angry, sad, relieved, weepy—all of those things. Her breasts hurt. As her body released the pregnancy hormones previously stored up she was subject to wild mood swings. Her hormones were going crazy, which she didn't know, and neither did he. Mostly she was in a state of profound depression. She saw man as the enemy. The woman always paid, while the man got away scot-free. Frank was the enemy. He had driven the car, sure, but he hadn't supported her in what she had had to do, and their relationship was doomed.

He was old enough to recognize a little of this, very little. No one had ever told him how a girl might feel after an abortion. No one in his presence had ever spoken of abortion at all, and he did not know what to do or say.

He was depressed himself, they seemed unable to communicate, so as they drove along he began to talk about his car. This was small talk, nothing more. He was trying to get a conversation going. Any conversation. He had been having trouble with his car lately, he said. When they got to the parking lot at the club he hoped it would start.

"Who cares," she said.

"Well—"

"It's a piece of crap."

They hardly spoke the rest of the way.

They had got a late start, and it was later still when he drove into the club parking lot. He pulled up beside his car. In a low voice she thanked him for having come with her, and he nodded and tried to smile.

"Don't look at me like that," she said. "It's Catholic girls who get married and have the baby. I'm not Catholic, and I never will be."

He called her about a week later to make sure she was all right. She sounded as depressed as ever. He made just the one call, the last one.

He did not see her again for five years.

ON THE FOURTH OF JULY Earl put on another comical diving exhibition at the club, and afterward danced a number of times with Rocky, he told Frank later.

"How was she?"

"Cheerful, full of fun. Why?"

"She seemed kind of depressed the last time I saw her."

The boys were all at Andy Troy's parents' place on the lake. Earl, Frank, Andy, and Gabe, the four recent graduates, the former freestyle relay team. It was a Sunday, and they were sitting on the float in the sun with their feet in the water.

"What happened between you two?" Andy Troy asked. "Why did you break up?"

"Ask her," Frank said.

"I did ask her," Earl said. "She said to ask you."

"It used itself up," Frank said. "It played itself out."

"She said she misses you," Earl said. "I asked her if she missed you, and that's what she said."

"Yeah."

"You should call her."

Frank said nothing.

"I thought you two would probably get married," said Andy Troy.

"So did I for a time."

"But not now?" said Troy.

"I don't think so, no."

"She said she's through with diving," Earl said. "She told her father she didn't want to do it anymore."

"How did he take that?"

"She said he accepted it. After I finished my show we did some dives together. You know something, she could have been really good, if she ever wanted to be."

"She never wanted to be a diver," said Frank. "In fact there were a number of things she didn't want to be."

"Maybe I'll take her out," said Earl, "if you're not interested anymore."

"Sure, go ahead," said Frank.

He worked one month for the advertising agency, then quit. For a few days he wandered aimlessly around. In September, feeling he had a lot to atone for, he entered the seminary.

THE INVESTIGATION

3

CHIEF DRISCOLL DECIDES, AS HE BROODS, that certain hypotheses can be dismissed out of hand, and certain others cannot be. For instance, Frank Redmond, if he was murdered, was not murdered by a chorus girl, or some rich wine merchant from Westchester, or in a dispute with his bankers over money. The one certainty, Gabe believes, is that the answers he is looking for will be found within the high-crime precinct in which Frank Redmond lived and died.

Therefore, he must start by asking himself who were Frankie's enemies—he is thinking of him as Frankie again, though he hasn't in years. Frankie was an active priest who tried to protect his parishioners from predators. He would have run up against enemies at every turn. Local drug dealers. Mafia guys. Junkies. Crazed teenagers. Even, perhaps, some freelance thief he had got in the way of. So who did he have trouble with who might have thrown him off that roof?

Gabe has considered other possibilities also, but discarded them. The jealous lover. The irate husband. Let Andy Troy worry about that kind of thing, which to Gabe Driscoll is a waste of energy anyway.

He has already identified some of Frank's enemies, probably not all. He has their names but is unsure what to do with them, for this is not his case. He is supposed to run Internal Affairs — other units too, but that is the principal one. He is supposed to lock up corrupt or brutal cops. He is not supposed to use his rank to interfere in a detective commander's murder investigation in an outlying corner of the city. And if he tries to interfere, the lower-ranking commander is within his rights, according to departmental protocol, to resist him.

The official investigation is being conducted out of the 32nd Precinct stationhouse on West 135th Street, which is one of the older houses in the city, built in 1931, and also one of the busiest. The Three-Two, one of three Harlem precincts, has been called from time to time the murder capital of the world. Of course the other two have been also, have had their turn. The Three-Two has a complement of 250 patrol cops in uniform, plus, working out of the squadroom upstairs, 19 detectives who cope, or try to cope, with the major crimes.

Chief Driscoll has himself driven up to the Three-Two, ordering his driver to park directly in front. He wants every cop who goes in or out to note the bristling aerials, to be aware that serious rank has come calling. If he should want or need something he wants no hesitation, no questions asked. He goes past the cop on security duty outside, who salutes him, and up the stairs to the squadroom. He knows this house from the past, and sees that it is as run-down and dirty as ever. Its last coat of paint dates from decades before Driscoll himself worked here, and the legions of cleaning women who have swept it out once a week over the years have sometimes remembered to empty the overflowing wastebaskets, the pyramided butts in the ashtrays, sometimes not. The air he breathes stinks of spilled coffee and stale smoke, of half-eaten sandwiches half wrapped in old waxed paper and left in drawers for days, and of the urine and vomit of strung-out prisoners. Also he can taste, it seems to him, the less tangible but still real odors of violence and fear.

The Three-Two Squad is commanded by a Lt. Begos, who, for this meeting, has called in the two detectives he has assigned to the Father Redmond case. Begos, Chief Driscoll senses at once, sees himself caught in the situation every squad commander dreads: a case that has caught the interest of someone powerful from "downtown." His reaction is a barely concealed hostility.

The four men take their places around a small conference table, and Begos introduces the two detectives, one of whom, Cliff Spadia, Driscoll knows from the past.

A man does not survive in the NYPD hierarchy if unable to read the undercurrents, which sometimes are unpleasant. There is a second reason for Begos's hostility. Although Gabe Driscoll has never met him before this minute, he is another of those who, as a matter of principle, do not like him. It is a reaction Driscoll is used to, which doesn't mean he enjoys it. To most cops his role in the department is unsavory. Locking up other cops is unsavory. Bad cops, maybe, but cops. He is seen as necessary. Which doesn't mean anyone has to like him. Or cooperate with him if, for personal reasons, he tries to take over someone else's investigation.

Years ago Chief Driscoll was assigned to Internal Affairs. A captain at the time, he has risen to command the division, but this has isolated him within the department, left him with associates, but no close friends.

"Which one of you geniuses told Redmond's pastor this was a suicide?" Driscoll begins. He knows better than to turn this meeting into a confrontation but he is angry and that's what he has done. Since Frankie's death, he realizes, he has been snapping at everybody. He doesn't seem able to help himself.

When no one answers he says: "You've been working the case three days, for Christ's sake. It's too early to tell, wouldn't you say?"

He watches Lt. Begos choose his words carefully: "We've checked out all the leads we had, Chief."

"I can think of about twenty you haven't checked out."

"If you have anything specific, Chief, we'd be happy to look into it."

"Did you find a note?"

Begos gives a shrug.

"Did you even look for one?"

Cliff Spadia says: "The pastor went through his things. He said there was nothing."

"Who's running this investigation, you or the pastor?"

"He wouldn't let us in the rectory."

"Did you ever hear of a search warrant?"

No one answers. Chief Driscoll wears a three-piece brown suit and a red tie. The dress code for detectives is coat and tie, so Begos wears a suit too, blue pinstripes, but it is not new, nor does it fit him very well. The two detectives wear sports coats with shiny sleeves and somewhat soiled ties that have been tugged into small knots too many times. They are aware of who Driscoll is. They look nervous in his presence, but Begos, for the moment at least, does not. The lieutenant is young, about 35. He pretends patience, but means Driscoll to see that it is thin and will quickly go thinner, because the brass, except for his own superiors, is not supposed to meddle in the way he manages his squad.

"So do you have something specific, Chief?"

He is newly made, Gabe Driscoll judges, a product of the most recent promotion. The two detectives, Spadia and the other guy, are older men, midforties. They might not understand how department command lines run, but Begos obviously does. His lieutenant's rank is protected by civil service. It will be years before he's eligible to take the captain's exam, and more years before he'll be considered on his merits for higher rank than that. By which time he figures Driscoll to be retired and out of the department.

That is, the three-star chief across the table can't hurt him much, and he knows it.

This realization greatly annoys Chief Driscoll, who has a habit of tugging on his ear when upset. The more upset, the harder he tugs. He is tugging hard now.

"What I'm asking you to do is try a bit harder." Since he can't order, Gabe decides for the moment to try to persuade.

"I got nineteen men, Chief, half of whom are sick or on vacation. Do you know how many cases I've got?"

"A lot, I'm sure."

Begos says to Detective Spadia: "How many open murders you working on, Cliff?"

"About twenty," Spadia answers.

Though this figure sounds normal to all four men, there are, elsewhere in the world, good-sized countries that don't see that many murders in an entire year.

"So you see where I'm coming from, Chief. A priest goes off a building, well — if there's no evidence to the contrary I'm perfectly willing to accept it as suicide."

"There are pigeon cages on that roof. Did you find the kid that owns them?"

"We're still looking for him," says Cliff Spadia.

"I suggest you find him. Did you canvass the neighborhood?"

"Chief, I've been a detective a while," says Begos. "Of course we canvassed. That's the first thing a detective does."

"You can canvass one building or fifty. Which was it?"

Begos falls silent. For the first time he begins to look intimidated.

Chief Driscoll's voice goes quiet, which makes him sound all the more menacing. "I think you should go back over the same ground again, don't you? And this time find somebody who saw something."

The two older detectives gaze at their hands.

"Have you examined his checkbooks yet, his telephone bills? When do you plan on doing so?"

"You're right, Chief," Begos concedes, "we should get inside the rectory, go through his papers."

"You wait long enough, evidence disappears."

Lt. Begos looks shaken. "You suggesting the pastor might destroy evidence?"

Chief Driscoll looks at him till his eyes drop.

"Never mind," snaps Chief Driscoll. "I'll do it."

Begos begins to fight back. "Why is the case so important to you, Chief? If I may ask."

"This particular priest was a friend of the department."

"A friend of yours, you mean."

Gabe Driscoll gives a slight nod. "He sometimes gave us important information."

Realizing that the case is personal to Driscoll, Begos's nerve stiffens, for detectives, like doctors, are not supposed to get personally involved. "He was an informant?" Begos asks.

"He was a parish priest."

"But he gave information?"

"From time to time he did."

"Did you register him?"

"So far as I know he was never registered."

"If he was an informant he should have been registered."

Driscoll is being lectured to by a man twenty years younger and six ranks lower, and he does not like it. Again his voice goes low, menacing. "Believe it or not," he says, "I was once a lieutenant like you. I worked out of that same office behind you."

He sees Begos's expression change. Men Begos's age imagine you were born 53 years old in command of Internal Affairs. When they find out you were once their age they're shocked.

Driscoll takes a folder out of his briefcase. "One day Father Redmond came in here with information. A guy selling guns to teenagers. Wanted me to make an immediate arrest. I was too busy to help him." Chief Driscoll pauses, then adds: "So he took the law, you might say, into his own hands."

Detective Spadia, grinning, says: "I remember that case. Helluva case."

"Tell him about it, not me," snaps Driscoll. "Has the name Malcolm Poindexter come into this investigation yet?"

"No, it hasn't, Chief."

"Find him. It's all in here."

"Judge ordered the perp—this mutt Poindexter—held without bail," says Cliff Spadia. "The priest testified at the trial. Mutt got seven to ten at Attica, as I recall."

"Poindexter may be out now," says Chief Driscoll. He studies Lt. Begos. "Two of his suppliers got sent up with him. Mafia guys. They might be out also. Any of them might have come looking for Father Redmond, been responsible for his death. I think you should check them out before you close the case, don't you?"

Begos gives a slight, intimidated nod.

"There were other cases too. Once he spotted a guy breaking into a parked car. He flagged down a taxi and followed the car to a junkyard in the Bronx—a chop shop. We raided the place the next day, arrested seven perpetrators, recovered about fifteen stolen cars. You look over those fives, you'll find their names."

"Car thieves are not usually violent," Begos says defensively.

"Check them out anyway. You'll find a number of drug dealers in there too, some of them locals, some Mafia. Cases he initiated. Made observations, photos, even buys. For a time he had a drug-free parish. I don't know if it still is or not. The last few years I didn't hear from him much."

"You've given us a helluva lot of work, Chief."

The form for ongoing case reports is numbered DD-5. "From now on I want copies of all your fives," Chief Driscoll says. His tone is almost threatening. "I'll call you from time to time so you can keep me up to date."

He gets up, tosses the folder onto the table, and stomps out.

CHAPTER THREE

COLLEGE WAS OVER, THE RELAY TEAM DISSOLVED. But the four young men, having accepted their diplomas, went back to school.

Only Andy Troy's school was informal. His classroom was the block-long newsroom on West 43rd Street. There, five nights a week from eight P.M. to four A.M., Tuesdays and Wednesdays off, he learned the newspaper business. He was a copyboy, one of about a dozen at any one time, but the shifts were staggered, and late at night, meaning most of Troy's shift, the ranks thinned out.

It was Troy's job, and the job of the others, to answer to cries of "BOY!" which, especially as deadline neared—and there were three deadlines per night—were all around him. Reporters cried, "BOY!" held up pages, and went on typing one-handed as he or another ran up, grasped the pages, and ran them to the copy desk to be edited. Or a copyeditor or makeup man cried "BOY!" and held up pages, and these were to be run up to the composing room one flight above and handed to a lineotype operator.

There was a teleprinter room where stories rattled in from the paper's correspondents abroad, or from the wire services, and these had to be ripped off and distributed to whoever was waiting for them.

The composing room was a different world, almost a different business. Though as big as the newsroom just below, it was strangely muted, no one crying out. The smells were different, hot lead mixed with hot ink, the sounds different as well, mostly the clack of lead type dropping line by line out of the machines into the long narrow trays.

Back in the newsroom there were cries of "BOY!" even when deadline was far off, even during the quiet half hour after each edition went to press—a reporter or editor who wanted his pencils sharpened, or a coffee from the cafeteria upstairs, or a file from the morgue. Several times Troy was sent out to the bar across the street to bring back beer, which technically was not allowed and not part of his job but which nonetheless he did, for it seemed to him he had no choice.

Very few reporters or editors even looked up as he handed them what they had sent him for, or snatched pages from their hands.

At that time there were three editions each night, starting with the City Edition which closed at 9:00 P.M., and was marred by typos, rushed stories, and ill-fitting headlines; the Late City Edition closed at 11:45 and was much cleaned up, many of the pieces and headlines rewritten; the Late Late closed at 2:40, though breaking news could be added to it later, and was as close to perfect each night as the men could make it. Men only. There were a few women on the paper then, very few, and they worked days, as if to keep them out of everyone's way. Journalism was considered a métier for men, and by nightfall the newsroom had become an all-male club.

The night managing editor would give the good night at three forty in the morning. The paper would close down, empty out. Troy would go out onto Times Square and be amazed at how quiet the city had become, the only noise the banging of garbage cans being emptied into trucks some blocks away.

Troy saw his job clearly. He was an errand boy with a college degree, neither more nor less, he hated being a copyboy, and sometimes he imagined they were rating him on how fast he ran. But newspapering had its traditions, which were iron-bound, and this was how you started.

The pay was derisory, $29.50 a week, plus a night differential of $2.50. He still lived at home, had to. He had no car and could afford few dates. Many young men came to work as copyboys. Few lasted. The bad pay was no doubt part of the weeding-out process. Only the dedicated were wanted. Only the dedicated stayed.

Plus a few others who, though his age, were treated like first draft choices on a sports team, and who were promoted to reporter almost at once. The former editor of the *Harvard Crimson*. The former editor of the *Yale Daily News*. Troy had been editor of the *Fordham Ram*. Not the same.

The paper on Sundays was an inch and a half thick containing many sections. On his own time Troy began to write pieces for one or another of these sections. He wrote a piece for the Drama Section on a starlet appearing in her first big movie. He met her in a suite at the Plaza Hotel on Fifth Avenue, the first stop on her publicity tour. She was beautiful, earnest, and just as nervous as he was. Across from them, listening carefully, watching, sat a middle-aged press agent, the girl's eyes flicking toward him from time to time as if seeking help or encouragement. Troy did not yet know enough to order press agents from the room before interviewing someone, though he would learn this in time.

The piece was a success. He got $40 for it. At copyboy rates this counted as more than a week's pay, though by any other standards it was a poor wage. The paper prided itself on how well it paid its reporters. Freelancers, the category Troy fit into, were mercilessly exploited.

The Drama Section, pleased with him, offered other assignments at the same price. He wrote about a singer, a dancer, a radio personality. For the Sunday sports section he wrote some profiles of ballplayers.

In those days players would talk to individual reporters. The time would come when it was impossible to get close to such rich, spoiled, and famous young men except for formal press conferences to which they submitted, usually, with bad grace. But not yet. All that was required of Troy was that he know the player's exact batting average, and parrot it back to him, and then talk knowingly of games the player had broken up with a timely hit. Once he had done these things the interview would go smoothly. The player would usually talk his ear off.

All these pieces Troy wrote, and got badly paid for. But around the paper he was becoming noticed.

Other copyboys came and went. Troy stayed. He was promoted to clerk and put in charge of the weather page. Today's weather, tomorrow's, next week's, all of it sent over by the Weather Service. Day after day. He had only to arrange it in the paper's format and send it up to the composing room.

Finally, at the age of 25, the executive editor called him into the big corner office and, sounding expansive and generous as he did it, promoted him to reporter. Troy—at last—was on the staff.

It had taken him four years. There was still a long way to go. He wanted to write important stories but knew he would not be given any for a while. Troy saw journalism as a calling. He wanted to make a difference in the world.

DURING THESE SAME FOUR YEARS Earl Finley worked toward a Juris Doctor degree at Fordham Law School. Many of the law professors were Jesuits, but others were practicing lawyers—Catholic lawyers, usually—giving one or two nights a week back to the next generation. Earl, too, soon realized that a Fordham Law degree, when and if he got it, would not result in a clerkship with a prestigious judge. Nor would it lead to a big-money job with one of New York's whitebread law firms. Probably it would not even get him an offer from the U.S. Attorney's office, which, staffed mostly with lawyers from

Ivy League schools, worked only federal crimes, many of them of a financial nature.

That is, Catholic universities were highly regarded inside Catholic circles, but not outside. The general public tended to see them as football schools, their teams stocked with burly youths from the Pennsylvania coal towns, most of them with unpronounceable Polish names. Fordham no longer played football, but had, and the reputation lingered.

It was now that Earl realized this for the first time.

Only a limited number of doors would spring open at the push of a Fordham degree. The FBI was one. Certain other anti-Communist bastions, as well.

And the Manhattan District Attorney's office, which was what Earl wanted, for he had formed the notion that his true place in life would be in court arguing cases. He wanted to be on trial all the time, or as much of the time as possible. Perhaps he saw the law, or even life itself, as competition. The former diving champion wanted a role in which he would champion the good and the true, and thereby become a champion himself. He wanted to pile up victories.

Since he had no money, no scholarship either, no one to pay any of his bills, he was obliged to attend law classes at night, while holding down a full-time day job. To graduate he needed 83 credits, but evening-division students could take a maximum of only twelve per semester, which meant adding a year, perhaps more, to the length of time it would take him.

His first two semesters he worked as a laborer on a construction site, and ate mostly in the Automat on 57th Street, pushing nickels into the slots, then opening the little doors and withdrawing that night's feast, beef-stew pies and ginger cakes often enough. He would carry his tray to an empty table, and eat, usually, alone.

Over the years his diet did not change much, but his jobs did. With a year of law school behind him he was able to get an internship at

Belfast, Knapp and Curran, a Midtown firm with 60 partners and over 100 lawyers in all. The firm did contract law, divorces, and civil litigation and the partners, it seemed to him, spent most of their time sipping coffee in the halls and yakking about whatever they were working on. This counted as "consultation," and when the cups were empty the lawyers would go back inside their individual offices and each of them would bill clients at the rate of hundreds of dollars an hour for the time they had just spent considering their cases.

Earl detested this type of lawyering.

The firm had several floors of a Midtown skyscraper. In the halls Earl met many girls and young women. They were interns like himself, or secretaries, or even young associates, most of whom, being women, would never make partner. To his surprise a number of these girls and women seemed to find him cute. Earl, who had had almost no previous sexual experience, now developed a taste for it. Or at least as much of a taste as his limited money, time, and the size of his studio apartment would permit. He was surprised to find that girls liked sex too. He became rather experienced rather fast.

As a student he concentrated almost exclusively on criminal law. After a survey course on New York criminal procedure, he studied search and seizure, interrogations, identifications, rules of evidence, plea bargaining. There was so much to learn, but the new knowledge, the learning itself, enthralled him. He took seminars on rape and violence. He studied grand jury practice, the rules of discovery, jury selection, double jeopardy. He took writing courses: how to write motions, briefs, indictments. He learned about habeas corpus and Fifth Amendment safeguards, about trial advocacy and professional responsibility. The classes were long, the years were long, and he accorded them the same dedication, the fierce concentration that had once gone into the incredibly difficult dives he had learned, had sculpted into his brain, into his being, to the point where he could have executed them in the dark.

His final year in law school he worked as an intern at the Manhattan DA's office on Centre Street. He was paid almost nothing. The job did come with the promise that he would be hired as an assistant DA as soon as he passed the bar exam. He would have to sign on for four years. Assistant DAs were paid almost nothing also, certainly not a living wage, hardly more than Andy Troy earned as a copyboy at the paper, and most of them, the day the four years were up, quit for jobs with lucrative law firms. Earl was one of the few who had no intention of quitting ever.

Summer weekends he continued to perform his comical diving act at country clubs throughout the tristate area, changing and improving it year by year, adding first a straight man, and then a second diver, and of course raising his price. He was paid directly now, his days as an amateur athlete were over, and the money he earned, most of the money he earned all year, he salted away against the bad times he knew were coming. The first years as an assistant DA would be financially bleak, he realized, and he wanted to be ready for them.

At most of these clubs his act was the high point of the summer, and the Glen Garry Country Club wanted him twice, first on the Fourth of July, and again on Labor Day. He began to look forward to seeing Roxanne Harley there. In the evening they would sometimes dive together. She did not practice anymore but still dived well, and he even invited her to join his troupe, but she smiled and refused. Afterward they would have dinner together at the club, then go for a walk on the golf course in the night. At first she always asked about Frank Redmond, and seemed to want to talk about him. Then she didn't anymore, and when they walked on the golf course they held hands. He invited her out a few times, usually to the movies, or a party at someone's house. Eventually he took her to a motel where she felt obliged to apologize, as she lay back, for not being a virgin, though she was by then 22 or 23 years old. But those were the morals of the time. Earl didn't care about her virginity, or lack of it, especially not at that moment, but she seemed to. It was only one boy once, and no one he knew, she explained, trying to diminish it, lying under him and to him on all counts. She had graduated from college but was still living at home. She worked as an assistant buyer at her father's flagship store, liked the job and was good at it, she said, but business was bad, her father was worried and tense all the time and snapped at her constantly.

They went back to that motel, or another, regularly from then on.

Earl had given up going to church, principally because sex did not seem sinful to him. He had never believed very much in his religion anyway, and unlike his friends had received no religious pressure at home, where he had had only his mother, who was rarely there. The strict Jesuit morality was imprinted in his soul, but not the pious, churchy parts that went with it. When he asked Rocky to marry him this was an advantage, for there were a number of stern interviews with her father, which he was able to pass, stating bluntly: "I am not a practicing Catholic. Case closed."

He had passed the bar and was an assistant DA by then. His new God was the law, which was not a perfect instrument by any means but was the best man had been able to devise so far, better than the notion of God which, as Earl saw it, man had also devised. That is, far more evil had been perpetrated in the name of God than in the name of the law, and for far longer. He was not interested in being the kind of lawyer who worked at Belfast, Knapp and Curran, people who manipulated the law to suit rich clients. He would manipulate it to put bad people away. Earl wanted to wear the white hat, to work on the side of the angels—there were a number of clichés to describe it. He believed there was right and there was wrong—his Jesuit education had penetrated far deeper than he knew. There were predators out there causing pain, and it was his job to put them in a place where, at least for a specified time, they could hurt no one.

At first he was assigned to the bottom rung, arraignment court on the late tour, where he was able to accord only a few minutes to each of the dozens of arrests the cops brought in each night. He would have to work his way up. There were over 400 assistant DAs ahead of him, this was in Manhattan alone, with the elected DA on top. At the highest echelons, if he could get there, he would at last be decently paid. And one day, with luck, he might even run for DA himself. Might even be elected.

GABE DRISCOLL WAS IN SCHOOL most of these years as well. Not one school, but several, beginning with the Police Academy. The NYPD had no proper Academy building yet. The politicians were still arguing over where to build one. In the meantime a former warehouse at the edge of the Hudson River was in use, and had been for some time. It was a patched-up building that had been fitted out with classrooms. It seemed to carry the odors of every product that had ever been stored there. The odors changed from room to room. All were strong. Some were only disagreeable, others downright unpleasant.

The recruits wore gray uniforms and already carried shields and guns. Sometimes they were brought out to the street to help control crowds. Parade duty, ball games. Otherwise they were full-time students.

Gabe was there by accident. Midway through senior year at Fordham his father's brother, a police sergeant, had come to the apartment where Gabe still lived with his mother. The police department entrance exam would be given in two weeks' time, Uncle Jack said. Gabe should sign up for it. The family's police tradition should not be allowed to lapse.

Gabe said he wasn't interested.

His uncle came back the next night with the application and more or less forced him to sign it.

Along with 9,000 other young men sitting at desks in public schools all across the city, Gabe went on to take the test. His purpose was mostly to keep peace in the family. He passed easily, then forgot the whole thing.

By June he had a college degree but no notion of what he wanted to do with his life. He applied for jobs at Xerox, and at New York Life, and was told his application would be kept on file. He tried for the training program at a drug company, and also at IBM, but did not hear back from either. At this point he received a letter appointing him to the next Police Academy class. Still without a job, thoroughly discouraged by what he was finding out about how hard it could be to get one, he took it.

He found the Academy much like college, though in important ways different. Cosmology and calculus were out. In the classrooms, the principal textbook was the New York State Penal Code, which was thick and would have to be virtually memorized, but this would be no harder, Gabe judged, than learning Latin. Dozens of official forms were presented for study. He had to become familiar with each one, learn how and when to fill them out.

There were integrity courses too, at which some of his classmates scoffed, not Gabe, for police integrity was based on the same ethical principles the Jesuits had been teaching him at Fordham, no different. He was about to drift away from the Catholic Church, but not from most of the standards it imposed.

The odorous warehouse had no gym or shooting range. For physical training the classes were bussed up to the 68th Street Armory, where, after calisthenics, they began to be taught how to arrest, disarm, handcuff, frisk subjects. How to subdue prisoners who did not wish to be subdued. Rough and tumble police tactics. Courses colleges didn't give.

At the department's outdoor range at Rodman's Neck in the Bronx, also reached by bus, Gabe scored fourth highest with the .38. He liked the heft and feel of the gun, the recoil when he fired it. The noise. The power of it. As a boy he had been given his father's gun to handle from time to time, but had never fired one before now.

One day the police commissioner came to lecture them about the policeman's role, which for the most part, he said, had nothing to do with shoot-outs, or wrestling malefactors to the ground. Mostly it had to do with helping people: the rape victim, the battered wife, the old man who had collapsed on the sidewalk. The quality most demanded of a cop was not bravery but compassion, the PC said. It was the cop's job to intervene in family fights, to find lost children, to serve as a role model for teenage boys who might otherwise get in trouble. Yes, a cop arrested bad guys from time to time, took them off the street, but mostly he responded to people who needed him. He was the most important social worker we have, the PC said, more important most times than a doctor or a priest. Being a cop was a chance really to help people. It was a noble calling, or it was nothing at all.

The PC spoke with fervor. The class had become very still. Being a cop was a vocation, the PC said, and Gabe believed him. Being a cop was a chance to serve. Gabe had never thought of it in that light before. But he could see that it was true. Or could be true, if a young man cared enough to make it true. For himself he meant for it to be true. He wanted to help. Wanted to serve. He was at a susceptible age, and he came from a black-and-white, ethical, structured world, namely Fordham. The police department would be more of the same.

The PC's words went in deep. Gabe had come to this lecture already enthralled by his first weeks in the Police Academy; the course work, the physical work as well. And now this. Of course he found the PC, this tall, baldish man with the big teeth, very old, 50 at least. He also found him impressive, persuasive, honest, and he made of him an instant hero.

Most of all the PC's lecture convinced the young man that in becoming a cop he had made the right decision.

The lecture lasted about an hour. In the course of it Gabe had perceived one thing more. That the NYPD could be a real career. His father, before being invalided out, had not got very far, nor had Uncle Jack. But this man on the dais had one of the most responsible jobs in the city, was respected by all, and got good money. Gabe, if he worked hard, studied hard for the promotion exams, could do the same.

There was applause as the PC stepped down from the dais, and some of the older, braver recruits in their gray uniforms stepped forward to shake his hand, but not Gabe, who, musing about the future, did not quite dare join them.

He was twelve months in the Police Academy, longer than most classes had lasted previously, or would last in the future. He graduated at the top of his class of about 300, and to the ceremony wore his brand-new blue uniform and white gloves, they all did. The PC swore them all in again, and the mayor made a speech.

Gabe's idealism lasted only a few days.

He found himself assigned to the 25th Precinct, East Harlem. Spanish Harlem it was sometimes called. Many Hispanics there. Many mostly aged Italians as well. It was a Mafia bastion. The Mafia was as strong a presence as the police. It ruled with an ethic of its own. Predators who preyed on its people were dealt with. This was fine with the cops.

Gabe had a footpost for a time, then was given a seat in a radio car with a mentor beside him, a 42-year-old patrolman who smoked cigars. The NYPD has never favored corruption, and there have been periodic purges which have wiped out virtually all of it. But at other times enforcement has become lax, and it has crept back in. This was one such time.

Gabe and his mentor were working a split tour, eight at night to four in the morning — at the paper across the city so was copyboy

Andy Troy—when they responded to a past burglary. A clothing warehouse next to the East River had been broken into. When they got there Gabe saw that the warehouse door hung half off. Other radio car teams had already come on the scene. Cops were carrying goods out of the warehouse and stuffing them into the trunks of the sector cars. Gabe's mentor hurried into the warehouse to grab his share while Gabe stood on the sidewalk wondering what to do.

As most cops saw it, it wasn't even stealing. The insurance would pay.

Gabe got back in the car and drove away. His mentor, when he came out with his loot, had no car to stuff it into. Later Gabe explained to him that he had been taken sick and had had to hurry back to the stationhouse urgently. His mentor looked at him suspiciously, but said nothing.

Internal Affairs was a fairly small unit at the time. Gabe went to talk to a captain there. The captain promised to look into it, but as far as Gabe knew, nothing ever was done.

A week later came a cardiac arrest in a tenement on First Avenue. Gabe was driving, his mentor beside him.

They entered the apartment. An old woman weeping. An old man on the floor. Gabe wanted to start artificial respiration but his mentor stopped him. "He's DOA," he said, giving a slight kick to the unresponsive leg. "What else do we have here?"

What they had was money on the dresser. Bills and coins, not very much because these people didn't have much. Gabe sat down to start on the paperwork that accompanied a DOA, a patrolman's nightmare. The mentor waited until a neighbor had led the weeping widow next door, then scooped up the money.

"Put that back," said Gabe.

"Don't worry, you'll get your share."

"Put it back."

"Half is yours. It goes without saying."

"Put it back."

Word of this spread too, followed by rumors of a corruption investigation. Gabe's mentor hurriedly retired.

From then on Gabe was semi-ostracized in the precinct. Also he acquired a reputation for probity that resulted, many years later, with him being appointed to command Internal Affairs.

The precinct captain, who saw Gabe as dangerous to himself, could not get rid of him fast enough. Corruption in a precinct was seen by headquarters as the commander's fault. He could lose his post, lose any chance of being promoted to deputy inspector. So this commander did not want Gabe around.

To put on it the best face possible, he arranged for Gabe to be advanced to the detective division.

The young cop of course was delighted. He now had the gold shield, which was every patrolman's dream.

He was sent back to the Police Academy to detective school. He and the other new detectives were led deeper still into the penal code, were taught how to request legal wiretaps and bugs, and how to plant them, how to interrogate prisoners and tail suspects, how to shake a tail on themselves. For weeks they studied all the arcane tricks that, as detectives, they would use every day.

There were two more schools in Gabe's immediate future, the first of them a private training program that offered instruction to cops studying for promotion exams, in Gabe's case the exam for sergeant. There were several such schools, all run by ex-cops. On his own time Gabe attended one of them.

The department was expanding at this time. Sergeants were needed. Therefore a number of time-in-grade requirements were waived. Gabe was permitted to take the sergeant's test, which he passed with the third-highest score overall.

While waiting for a specific vacancy to occur Detective Driscoll worked homicides out of the 9th Precinct in the East Village, a dangerous place, for the city's racial groups were all mixed up there, whites, blacks, Hispanics all crowded in together, everyone poor, murders and assaults as common as in the city's black ghettos, sometimes even running ahead.

He and 40 others were promoted to sergeant. There was a ceremony at which Gabe was obliged to wear his uniform and white gloves again, and at which the mayor made another speech. Afterward he was ordered back to the Police Academy for sergeants' school.

He was 25, possibly the youngest sergeant in the department. He was still a well-muscled young man, but was beginning to lose his hair and this concerned him more every day.

GABE'S VARIOUS SCHOOLS, EARL'S LAW COURSES, Troy's newsroom all allowed a certain flexibility. Frank's school — the seminary — did not.

The seminary was in Yonkers, a 17th-century French chateau built in the 1890s. Its stone walls looked like what they were: impregnable. One turret had a golden dome surmounted by a great gold cross.

For four years Frank lived in a bare cell of a room. Above the first floor, silence was mandatory at all times. No one was allowed out of his own room except when wearing his cassock. No one was allowed in anyone else's room under pain of instant expulsion. The silence between night devotions and the following dawn was called Magnum Silencium, the great silence.

Lights went out automatically at 10:00 P.M., then on again automatically at 5:30 the next morning, at which time the seminarians had 30 minutes to wash, shave, dress, and make their beds. In winter it was still dark outside. But when the days got longer the windows were open, and they could hear birds. Frank thought this a lovely time of day. The whole world made new.

He and the others trooped into the chapel, the day's first stop, for half an hour of collective meditation directed by the spiritual director, followed by the first of two daily examinations of conscience.

Then mass, early morning singing, the taste of holy communion on his tongue.

Fifteen minutes for breakfast. Lumpy oatmeal.

Twenty minutes' recreation before classes. Time for a smoke, if the rector had given permission that day, which was rare.

Bells rang, signaling the rush to classrooms. Courses in scripture, liturgy, canon law, sacred music, dogmatic and moral theology, homiletics, and pastoral counseling; the dogmatic, moral, canonical, and social aspects of matrimony; the psychology, morality, and supernatural value of human acts in general, which led into the division and distinction of sins.

There were maps that pulled down over the blackboard, sometimes springing back again with a crash. Maps showing Palestine in Christ's time, with the locations of his miracles marked in. Maps showing the journeys of St. Paul through Asia Minor to martyrdom in Rome in A.D. 67. The desks were exact replicas of the desks at West Point: straight, square, and in use in these two places and nowhere else.

From 3:15 to 4:30 each day compulsory recreation outdoors. Touch football, basketball, softball. Collars on a bench, cassocks tucked up into trousers. Running and running. Laughter sometimes, bitter words other times. A few seminarians discussing the new philosophers, Kung and Schillebeecks under the trees, to the contempt of those playing ball.

During meals in the refectory a lector read pious tomes. The lives of saints, usually. Boiled codfish, boiled succotash in the separate compartments of an aluminum tray. Each saint's life ended with a punch line. "His resolution — death before sin — has become the rallying cry of Catholics."

A pause in the clink of cutlery while, as they were supposed to, the seminarians chanted: "Deo Gratias" on cue.

Warm comradeship. Gossip in the corridors. Who was having

trouble, who not. Which teachers might be replaced. Who would the rector select as his personal sacristan? An important question, for selection virtually assured ordination. In later years there would be a shortage of candidates to the priesthood. Parochial schools would have to be closed. The seminary would have to accept whoever it could get. But not then. The New York Archdiocese had more candidates than it could handle. Frank and the others knew this. They were replaceable. Ordination was no sure thing. Many young men were told to pack their bags and leave, more often for insubordination than for doctrinal failings. Dissent was not tolerated. "If you want to be ordained," they told each other, "toe the line."

Back to the chapel for night devotions. A second examination of conscience. Loud singing.

The rector watched to see who stayed behind to pray on his own, as coaches watched to see who stayed out practicing after practice was over. Who really wanted to make the team?

Upstairs, alone in their rooms, they studied. All was silent. They watched the clock as the needle advanced toward lights-out. Wooden clogs clip-clopped down the corridor to the shower room. Cassocks in place but naked underneath. One seminarian wore bathing trunks in the shower so as not to be tempted by his own body, or tempt others. Frank Redmond had never heard of a case of homosexuality among priests and so assumed there had never been one. Which meant that such rules were silly. But a rule was to be obeyed. From Fordham Prep on he had been taught the value of discipline for discipline's sake, of the value of self-denial, of obeying rules. And he wanted to be ordained.

At 10:00 P.M. came the sudden darkness. Frank knelt beside his bed trying to pray, failing some nights, the words sounding empty. But one knelt saying them in the hope that when grace came, one would be ready for it.

Exhausted from the sports, the study, the constant consideration of eternity, he got into bed and slept. Most nights his sleep was dreamless and he awoke feeling totally refreshed.

The course on marriage came during the final year of theology. "Marriage and the Eucharist are sacraments of unity. Marriage finds its closest parallel in the Eucharist as an effective sign of Christ's presence," the professor intoned. Notebooks had to be filled, and blue-books later. The textbook was entirely in English except for one chapter in Latin, the one entitled "De Sexto."

"The erotic is essentially an embrace on the surface of being," the professor continued, "a palpitation, a fascination with the flesh, with the immediate, with outward appearance. Ontologically speaking it is a place of absolute solitude, two beings together in complete solitude, so situated that they are parallel to one another and cannot be joined."

The professor, a middle-aged priest, stood on the dais in front of the blackboard. He had a piece of chalk in his hand, and chalk dust on his cassock. "The child who bursts forth seems to be hurled at this union as its negation," he said. "Actually the child is its affirmation. The child is a symbol of transcendence which by its presence in the interior of the couple obliges them to open themselves to universal love."

Because the words were meaningless to Frank, or virtually so, it was easy to memorize them, no questions asked.

He did not know much about marriage, almost nothing, but did know something about sexual love which, he imagined, the professor did not. In any case the priest had not come close to describing the emotions Frank had once felt for Roxanne Harley. He seemed to be insisting that they did not exist.

Frank tried never to think of Rocky, and most days succeeded. Sex was a drug, he convinced himself. Like other drugs it was habit forming. But you could wean yourself off it, which he believed he had done.

Ordination day came. The ceremony was in St. Patrick's Cathedral, the cardinal presiding, the pews crowded with family and friends. He and the other seminarians prostrated themselves on the altar. An auxiliary bishop anointed them with oils, laid on hands. Frank's parents were there, so were Andy, Earl, and Gabe. Afterward came much hugging, kissing, congratulating, and shaking of hands.

Frank was now a priest. People called him Father. He was 25 years old.

Andy, Earl, and Gabe were 25 also. All four of them had reached, from one day to the next it seemed, a level of professional competence that could not be denied. Andy was a staff reporter, Gabe a sergeant, Earl an assistant district attorney, and Frank a priest. For the first time the generation above seemed to accept them as fellow adults who could be allowed out alone, who could be allowed to function, at last, without supervision.

FRANK WAS ASSIGNED TO THE Church of St. Pius X in Scarsdale, possibly the richest town and parish in the archdiocese, a place of more mansions, more corporate executives than anywhere. The amount of the collection take each Sunday shocked him.

It was one suburb over from Larchmont, where Rocky lived, and he hated it there, though not for that reason. Parishioners came to him for help, which was what he was there for, but the help they needed he was unable to give. Scarsdale was a place where teenagers were given sports cars as birthday presents, usually as soon as they learned to drive. Their pocket money was sufficient to buy the latest designer drugs. Their cars, at great cost to themselves and others, they frequently wrecked. The drugs they bought put them in the hospital or jail. Focused on the companies they ran, the fathers were rarely home. Though loaded down with money, the mothers felt abandoned and did not know which way to turn. So they turned to the new priest, who seemed more sympathetic than the ones who had been there awhile.

The teenagers were defiant and could not be talked to. The mothers sobbed a lot. Frank came to feel completely ineffectual.

He petitioned the Chancery for a change, but none came. He wanted a ghetto precinct. The poor he thought he could help. The mess here would have to be cleaned up by the people themselves. An outsider, especially a newly ordained outsider, could do nothing.

And then Earl came to him to announce that he and Rocky were getting married. "What do you think? Do you think it's a good idea?"

What was he supposed to say to this?

So he tried for a jocular response. "Are you going to be able to support her? You don't get paid much, and wives are expensive."

"That's the good part. She works, she earns a nice salary."

"You don't get paid as much as I do, and I'm just a parish priest."

"Without her salary we couldn't afford to get married. With the two together we can get by."

"Suppose she gets pregnant?"

"In a couple of years I'll be making enough."

"You've got it figured out, I guess."

"So do you think I should do it?"

Again the question bothered him. "Do you love her? Does she love you?"

"Sure."

"If you love each other you should do it."

"Will you perform the ceremony?"

"Is that what you both want?"

"It's what I want."

They were again sitting on the float, feet in the water, at Andy Troy's parents' summer cottage.

"What does she want? Have you asked her?"

"She'll be delighted. She still talks of you."

"I haven't seen her in a long time."

"She likes you a lot."

"Does she?"

Frank had been aware of the ongoing courtship. Nonetheless the announcement had set him back. He imagined Rocky in a long white dress, saw her lifting the veil off her face and pledging her troth to another.

"The only thing is," Earl said, "it can't be in a Catholic church. You know her father, I believe?"

"Yes, I know her father."

"It has to be in the Presbyterian church in Larchmont. Does that pose a problem?"

"Well, it would be perfectly legal," Frank said with a smile. "If that's what you're worried about."

But technically it did pose a problem. Ecumenism had not yet started. Technically he was not permitted to enter a Protestant church or take part in ceremonies there. He would have to request permission from the Chancery, which probably would deny it.

So he could tell Earl no, could beg off if he wished to.

On the other hand he could ignore the Chancery, inform nobody, perform the ceremony. Someone, some pious woman, would probably find out and report him, and he'd be in trouble. What did he care? What could they do to him?

He stirred the water with his foot.

So he thought he would do it. He owed it to Earl. How much would watching Rocky get married upset him?

"Let me see what I can work out." Frank stood up. "Race you across the lake," he said.

They plunged in and started thrashing.

The next day he drove to Glen Garry Country Club. It was Sunday, sunny, hot. He wore black pants and shoes, and a red and green striped sports shirt. He thought Rocky would be at the club, and looked for her, but she was not at the pool, nor on the tennis courts, and the restaurant was empty. He asked the caddy-master, but she was not playing golf.

Sitting in a deck chair he waited a while, but she did not appear. Despite the five years that had gone by he remembered her phone number perfectly well.

He phoned her house and, when she came on the line, identified himself.

After what sounded like a shocked silence she said: "Yes, I remember your name." Then: "What do you want?"

"I'm at the club. I thought you might be here."

She did not respond.

"There was something I wanted to discuss with you."

"What?"

"Are you busy? Could you come over for a few minutes?"

"What could we possibly have to talk about?"

"Or I could come there."

"That definitely would not be a good idea."

After a pause she said: "As it happens I was planning on coming over in about half an hour, anyway. Because I have to meet someone."

"I'll wait for you."

He drifted about the club, watched the swimmers for a while, watched the golfers teeing off. He saw her come into the parking lot in the same little sports car, and get out. She was wearing a T-shirt, shorts, and sandals. Her thick dark hair was tied back.

He offered his hand. After a moment she shook it.

They stood looking at each other. She said: "Let's get in the shade. It's hot out here."

So they moved behind the clubhouse under some trees.

She said: "Are you allowed out dressed like that?"

"Of course."

"I thought you'd be wearing a cassock. A roman collar."

"No."

He tried to decide on an adjective to describe the way she looked to him. But no single word seemed adequate.

He said: "How long has it been since we've seen each other?"

"I have no idea."

Frank could have told her.

"What was it you wanted to talk about?"

"Earl asked me to officiate at your wedding."

"So?"

"I wondered how you felt about that. About me being on the altar."

"Whatever Earl wants. You're his friend, not mine."

"About getting married in front of me."

"Why should I care, one way or the other?"

"Well, if Earl found out."

"How do you know I haven't told him already?"

"I think he would have mentioned it to me. You haven't, have you?"

"No."

"That's one good thing."

"Who's going to tell him?" she said. "You?"

"No, of course not."

Seeing him again she was as shaken as he was, but it did not show and he never guessed.

When a young woman called to Rocky from the clubhouse terrace, she looked over and waved. "I have to go," she said.

"So what should I do?"

"I don't care what you do," she said. "You're nothing to me."

Turning, she walked toward the terrace.

"Nice to have seen you again," Frank called out to her back, hoping she might turn and smile at him.

He drove to his rectory. In there, until such time as he ventured forth again, nothing could hurt him.

———

THE WEDDING TOOK PLACE ON A SUNDAY AFTERNOON in the Larch-mont Presbyterian church. A Protestant minister officiated. Father Redmond in his clerical suit sat amid Earl's other friends on Earl's side of the church. The church was crowded, mostly guests of the large Harley family. Earl had no family, only friends from college, and from the DA's office. So his side of the church looked a bit empty. The bride, wearing a long white dress, a kind of tiara, and a veil, was led down the aisle by her father. Upon reaching the altar where the bridegroom waited along with his co–best men, Gabe Driscoll and Andy Troy, she lifted the veil off her face.

Prayers were said, vows exchanged. Rocky looked solemn. Earl looked pleased with himself, smug, the way he had looked after winning the dive at the Nationals.

Rings slid onto fingers. The bridegroom kissed the bride, then the minister did.

Outside on the church steps additional kissing took place, but not by the priest, who only shook the bride's hand.

The reception was held at the country club. An orchestra played too loudly. The cake was big enough to cut with a sword, and one lay on the table, waiting. There was too much to drink.

After a time Rocky came over to where Frank was talking to some people.

"Dance with me," she said, threw the train of her dress over her arm, and led him onto the floor.

They danced. At first the music was fast. Fast and loud. Rocky whirling, the gown over her arm. Her face red. His too, he supposed. Black suit, white gown, they moved in sync but hardly touched, for that was the popular mode of dancing that year. Amidst such noise they certainly couldn't talk. It isn't as if I'm holding her in my arms, Frank told himself. She no longer affected him the way she used to, he told himself.

But the next song was slow. He glanced around, planning to leave the floor, but she came close, and then her body was against his and he was breathing into her hair.

The music had turned sweet and old-fashioned, though as loud as ever. He looked over and saw Earl dancing with Rocky's mother.

Sweetheart, they're suspecting things.
People will say we're in love.

"The last time we met I was rude to you," Rocky murmured close to his ear.

"Rude? No, not at all."

"I said you were nothing to me. It isn't true."

"Well —"

"I was trying to be cruel to you, and I'm sorry."

An hour after that the orchestra went silent, the dancing stopped, and Earl raised the sword over the cake. A trumpet fanfare, a roll of drums, and he brought the sword down like an ax, severing the cake, which fell heavily into two massive parts. Laughing happily, the swordsman pretended to lick the blade.

Rocky again came toward Frank, this time with a piece of the wedding cake which she rammed into his mouth.

"Isn't that delicious?" she said.

He saw that she was a little drunk.

"Look at Earl over there," she said. "Don't you think he's handsome?"

Frank said: "You're going to be very happy together."

"Does Earl have a nickname?"

"Not that I know of, why?"

"He told me you boys used to call him something."

This information was true, and Frank wondered where she was going with it.

"What do the letters H.C. stand for?"

"I don't remember," he said.

"I know what it means," said Rocky.

"Do you, now?"

"He told me."

"Hmm."

"Aren't you ashamed?" she asked archly. "You could have given him a complex."

He remembered being 16 years old, a group of them standing in many shower rooms together. To all these boys Earl had seemed well endowed. And so for a time they had called him Horsecock. H.C. for short.

"Anyway, for your information he's no bigger than anyone else." And she smirked at him.

He realized that she wanted him to know that she had been to bed with her new husband in advance of the wedding. Earl and how many others?

He tried to think up a nonchalant reply, but couldn't.

He delivered Rocky back to Earl, and shook hands with both of them, planning to leave. I've got to get out of here, he thought.

But he did not leave. A little later Rocky and Earl reappeared, she in a pink suit over a black silk blouse, Earl in blazer and slacks. Everyone congregated on the clubhouse stoop. A Cadillac waited, engine running. Rocky tossed her bridal bouquet backward over her shoulder.

Rice rained down. The bridal couple scurried into the Cadillac, which motored away.

In Vietnam that year the war approached its ugliest phase. Rocky and Earl went to Paris on their honeymoon, a gift from the bride's father. Before they got back Frank had enlisted in the Navy as a chaplain attached to the Marine Corps. He did not see them again before shipping out.

THE INVESTIGATION

4

SATURDAY AFTERNOON. CHIEF DRISCOLL, who lives on West 67th Street, decides to take his wife for a walk in Central Park. When he suggests it to her she is delighted. Her face lights up and she claps her hands together. He bundles her up carefully for it is a crisp winter day outside, and helps her into the wheelchair. She can walk around the apartment holding on to things. She can move from one armchair to another by herself, but crossing streets would be beyond her. He gets out a hat she likes and puts it on her, wraps a scarf around her neck, and then takes her down in the elevator and wheels her out onto the sidewalk and across to the park, entering past Tavern on the Green.

There is another street to cross inside the park. This one is closed to cars on weekends but bicyclists, roller skaters, and joggers rush by, some of them at considerable speed. "It's worth your life to get across," Gabe tells his wife.

Though there are patches of thin snow here and there, the Sheep Meadow is crowded too. Frisbees sail into the sun. Touch football games are being played. As he pushes her along he listens to the noise footballs make slapping into hands. They talk about Frankie. Or, rather, it is he who talks mostly, while she listens, for lately she has trouble forming her words.

"I liked him so much," she says.

"He was the best of us," says Gabe, meaning it. "The best looking, the smartest, the most giving. The best swimmer too."

Once they were four boys together, but life has not been kind. Frankie is dead, and Gabe flinches from remembering what happened to Earl. Andy and his wife have nothing together, hardly talk to each other anymore, and he himself has a wife with an incurable illness, but their marriage, as Gabe sees it, has been good all along. So perhaps this makes him the luckiest of the four.

When he wheels his wife back into their apartment the phone is ringing. Lt. Begos. They have found Keershawn Brown.

"Congratulations," says Driscoll into the phone.

"You don't have to be sarcastic, Chief. His mother is bringing him into the stationhouse in an hour."

"I'll be right there."

Begos says stiffly: "I think I'm capable of interrogating the kid, Chief."

"Just hold him until I get there."

Chief Driscoll calls for his department car. One or the other of the drivers assigned him is on duty around the clock.

While waiting he prepares dinner for himself and his wife. Their children are in college, one in Chicago, the other in Miami. During the week he has a woman who comes in. Weekends he manages alone.

The doorman signals that his car is downstairs.

He establishes Barbara in front of the television, making sure the remote is working and in her hand so she won't have to struggle to her feet to find it. He promises to be back in an hour.

"I'll be fine," she tells him. "Don't worry about me."

He goes down and gets into his car, and during the ride uptown moves the police radio from one band to another, listening for whatever might be happening in the city.

Keershawn Brown turns out to be a tall, gangling kid, and he is terrified. He seems to think he has been arrested for keeping pigeons on the roof, and will go to jail. Chief Driscoll must spend the first 20 minutes trying to calm him down. His mother sits in the corner and says nothing, no matter how often the boy's eyes turn beseechingly in her direction.

"This is not about you," Chief Driscoll tells him, "it's about Father Redmond, whom you must have seen on that roof from time to time. What can you tell me about him?"

Now the boy imagines he is being accused of pushing the priest off the roof. His Adam's apple jerks spasmodically.

Gabe must take him out into the street, walk him as far as Adam Clayton Powell Boulevard, talk to him first about baseball, and then about Powell, the former Harlem congressman who died in 1972. The night is cold. Gabe's words rise up like smoke. Powell was elected to the House almost two dozen times, he says. He was the first important civil rights agitator, and he paved the way for Martin Luther King Jr., Malcolm X, Jesse Jackson, and all the others. And now we have this street named after him.

Against the curb lie patches of dirty ice.

"You warm enough?" asks Chief Driscoll, for he can see that the kid's coat is thin.

"I's fine."

Driscoll continues to talk of Powell. He can see the kid getting interested, getting relaxed. Powell was other things too, the detective reflects. He was accused of tax evasion, of taking kickbacks; he was expelled from the House. But Driscoll mentions none of this.

"You might say he integrated the House of Representatives," Chief Driscoll continues as they walk along. "The House barber wouldn't cut his hair. The House restaurant wouldn't serve him. He forced them to."

They stand for a moment watching the traffic go by, then turn back. "So what did you and Father Redmond talk about on that roof?"

"He had this camp chair he bring up there. He sit and look off at the lights on the George Washington Bridge. He look at the stars. He tell me he meditating. I didn't know that word." The boy adds proudly, "I do now. I looked it up."

"What else did he say?"

"He keep telling me to stay in school. He tell me practice my reading. He give me books to read sometimes. I try them, but they too hard."

"Was there ever anyone on that roof besides you two?"

"No one else have a key."

"Did you ever hear of a guy named Malcolm Poindexter? Have you ever seen him around?"

Keershawn didn't and hadn't.

"He was arrested near here some years ago," Gabe explains. "He was selling guns to kids."

Keershawn, who would have been six or seven years old at the time, shakes his head.

As they walk back to the stationhouse, the detective continues to probe, but the boy has little more to tell him.

"Did he ever talk about bad guys in the parish?"

"He tell me stay away from them."

Driscoll hands over his business card and a five-dollar bill. "If you hear anyone talking about Father Redmond, hear anything at all, you go to a pay phone and you call me up. When you use up that money, Keershawn, I'll give you some more."

In front of the stationhouse the night seems darker, colder, quieter than it was.

"Wait out here," Gabe Driscoll tells him. "I'll send your mom down to you." No sense scaring the kid again. No sense making him reenter what is to Driscoll just another office building, but to the boy the lion's den.

From the sidewalk Driscoll watches mother and son walk off together. Most leads lead nowhere. Keershawn has led nowhere. Then he tells himself not to be discouraged. Investigations are slow. But he feels like someone whose pockets have been emptied. A detective must be above all things patient, he tells himself. Most times he can only wait until his quarry steps into the web.

His car is at the curb, his driver holding open the door. He gets in and goes home to his wife.

Chapter Four

IT WAS LATE AFTERNOON WHEN THE EXECUTIVE EDITOR sent a copy-boy to get Andy Troy.

Troy, who was on deadline, was seated at his big Underwood pounding out a story about a major water main break. Although he now had under his belt two years' experience as a reporter, all of it assigned to the Metro staff, this was as important a story as he had been given so far. If the photographer had got some good pictures it might even make tomorrow's front page, which would be the first time for him. With the copyboy standing over him, he rose to his feet and stood glancing from his typewriter to his watch. He had only about 20 minutes left to finish the piece and hand it in. He wore a button-down shirt with his collar open, tie hanging. A tall slouched figure, his hair hanging down almost to his glasses, he strode toward the big corner office on the 43rd Street side, and he wondered if he had done something wrong.

"How old are you now, Andy?" the executive editor asked. His name was Dodd, and he was, to Troy, an old, old man, 55 at least.

"I'll be 28 next month," Troy answered.

"Married?"

"No sir."

"How would you like to take over our Vietnam bureau?"

Troy had done well in Metro. He was fast, accurate, he wrote vivid prose, and he had become known as a reporter who got his nose close to every story he worked on. He knew this. He had worked hard to impress, which was not easy, given the innocuous stories he was assigned to cover. He knew he was the right age for Vietnam as well. Experienced correspondents were assigned to Paris and Rome. Often it was the young ones, full of energy and willing to take risks, who got sent to wars. The paper did not want to see its reporters killed, but if it happened it was good for the paper's image. And for as long as the young reporter lasted he would file eyewitness stories.

The executive editor, waiting for Troy's response, drummed impatient fingers on the desk.

Of course Troy wanted Vietnam, but there was a problem. The problem was his fiancée. Her name was Maureen Donnelly. She taught second grade in the parochial school in the parish in which they had both grown up. "Fiancée" at that time had a formal meaning: engagement announced, marriage scheduled for a date some months ahead. It did not then mean what it came to mean later. Maureen still lived with her parents. Troy had only recently rented an apartment of his own, which he was slowly furnishing, and into which they would move when they were married. He saw her weekends. That is, they did not live together, and their sexual intimacies, if any, were kept secret from the world, including even close friends, lest Maureen seem "cheap." Lest, also, she lose her teaching job. There was a new generation coming along that would change all this quickly, almost violently, a change, some said, caused by the Vietnam War itself, and the civil disobedience it engendered. But this change had not happened yet.

That reporters burned out fast in war zones, Troy also knew, and the paper's man in Saigon, Mulholland, judging from his dispatches, had burned out long ago.

As he contemplated the big career he had always dreamed of, and that this one assignment would open up, Troy was trying to weigh what the personal costs to him might be. But he did not have much time to think. He was on deadline, he had a story to finish. That he could get killed in Vietnam was not part of the equation. He would not get killed. He would be gone two years at least, maybe more. What about Maureen and the marriage?

"Fine," he said, "how soon?"

"As soon as possible."

"I need three months in a language school, maybe more."

The executive editor nodded.

"Now if you'll excuse me, I'm on deadline."

He called up Earl that night, and after him Gabe. He bragged about his assignment. He was gleeful. He was about to become the paper's bureau chief in Vietnam. The others congratulated him, said they were excited for him, after which the conversation turned to Frankie because he was already there. They had all had letters from him. Frankie was up by the demilitarized zone with the Marines. Troy promised to look him up as soon as he got straightened out in Saigon; he would send them a report.

Troy had trouble ending both conversations. He was so happy he was chortling.

But it took him two days to get up the nerve to tell Maureen.

He rang her bell. It was night. Because her parents were there they went out, crossed Seaman Avenue into the park, and walked as far as the river.

"We could advance the wedding," Maureen said. "You have three months, you say."

"I could get killed over there, leaving you a widow, possibly pregnant."

"That would be my worry, wouldn't it, not yours."

"It doesn't make much sense, is all."

The river was silver and black. They watched it move by.

"I could be pregnant already, for all you know. Or care."

"Are you?"

"No."

Maureen was a tall young woman with a rather long face. Together they towered over other couples they knew.

"I have to be able to support us, and however many kids we might have, for the rest of our lives," said Troy. "To do that I've got to get my career going. And Vietnam, don't you see, is the chance of a lifetime."

They turned away from the river, walked round and round the ball fields.

"Am I supposed to stay engaged to you for however long you're gone?"

Troy, who hadn't confronted this idea in advance, was stuck for an answer. "If you want to," he said.

They had been walking hand in hand. "Don't worry," she said, having shaken her hand loose. "I'm breaking the engagement right now."

"Okay," said Troy.

"You don't love me, and you don't want to marry me. Why don't you admit it?"

Another girl, Troy supposed, would be in tears, but not this one, who was fighting back, and he found that he liked her for it, liked her more than ever. It was just that he wanted a career more.

"I do love you. But with me gone you ought to be free to do what you want to do."

"Go to bed with another guy, you mean?"

This idea caused him a jealous pang. "If that's what you want to do." He had always found her sexy, never more than after a remark like that. He thought her serious, generous, loyal, and she had nice legs, nice breasts. People called her attractive. No one ever called her beautiful. She wore her hair in bangs. He had proposed to her because physically he thought he could never do better, and because he had judged it time for him to get married and start a family.

Now of course the game had changed.

They walked back to her house. At her door he kissed her. Her lips were dry and she did not respond. Her door closed on him.

And so the wedding was "postponed," until such time as the bridegroom returned from Vietnam. This was the official line as given out by Maureen's parents. It fooled some people, not others, but in fact it proved to be true. When Troy returned three and a half years later, Maureen broke off her engagement to someone else, and moved in with him, which by then was possible without too much scandal. Later they were married. There were children, they lived in various countries. But although the marriage lasted, it was never a comfortable one. Their broken engagement, Troy's years in Vietnam, had left Maureen with more scars than either of them imagined. The memory would not die. Increasingly it made her feel that his love for her was shallow, or perhaps did not exist at all. She found she could not trust it or him. She felt diminished in his eyes. His ambition was a rival with which she could not compete. This caused her own love to dry up, which Troy soon realized. It sent him looking for other women. By the time they had been married 20 years, though they stayed married, they were barely speaking to each other.

But on the day that Troy's plane landed at Tan Son Nhut, as he descended the steps into Vietnam's crushing heat, all this was in the unknown future, and he knew only a kind of soaring elation. Already he saw the war as the defining experience of his generation, and he was in it. He was one of the ones defining it for the world. At 28 he was a foreign correspondent, and he was here, sitting on the biggest story there was. The summit of his childhood dreams already achieved.

At the bureau he met Mulholland. Also the bureau's secretary, its translator, and its driver, Vietnamese all. From now on these people worked for Troy. In the afternoon Mulholland took him to the daily press briefing at the army compound out by the airport that was known as Pentagon East, and for the first time but not the last Troy listened to rosy reports of the light at the end of the tunnel. A colonel spoke for 20 minutes, then answered questions.

"Will you write it, or will I?" asked Mulholland, when they had got back to the bureau.

"You better do it," said Andy Troy carefully. "You have so much more experience than I." He was not going to start his career in Vietnam by signing his name to the gibberish he had just been listening to. Mulholland, he decided, was a corridor journalist—there were plenty of them in Saigon and everywhere else—a reporter who never went to see anything if he could help it, but waited in the corridor for a spokesman to come out and hand him a press release. Troy saw the job differently. He intended to go where the shooting was. He wanted to report the war from up close. He wanted to go places other reporters had not gone to, were afraid to go to. Dangerous places where there were stories readers hadn't read yet. That was how you made a reputation in a war zone, got yourself talked about, won prizes.

Over the next three days Mulholland introduced him to his contacts, none of whom impressed Troy very much—various Army press officers mostly. The press officer at the presidential palace as well. Troy needed better sources than that. I have to find people who are disgruntled, he told himself. This was the first rule of journalism, find those who are unhappy and who will tell you the truth, as opposed to the official version. Listen to their complaints, then check them out. That was how the important journalism got done.

"Be careful where you place your feet," Mulholland advised him just before leaving for the airport. "There are mines everywhere. The roads are not safe. They remove a square of tarmac, put a bomb in, and put the square back. When your car goes over it some guerrilla hidden in the bushes detonates it, and your head makes a hole in the roof."

There was more of this nature, but Troy stopped listening. They shook hands, then Mulholland was gone. Troy went out and walked along. Tree-lined boulevards. Hordes of bicycles. Ancient cars and buses spewing smoke. Outdoor cafés. Colonial architecture. Red-tiled roofs. Sampans on the river. This was his domain now. He was ebullient. He was not a sentimental man, he prided himself on it, but as he walked along his happiness was such that he burst suddenly into tears.

Within two weeks he had found the sources he was looking for, one an Army lieutenant colonel who deplored the way the war was being fought, deplored the fictitious body counts, and who showed him official statistics, orders of movement, and other documents, none of them rosy, to prove his point. The second was a civilian who worked for AID, the agency responsible for the pacification program in the villages, according to whom this program also was not working. Troy had a way of convincing such people to talk to him; he would treat them as confidential sources, he promised, would never use their names or in any way hurt their careers, and they believed him.

Later he found other, similar sources.

Often he drove down into the delta where there were gunboats on the river, and constant pitched battles, some of which he watched from as close as he could get to where the shells were falling. He drove north toward Phuoc Long where the Michelin rubber plantation lay in ruins, and where other battles took place. He would get covered with dirt from the explosions, for he was always that close, then wear the dirt home like a medal. He had not yet had time to fly up north to see Frank Redmond.

And then one day he came back from the delta and Frank was sitting in his office waiting for him. Troy was delighted to see him. He had Frank by both shoulders and was shaking him, though getting only a wry smile in return. This sobered him somewhat, and he pondered it as he sat down to write that day's story, making Frank wait for him while he did.

"Let's go have dinner," he said. He had come out into the anteroom, his story written and filed. There was an ashtray next to Frank and it looked half full of butts. "Frank," Troy said, "I am so glad to see you."

As they went down the stairs and out into the crowded street, he described part of the story he had just filed. It concerned the pacification program as it worked—did not work at all—in a specific village. "We pacify the village by day, but at night the guerrillas come back in," he told Frank as they walked along. Frank was tall, Troy taller, and they were giants compared to the Vietnamese. "What's it like in the north?"

"What we're doing up there isn't working either," Frank said. "We're supposed to stop North Vietnamese army units from infiltrating into the south. There are two Marine divisions and a Marine air wing up there, the country's only fifty miles wide, and they keep coming."

"We're losing the war," said Troy.

"Yes, I think so."

Troy took him to a restaurant on the river. The menu was in English, what else, and in English they gave their order. Andy, who knew dishes he liked, ordered for Frank, who, to his surprise, had not yet eaten in a Vietnamese restaurant. They sat on the terrace overlooking the water, and waited to be served, Frank still smoking nervously, while watching the sampans ply the river. Frank wore khaki trousers and a red and blue sports shirt. Almost any onlooker, Troy thought, would see him for what he was, a military man but off duty. In any case he did not look like a priest.

"Are you allowed to be out of uniform like that?" Andy asked.

"I don't know and I don't particularly care. I don't think anyone is likely to court-martial me, do you?"

"You sound bitter."

"No. Tired is all."

Troy himself wore jeans and a yellow polo shirt. He had been in Vietnam a month, Frank much longer, and without taking notes he began to interview his friend about the war in the north.

"We do 'search-and-destroy missions,'" Frank Redmond said. "Words I have come to detest. The military speaks in acronyms and code words almost always, as I suppose you've noticed. Another word I detest is 'obliterate.' Every day we try to make contact with the enemy so as to obliterate him. That's a Marine word, used by officers and enlisted men alike. Trouble is, people's houses get obliterated also, sometimes whole villages, not to mention men, women, and children, not all of whom are armed combatants."

Frank was attached to the 2nd Battalion, 3rd Marines. They patrolled just under the demilitarized zone, he said. In battalion strength, 800 to 1,000 men, depending. They went out for six weeks at a time, once for two months, moving constantly. They patrolled wherever they were told to. The country was flat near the coast, hundreds and hundreds of paddy fields, farmers in flat conical hats, water buffalo, hamlets. Then came fields of elephant grass higher than their heads and sharp as spears. The grass sliced open arms, faces, any unprotected flesh, causing wounds that festered and would not heal. Through this grass ran thin paths that they were obliged to follow, sometimes into ambushes. Farther west came jungle-covered mountains, most of whose villages had been abandoned long ago, the people had fled to the coast, no one there except the enemy, who was well hidden, well fortified, unseen.

Mostly they patrolled in or near these mountains under the triple-canopy jungle. Two or three times a week they made contact, came under fire, returned fire, but these fights they did not always win. The trees were so thick the medevac helicopters couldn't set down, but had to hover, lowering their litters on lines to the ground. Two or three gunships always hovered near them. Like bodyguards, they were ready to blast anything. Laid on the ground in rows waited the dead in their body bags, and the wounded with faces showing. As soon as the lines went slack the wounded one by one were strapped into the litters and sent up. When the wounded had been lifted out it was the turn of the dead. Frank witnessed this scene many times, watched the lines tauten, his eyes following the litters until they cleared the trees and dangled in the sky. Morphine swimming through their veins by then, the wounded made no sound usually, and of course the dead did not, though the medevacs and gunships overhead, rotors beating the air, made plenty. An advertisement that was entirely too blatant. As they worked the lines, the litters, the straps, the troops hurried, expecting each moment to receive incoming. The litters swayed, sometimes slapping at branches on the way up.

Afterward the patrols went out again, usually four company-sized units in different directions though always close enough one to the other to give support if necessary.

Frank was 28 years old when he arrived, older than most of the troops, younger than some of the officers and NCOs, and he had gone to the battalion commander the first day requesting permission to go out with the patrols.

"Negative, Father," he was told. "You are part of the staff. Your job is to remain in the command post."

After a few days Frank ignored him, went out anyway. He had been trained at Newport, then Camp Pendleton, could tie off wounds, plunge needles into flesh, field-set broken bones as well as any corpsman. More than this, the men were not going to trust him, were not going to bring him their fears and their doubts, unless he was with them, seeing what they saw, sharing their discomfort and fatigue, their pain, their grief, their terror. When they came to him he would not have many answers, perhaps none, but a panicked or shell-shocked Marine was a danger to all, and having the chaplain there was better than having no one.

One other thing. His presence could perhaps prevent atrocities — the murdering of prisoners or villagers, for instance. He knew it had happened in other units from time to time. It wasn't going to happen in this one while he was there.

Each afternoon the battalion command post moved about 2,000 yards forward or to the side. This was to make it more difficult for the enemy to fix their position, but at night the mortar rounds found them often enough. The men would come in from patrol and their first job was to dig their holes, Frank too. In a six-week patrol he dug 40 holes, more or less, everybody did. Often young Marines would offer to dig Father's hole for him, but he would shake his head, smile, and claim he needed the exercise. During the days, if the climbing was steep, or the heat especially bad they sometimes offered to carry his pack too. Again he would refuse.

They slept above their holes. If it rained at night, too bad, though a mortar attack was worse. Those who were awake would hear the *crump-carumph* a mortar makes, would scream "incoming," and every man would tumble into his hole. Seventeen seconds would then elapse — mortar rounds went up very high — before the first of the concussions buried them in dirt. They would call in artillery to silence the mortar, or a patrol would go out and find it. Sometimes that was the extent of the cost — a lost night's sleep. Other times rounds fell into holes with Marines in them, ruining the holes as well, and someone, looking down, would say: "It wasn't their day." This too Frank saw. He would put his stole around his neck and read the required prayers, not so much to help the dead across — before long he didn't know if he even believed in that anymore — but to console the living. Most of these so-called tough Marines were kids, believers all, and needed to talk to grown-ups that they were not afraid of.

He wore what they all wore, loose camouflage trousers tucked into shin-high boots, and a loose camouflage jacket. Plus helmet and flak jacket. Most days the temperature reached a hundred degrees, the humidity intense. Most of the men had cut holes in their sleeves, their pants legs too, hoping to catch any movement of air, and they wore no underwear, for it was cooler without. Before long Frank copied them. His hands and arms, his face, became caked almost permanently in mud. There was mud in his hair. He got used to this. Within an hour each day he was wet with sweat. He went six weeks, two months without a bath, and got used to that too. About halfway through each patrol the helicopters dropped bins of clean fatigues which they rummaged through looking for a fit. What they took off they buried. If my parishioners could see me now, Frank often thought, before correcting himself. His parishioners had become these boys. He tried to shave every day, if there was water. All the officers did. And when they came to a stream, of which there were many, he would rinse out his spare socks, wring as much mud as he could out of his jacket and, if there was time, and if there seemed to be no enemy nearby, he would strip and sponge himself off, many of them did that too, not all.

He carried a .45 caliber pistol he had no intention of using. He had rubbed the shine off the insignia of rank at his collars, blacked out the one on his helmet. Although he was never sure why he had chosen to be in Vietnam at all, beyond a vague notion that he wanted to be where he was needed, still he had no interest in making himself a target for snipers.

He carried about 20 pounds on his back under which he walked all day most days: a poncho, a polyester blanket, rations. He was not burdened with a rifle and ammo, but in exchange carried a medical pack, plus a chalice, a box of unconsecrated hosts, and enough wine to be able to say mass regularly. His total load each day, including helmet, cartridge belt, flak jacket, and water, was close to 50 pounds.

Helicopters supplied food and ammo every two days. Boxes of rations were dropped to them, boxes of cartridges and grenades, water in five-gallon cans. The cans had to be carried, and they weighed 30 pounds each. The empties had to be stockpiled as well, for the helicopters came back later to retrieve them, a risk both to the helicopters and to their position. When a new commander was dropped in he stopped the water immediately, told the men to fill their canteens in the streams. The men grumbled and came to their chaplain for help. Father Redmond assured them that two iodine tablets added to each canteen would prevent sickness. They believed him — they had not believed the new commander — and the grumbling stopped.

For six weeks at a time, sometimes two months, he ate out of ration boxes — care packages, the men called them — meals that were sometimes edible, sometimes not; ham and lima beans, spaghetti and meatballs, disgusting sausage patties he could not get down no matter how hungry. An accessories can contained gum, candy, crackers, toilet paper. Sometimes, out in the middle of nowhere, in the midst of the killing, maiming, and wanton destruction, the drop included beer and ice cream too.

More and more enemy soldiers were "obliterated," sometimes whole units. When he looked down at their smooth young faces, their savagely treated bodies, he saw that they were no older than his Marines, and even less able to cope with what modern war had become.

Marines died in fewer numbers, but they did die. Boys were killed in firefights or ambushes, or by mortars or artillery, or they stepped on mines. One boy killed another while they sat side by side cleaning their rifles. Each time Father Redmond would officiate at the grisly ceremony that followed.

The mail arrived regularly, and went out regularly. One night a group sat around decorating their helmets much as World War II pilots had decorated the noses of fighter planes. Someone had produced a Magic Marker, which worked excellently. After girlfriends' names or brave slogans had been scrawled on the steel, the helmets were held up for general approval. "Maryann," wrote one youth, who then wanted himself photographed so he could send his girl the picture. The other boys began calling him Maryann, and it stuck. Before long no one called him anything else. "Avenging Angel," wrote another boy. "The Harlem Globetrotter," wrote a third, who was black. A boy named Bushmaster wrote: "You and Me, God, Right?" and then went to Father Redmond, showed his helmet, and asked if this was blasphemy.

"No," said Frank.

The boy sat down beside him on the dirt. "If I get out of this alive," he said, "maybe I'll become a priest."

"That's interesting," said Frank. "How old are you?"

"Eighteen, Father."

After a pause, the boy said, biting down on his lip: "The real reason I want to get out alive is so I can find out what it's like to have a woman. It wouldn't be honest to deny it. Is that a sin, Father?"

Though he wanted to smile, Frank answered with the seriousness the boy deserved. "No, of course not."

At Division there existed an intricate scientific instrument called a Seismic Intrusion Device that could measure the impact made by the boots of troops moving across ground miles away, and the morning came when Battalion was alerted to such a movement in its sector, and given the coordinates. Of course it could have been a herd of animals, no way of knowing. This was in high elephant grass, and nobody could see anything. Behind the battalion command post stood a ridge, and from there the forward air controller was able to put a radar beacon on the supposed spot. This done, he called in an A6 Intruder to "obliterate" it with a stick of 500-pound bombs.

But a 700-foot-high outcropping known as the rockpile rose up to one side, and the magnetic properties of the rock, it was later theorized, bent the radar beam. Or else the coordinates were wrong. The stick of bombs fell on 3rd Platoon of F Company, 35 men who, concealed by the high grass, had been moving in a spread-out column along a narrow trail well to the east.

The concussion blew Frank ten yards into the elephant grass. He scythed it down with his body. He got up dazed, momentarily deafened, most of his shirt torn off, and bleeding from a leg wound, shrapnel perhaps, that he had never felt. Half on the path, half in the grass he went running back toward the tail of the column. The grass lacerated his arms and neck, which he never felt either, and he came upon the platoon commander, Lt. Ross, screaming into his radio, "We've just received incoming, we've got casualties, send the medevacs."

Frank kept running, skirting three men — badly wounded apparently, but already being cared for by others — until he came to an enormous crater, on the lip of which, at the crazy angles the dead assumed, hung Maryann and the Harlem Globetrotter, one boy faceup, the other down. Beyond that was a swath through the grass that a flying body might have made, so he followed it until he nearly tripped over a severed leg. The rest of the body lay just beyond. It was Bushmaster, who, in the few seconds that had elapsed, had bled out. A few seconds earlier, thought Frank, and I might have saved him. Beside the boy lay his helmet still reading: "You and Me, God, Right?"

Frank was bleeding so badly from the grass, and from the leg wound, that the medevacs, when they came, wanted to evacuate him too. He let them bandage him up but refused the ride out. Even before they left with their bitter load Lt. Ross had been advised by base that his unit was not under attack, but had been hit by friendly fire, and he was ordered to form a defensive perimeter, and wait for the arrival of the command staff. Silent, stunned, the platoon did as ordered.

The battalion commander, a man named Quaid, met Frank as they came in. Quaid was a lieutenant colonel, 36 years old, a career Marine officer. "From now on, Father," he told his chaplain, "you stay with that platoon. They're going to need you."

Frank was fine that night, and all the next day. He sat with the boys, listened to them, gave them what consolation he could. There had been a terrible accident and the platoon had been caught in it, he told them. It was nobody's fault. Accidents happened all the time. People were people. They made mistakes. It was like a very bad car crash. Car crashes shook people up too, but they got over it. In this case the dead had not suffered and the wounded would recover.

Words, he thought. Useless words. That's all I have been able to give them.

By the end of the week he was not eating and could not sleep. An accident, he told himself. Think of it as having nothing to do with war, he told himself. But he couldn't. It had been too calamitous for that, too incomprehensible as well. He began to dread the night. Two or three hours of bad dreams and he was awake again, hating the dreams, fearing the darkness. He would get up and pace the command post, but this was no good. The nights were too dark, there were too many holes, too many sleeping forms. He took to going outside the command post until one night Colonel Quaid caught him coming back. Quaid was good, meaning that he was always watching, saw everything. He said: "You keep doing that you're going to get shot by your own men."

"I couldn't sleep," said Frank.

The commander knew or sensed what he was dealing with. He said: "How long have you been in the field, Father?"

"Eight months."

After half of their 385-day tour all personnel were entitled to five days' leave. "You didn't put in for R & R?"

"No."

"Why not?"

Frank shrugged. He couldn't see Quaid's face very well, but felt the commander's scrutiny.

"Your leg all right, Father?"

"Yes."

"Show me your arms."

"I have a little jungle rot." Frank's arms were covered with festering sores from the elephant grass. The sores were long and had formed a rash.

"You better go to Da Nang, have that looked at," Quaid said. "You come back in a week or two, you'll be fine."

The next morning Quaid saw him off—made sure he left. "I'm awarding you the Purple Heart," the commander said.

"Don't do that, Colonel. I didn't do anything."

The commander studied him.

"Please," Frank said.

Quaid watched Frank get into the helicopter. "Spend some time on the beach," he advised. "The salt water is great for that jungle rot."

At Division, Frank changed from helicopter to jeep. By noon he was in Da Nang, the major U.S. installation in the north, where he secured an appointment at the base hospital for midafternoon. While waiting he entered the PX. There was nothing he wanted to buy, he just wanted to see it, this gigantic American department store implanted in Southeast Asia, only ten or fifteen miles from the carnage and destruction that was behind him. On sale were all manner of exotic goods at giveaway military prices: hi-fis, toasters, hair driers. He picked up a hair drier, looked at it, then put it down again.

He kept his appointment at the hospital. The doctor gave him a tetanus shot—he didn't know why—and some salve for the jungle rot, a prescription for antibiotics, and told him to come back in two days. He nodded as if he would obey though he did not intend to. In the street he threw the prescription away and went out to the airfield where he hitched a ride to Saigon on a C-123.

Andy Troy had reached Vietnam by then, he knew. Letters between them had passed back and forth. Frank went to Troy's office. According to a Vietnamese secretary, he would be back later.

Frank knew no one else in Saigon. He took a room in the Continental Hotel where he stood under a hot shower trying to scrub Vietnam out from under his fingernails, out of his head as well.

"AND SO YOU CAME TO SAIGON TO FORGET THE WAR," Andy said when dinner had ended.

"I came to see you."

"Admit it."

Frank laughed. "You're nuts."

"The traditional method of forgetting is the bottle —"

"I can't drink," said Frank. "You know that. Two drinks and I get sick."

" — or a woman."

"You know my answer to that, too."

"It isn't permitted, is it?" said Andy.

Frank was silent.

Andy stood up. "Come with me, I know something else."

He took him to a room over a restaurant on a dark street back from the river. They entered through a door on the side and could smell the opium before starting up the stairs.

Frank knew what it was without being told, and drew back.

"It's not a brothel," said Troy, "it's an opium den."

"How do you know about it?"

"I'm a foreign corespondent. It's my job to know about everything."

Troy's hand was on Frank's shoulder. He was trying to propel him toward the stairs, but the priest's shoulder was resisting.

"You didn't take a vow against opium, did you?"

"Of course not, but—"

"So relax. This is what you need, believe me."

"You've done it?"

"Sure."

"Is it addictive?"

"Not a couple of pipes, no."

They were greeted by a middle-aged Asian woman, her face painted, who wore floor-length pajamas of flowered silk, and she gushed over Troy, and then over Frank, who only looked increasingly nervous.

Troy talked to the woman in a combination of French and Vietnamese. He was not very good at either, Frank judged, but did make himself understood.

"She says that since it's your first time," said Troy, "you should smoke four pipes maximum. Any more might make you nauseous, spoil the whole thing."

She led them down a corridor into a room and left them there.

The rest of the experience, to Frank, vanished into a kind of dream. Afterward no detail seemed vivid, only the drowsiness that made the whole world seem to glow. The room itself he was able to recall only vaguely. Dim light from a spirit lamp on a stool in the corner. A bed. No, not a bed, a hard couch. A pillow under his neck, leather covered but hard as a log. The room was not only dim but small, the air close, and reeking of old opium. This was the way it looked as he came in. He didn't recall leaving it at all.

"Lie down there," said Troy.

A man joined them, or perhaps two different men separately, though in what order he did not know. He—they—were old and emaciated, as if they had smoked too much of their own product. He—they—wore flowered silk pajamas also. Troy was gone, and Frank was being served green tea in a small lacquered bowl. Before smoking? During? After? He seemed to remember sitting up to drink, then lying down again. Or perhaps he had sat up only to smoke.

At the stool in the corner a man was heating opium over the spirit lamp. It was like brown gum. He kneaded it into small balls, injected it into the pipe, reversed the pipe over the flame. The odor was tantalizing. It began to bubble.

Frank held the pipe. "You inhale it all at once," Troy had instructed. "You only get one hit per pipe." He remembered just in time.

One long inhalation and it was gone. The man in the pajamas brought him another pipe.

Which pipe was it that brought on the immense drowsiness? Not the first, surely. The second, the third? For the first time in weeks Vietnam was gone from his thoughts, the war was gone, time and place were gone. He existed only inside himself, inside a kind of haze. The burden of celibacy, and the sometimes terrible loneliness that went with it, floated away. He was drowsy and yet alert. He wasn't a priest anymore, just a man, wondering what life was all about. He thought that if he looked he could find the answers that everyone had been searching for so long. What was good, what was evil, he asked himself. But the questions did not trouble him. Nothing troubled him. In a world as perfect as this one seemed to him at this moment to be what did it matter?

Four pipes, he supposed it was four, and it was over. He drifted from the room. On the way out he found himself speaking perfect French, though he had not studied the language since high school. How voluble he was, how incisive his thoughts. Then he was on the street with Andy Troy, who wanted to know how it had been, how he felt.

"Tell you tomorrow," he said. They walked side by side. The streets were empty. A motorcycle started up across the city. Otherwise Saigon was quiet. Frank moved along, one step after another, but in a trance that he was unwilling to disturb.

Presently he lay in bed in the hotel, totally calm yet as alert as he had ever been, and in all the directions in which he looked there was only goodness and beauty. Why had he never recognized this before?

He fell asleep, woke up totally refreshed, and was amazed to find that only twenty minutes had passed. Again he lay in total calm, and fell asleep, and again woke up soon after, feeling as if he had slept ten hours, perhaps more.

The next day he tried to explain his sensations, this first opium experience, but Andy Troy only laughed at him. "I know, I know," he said.

"How often do you go there?"

"Whenever I get down on myself. If the desk edits one of my pieces to death, for instance. Want to do it again?"

"When?"

"Tomorrow night, or the night after."

"We'll have to see."

"I know some other places, if you're interested."

Two nights later Troy took him into the *paillote* district, a place of thatched roofs and garbage in the streets. They knocked on the door of the *fumerie*, and were led to rooms in back. This place, Frank judged, was a little more luxurious, or a little less, he wasn't sure which, because it didn't look clean. He sat down on a double bed. A four-poster. The sheets looked fresh enough, and a woman came in and began preparing the pipe. She was young, rather pretty though even in voluminous pajamas she looked skinny. Hungry too. By this time Frank knew that a pipe prepared by a woman was considered more sweet. After handing him the pipe she began to massage his neck and back until satisfied he understood she was there for his pleasure.

He was not very experienced, neither with women nor opium, and it took him time to realize this, and more time to convince her he wanted only the pipe. He was angry. Had Andy Troy set this up? The girl pouted, but moved away.

As a result he smoked only two pipes which did nothing for him, waved away a third pipe already prepared, handed her a wad of piastres and left hurriedly. Out on the sidewalk he was obliged to wait for Troy to finish. He was ready to accuse him of a monumental betrayal of their friendship.

His face wearing a beatific expression, Andy came out of the building some time later.

"How was it?" he asked.

"Not as good tonight."

"That sometimes happens."

Frank peered at Troy in the gloom, searching his friend's face for guile but not finding it. So for the time being he decided to say nothing.

A battle erupted near the parrot's beak where Cambodia juts into South Vietnam. Andy Troy ordered his driver into the backseat, and with Frank beside him, drove toward the battle at 70 miles an hour along the two-lane Route 1, speeding past bullock carts, motor scooters, bicycles, his hand on the horn, forcing the oncoming trucks, bicycles, and bullock carts to veer almost into the ditch to let him by.

Frank was holding on to his seat with both hands. Once he smiled and said: "This is the most dangerous thing I've done since I've been in Vietnam."

They heard the gunfire as they got close, and when they had stopped and jumped out running they could see the gunships sweeping over close to the deck blasting away. Andy was running hard, Frank just behind him. They got within two or three hundred yards of the battle, taking cover behind a fallen tree. Andy had his notebook out and was describing what he saw. The terrain, the action. Jotting fast.

A South Vietnamese battalion was pinned down. Small figures. Too far away to see faces. Only one or two men firing back. The rest, six or eight hundred men, crouching, hiding, waiting to be overrun.

"Look at them," said Troy. "They don't do anything. It's always that way. They won't fight. Their officers don't make them fight. That's why our side is losing the war."

"If they get overrun, we get overrun too," Frank told him. "You know that, don't you?"

The excitement, the danger, were delightful. "I like it here," said Andy Troy, "don't you?"

Frank felt as if they were two kids playing at war. Admit it to yourself, he thought. He's right. You like it too.

With so much combat experience behind him, Frank was able to read the battlefield and explain it to Troy. The enemy, said the priest to the journalist, was hidden under the bushes and trees along the dikes edging the paddy fields.

"How many, do you think?" said Andy.

They were invisible. Only the flashes from rifles and automatic weapons could be seen.

"Battalion, maybe," Frank said.

One helicopter was already down. Another crashed as they watched.

Shells were falling uncomfortably close.

"Mortars," Frank said. "Sixty-ones, probably. Aiming at the downed helicopters but overshooting. We're in a direct line. This is the wrong spot. Follow me."

Andy Troy refused to budge.

"Staying here is suicide," the priest cried. At last Troy followed him, and the two men ran crouched over, running hard down a gully and into the protection of a line of dikes. A moment later a shell landed where they had been.

"I never imagined I would get out of this war alive," Frank said. "But if you go on like you're going you definitely won't."

They watched the arrival of more helicopters who brought in American reinforcements, landing them behind the enemy. In an hour the battle was over. The enemy had evaporated. Andy and Frank moved forward over the suddenly safe battlefield. There were wounded, some moaning, one or two screaming, the rest quiet. They moved among corpses. Many South Vietnamese dead, a handful of Americans, and almost none of the enemy. Andy touched one of the enemy bodies with his shoe. "North Vietnamese Army," he said. "Not guerrillas, regular troops. That's my story, and I'm the only one here that's got it."

On the way back to Saigon they stopped at a decrepit cantina beside the road and reached into a rusty old cooler where bottles of Vietnamese beer lay in dirty water beside a block of diminishing ice. They drew out four bottles which they drank in the shade of a thatched arbor. It was not until the beer was almost gone that Frank decided at last to speak.

"In the *fumerie* last night," he said, "there was a girl in my room. At my service, if you understand me."

Andy looked shocked. "And you thought I put her there?"

"Well," said Frank, "I wondered."

"No, you actually thought I would do such a thing to you."

"Yes."

"You had a right to think so, I guess. But I didn't." Troy was apologetic, swore he had nothing to do with the woman. "Please believe me, Frank."

Again Frank looked for guile in his eyes, and again did not find it.

"All right, I believe you." And he did. "Let's forget the whole thing. But if we want to smoke any more opium, we won't go back there."

Troy laughed. "No, of course not."

Both men were silent for a moment. Then Troy said: "Have you ever had a woman, Frank?"

Frank smiled. "No comment."

"You don't hate me for asking?"

"Of course not." To Frank they were as close as brothers, closer. A brother had the right to ask any question he liked.

Frank said: "What you're really asking, I think, is how do I do it. Keeping busy is one answer. If my mind goes in that direction I force myself to think of something else. Is celibacy hard? Yes, very hard. But I made a vow of my own free will and I intend to live up to it. I'm strong enough to live up to it."

"It isn't necessarily a question of strength, perhaps."

"It is for me. Maybe not many people could do it, but I can. If you told me nobody else could do it, I'd still say I can. I'm strong enough. And so far I have been."

They got back to Saigon very late. Troy went to his office to write and file his story. Frank at his hotel ate two sandwiches at the bar, drank another beer, then went up to his room and slept.

Colonel Quaid had given him two weeks off. But the rest of the battalion got only five days, and Frank's five days were up. He would have to go back. He studied his lacerated arms. They were a little better, not much. They did not, to Frank, justify staying away two weeks. Troy drove him out to Tan Son Nhut where, as they waited, they promised to see each other regularly. They even made plans for Troy to come north in a month's time. They would spend a week in the field together. Frank would arrange it with Colonel Quaid. Frank would continue instructing Troy on how not to get killed in these battles he seemed to enjoy so much. They laughed about this.

A MILITARY PLANE LEFT FOR DA NANG 30 minutes later with Frank sitting in a bucket seat in an otherwise empty fuselage. By evening he was back with his battalion.

THE INVESTIGATION

5

"WE SAW EACH OTHER FAIRLY REGULARLY AFTER THAT," says Andy Troy.

They are in Chief Driscoll's department car, the snow coming down, the traffic barely moving.

"He did three tours, I think," says Gabe Driscoll.

"A little more," says Troy. "At the end of his first tour he was at the airport with his orders in his hand, waiting for a flight back to what the troops called 'The World.' His 385 days were up. Suddenly he turns around and walks out, his barracks bag over his shoulder. He's staying. It's completely against regulations. He could have been court-martialed. He never worried about things like that. He goes to Marine Corps Headquarters and causes a cable to be sent to the Chief of Naval Chaplains. His request is going to take time to process, so he puts on a sports shirt and comes to Saigon. He could have been court-martialed for that too. We spent a couple of weeks together, smoked some more opium, palled around."

The car inches forward under the snow.

"About a month later," says Gabe Driscoll, "he gets the Navy Cross. What was that all about?"

"The platoon he was with got ambushed, the radio blown up, the NCOs wounded or killed, the lieutenant with his leg shot off. Instead of taking cover Frank rushes about tending the wounded, including the lieutenant. He ties off the lieutenant's stump, saving his life, fills him full of morphine. Suddenly he sees that nobody is in command of the platoon. The survivors are in a panic, all grouped together. A single mortar round can wipe out everybody. So he takes command. He gets the men calmed down, deploys them, forms a perimeter. There is a terrific firefight."

The snow cakes to the side windows. Soon they can barely see out.

"Frank is in full view of the enemy, trying to give confidence to his men," Troy continues. "Bullets are flying all around him, and he isn't touched."

"Is he firing a weapon himself?"

"Apparently not. He's running from group to group, jumping into holes, bandaging the wounded, giving the last rites to the dying, and at the same time barking orders to his Marines, and they beat off the attackers. When the fight ends he collects the wounded and dead and leads them back to the base. The lieutenant gets to the hospital in time and survives. In bed he writes him up for the Medal of Honor."

"He didn't get it, though."

"He got the Navy Cross, which is the second highest, because the lieutenant was a lousy writer. If I'd written it up he would have got the top one."

The rectory is a red brick building next to the church. It is narrow, three stories high. Tall windows with snow piling up on the sills. Chief Driscoll's car pulls up in front, and they get out. The church looks small too, not much broader and about the same height. There was never any need for big churches in Harlem, and probably less now than before. On the other side, boarded up, is the former parochial school. The city is supposed to make a public school out of it this year or next.

The snow on the steps to the rectory has already been stomped down. As Driscoll and Troy go up they are met by movers coming out, two men embracing cartons higher than their faces, and attempting to march on past. In the street stands a double-parked Salvation Army van.

Chief Driscoll pulls out his shield and flashes it.

"I was afraid of this," he says to Troy. "Police," he tells the lead mover. "Those boxes are part of a criminal investigation. Put them back where you got them." When the man hesitates, he says: "Immediately, got it. That means now!"

The snow is coming down harder. The sidewalks are white, as is the top of the van, but not yet the slushy street. Cars go by.

They follow the boxes back into the rectory, where the housekeeper Driscoll met previously makes a brief attempt to bar their entrance. When the detective chief pushes past her she stands aside looking nervous. Up the stairs go the boxes, and into a small room in the back, almost a cell. It contains a bare desk, a chair, and a bed that is narrow as a cot. Frankie's former room, apparently. The bed has been stripped of its linen. The mattress is gray and lumpy, the pillow old and thin. There is a crucifix on the wall above the bed. On the floor, waiting to be moved, are two additional cartons.

"Put the boxes on the bed," orders Chief Driscoll. "Good. Now get out of here." But the men only look confused. "You're excused, understand. Beat it. Go move your truck before I give you a summons for illegal parking."

The movers go down and out of the house.

"The pastor must be out," Gabe Driscoll says. "We're lucky there." He imagines the housekeeper at the foot of the stairs, waiting nervously for the pastor's return.

"Let's see what's in the boxes," he says, upending the first of them onto the bed.

Out tumbles clothing, none of it neatly folded.

"Is this all he owned?" asks Troy. "Four boxes?"

"I don't know."

"Fifty-three years old, and his entire estate fits into four boxes."

"I phoned the pastor we were coming."

"You gave him time to call in the Salvation Army," says Troy.

"He tells me it's his rectory and he won't let us in."

"Looks like you shouldn't have called him."

"How was he able to get the van here this quickly?"

"Maybe it's not even the first van."

"Yes, he's had several days."

"Who knows what else he got rid of."

Troy upends a second box. Same result.

"We're looking for phone bills, checkbooks, letters," says Gabe Driscoll.

"I begin to sense we won't find any."

Presently the bed is piled high with Frank Redmond's clothes. Also a pair of scuffed sneakers, a pair of black shoes, and, buried deep in one of the boxes, two framed eight-by-ten photographs.

"Go through the pockets," says Gabe. "Maybe there's something."

But there isn't. They contemplate the clothing, the shoes, and the photos, nothing more.

"Where are all the swimming medals he won?" says Troy.

"The medals in Vietnam too. Where are they?"

"Perhaps he felt a priest has to travel light."

"Or else the pastor got rid of stuff before we got here."

Chief Driscoll picks up one of the photos. Judging from the stain on the wall it had hung above the desk. Dating from the wedding of Earl Finley and Roxanne Harley, it shows the bridal couple plus Father Redmond, and to either side Gabriel Driscoll and Andrew Troy, the joint best men. Rocky in her long white gown with lace trim. The boys in tuxedos. Frankie in his clerical suit. He is the only one in the photo not smiling.

The second photo shows Frank with Andy Troy in Vietnam. There is no matching stain on the wall, so perhaps it stood on the desk. In it Troy wears an open-necked shirt and slacks. Frank is in combat fatigues, boots, helmet—the field uniform of a Marine chaplain.

"This was taken just before some mortar rounds came in," Troy says, holding it. "He thought he would probably be killed in action. I thought I was hot stuff and expected to win the Pulitzer Prize that month or the next."

Troy stands the photo back on the desk.

"In Vietnam," says Gabe, "did you ever see him with a woman there? A nurse, maybe?"

"No. He believed in being a priest. At least then he did."

"I keep remembering what the pastor said. About Frank and women."

"I never saw him with anyone."

"Why would he keep only two photos, and why these particular two?"

They hear the front door open downstairs, followed by voices in the hall: the pastor being greeted by his frightened housekeeper. Like schoolboys caught where they aren't supposed to be, the two men gaze at each other.

Then comes the pastor's voice on a rising angry note. They hear him on the stairs, his voice preceding him upward. "Who let them in? This is church property. They have no right in here."

At remarkable speed for a man his age, he follows his voice into the bedroom of his former curate.

"Out," he cries, pointing first at Gabe, then at Andy. "Out."

"Sit down," orders Chief Driscoll.

"Get out at once."

"I said sit down." Gabe pushes him down on the bed.

"There's separation of church and state."

"You've got some explaining to do, Pal."

"It's in the Constitution."

They are shouting at each other, voices overlapping. The pastor keeps struggling to rise, but the detective keeps pushing him back down. The scene is almost funny. "One more word out of you," Chief Driscoll cries, "and you're under arrest."

"For what?"

"How does obstruction of justice sound to you?"

"Don't make me laugh."

Gabe's method, Troy observes, is confrontational. He is used to browbeating subjects, most of whom are terrified or in custody or both. The pastor is neither, and the confrontational method that works elsewhere is not working here.

The journalist's own method is different, for the people he interviews are not obliged to answer him and sometimes don't. He must coax them, make them into collaborators. Make them want to cooperate.

Now he interrupts. "We're the executors of Father Redmond's will, Monsignor." Troy's tone is mild. "We need his bank statements, his canceled checks, his telephone bills."

"You're trying to bring scandal down on the church."

"Oh?"

"My only interest is to protect the church." As his voice rises, Monsignor Malachy's Irish brogue becomes more pronounced.

"We really need to see his records," says Troy patiently. "Can you tell us where they are? What happened to them?"

"I threw them out."

"Everything?"

Mouth set stubbornly, the pastor does not reply.

Despite himself, Troy's tone becomes crisp. "What gave you the right to do that, if I may ask?"

"As his pastor I have every right. A curate's role is total submission to the will of his pastor. Curates have no rights except as their pastor chooses to accord them. That's canon law. In my rectory I have the right to do anything I please."

"Jesus," says Gabe. Although he has stepped back to let Andy do the questioning, he is unable to keep silent. "The arrogance of the Catholic Church."

"Were there letters, as well?" Troy asks the pastor.

Again the stubborn, set expression.

"What happened to them?"

"They were trash, so that's where they went, out with the trash."

"Did you read them before you threw them out?"

The pastor does not answer.

"Probably read them before Frank did," says Gabe. "Steamed them open and read them, resealed them, and handed them to Frank."

"In what way," inquires Troy, "do you imagine our purpose here is to bring scandal down on the Catholic Church?"

"That man was a scandal waiting to happen. He still is."

"Frank Redmond a scandal?" says Troy. "I really can't believe that."

"The faithful need to see a Church, a priesthood, that is without flaws." The brogue has come on strong. "You fallen-away Catholics are all the same. You're trying to dig up something unsavory about the Church. You'll get no help from me."

"We're wasting our time with this guy," mutters Chief Driscoll.

He gestures toward the piles of clothing, some on the bed, some on the floor. "You want any of this?" he asks Andy Troy.

The journalist gazes at what, a few minutes ago, he described as his friend's entire estate. He even, as Frank's death becomes vivid to him, lays his hand on some of it. "No," he says finally. He finds himself sad beyond words. "I'd like to keep the picture from Vietnam, though."

"Take it then, and let's go."

Gabe Driscoll takes the other picture for himself, and they leave the rectory.

On the sidewalk they stand in the falling snow, and Gabe begins cursing the pastor.

When he stops, Troy says: "What do we do now?"

"The phone company can give us bills matching Frank's telephone number. They may demand a subpoena first, they may not. We'll have to see. Assuming he paid his bills, probably they can tell us also what bank his checks were drawn on. Then we go to the bank and get his canceled checks. The bank will certainly demand a subpoena, meaning a detective will have to spend half a day in court. It's a lot of work, but it can be done." Then he adds: "I'll put some detectives on it right away."

Chief Driscoll's department car waits at the curb, so much snow on the windshield they cannot see the driver. They get into it and the driver starts the windshield wipers, then turns and asks: "Where to, Chief?"

Troy wants to return to his paper, so Driscoll gives the address. They sit back, the streets begin to pass, and the snow falls.

Chapter Five

FRANK REDMOND, TECHNICALLY, WAS A NAVAL OFFICER, for the
Marines have no chaplain corps of their own. He went in as a lieutenant junior grade, served more than five years in all, mostly in
Vietnam, and came out with the rank of lieutenant commander, two
grades higher. During his time off in Saigon and elsewhere, he
could have worn impressive ribbons had he chosen to, which he did
not. In combat he had spent almost nothing. His pay, including the
combat bonuses, had gone into the bank, where it stayed.

It was 1970. Separated at Camp Pendleton, California, he was
given a travel allowance to get him back to New York, but he threw
this into the purchase of a used car, slung his barracks bag in the
trunk, and started east by road. He had no specific plan. He would
stop each night wherever he happened to stop. No one was waiting
for him. He had time. No one cared how long it took him.

It took more than a month.

He had asked no one to accompany him. He was alone. It was the
end of summer, hot at first but getting colder as he drove north, and
as the season shortened. He had with him several pairs of khaki pants
and some sports shirts. He did not have a clerical suit. When he got
into the mountains he had to buy sweaters.

He did not want to go home, he did not know why. Perhaps because he had no home to go to.

En route he saw the sights, which he did not much want to do either. The Grand Canyon. The Rockies. He saw what everyone sees. The Great Salt Lake. He slept in motels beside the road, the cheaper the better, for he was unused to luxury. However lumpy the beds they were better to lie on than the pile of dirt and stone above a foxhole. Being unused to fine food also, he ate in diners and truck stops, happy just to look at food on a plate, and not have to fork it out of boxes.

He did talk to people at times. A ranger in Yellowstone Park. A gas station attendant from whom he asked directions. One or two individual tourists who crossed his path and who spoke to him first.

Mostly he avoided other people. The war behind him still had years and years to run.

On Sundays he would drive into a town, find the church, knock on the door of the rectory next door, and ask permission to say mass. Usually the local priest or priests would press him to stay, at least for lunch, but he would smile and refuse. He was in a bit of a rush, he would say, and he drove on.

Once a week he phoned his mother. Many priests develop an obsession with their mothers, but he was not one of them. He would see her soon, he promised her. He had obligations toward her, he recognized this, and would fulfill them the best he could. For the time being the phone calls would have to do.

He drove as far north as Montana, where he made a kind of pilgrimage to the Little Bighorn, because a movie about Custer's last stand had impressed him as a boy. Getting out of the car, he walked uphill to the monument, and thought of the men who fell here. As a grown-up it was easy enough to see the movie as romance, not life. Legends have no real existence, he told himself. A massacre is a massacre. He did not see this as a big idea, only, at this stage of his life, a persistent one. Life never measures up to romance, does it, he thought, an observation that made him laugh suddenly, so that a nearby couple glanced at him strangely.

He drove east through the Black Hills. At Mount Rushmore he stared up at the four immense faces, and wondered what kind of men those presidents had been, really. He was in no mood anymore to believe in heroes.

The country was immense, no mass graves anywhere, no bomb craters that the monsoons turned into ponds which, when you looked at them, seemed almost natural, except that there were so many of them in so many shapes and sizes and, often, so close together.

Above St. Louis, standing at the confluence of the Missouri and the Mississippi, he watched the two rivers pour one into the other.

It was there he decided that he had postponed the future long enough. Let's see what happens next, he told himself, and got back in his car and pointed it toward home. Insofar as he had a home.

In New York he stayed with his parents in his old room in the apartment in the Bronx. He felt like a man under indictment. Sooner or later he would have to turn himself in to the Chancery. And be reassigned, probably, back to Scarsdale. Or someplace like it.

Andy Troy had only recently arrived home himself. Both were invited to dinner at Earl's house the following Saturday night.

"HE LOOKS LIKE YOU, EARL," said Barbara Driscoll, Gabe's wife, gazing at Earl's son.

"I just hope he won't have Earl's bow legs," said Rocky, the proud mother. She laughed. They all did.

They were seven people crowded over a three-year-old boy with his thumb in his mouth, asleep on a cot beside the double bed. Gabe was getting a bit heavy, Frank Redmond had noted, and he was losing his hair. The women had all wanted to see the baby. The men had been obliged to troop in there behind them.

Frank looked from the sleeping boy to Earl to Rocky. There was a sister, he knew, about three years older, staying tonight with her grandparents. He was trying to imagine Rocky pregnant, her stomach puffed out, her face and breasts a bit puffy too. Rocky as a doting mother.

Earl and Rocky were living on the Upper West Side — not then the fashionable address it was to become — in a three-room, rent-controlled apartment just off Broadway. Seven for dinner was about as many as could be crowded in. The building was old, with stores at ground level. The apartments inside, which were small, had never been renovated. There were so many coats of paint on the walls, Frank saw, glancing around, and they had been so heavily and sloppily applied over the decades that the definition of the wall and ceiling moldings could barely be discerned. He realized that the Finleys could afford no better. Rocky had been unable to work since late in her first pregnancy, and then in her absence her job had disappeared as her father fought with his stockholders, was forced out, and later went bankrupt.

Tonight's dinner guests had been asked to bring food to the party. Gabe and Barbara, who was seven months pregnant, were responsible for the dessert, and that afternoon Barbara had made two peach pies that they had carried in with them. Andy, who would be accompanied by Maureen Donnelly, was supposed to bring the salad. They all remembered Maureen from before Vietnam, and she arrived embracing an enormous wooden salad bowl closed off at the top with Saran Wrap. And Frank, who of course came alone, had been told to bring the wine, which he did.

All had been asked to come late so the child could be put to bed first.

Once the viewing was out of the way Earl brought forth a pitcher of manhattans — cocktails that year were what most people liked to drink before dinner. He had concocted a potent mixture, and they all got a bit high. All seven of them were smoking. Smoke hung above their heads. After a time Rocky had to move through the room emptying ashtrays.

At dinner they talked about Vietnam for a while, and then about babies. Frank found himself unwilling to contribute to the first of these subjects, and felt left out of the second.

When the dishes had been cleared away the party split in half. The women pushed into the tiny kitchen where Rocky was cleaning up, while the four men clustered together at one end of the big room where they smoked, sipped highballs, and talked of a case Earl and Gabe were trying to put together against a man named Rienzi, who was running for mayor. It was the good guys against the bad guys again, Gabe explained to Frank in an aside. Frank was distracted. The women were all laughing, and he kept glancing in that direction, from time to time catching a glimpse of Rocky.

Congressman Rienzi used to be a detective. Used to moonlight as a Mafia hit man too, according to Gabe. As a congressman he was an extortionist, according to Earl. A bad, bad fellow, according to them both. He had to be stopped, they said, and they wanted Andy Troy to write articles that would help them do it. But to Frank's surprise Andy refused. He had ethical objections, he said. Something about the adversarial role that existed between the press and law enforcement. This role was sacred, according to Andy, and must be protected at all costs.

The cigarettes flared and subsided, the smoke rose toward the ceiling.

Frank, who had been out of the country for most of five years, and out of New York even longer, barely knew of the upcoming election. He did not fully understand what an assistant district attorney and a police sergeant could do about the mayoral candidate at this stage, and he did not grasp Andy Troy's ethical objections either, for he was trying to fit them into a moral equation he was familiar with, just as he had tried to do over and over again with the war.

The women came from the kitchen. "Your wife wants to go home," Rocky told Gabe.

"In a minute," said Gabe.

Rocky turned to Frank. "I thought you'd be wearing your, well, uniform."

He had on brown slacks and a red sweater. "My uniform?" he joked. "My dress uniform, my combat fatigues, or what?"

"Or your other uniform," Rocky said to him. "Your cassock, or whatever you call it."

"I decided not to. I was afraid you'd feel obliged to call me 'Father.'"

She gave him an intimate, secret kind of look, or so it seemed to him. "Somehow I've never thought of you as my father," she murmured, and she laughed.

"The press cannot operate in cahoots with cops and prosecutors, or with any arm of government on any level," Andy stated.

"It's time to go home, Gabe," said Barbara Driscoll.

"Another couple of minutes," said Gabe.

"My back has started to ache."

"Not mine," said Maureen Donnelly with a laugh. "I'm not even married yet."

"At least think about it," said Gabe to Andy.

"All right, I'll think about it."

And the party broke up.

But the conspiracy had been joined. The impact on the lives of all of them would be heavy, though in Frank's case deferred.

ALL THREE OF THE MEN DETECTIVE RIENZI had killed had criminal records, all were black, all were said to be drug dealers. The killings were not shoot-outs but Mafia-sponsored executions, the black community had charged. Grand juries had looked into all three killings, as was routine, and had judged them to be line of duty. Treated as a hero, Rienzi was given medals.

Detective Rienzi owned a house in the suburbs and drove a Cadillac. He wore a gold watch and expensive suits. But when asked about this he explained that his wife came from money. Occasionally a reporter would look into his wife's background, and find no money there. No one ever acquired enough information on which to base an exposé.

At 42 years of age Detective Rienzi resigned from the department and ran for Congress in Spanish Harlem, one of the poorest, most ravaged sections of the city, using his police department record as proof of integrity, and promising law and order. He was elected in a landslide that year, and every two years afterwards, eight straight terms, and now was Democratic nominee for mayor. In heavily Democratic New York City he led in the polls by 20 points.

Assistant District Attorney Earl Finley had resolved to bring him down.

Though still a junior prosecutor, and still atrociously paid, Earl had escaped from arraignment court, and was now attached to the Rackets Bureau. He wore dark three-piece suits as lawyers were supposed to. His suits were well cut and always beautifully pressed — Rocky's responsibility, one of them. The Rackets Bureau was the first career move he had made, and he needed a big case to solidify it.

One day his bureau chief handed him a complaint, saying: "Look into this and get back to me." The Manhattan DA's office received dozens of complaints each week. That is, the bureau chief had no special interest in this one, and after having spoken to Earl he could be seen entering one cubicle after another dropping complaints on desks.

The letter Earl gazed down on was handwritten in block characters, with many misspellings and no signature. It charged that Congressman Rienzi had promised American citizenship to the author of the complaint, a hardworking Hispanic father of four, and had demanded money in exchange. Though the money was paid, the congressman had done nothing. The writer now faced deportation.

Attached to the letter by a straight pin through the corner was the envelope it had come in, postmarked the week before, its return address inked out.

Earl knew of the rumors attached to the probable next mayor of New York. Some dated from his police career. But there were more recent rumors as well. Most had to do with immigration bills that he had introduced in the House by which the foreigner mentioned in the bill, sometimes several of them, became citizens by act of Congress. No waiting period, no residency requirements, or scrutiny. Other members introduced such bills as well. Usually they favored foreign-born executives, scientists, professors working for major American corporations or universities. Even important newsmen at times. Such bills were enacted into law on a simple voice vote — a courtesy members regularly did for each other.

The difference was that Congressman Rienzi had introduced rather more of these bills than his colleagues, there were no corporations lobbying him, and it had long been rumored that he charged fees to do it. Criminal extortion, if true.

To get started Earl needed help. The Manhattan DA's office had access to about 60 detectives who worked out of offices in the criminal courts building, and who were used usually on cases being readied for trial. This was known as the District Attorney's Squad. It was the squad's job to find and bring in missing witnesses, missing evidence.

But Earl decided to run what amounted to a private investigation. On mere suspicion of wrongdoing he was setting out to derail an election. Therefore he could not use these detectives. He could not even tell his bureau chief what he was doing, or hoped to do, because it might be seen as tampering with the democratic process.

In addition, if the case went anywhere some higher-ranking assistant DA, probably his own bureau chief, would step in and take it away from him.

Earl thought the police lab might be able to bring up the inked-out return address, so he put in a call to Sergeant Driscoll. Presently Gabe was back with the complainant's address. "Easy," he said to Earl. "Next time give me something harder."

Together they went up to Harlem. The complainant's name was Cayetano Gonzalez. They knocked on his door and showed their shields.

"Did you write this?"

It was a poor apartment on the fourth floor of a brownstone that had become a tenement. Outside its windows ran the elevated tracks of Metro North. Every few minutes as they interrogated Gonzalez, the room vibrated and their words were drowned out.

A Venezuelan, Gonzalez had entered the U.S. on a student visa, but had never attended any school. He had been able to bring in his family on similar visas. Now, having found him, Immigration had ordered him to leave. He had contacted Congressman Rienzi, who, friends told him, might be able to help, had gone to his district office and met with him, and had been told that citizenship would cost $5,000. He was to go to the Democratic Party's West 57th Street offices, and give the money in cash to a party official named Colesano.

A train rattled by the windows. When it had passed Gonzalez refused to cooperate in any investigation. In Harlem, he said, people were murdered for little reason or none. Congressman Rienzi was a powerful man.

He would not be alone, Earl told him. There would be other complainants. Rienzi would not be able to single him out. Furthermore, he would not be deported for as long as the case remained open, a year's respite, perhaps more.

Earl spoke earnestly, and never took his eyes off Gonzalez.

No matter how much he needed their cooperation, Earl was determined never to lie to subjects. Once jailed, he told Gonzalez, Rienzi would be unable to hurt him. And at the end of the case Earl would speak to them at Immigration. He would perhaps be able to get Gonzalez a green card; it wasn't sure, but he would try. The grateful government might see to it that Gonzalez could stay in New York.

They talked to him more than an hour. Señora Gonzalez, a tiny woman who spoke almost no English, served tea.

EARL NEEDED THE NAMES OF OTHER BENEFICIARIES of Rienzi's immigration bills, so this was the first of the jobs he wanted Andy Troy to perform. Go to Washington, find out how many bills and whom they favored.

They had met for lunch in a restaurant near the paper. Andy shook his head decisively. "Sorry, I can't do it."

Earl showed him the Gonzalez letter, described the interview, then promised Andy exclusive access to the case. "You could be sitting on the story of the year."

"Pulitzer Prize," said Andy with a grin. "I already won it twice in Vietnam, only I didn't get it."

"If we can knock this guy out of the mayoral race you'll certainly get it."

Two days later Troy did go to Washington. He did come back with the names Earl needed, but he handed them over with misgivings, saying: "This stuff is all public record, so I guess it's okay. Just don't tell anybody I gave it to you."

However, in Washington Troy had had to dig so hard that word reached Rienzi, who phoned Troy's publisher. "You're trying to influence the election with rumor and innuendo," he accused. "Who is this reporter? What are you people plotting?" He was furious. "If you're trying to ruin my candidacy I'll denounce you to the city and the world."

The shaken publisher called down to the third floor, asking his executive editor to come up.

"Who is the reporter? What does he have?"

Back in the newsroom the editor sent for Troy. What was he doing in Washington, and what was he doing with those names?

"The Manhattan DA has an investigation going into bribe soliciting by Rienzi," Troy answered.

"How do you know this?"

Troy stood with his shirt collar undone and his tie hanging to his waist. His success in Vietnam had given him two things, the beginnings of a reputation, and belief in himself. But he was not confident now. "I have a source in the DA's office," he said.

"Who?"

"I'd rather not say."

This answer fell within the journalistic code, and the editor decided, for the moment, to accept it. "Someone you trust?"

"Absolutely." But it made Troy wonder how much he trusted Earl. He would have trusted him with his life, but was it safe to trust him with his career?

The editor was nervously cracking his knuckles. "We're on dangerous ground," he said.

On the other hand it was the type of investigation on which newspapers made their reputations.

The editor said, "Go on with it then. But be very, very careful."

The worried Troy immediately phoned Earl. "You better be right."

Earl laughed. "Of course I'm right."

Sergeant Driscoll in uniform was out every night looking for the men on the list. He located five, and he and Earl interviewed them all. It was not hard to trick them into admitting they had paid bribes to Rienzi. But they were afraid they would be indicted themselves, or lose their new citizenship, or both. Or Rienzi might have them killed.

All refused to cooperate further, and Earl did not blame them.

After each interview Gabe Driscoll went home to Barbara, while Earl returned to the office and considered his next move. He had no clerk to research the law for him, no secretary to type out the subpoenas he was planning. In addition he was responsible for other cases as well, for which he was obliged to file motions, and interview witnesses. He worked most weekends, and was rarely home, a pattern that was to continue as his career advanced. Rocky began to nag him about being left alone so much.

Home, to Earl, became a place where he could not concentrate because his wife nagged him and his small son cried a lot. He might have explained the Rienzi case to her. But it was after all secret—secret even from his bureau chief—and he decided she wouldn't understand it anyway. So he told her nothing.

Rocky began to complain that he bought himself new suits, but nothing for her. She hadn't had a new dress since—

They couldn't afford new dresses right now, he retorted. As for himself, he was a lawyer and had to dress like one.

She became unresponsive sexually, which bothered him, but he did not know what to do about it. He began to feel isolated. He had become a kind of priest. He stood for truth, for justice. A different priest from Frank Redmond, but similar.

At night he would ride uptown on the Seventh Avenue subway as it was then known, coming up on the sidewalk at 72nd Street, and walking the few blocks home. But one night he stayed on the train several more stops, getting off at 116th, where he walked downhill toward the river and sat on a bench under the trees and looked up at the tenth-floor windows where his grandmother used to live.

She had died when he was eight. He still remembered her phone number, the first he had ever dialed by himself. He had sometimes stayed with her for months while his mother was off somewhere, and during this period would have to attend a different school. He called her Nana, and liked the way she smelled when she put him on her lap. She always praised him, told him what a good boy he was. He would bring her his report cards each month, riding up on the subway alone, and she always gave him a half dollar piece, which made him feel rich, and which he never spent but kept in a stack in his drawer, until he had enough for a five-dollar bill. He remembered the way she looked when laid out. He remembered realizing she wouldn't be there anymore. Small as he was, he saw that from now on he was alone. A man named Jack Pepper had moved in with his mother, and it was Jack Pepper who signed his report card that month. He remembered having to explain to the teacher who Jack Pepper was.

He turned away from his grandmother's windows. The election of Rienzi had to be blocked. Nothing else counted.

If the district attorney learned of the investigation he might stop it, stop Earl, for he was running for reelection on the same ticket as Rienzi and had debts to the party. To forestall this possibility Earl decided to take several low-ranking colleagues into his confidence, enough of them, he believed, to start rumors down the hallways. The DA would hear these rumors, would have no idea how far they had spread, were spreading, and, being faced with an election, would not dare order the case quashed. In law enforcement, every case was bizarre. The more secret, the more rumors they engendered. On the eighth floor there was no way of stopping any of them.

And Earl primed Andy Troy.

Presently he took his case folder into the office of his bureau chief, a man named Conroy, and watched him thumb pages.

"Jesus," Conroy said. "Do the reporters know about this?"

"One does," Earl was careful to say. "Andy Troy got on to it, I don't know how."

Conroy was silent, but his face showed almost terror. Then: "You bring a case like this, you better win. You lose, and Rienzi wins the election. Once he's mayor he'll eat you alive. He'll eat all of us alive."

"Do you want to take over the case?" Earl offered, knowing Conroy's answer in advance.

"As it happens, the boss will be out of the office campaigning the next two weeks. I'll be with him. What you do is your affair. I don't want to know anything about it."

Earl began to present his case to the grand jury, 23 men and women sitting three mornings a week in tiers in a small amphitheater, looking down on Earl and whatever witness he was examining. Grand jury proceedings were secret, and were mostly a formality. No lawyers were present except the prosecutor himself. If he asked for an indictment, he would almost always get it. A grand jury, it was said, would indict a ham sandwich, if the prosecutor told it to.

The election was less than a month away.

His first witness was Cayetano Gonzalez. Earl swore him in and warned him about perjury, but Gonzalez shook him off impatiently. The witness had names, dates, amounts written down on a card, and he read them off. He was good. He solidly implicated both Rienzi and his bagman, Colesano.

Next came the five reluctant witnesses. Gabe Driscoll brought them in one at a time. They too implicated Colesano, who had demanded and received money from them. But the congressman himself could be perceived only at a distance. He had sent them to Colesano promising only: "If he says it's okay, I'll see what I can do."

These witnesses gave Earl pause. His case against Rienzi was getting no stronger.

A subpoena was served on Colesano, and he was brought in. He denied everything. Earl made him sweat, made him lie.

After studying the minutes of the testimony Earl became convinced that, with six victims testifying against one lying bagman, he had a solid perjury case against the bagman, and a medium-strong case for extortion as well.

But it wasn't the bagman he wanted, it was the future mayor.

ANDY TROY HAD WRITTEN HIS STORY. It was filled with details no other reporter knew. But the executive editor refused to run it.

"Anyone else got this story?"

"No."

"In three weeks the guy will be mayor, for crissake," the editor told Andy. "We can't afford to be that far out in front of everybody else."

Trying to get the piece into the paper became, for Troy, harder work than writing it in the first place. For two days he argued, pleaded.

But the editor was adamant.

The two childhood friends found themselves unable to help each other.

EARL'S ONLY CHANCE, IT SEEMED TO HIM, was to throw Rienzi before the grand jury, pressure him, force him to lose his cool, make admissions, trip himself up, lie.

As a courtesy, elected officials are almost never subpoenaed, but simply telephoned and asked to come in. But Earl ordered a subpoena served on Rienzi in public — not at his office or home but during a street rally on Fordham Road in the Bronx in front of a crowd of approximately 500 voters and the press corps.

Now, with the other papers and TV news shows revealing what bits of information they had been able to acquire, the editor decided to go with Andy's detailed story, and it appeared the next morning on the front page.

Its impact on voters would not show in the polls for some days. But its impact on Rienzi was immediate.

Earl had just got in. Rienzi came storming onto the eighth floor. Armed with an empty, not particularly clean coffee mug, Earl was halfway out of his cubicle en route to the coffee machine. Rienzi nearly knocked him down.

"You have to send me a subpoena?" the congressman raged. "You never heard of the telephone?"

"This case has become a bit too big for that, Congressman."

Earl went back behind his desk. He sat down, put down the dirty coffee cup.

Rienzi was a big man in a dark silk suit. His hair was thick, wavy, and still almost entirely black. He stood in front of the desk, his face red. "You know what an election is, Dickhead? I've won eight straight elections."

"But not nine," said Earl.

"Who elected you, Scumbag? Somebody elect you? Who gave you the right to interfere in an election?"

Rienzi waved fists covered with black fleece. "I want you off my back. What do I have to do to get you off my back?"

"Well," said Earl coolly, "you can drop out of the mayoral race. That would be a good start."

"What? What?"

"You're not going to be mayor, Congressman, sorry to say."

"I'll ruin you, Fuckface."

Over the top of a pencil Earl studied him. This man had killed — probably murdered — three people. "No, it's the other way around. I'll ruin you. In fact I already have."

"You prick."

There was more dialogue of this nature, Earl calm, Rienzi in a rage. "I'll have you fired. Where's your boss's office?"

Earl smiled at him. "The DA's campaigning today. To see him you'll have to come back next week, though that might be too late, I admit."

Rienzi was sputtering, too angry to speak.

"So I'll see you tomorrow in front of the grand jury," Earl said. "Nine A.M."

"I've got a street rally at nine A.M."

"Better cancel it. Don't be late, now. I'd hate to have to issue a warrant for your arrest."

Still sputtering, Congressman Rienzi spun on his heel and departed.

Behind him, Earl began to laugh.

The next morning Rienzi sat in a chair below the jurors in their tiers, and began to answer Earl's questions. His manner, as he answered, was subdued. Most of all it was careful. How much did this prosecutor already know? Troy's article had listed the complainants, whose names Rienzi did not remember. He knew others had testified before him, but not which ones. What had they said? The congressman's silk suit today was powder blue.

Perjury was what Rienzi feared. Perjury was like a hole so deep that if he stepped into it he might disappear.

And so he answered with increasing care. Wherever possible, his responses were pious: "I don't recognize the name you mentioned. Did I help him become an American citizen? If you say I did, then probably I did. Why did I do this? Because it's my job to help the underprivileged, the poor, the downtrodden of my district, and I do this every chance I get."

But when Earl's questioning became more insistent, more specific, Rienzi began to squirm, to clench and unclench his fists, to become evasive.

But Earl had names, dates, amounts.

Abruptly Rienzi asserted his Fifth Amendment constitutional rights: "I respectfully decline to answer on the grounds that my answer may tend to incriminate me."

From then on every question drew the same answer: "I respectfully decline to answer—"

In all he took the Fifth Amendment 19 times.

The stalemate lasted more than two hours. Finally, having gained not even a step, Earl dismissed him. The congressman got up smiling, shook hands with the jurors in their tiers, and went out the door. Earl gathered his papers and followed.

Reporters and TV crews waited in the corridor. Earl saw microphones hanging on booms, and the glare of lights made him blink. But it was all focused on Rienzi's smiling face. No one was interested in Earl. There came a clamor of blurred questions, and then Rienzi's pontificating voice.

"Today's exercise in futility was a fishing expedition pure and simple by Mr. Earl Finley, a junior assistant district attorney, whose political leanings may favor my opponent, and who on his own authority has attempted to influence next month's election. But it didn't work. He went fishing, but there were no fish there."

This would be the sound bite on tonight's news broadcasts. Everyone laughed, except Earl.

"There is no evidence that I committed any crime. There is no evidence that any crime was committed." Again his audience laughed.

In the group of reporters taking notes stood Andy Troy, who caught Earl's eye and gave a sad, sympathetic grimace.

"I answered every question frankly and unequivocally," Rienzi said into the microphones. "Answered them all. End of case. Case closed."

He's lying, Earl wanted to interrupt. The man had taken the Fifth 19 times. If the city could be told he would lose the election. Constrained by law Earl could say nothing. To reveal grand jury testimony was a felony. He would go to jail. All he could do was give Troy a vigorous, negative shake of his head which he hoped would alert his friend that there was more to come. For a plan was taking shape in Earl's head, and Troy was part of it.

"Now let's get on with the electoral campaign," Rienzi said. The glare of lights shut down. Earl watched the congressman's back receding down the corridor.

BECAUSE HE WANTED NO RECORD OF the call he was about to make, Earl went out into the street looking for a phone booth. The first two booths he stepped into stank of urine and the phone cables were ripped half out of the wall. In the third booth the phone worked, so he closed the door on himself, dropped in his dime, and dialed Andy Troy. Their scheduled interview was off, he told him. He would not be able to talk to him at ten A.M. tomorrow as scheduled. His bureau chief, Conroy, would not be there either as he was campaigning with the DA. And he hung up.

The two men had no scheduled interview at ten A.M. or any other time. Earl was betting that he and Troy were so attuned to each other that they could communicate even in a code neither of them knew.

When he got back to his office Gabe was waiting, but he sent him away. "You're out of it, Gabe, go."

Gabe too understood.

There was going to be a stink when this was over. A terrific investigation too — not of Rienzi but of himself, Troy, and Gabe, and Earl was trying to protect all three in advance.

JUST BEFORE TEN THE NEXT MORNING Troy entered the criminal courts building, showed his press card, signed the logbook and stepped into the elevator.

On the eighth floor he walked along until he came to Earl's office. A number of people saw him, one or two nodded, but no one questioned him. With over 400 assistant district attorneys working on that floor and adjacent ones, with cops, defense lawyers and witnesses coming and going at all times, this was not surprising. Even the people who worked there every day did not all know each other. Troy came to Earl's office which was locked, then moved along until he found Conroy's, and this door, when he turned the handle, opened.

He had with him an early edition of the *New York Post* whose front page headline read:

GRAND JURY EXONERATES RIENZI
CANDIDATE ANSWERS ALL QUESTIONS TRUTHFULLY

Troy put the paper down on the desk. In Conroy's IN basket he found the minutes of Rienzi's testimony which, sitting down in Conroy's chair, he calmly read through. He had with him a small tape recorder, into which he now began to dictate.

Within ten minutes he had finished. He put the minutes back in Conroy's IN basket, exactly where Earl, or a legal secretary, must have placed them, and listened momentarily at the half-closed door. Hearing no hallway traffic, he stepped outside and moved to the elevator. Downstairs he logged out.

Twenty minutes later Earl arrived downstairs and logged in, his signature separated from Troy's by about ten intervening names.

As soon as he had got back to the paper Andrew Troy began writing his story. According to sources high up in the district attorney's office (for Troy too had footprints to smudge) Rienzi's public statements were a lie, he wrote. In actual fact, the candidate for mayor had not been exonerated by the grand jury as he claimed, and had not testified frankly. On the contrary he had refused to answer every question relating to possible bribe soliciting, resorting to the Fifth Amendment in all 19 times.

When he had finished Troy carried his story into the executive editor's office and waited while he read it.

"These are grave accusations. Who are your sources? You know the rules. You need two sources independently corroborating each other, or we can't run this."

"I know that," said Troy.

"So who are they?"

"I only have one," said Troy. "Me. I've seen the minutes myself. I've read them from beginning to end."

He turned on his tape recorder and let the editor listen to the testimony line by line.

"Hmm," the editor said. Then: "Find Rienzi. Tell him we're running the story tonight and give him a chance to comment."

Troy found the candidate in the back of a hall in Brooklyn about to address a gathering of Hasidic Jews. He was practicing some words in Yiddish, or perhaps Hebrew, when Troy interrupted him, and handed him a copy of his story, which he read.

"You scumbag," Rienzi said, "where did you get this stuff?" He tore the pages to shreds, threw them on the floor, and in a low menacing voice began to berate Troy.

Rienzi was announced as the next speaker and the interview broke off.

Troy went out front and listened to his speech. The man sounded as confident as ever, and the audience seemed to hang on every word. He was like one of those heavyweight fighters with an iron jaw. Troy had hit him with everything and he still wouldn't go down.

The next day, with Troy's front-page story on the street, Rienzi called a press conference at which he charged "this scheming reporter" with writing lies, and he offered to "waive his rights" to grand jury secrecy by showing his testimony to a three-judge panel. The panel would attest to who was telling the truth, himself or Andrew

Troy. He demanded only the right to name two of the three judges who would compose the panel.

This idea was a useful stall, but it did not seduce the media, for clearly the election would be over before it could be arranged. Why didn't Rienzi just release the minutes himself?

At the same time the candidate called for the district attorney to investigate at once. Who had leaked this inaccurate version of secret grand jury testimony? Whoever it was had committed a felony, and should go to jail.

The politician was scrambling and the media, as always, was delighted to watch. The suggested investigation sounded good too, for it kept the presses turning.

When the *New York Post* discovered that Sergeant Driscoll, the principal investigator on the case, and reporter Andrew Troy and Assistant District Attorney Earl Finley were all childhood friends the case got even hotter.

A judicial investigation became inevitable.

A subpoena was issued for Troy; he was to bring all his notes and first drafts to court. When he refused to appear he was threatened with contempt, and a possible jail term, but he refused to appear anyway. His paper sent four lawyers to court to defend freedom of the press, and Troy personally. They presented motions to quash that ran to more than 100 pages. The judge, who recognized political clout when it was thrust into his face, announced it would take him some time to review all this.

The paper promptly sent Troy to Paris, putting him out of range of any more subpoenas, or a possible jail sentence for civil contempt. Maureen Donnelly quit her job and went with him. They were married there a month later. Ultimately Troy never appeared in court and was never cited for contempt.

The DA had expected no better in his pursuit of Troy, whose paper wielded far more power than any elected official. He now focused on his own men, starting with Detective Sergeant Driscoll, who was forced to testify under oath about the freelance investigation he had conducted on his own time. But Gabe knew nothing about the leaked minutes, he swore, had never seen them and still didn't know what was in them.

This was public testimony, and Sergeant Driscoll was pilloried for it by the media, who accused him of unauthorized snooping on private citizens while off duty. The outcry against Gabe was so loud that it frightened the mayor, who then frightened the police commissioner, who decided Sergeant Driscoll had committed a grave breach of regulations. Accordingly, Gabe was put on trial in the department trial room in front of the deputy commissioner of trials. The deputy commissioner, being sole judge and jury, reached the verdict that he saw was expected of him. He found Detective Sergeant Driscoll guilty as charged. Gabe was fined five days' vacation, flopped back to uniform, and reassigned to the East New York section of Brooklyn. He just missed being dismissed. His career was severely damaged and would not recover during the present administration, if ever.

When it was his turn to appear in court, ADA Earl Finley swore that he had come to work late the day Troy was known to have been snooping around the eighth floor, had not been in the building at the same time as Troy; and that his own copy of the minutes had been in the office safe all the previous night. There were no phone records linking himself and Troy, and he had not even seen him during those days, except in the crowd after the hearing; he had revealed to him nothing of what was in those minutes, not then, not ever. So he swore.

The assistant DA examining him was Conroy, who was sick of Rienzi's posturing and lies, and of the trouble he had caused. Conroy knew very well that the benches behind him were filled mostly with reporters hanging on every word. So he phrased his final question this way: "But the version of the minutes that appeared in the paper was essentially accurate. How do you account for that?"

"Good reporter," said Earl.

"I have no further questions," said Conroy.

The newsmen rushed out of the courtroom. Their segments and stories, appearing that night and the next morning, were like multiple punctures in a rubber dinghy. No political candidacy ever deflated and sank more quickly.

Five days later Rienzi lost the election by eight points.

The district attorney decided to take no further action against Gabe, Earl, or Conroy.

Earl took the following week off, the better to bask in the applause he was giving himself. At home Rocky still cooked for him, still did his laundry, but often when night came and the kids were asleep, she put on her coat and told him she was going out. She never told him where she was going. In fact all she did was walk along Broadway looking into whatever shop windows were still lit. But it was always close to midnight, Earl already in bed asleep, before she got home.

THE INVESTIGATION

6

"THE DEATH OF FATHER REDMOND IS A PUZZLE," Chief Driscoll says. "I've got some detectives trying to figure out what happened. I thought maybe you might know something that could help us."

He sits in a big corner office, the furnishings expensive, with a view over Fifth Avenue. The man across the desk leans back, his leather armchair tilted, hands behind his head, and he gazes at Gabe without speaking. They are about the same age, and there is a quality about him Gabe recognizes. Like Gabe himself, he exudes power. A man used to commanding other men.

An American flag pokes up in one corner, a New York flag in the other. On the walls hang blowups of the man's superiors. This could be a law enforcement office, the police commissioner's, say, or the attorney general's, or any of the other important offices Gabe frequents. Only the artwork is different. This man, whose rank is bishop, sits amid blowups of the New York cardinal, who is smiling, the Roman pope in a somber mood, and a giant version of the holy picture known to every Catholic as the Sacred Heart of Jesus: Jesus facing the artist, fingering his exposed, bleeding heart.

Gabe is a supplicant here, a role he does not like. According to protocol, he is supposed to address this man as Your Excellency. Your Grace. Something like that. But he doesn't do it.

It should be Andy Troy performing this interview, according to the way he and Gabe have divided up the work. But Gabe has a relationship of sorts with this bishop, or so he has imagined. When Frankie's pastor tried to block the funeral, Gabe phoned this man, whose name is Ahern, whom he did not know. Ahern seemed cordial that day, and immediately ordered the pastor to let the funeral proceed.

So Gabe and Troy decided Gabe was the one to talk to Ahern now. But his reception so far has been frosty.

"So I have a few questions for you."

"Why come to me? What do I know about it?"

"I talked to his pastor. This Monsignor Malachy. He said some things. I don't know how true. I thought I should check them out with you. Maybe you can help move the investigation forward." A long nervous speech, though why? Why does this man make him nervous? As a child Gabe was taught to revere priests, an instinct that, perhaps, one does not get over. And this man, you might say, is a superpriest, is he not?

Or does Gabe, given the frosty reception, fear the answers he might be about to hear?

The bishop wears black shoes—Gabe can see them beneath the desk—black trousers, a collarless white shirt, and, over it, a red cardigan. There is a coat tree in the corner from which hangs his black suit coat on its hanger, and his roman collar.

In Gabe's line of work, interviews are almost always adversarial, the detective probing, the subject on his guard, concealing something. Answers tend to be self-serving, if not outright lies.

So it is best, Gabe knows, always to begin with easy questions. Put the subject at ease. Perhaps an important detail will slip out before the subject can call it back. This is what one hopes for, but the technique does not always work.

"So why did you send Father Redmond to that particular parish in the first place?"

"I thought it would do him good."

"You make it sound like a punishment."

In theory this particular interview should not be adversarial at all, and yet Gabe senses that it is. He just doesn't know why.

"It was the type parish he deserved."

"I'm not sure I understand."

"Look, we had him in a rich suburban parish. Most priests would kill for that. No drive-by shootings and you get invited to dinner in nice houses. What does he do? He goes into the military. He didn't ask permission. He just did it. Years go by. Then we find out he's in Africa. He didn't ask permission for that either. Made a connection with an order in Canada, Missionaries of Africa. Ever heard of them?"

"No."

"More years go by. Finally he comes back. Comes in here asking for a job. So I sent him to St. Ambrose in Harlem, which is a place no priest in his right mind would want to go."

"Why is that?"

Ahern ignores the question. "He was sick, which I didn't realize. Though he got better soon enough. He thrived in Harlem, which surprised me. Did an excellent job too, I believe."

Gabe sees well enough where this man's power comes from. The New York Archdiocese includes all of the city and much of upstate, hundreds and hundreds of priests. This one man controls their lives, where they live, how they live, and from his decisions there is no appeal.

Gabe decides to say: "The pastor told me he had asked you to remove Father Redmond, and that you had promised to do it."

"Can I speak to you off the record?"

Gabe nods, already dreading the revelation he imagines is coming next.

Bishop Ahern in his red cardigan pauses to light a Marlboro. He blows out a lungful of smoke, and for a moment watches it rise.

"Filthy habit," he apologizes, gazing at the cigarette between his fingers.

Gabe imagines he has changed his mind. The revelation, whatever it is, is not to be divulged.

"That man Malachy should not be a pastor," Ahern says. "He makes his curates' lives hell. He's been demanding that I remove them, one after another, since I was a monsignor. Eventually the curate himself will come in here and beg me to reassign him. When he does, if I think he's been there long enough, then I transfer him. Most of them I make pastors. They've put in their hard time with Monsignor Malachy, and they deserve it."

"But you didn't transfer Father Redmond?"

"He didn't want to be transferred. He actually liked it up there. Fine. One less headache for me."

Now it is time for the hard questions. Gabe gets a clipboard out of his briefcase and pretends to study it. The clipboard is theater. It allows him a moment to decide how to proceed, and perhaps gives the impression that none of the questions on it is more important than any other.

"We've been studying Father Redmond's personal bank statements," Gabe begins.

It seems to him that Bishop Ahern immediately stiffens. The movement is very slight. He cannot be sure.

"What's that got to do with me?"

"There seem to have been a number of deposits and cash withdrawals these last few months."

"And?"

"We can't seem to find an explanation for them, and wonder if you might be able to help."

"Well, I can't."

"Father Redmond received a salary, I believe."

"Diocesan priests do not take a vow of poverty."

"In any case," Gabe says, "the salary was not very much."

"Meaning what?"

"You don't pay your priests very much."

"The church takes care of them from ordination to the grave," Ahern says sharply. "They're fed, housed, medical bills paid. They've got no wives, children, or dependents. When they get old they go into one of our homes for retired priests."

"On the bank statements we see a pattern of small deposits and expenditures," Gabe persists. "Then all of a sudden these big ones."

"Apart from buying a new shirt once in a while, a priest doesn't need money."

"Exactly," says Gabe.

"He's got nothing to spend it on."

"So what could it be?"

"Go ask Monsignor Malachy, don't ask me."

"I did ask him. He stonewalled me."

Bishop Ahern's chair comes forward. Body language, obviously. But Gabe can't be sure he reads it accurately.

"What are you trying to accuse me of?"

"You personally? Nothing. I do have one or two more questions, though."

"You've got about another minute."

Gabe brings forth the one he has dreaded having to ask. "Did he have access to parish funds?"

"No."

"The Sunday mass collections? Money to fix the church roof?"

"That's it." The bishop is on his feet, ushering Gabe to the door. "I don't know what you're getting at, but you've run out of time."

IN HIS DEPARTMENT CAR IN A NO-PARKING ZONE opposite the paper's entrance Gabe waits for Troy. His driver, a detective, has spread the *Daily News* out on the steering wheel. He reads it by the light above the mirror. Snow is falling. The windshield is covered over. The city is entirely muffled. Pedestrians move by heads down. Snow decorates their shoulders, their hats. It falls through cones of light. Except for the detective turning pages there is no noise in the car.

The car is cooling fast.

Gabe says: "Put the heat back on, Louie."

"Right, Chief."

Driscoll and Troy have formed the habit of meeting each evening, usually in this car in this spot. After comparing notes, they will go their separate ways.

At last the door opens, and Troy slides in.

"How did you do?" he asks Gabe.

"This Bishop Ahern, do you know him?"

"No."

"Told me nothing, then threw me out."

Troy laughs. "Seemed a little haughty, did he?"

"A little, you might say."

"But that's been the Church's way for 2,000 years. Tell the faithful nothing."

"They do tell us a few things. Not to fornicate and all that."

"And how much money we have to contribute."

"I should have arrested him for obstruction of justice."

"Why didn't you?"

Gabe laughs. "Because officially this isn't my investigation. I would have been in more trouble than him."

"It would have made an interesting headline though: 'Stonewalling Bishop Led Away in Handcuffs.'"

"First time in history."

In the front seat the driver says nothing. The pages continue to turn. He is like an old-world servant. He is there, but expects to be treated as if he isn't.

"What did you find out from the bank?" Gabe Driscoll asks.

"The money went into Frank's account via cashier's checks, and it went out the same way. Which is not the way one usually does it."

"It was when I started talking about money that the bishop threw me out," says Gabe. "There's something there, but what?"

"It's going to be hard to find out."

"Cashier's checks are almost impossible to trace."

"It sounds almost like he was paying blackmail."

"If it wasn't Frankie we're talking about, I'd say the same."

"What did Frankie have that anyone could blackmail him about?"

For a moment both are silent. "Frankie was into something, obviously," Gabe says.

"But we don't know what."

Gabe says: "If we could find out, it might tell us how and why he went off that roof."

"Maybe."

"I've got to get home," Gabe says.

"Me too. Maureen has invited people to dinner. That's almost the only time we talk to each other, these days. At dinner parties." He gets out of the car. "See you tomorrow," he says. Snow falls on the back of his coat. He straightens up, and slams the door shut.

As he is being driven home by Louie, Gabe gnaws at his thumbnail, thinking: We're not gaining any ground on this thing.

Chapter Six

In Africa he lived in a village at the edge of the Zambezi River. The village was shabby, unordered, scattered. One-room shacks, the better ones with corrugated roofs. Others of black mud walls with thatch on top, like swollen chocolates under straw hats. Chickens nosed about scratching. Dogs scavenged in the garbage. Older children in ragged clothes, younger ones naked. Women in brightly colored dresses, with heavy tins of water on their heads. A post office built when the British were there, and not maintained since. Some small stores. A market shed in which some of the merchants had stalls. Others squatted behind mats that were tattered, and on which was laid out whatever they had to sell. Used clothing. Gasoline in whiskey bottles. Individual cigarettes laid out in rows to be sold one at a time.

The clinic stood opposite the church, both of them covered by thin corrugated roofs, the one with beds always full, the other with pews mostly empty. A school that contained two rooms, two blackboards on wheels. But books were scarce, and sometimes there was no chalk. The teachers were barely schooled themselves. One had gone as far as the sixth grade, the other not even. Dirt streets. Rusty pickup trucks parked here and there. Bicycles. The carcasses of cars that had been stripped of whatever was usable, even the doors gone so that one could walk right through them, the doors serving now as people's garden gates. Other derelict cars still ran, more or less.

When engines started the noise was audible all over the village. Black smoke came forth, and when they moved, a halo of dust hung over where they had been.

There was a headman who ruled over the village. He was judge, jury, and police chief. When disputes arose it was he who heard the case and dispensed justice. The winner, the loser, the amount of the fine to be paid in cattle. He was about 60, tall, skinny, and because he was a drunk no one could predict what his judgments might be.

There were ceremonies whose origins were lost in time. The reed dance of the virgins, for instance. The girls were taken to the edge of a field, stripped naked, and examined for virginity by the women of the village. Then, to prove the purity and beauty of their young bodies, wearing only short bead skirts and carrying long reeds from the river, the girls weaved through the dirt streets in a ritual dance. Most years Father Redmond watched, but from a distance.

To one side of the village was the great river, to the other side a dirt road. The river hurried on by, always hurrying, never stopped. It didn't know the village was there. The dirt road ran toward the capital in one direction, toward more villages in the other, but whole days could go by with no traffic at all. Across this highway stretched fields of cassava and maize, the villagers' staple foods, and also pasturage for the cattle.

The clinic had electricity from a generator, and contained rows of beds that had been donated. The patients who occupied the beds suffered from all the usual tropical diseases, but also from a mysterious new ailment which had no name or cure, and which would later become known as AIDS. Life expectancy in this country was one of the lowest in the world, 38 years for men, 39 for women. The clinic was staffed by a doctor from Médecins Sans Frontières, and by the village midwife, a gigantic fat woman who was not seen to wash her hands too often. Some African nuns served as nurses. But there were few medicines and the doctor, whose name was Goddet, moved about in an old Land Rover. He was responsible for several other villages as well, and did not live in this one. In his absence the tribal witch doctor sometimes appeared in the clinic either to cast a spell or remove one.

The clinic held also the village's only telephone which, when it broke down, could be out of service for months.

Father Redmond's house was one room on stilts just back from the river. Access was via a ladder with twelve rungs. The roof was thatch. The walls were mostly open, and monkeys got in. When it rained there were no windows to close. The thatch overhung the roof on all sides, so that even during the November to April rainy season, unless there was a big wind blowing, he was dry enough. Mildew was another story, every surface slick, turning green.

He had a table, some chairs, a chest he had made himself to protect his food from the monkeys. He had a battery-powered radio. He had some bookshelves, also self-built, and was filling them with books his friends and parents sent him regularly from America. At night he slathered on insect repellent his mother sent him, and read by the light of kerosene lamps. During the rainy season, the climate was unkind to books, which thickened. Covers warped. He had built himself a long low table, had brought a mattress in from the capital, had hung a mosquito netting over it, and that was where he slept.

He was known to his parishioners as the White Father. Many of them thought he had magical powers. One of his jobs was to keep telling them he didn't.

The river was about a mile wide where it passed in front of his house. It had come nearly a thousand miles trying to reach the sea, and had another thousand to go. By day there was traffic out front. Produce moving across. Fishermen. Ancient workboats, old square launches, most of them rotting, barely afloat. The river upstream and down was full of crocodiles and hippos, but not so much here because of the boat traffic. But at night, if Frank had to use the latrine he had dug, he came down his ladder slowly, attentively, fully awake, shining his flashlight back and forth, looking for whatever creature might be down there. He was unwilling to serve as something's meal. Even by day he approached his ladder with care.

When he first came to the village he had painted his church inside and out. He had spruced it up as much as he could. He said mass every morning, often to empty pews. But Sundays people came, not many at first. He knew if he wanted better he would have to work for it. These people had their own religions, even those nominally Christian did, dark cults extending backward into the roots of whatever tribes they came from.

It was a country then of about eight million people, 60 or more different tribes, speaking at least that many dialects. Everybody spoke English, officially, supposedly. Most did speak it, more or less, for the British, though now gone, had been there a long time. On Sundays he would step in front of the altar and talk to them. His church sounded tinny to him. His voice sounded tinny. He spoke slowly and simply so they could more easily understand, but also vividly, mostly in stories, including parables from the New Testament in which he transposed the characters into Africans, and the Holy Land into this village on the Zambezi. Christ walked not on the Sea of Galilee, but on the river out front. The Good Samaritan became a man from a certain neighboring tribe they had been taught from childhood to distrust and despise; but only this man was decent enough to lend a hand to his neighbor in distress.

These were not sermons exactly. He never spoke of doctrine. He was trying to attract them not to Catholicism but to basic Christianity. He believed in the Catholic Church. He saw it as the greatest single force for good in the world. But a missionary's primary goal had changed, it seemed to him. It used to be the aggrandizement of the Church. That was secondary now, perhaps further back than that, and other missionaries he met had agreed with him. The primary purpose now was to spread — try to spread — the virtues Christ had taught: peace, justice, solidarity among peoples.

And so he did not proselytize. That wasn't what these people needed. At Catholic Fordham he had been taught to admire St. Francis Xavier, a 16th-century Jesuit who, so the story went, had once baptized 5,000 people in a single day. Frank had believed the story as a boy, though not since. Or, if something equivalent had actually happened it was not religion but mass hysteria. He would get into the subject of baptism later, he decided, and would baptize only parishioners who believed, and who wanted it.

Instead he talked to his increasing congregation about duty and responsibility. To support family members who depended on them represented one of their duties. Keeping their children in school was another, for only educated children could grow up to take their places in a world that was increasingly fast and complex. He talked to them of Christianity in general, of living a just life, of a God who wanted them to care for one another, to help one another. He talked against vengeance and jealousy as dominating emotions. He talked against drunkenness. He talked of a God who would not be taken in by prayers and devotions, but asked instead for positive actions that made life less onerous, a bit more pleasant for those around them. There was joy in helping others, he preached, try it and see.

He went often into the school, and when he noticed gaps in the curriculum, geography, for instance, he called the two teachers together and offered, with their permission, to help. This was accepted. He went to the capital and came back with another generator, and with a used slide projector and a used travel program — even in the capital very little could be bought that was new. Thereafter he showed the Himalayas to children who had never seen mountains, never seen snow. He showed images of America, of buildings that were unbelievably high, of traffic that was unbelievably dense. He taught them about their own river, and about rivers similar to theirs in other parts of the world. Where these rivers came from, where they went, how people used them.

Geography could be made to spill over into much else. He gave them a history of Africa. He taught them about America: where it came from and how it worked.

Before long most children wanted to attend only classes he gave, so that the two teachers became resentful, and asked him not to come to the school anymore. He looked into their faces. The eyes of frightened, vulnerable young men stared back at him. For more than a week he tried to change their minds. He coaxed, cajoled, but got nowhere, the resentment had spread into the village and finally, to preserve peace, he stepped aside. To do otherwise would have obviated, it seemed to him, all he had been trying to teach them in his sermons. His decision left the two teachers and many of the villagers pleased, the children disappointed, and Frank frustrated and unhappy. From then on he tried to think of a way to get back, an argument that might work, an appeal to someone, but who?

He went often to the clinic where, because of his Vietnam training, he could be useful. He could comfort patients, sure, and listen to their troubles and complaints, write letters they dictated. But he could give injections, too. He could set bones, sew up wounds, assist at operations. Gouts of blood did not frighten him, and in an emergency he could work quickly and without panic. Increasingly the overworked Dr. Goddet gave him jobs to do, gave him instruction in areas that were new to him, in time inviting him to help deliver babies. At this Father Redmond hesitated. He did not want to be intimate with women. But as soon as he watched his first birth he realized there was nothing sexual about it. When calves were born, impala, even zebras, the offspring slipped out and to the ground, and a minute later the female was on her feet grazing, more or less ignoring the newborn who stood suckling between her legs. He had seen this often enough. Why then was human birth a thing of such violence and trauma, almost an explosion? Why were women — in this village they were mostly girls — obliged to go through that? But to questions like this he found no answers.

In time Dr. Goddet permitted him to deliver a baby by himself. "Excellent," the doctor told him. "You are going to be good at this." Frank was elated to have done it, elated at the praise.

"Maybe the competition will make that midwife start washing her hands," the doctor said with a smile.

Or words to that effect. Goddet was Belgian. He spoke French, Flemish, and painfully little English. The two men could not really converse. But often on those days when he was in the village Dr. Goddet would make his way to Frank's ladder at sunset bearing with him ice from the clinic and a six-pack of beer, or a bottle of scotch, and they would sit looking out at the river and sip their drinks, and chat as well as they could, mostly in small phrases. Except for the company of children this was almost the only social life Frank had. The children flocked around him, but the adults treated him with such deference that it sometimes seemed impossible to get close to them.

He owned an old motorbike and an even older rowboat. There were conferences at the missionary order's field office in the capital to which he was regularly summoned. The motorbike took him there, more than two bumpy hours each way. His behind always ached by the time he got there, his hands and thighs too from squeezing hard to keep from being thrown off. The men who had sent him to Africa, the bureaucrats back in the developed world, wanted converts. At each of the conferences he was asked what was his body count. How many new Catholics could he claim? But his body count was not much and he thought it best if he avoided answering as much as he could.

Like Dr. Goddet he was responsible for outlying villages as well, the roads to which were equally rutted, though shorter. They seemed to loosen his teeth. He would say mass, and preach similar sermons. Sometimes he would perform marriages, or funerals. If he had medicines he would distribute them to those in need. His appearances always caused a stir. People brought him their problems, most of which he could not solve. But he could listen, and sometimes he could help.

He kept his rowboat pulled up on the mud under his house and tied to one of the stilts. He liked to fish. He had a rusty outboard, a fishing rod, and a net, all of which he carried back up the ladder each time. He liked to be on the great river, usually at sunset, the sky immense, the colors stunning. To be alone with himself. Alone trying to comprehend the immensity of Africa, the distance to eternity. Alone with concepts too big for any man. Perhaps he was looking for some sort of out-of-body experience out there. One sunset was almost monstrous in its beauty, the sky turning from pale washes to beet red to purple — a double sunset for the same colors were reflected in the water. It caused in him an emotion so intense that he fell to his knees on the floor of the boat, his arms outstretched, and thanked God for it. Afterward he thought this the most mystical experience of his life so far.

He caught tigerfish, bream, yellow bellies, for the river was alive. He caught enough for his dinner or, if he had been invited by one of his parishioners, enough for everyone's dinner. This done, he liked to motor upriver to where the hippos were bathing. He would shut the engine off and watch them awhile, even as he drifted back down. When the hippos were out of sight he listened to the silence. Sometimes, once he reached the level of the village, his motor would not restart, and he would have to throw the oars in the water and row in hard against the current.

When the spring rains fell on the tin roof of his church he made his sermons shorter, for he could barely make himself heard. He found himself wishing he had a better church, then chided himself thinking: You sound like priests everywhere, it isn't the building that counts, it's what goes on inside it, your church is good enough.

The day came when a 20-foot-long crocodile scurried up onto the bank where some children were playing, clamped its jaws on a six-year-old girl, and dragged her back into the river, the girl screaming all the way. When the water closed over her head her screaming stopped. A number of other children had witnessed this, and within minutes half the population of the village had gathered on the bank, the mother weeping.

Boats were mobilized, including Father Redmond's.

Not far away a sagging, half-decayed dock extended 30 or 40 feet out into the river. The children ran out onto this dock to watch, and it was they who cried out that the girl's body was under the dock.

The edge of her skirt, floating on the surface, could be perceived between the planks.

The boats congregated quickly. The spectators too ran out onto the dock which began to shiver from so much weight. The men in the boats reached out with oars and a gaff trying to dislodge the girl, but she would not come loose, for the crocodile, as is their way, had first drowned her, and then wedged her amid the pilings until such time as her flesh would become ripe and, for the crocodile, tasty.

Clearly someone would have to go in under the dock and get her out.

No one wanted to do it. Boats had begun to withdraw. On the dock and on the embankment men turned away. Some started back to their houses.

Those who remained watched Father Redmond.

He did not know what to do. Where was the crocodile? Not on the surface, obviously, for he studied the water all about, and it was smooth. It was unroiled also under the dock, as far as he could tell, for the current seemed to move smoothly around the pilings.

Could the crocodile be under there, watching over what had become its larder? Yes, of course it could. Was this likely? Probably not. There was no sign of it.

He looked into people's faces and saw what they wanted from him. Their headman was not present, probably lying passed out on the floor of his house. At least for the moment their headman had become by default Father Redmond. It was up to him to do what had to be done.

He had no desire to jump into the water with a crocodile, but did not see where he had much choice. If he did not do it he would lose all, or at least most, of what he had gained with these people. They probably did not even see the job as dangerous. Even if the crocodile should still be in the neighborhood, surely the life of the White Father would be protected by his God.

Frank took off his black shoes and socks, then stood up in his boat, which earlier he had tied to a piling. He stepped out of his black trousers, unbuttoned his short-sleeved black shirt. He made a small pile on the seat of his boat, his roman collar on top.

He stepped over the side. Taking a big breath he plunged beneath the dock. The pilings were barnacle encrusted in some places, slimy in others. He cut both his hands badly. He kept imagining the crocodile swimming in under him. The girl was wedged tight. He bumped against a piling and felt it cut open his thigh. Several times he was forced to come up for air.

Suddenly, one of the young men of the village plunged in beside him. "I help you, Father," he said.

Together they managed to free the girl's body. They dragged her out from under. The crocodile wasn't there, or at least did not attack. Frank swam the girl to shore. Lifting her in his arms he walked up the embankment and laid her in the arms of her weeping mother. The next day he conducted the funeral, which was accompanied by much wailing and keening.

Afterward, when he passed people in the streets he saw in their eyes how high his stature had risen, which was not why he had done what he had done. It seemed to him only a question of time before they began bringing him their disputes to settle. Not a good idea. But what to do about it? He longed to get away for a few days, give this emotion time to die down.

He had had a letter from Andy Troy, who had recently arrived in Johannesburg to take over the paper's South Africa bureau. Though on the same continent, they remained hundreds and hundreds of miles apart. Now a second letter came. Troy had been assigned to write a piece about Victoria Falls, which was very much closer. Could Frank meet him there? Money was not a problem, Troy wrote. If Frank served as guide the paper would pick up all expenses.

Frank arrived first and found a room reserved for him in the Victoria Falls Hotel, a two-story Edwardian structure dating from 1904. It was big, almost 150 rooms, and was surrounded by lush lawns studded with baobab trees. Black servants brought drinks to white tourists seated in wicker chairs on the veranda. The view from there was not of the falls but of the gorge into which the river took a header as if trying to commit suicide. The great split in the earth was filled almost to the top with whipped cream, while above the falls the spray rose up and was illuminated by rainbows a thousand feet high.

Two servants led Frank to his room, one to carry his small suitcase, one his key. They called him Bwana, and accepted their tips with deferential bows.

Hot water. Thick towels. The hotel seemed to Frank the most luxurious place on earth. He had forgotten such luxury even existed. The first thing he did was run a bath. He had not had a hot shower since coming to Africa, much less a hot bath. The tub was deep and he lolled in it, writhed in it, sighing again and again with pleasure.

But presently, like a periscope rising, a part of him broke the surface of the water. This surprised him. Well, he thought, I haven't seen you in a while.

What could have brought it on? he wondered. But he knew what to do. At times like this a priest should sublimate, they had been advised at the seminary, and so he sublimated, switching his concentration to sports, specifically to the race that had given him his first city championship, digging deep into the memory of it, and in a few moments the periscope had slid back into its conning tower and he was calm again. But he thought he should get out of the tub right away, and did so, drying himself off as roughly as he could, making his back and shoulders tingle.

Troy arrived two hours later, and checked into his own room, after which they sat on the terrace sipping gin and tonics, delighted to be together again, recounting all they had done, since the last time, already several years ago, that they had seen each other.

Troy had with him guidebooks and binoculars. "Bungee jumping," he said, "that's what the tourists do here. Highest one in the world, 366 feet." He focused his binoculars on the bridge that crossed the gorge. "There goes one of them," he said. "The thing is to brag to your children you jumped off Victoria Falls." Then he added: "Sorry, I forgot." But he recovered quickly: "Well, you can brag to my children."

To Frank at this distance the bridge was thin as a pencil sketch, and the jumpers — even through the binoculars he could barely see them — looked like specks at the end of threads.

"That's what we'll do tomorrow," said Andy decisively.

"Not me, Pal."

"Oh yes, can't leave without bungee jumping off the falls."

Frank laughed. "Without your glasses you can't even see your feet. What will you do with your glasses?"

"Tape them on."

Frank was laughing.

"Tonight we take a cruise on the river," Andy said. "Languid, dreamy. Watch the sunset."

"That doesn't sound like you," Frank joked. "You're more the adventurous type, from what you've been telling me. A bungee jumper and all that."

They did take the cruise. There was nothing dreamy about the "river launch" promised in the brochure. It turned out to be plastic chairs nailed to planks nailed to Styrofoam pontoons and powered by an outboard. Seeing it, Andy looked perplexed. The captain and sole crew member was an African in shorts and a dirty T-shirt.

"How safe is this ship?" Andy asked the captain. "Are you sure this ship is safe?"

This too made Frank laugh. "You're new to Africa, I see. You were expecting maybe the *Queen Mary*?"

As they stepped onboard the flooring wobbled, but righted itself. The captain pushed off, and after about twenty pulls his motor started up. As they moved slowly upriver the outboard exuded irregular noises and gouts of black smoke.

There was a rusty beer cooler with no top into which Andy peered. Water, a chunk of ice, some bottles lying on their sides. "Guy's got some beer anyway," he said, taking out two and handing one to Frank. "We won't drown thirsty."

As they sipped their beers they talked of Gabe Driscoll and Earl Finley. Troy had seen them both just before leaving America. Congressman Rienzi was in jail, Troy said, and the trouble their two friends had been in seemed over. Gabe had made lieutenant and now commanded his own detective squad in Harlem. Earl had been promoted to head the DA's Homicide Bureau.

Frank asked about Andy's wife, Maureen, and Gabe's wife, Barbara. Both were fine, Troy said.

"And Rocky," said Frank, "did you see her? How is she?"

"She looked very good," Troy said. "Not particularly happy, though. The marriage is not a good one, apparently."

"I'm sorry to hear that," Frank said.

"Neither is mine," said Andy.

After a moment Frank said: "I'm sorry to hear that, too."

Andy shrugged. "Well, we're not getting divorced or anything. Not yet anyway. She and the children are with me in Johannesburg. It's just that—"

Frank waited.

"—that when I went into marriage I hoped for better."

Behind them Victoria Falls still threw its immense mist into the sky, but soon they were far enough away that its enormous racket had faded out. That is, they could still see part of its effect on the world, they just could no longer hear it. The sun, meanwhile, seemed to have set fire to the entire countryside. The river at this hour was indeed languid. They saw a crocodile taking the sun on a rock, an elephant ripping branches off a tree near the bank, some hippos, only their snouts showing, turning toward them and giving their gaptoothed yawn. As the sun began to go down it seemed to diminish in size, turning at the end into a red-gold lollipop that the river licked at for a while, and then swallowed whole.

"That was nice," Frank said.

"Yes, it was," said Andy, sounding moved. But he was not one to stay somber long. "Turn this yacht around, Ahab," he said to the captain, "let's go home."

Soon they were approaching the dock: "Now we'll have a nice long drink on the veranda," Troy said, "and then go into the restaurant and have a lovely dinner. How's that?"

"A restaurant," said Frank. "A real restaurant. I can hardly believe it."

"And tomorrow we'll go bungee jumping."

The idea still made Frank laugh. "You mean you'll go bungee jumping."

In the morning, as they walked toward the bridge, they could see the jumpers. Every few minutes a new one leaped into the void. They came to the bridge and walked out onto it. A railroad bridge, narrow. In the center a platform had been welded outside the guardrail. About 20 people stood above it, watching. All were white. Hippie types, Frank judged. Backpackers. Late teens, early twenties. Much younger than himself and Troy. On the platform the jumpmaster was attaching the cord to the ankles of the next jumper.

"This is higher than I thought," said Andy, peering into the gorge, sounding much less sure of himself.

"Nonsense," said Frank, "you can't back out now."

"You better go first, tell me how it is."

The next jumper jumped. For a moment he hung in the air, legs and arms pumping like a man running the 100-yard dash. Then he fell. He fell screaming. Faster and faster. He fell unimaginably far. At the end the cord jerked him upside down and he began to bounce.

"Now you," said Frank.

"I can't take a chance on the paper losing me," Troy said. "If it were just myself, I'd do it."

"I thought you were going to write a piece about it."

"I'll write about you doing it."

In truth, the idea had begun to intrigue Frank. The previous jumper, who had been hauled up, stood there shaking, unable to speak.

"It costs $25 dollars," Frank said. "Can you put that on your expense account?"

"Of course. And don't forget the collateral benefit."

"Which one?"

"It will keep the hormones down. Guaranteed. All the blood will be in your head. There'll be none left over."

Frank laughed. "Pay the guy," he said.

He was weighed, his weight scrawled on his hand in red ink. His legs were wrapped in towels. He stepped over onto the platform, where the cord was attached to his ankles in what the jumpmaster called a dynamic knot. It could not come undone, he promised. The harder Frank fell, the tighter the knot would pull.

The safety harness was strapped on, and Frank hobbled to the platform's edge. "I want a big jump outward," the jumpmaster said.

Frank nodded.

"I'll count to three," the jumpmaster said, and started counting.

Actually Frank jumped on four, or five, Andy told him later. The wind screamed past his head. The river rushed up at him. When the cord stopped his fall he was jerked into the position of a man crucified, arms outstretched, upside down, like St. Peter martyred in Rome. He rocketed upward again, paused, dropped scores of feet a second time, then soared once more, a human yo-yo. The blood in his head gave him a colossal headache, and his body had begun to spin, which made him seasick and airsick both, and for a moment he wondered if he would vomit, and disgrace himself.

When he was hauled up to the platform, Troy said to him: "Aren't you glad you won't have to do that again?"

They both started laughing. Almost staggering with laughter they made their way off the bridge and back to the hotel.

Troy's principal beat was Apartheid, and the Afrikaans politicians who maintained it; also the imprisoned Nelson Mandela, and the atrocities committed by the South African police against the black nationalists. But he was also responsible for the rest of the southern half of the continent. This meant that he wrote also about the Bushmen, the Zulus, the diamond and gold mines, the dictators, the various civil wars. He went to places and informed himself and wrote articles that often made powerful reading.

He was expected to write about the animals as well. About herd management and poaching, and the new game reserves and national parks that were springing up everywhere. One of the new areas was the Liuwa Plains. It was so new no one had ever heard of it. There were not even any roads out there. Totally unspoiled. The world knew about Kenya and the Serengeti wildlife, but not this place. The Liuwa Plains would make a good piece, Troy decided. But he didn't want to trek all the way out there alone. His wife had no interest in animals, and his children were in school. He enlisted Father Redmond as company.

They had not seen each other in months. They met this time in the capital and flew west in a light plane Troy rented, landing near a lodge on the Luambimba River where they could rent a Land Rover and camping gear. They drove out onto the dry grassy plain, bumping over the ground, no people or settlements to be seen for miles, no human sign at all, the plain completely uninhabited, and they bounded along for mile after mile until they found a watercourse where they pitched their tent.

It was late October, meaning spring in that latitude. The rains began a week early that year, and they watched storms come into existence, the vast sky filling with piles and piles of clouds, dramatic formations in many colors, sky caps flying, the storms building and building until they seemed to explode into streaks of lightning wide as Broadway. The rains fell only an hour that first day. It was enough. Overnight the parched plain burst into a sea of wild flowers.

Behind the rains came the migrating herds in their tens of thousands, perhaps millions, the blue wildebeests, and the zebras, and many kinds of deer and antelope, and also the predators who followed them: lions, hyenas, and wild dogs. And above their heads wheeled the predator birds.

Each day the two men drove from their campsite out onto the plain looking for animals. Whichever man was driving clutched the wheel, while the passenger clutched the seat with one hand and the shotgun in his lap with the other. The shotgun was for protection, though the lions they saw ignored them and nothing else threatening was there; but also they shot meat to eat, an impala one day, a warthog another. They ate as much of both as they could.

They stayed a week, or until Andy decided he had enough for a long story for the paper's Sunday magazine, then returned to the lodge, turned in their gear and Land Rover, called in the airplane, and flew back to the capital. They had shared still another adventure, and the closeness between them was intense, though neither spoke of it. At the airport they shook hands. The journalist flew back to his family and bureau in Johannesburg. The priest went back to his village.

BEFORE SETTING OUT FOR AFRICA Frank had submitted to all the usual inoculations, and at the end of the first year had renewed them. He was safe from cholera, yellow fever, typhoid, and the rest. But from much else he was not safe. There was no inoculation against malaria. One day he felt headache, fatigue, nausea. This went into fever that lasted 24 hours, sudden chills, rapid breathing but no sweating. At last he did sweat, and the fever dropped. Every two or three days came another attack. This lasted months. He ignored the symptoms as much as he could, and went on with his work. Dr. Goddet told him he would never really be rid of it, that attacks might recur for the rest of his life. He gave him quinine, and finally the attacks petered out, and then, temporarily at least, stopped.

The next year he was bitten by a spider or a tick. It left an ulcer in his arm. Presently all his joints ached, and he began losing strength in his hands and arms. By the end of the second week he could barely lift a fork to his mouth. Dr. Goddet prescribed powerful antibiotics that were unavailable, even in the capital, and asked if he knew anyone elsewhere who could send them to him. Frank phoned Andy Troy. Having located the drug in Cape Town, Andy flew down there from Johannesburg, bought a two-month supply, and sent it to Frank air express, meaning that it reached him in only ten days. About two weeks after that the priest's strength began to return, though weeks more went by before he felt normal.

Two years later he became infested with bilharzia, parasitic worms or flukes. Some doctors called them microscopic snails. He contracted the parasite probably in the river. It entered his body through his skin, got into his bladder, then his intestines, then began to spread to other internal organs. Dr. Goddet, who had medication for this, said he had never seen a more ferocious case. Again Frank suffered lethargy, nausea. He had no appetite, had to force himself to eat. He lost more than 20 pounds, and even when the drugs had done their job, and every parasite in his system had presumably been killed, he had trouble gaining it back.

Dr. Goddet told him it was time for him to get out of Africa, that his resistance was permanently weakened.

"How many years do you have to put in here?" Dr. Goddet demanded, or so Frank understood.

To which he replied: "You're still here, aren't you?"

"I'm a doctor."

"And I'm a priest."

"Go home and recover your health before it is too late."

But Frank refused.

He came down with what at first seemed a mild case of jaundice. It wasn't jaundice but a virulent hepatitis. More weakness, vomiting, weight loss.

"It can ruin your liver," Dr. Goddet told him. "It can turn into cirrhosis. It can kill you."

When Frank refused to be hospitalized Dr. Goddet phoned Troy, who came at once.

"Andy," said Frank, "what are you doing here?" Frank was wringing his hand, delighted to see him.

"You're sick," Troy told him. "You're coming home with me."

"All right," said Frank. "For a week maybe. I'll be better by then."

At the Johannesburg airport, when Troy told him he was taking him to the hospital, Frank seemed too weak to resist. The sheets were clean and white, and most of the time he slept, but for some days got steadily weaker. Maureen Troy came to see him every afternoon. She was distressed by his yellowish pallor, amazed at how skinny he looked. He was still six feet three inches tall, but seemed to float above the bed as if he weighed nothing, and she held his hand and sometimes read to him.

When he was a bit stronger Troy came in and dropped an airline ticket on the bed.

"You're going back to America," he told him. "I've spoken to your father. He'll meet the plane. Your mother has promised to fatten you up. When you're better you can decide whether you want to come back or not."

Frank protested, but only feebly. "I'll pay you back for the ticket," he said.

On the day Andy and Maureen drove him to the airport he was still very weak. He embraced them both, then walked through customs without looking back. In the air he peered out the porthole, and watched an entire continent become small. He had been there nearly ten years, and he started to cry because he felt himself a failure. He hadn't been strong enough, or spiritual enough for the job he had set himself.

ABOUT TWO MONTHS WENT BY. He had gained most of his weight back by then, not all. He felt much stronger, and he telephoned the Chancery and made an appointment with Bishop Ahern.

He rode the subway downtown. At the Chancery he sat in an anteroom with his hands crossed, made to wait like a schoolboy summoned before the principal. All around him were offices housing the cardinal, the twelve auxiliary bishops, and countless monsignors, some of whom came and went through the room in which he sat. He was made to wait 30 minutes, then shown in.

For some minutes Bishop Ahern, who was writing in a ledger, did not acknowledge him.

Finally the holy man's eyes rose. "Yes?" he said.

Frank introduced himself.

"I know who you are."

"I've been out of touch for a while," Frank said.

"I'm aware of that."

Frank said: "I need a job."

"Hmm," said the bishop, and he leaned back and gazed at him. "I have just the place for you."

THE INVESTIGATION

7

THE CONFERENCE ROOM IS TOO SMALL FOR THE TABLE that some previous police commissioner, or some decorator working for the architect, ordered put there. The vast table seems to dominate not only the room but the 26 men (no women) seated around its rim. It crowds them against the walls.

This is on the 14th floor of police headquarters, adjacent to the police commissioner's office. Only two places are left, notes Chief Driscoll as he stands in the doorway, and the one at the head is for the PC, who has not yet made his appearance. The PC will enter through the communicating door from his office, the wall of which is two paces behind his empty chair.

Advancing toward the only seat left him, Chief Driscoll distributes nods and smiles in several directions. "Gentlemen," he says. And then, making small talk: "If we're all here it must be Monday morning again." He sits down.

Gabe is in civilian clothes. So are several other men who function as detectives. The rest are in uniform. Shoulders that glitter with stars, chests slashed by ribbons. The chief of department, the chief of patrol, the chief of personnel, the borough commanders, the chief of traffic, the division chiefs. A roomful of middle-aged guys with guns, Gabe Driscoll thinks, glancing around him.

They wait. Until the PC comes in the conference cannot start. The men make idle chatter, or drum fingers on the table.

Gabe finds himself seated beside Spinelli, the chief of detectives, who like himself wears a dark business suit.

Spinelli begins brusquely: "Are you investigating some of my men?"

"Specifically?"

"The Three-Two Squad."

There are yellow pads and pencils in front of each place. Driscoll begins to doodle on his pad. "Well," he says, "I'd have to ask my staff. Maybe someone has something going, but I don't think so."

"Not your staff. You personally."

"Me personally? No."

There are five bureau chiefs, Gabe, Spinelli, and three others; they hold the second-highest rank in the department. The chief of detectives is often thought of as first among equals, for it is he who directs the celebrated cases, and sometimes sees his name in headlines. But he operates in the open, and no one is afraid of him except criminals. Whereas Gabe operates only inside the department, and usually in secret. No one knows what he is doing until cops are arrested or his report filed. And so he is feared. Cops in the street, those guilty of questionable acts, do not fear ordinary detectives, but when detectives from Internal Affairs come snooping around they become terrified, as do their commanding officers, who could lose their posts if significant corruption is found. These same commanders fear also the second of Gabe's major units, the Inspections Division. If he sends men in to monitor the methods and efficiency of a commander's office, that commander is possibly in trouble.

"They say you've been up there," Spinelli persists.

Gabe is aware of all this fear. To his mind, fear carries more weight than fame, meaning that effectively he outranks Spinelli. And so he is surprised to be questioned in this way.

"They say you've been up there looking over their shoulders."

Spinelli's intensity bothers Gabe, and he attempts to deflect it with a laugh. "Naw. I was just pointing them in directions maybe they had overlooked."

"It sounds like more than that to me."

"I was just helping them out a little."

A lieutenant in uniform, one of the PC's clerks, sticks his head in the door, sees that all the chairs are taken, and ducks out again. This means that the PC will enter momentarily, and the meeting will start.

"They don't need your help," Spinelli persists.

Gabe hopes the PC will come in quickly. "Everybody can use help once in a while," he says. "Even you." The meeting cannot start soon enough to suit Gabe.

"They can't do their work."

"Sometimes some work is more important than other work."

"Why don't you let me decide that for my men."

"A priest up there went off a rooftop."

"A friend of yours, it seems."

"Maybe he was murdered."

"My men say it's suicide."

"Maybe it is. A lot of people up there knew him, cared about him. They want to know what happened. I think a thorough investigation is in order, don't you?"

Spinelli's voice has risen. The men to either side are listening carefully, perhaps the whole table, which Gabe does not like at all. One's place in the police hierarchy is fragile, his own and everyone else's. Not one of these men, in Gabe's opinion, gives a hoot about crime, or about the men under their command either. All they care about is protecting their turf, advancing their own careers, assuring their next promotion. Let a rival show any real or perceived weakness, and they will pounce on it and him in an instant.

One has to be careful not to show weakness. Not any, not ever.

Gabe has definitely encroached on Spinelli's turf, and his job now is to make it clear that he means to continue to do so. "Look, Joe," he says, "as chief of Inspectional Services, my job in this department is to make sure that all the little pieces fit together. From time to time I have to inspect the Three-Two Squad just like every other squad. Do they have too many men up there? Not enough? Are they getting proper direction from headquarters? Direction from your office, that is."

The thinly veiled threat. It is enough to cut Spinelli's ardor way down.

Spinelli should never have made an issue of this thing. But he had. Now Chief Driscoll has to end it without making an enemy. You never know who might one day get promoted over you. There is a saying in the NYPD, other places as well most likely: The toe you step on today might be attached to the ass you have to kiss tomorrow.

"Joe, let me ask you a personal favor. Let me have my way on this, and I'll owe you one. How about it?"

The door at the end of the room opens, and the PC enters. Everyone stands up.

The PC is a small man wearing a double-breasted blue suit and, at his throat, a red tie with a big knot in it. A former judge, never a cop, he approaches his chair while looking straight at Gabe and Spinelli. Perhaps he has been listening from behind the door.

He says: "Something I should know about?"

Gabe says: "We're arguing about a case we're both interested in, Commissioner. But I think we have it settled now."

"Right, Commissioner," says Spinelli. "Settled."

"Good," the PC says. He sits down. They all sit down. "So maybe now we can begin the meeting." He has with him a legal pad on which he has written out his agenda. After consulting it for a moment, he addresses himself to Wotcic, the chief of traffic. "You had some plans about Midtown congestion, Sid. Where are we on that?"

This opening topic does not concern Chief Driscoll, who, for the moment, shuts off his ears, shuts down his mind, even as he gives an interior sigh of relief. Spinelli will make no further issue of this thing. The investigation into the death of Frank Redmond will continue a while longer.

CHAPTER SEVEN

—————

FOLLOWING FRANK'S RETURN FROM AFRICA he and Gabe saw a good
deal of each other, and this went on for several years, for their places
of business, St. Ambrose Church where Frank was curate, and the
Three-Two stationhouse where Lt. Driscoll commanded the detective squad, were not far apart.

Frank Redmond, even as he moved into his mid-forties, was still
boyish looking, it seemed to Lt. Driscoll—boyish in some of his ideas
too. The detective, who was concentrated on running his squad, and
on pushing his career forward, who had a family to think about, and
who was studying for the captain's exam on the side, no longer had
time to go to the gym or work out regularly, but the priest did, obviously. Gabe had put on weight. Frank had not. He appeared no less
muscled and fit than in college. He looked, in fact, years younger than
his age. In Gabe's experience this was true of many priests. They wore
the faces of men who had never had to wake up to screaming kids, or
sick wives, never had to scrap for a living. They had soft mouths and
unlined foreheads—few age lines of any kind. Frank's life had not
been easy up to that point, Gabe Driscoll well knew. Nonetheless he
still had that kind of face, what Gabe thought of as a priest's face.

It was May, midafternoon. Lt. Driscoll looked up and Father Redmond was standing in front of his desk. In his clerical suit and roman
collar he had walked past the cop on security duty at the door, who

did not try to stop him, and into the building. There were still a few places in New York where a man in a roman collar could walk right in, no questions asked, and among them were police stations.

Though overwhelmed with work that particular day, Gabe was glad to see him.

Frank got right to the point. A guy was selling guns from the stoop of a tenement not two blocks from his church. He wanted Gabe to arrest him immediately, tonight if possible.

Like Lt. Begos some years later, Lt. Driscoll had 20 or more open murder cases on his hands—the murder total for the entire city approached 2,000 murders a year that year. In addition, for the past weeks the precinct had been plagued with stickups. Liquor stores, bodegas, fast-food joints. Owners and clerks stepping back against the wall, terrified, hands in the air, while some thug rifled their cash register. Even women were victimized, all of them poor, some of them old as well. They described guns thrust in their faces on the street, their purses taken, their welfare money gone. They were in tears. Different perpetrators, apparently, for the descriptions varied.

At first Gabe had half his squad on the murders, the other half on the stickups. He kept taking detectives off the murders and putting them on the stickups, but they were getting nowhere, he himself was out of ideas, and he kept calling meetings hoping one of the men would come up with something that would work. Two days in a row the Chief of Detectives had phoned him. Do something. Show results. Catch those guys. A Harlem politician had leaned on the chief, and he in turn leaned on Lt. Driscoll. The pressure had got to Gabe days ago, so now, even though Frank was his oldest friend, he brushed him off. Told him he couldn't arrest the gun dealer just on his say-so, it wasn't done that way.

Frank didn't see why he couldn't.

The law required hard evidence, Gabe told him. There would have to be observations, undercover buys. Several of each, or the arrest wouldn't stick. It would take men, it would take time, and he didn't have either.

Other citizens had stood before his desk, just as Frank did. They too demanded instant action. In most cases, when they had heard him out, that was the end of it.

But not this priest. For a minute or two, Frank argued calmly. Mentioned the recent stickups, which were the talk of the parish, of the precinct. Where did Gabe think the guns were coming from?

"Most of the stickup men are kids, Gabe. The guy is selling guns to kids."

When his arguments didn't work, Frank got angry, and screamed at Gabe. Above the roman collar his face got red. Didn't Gabe care?

Of course he cared, Gabe told him, he just couldn't do anything about it right now. Maybe next month, if the crime rate ever calmed down around here.

Cops passing by on the stairs had begun looking into the squad-room, wondering who was shouting at whom.

Everyone in the precinct knew the gun dealer was out there, Frank raged. They thought they knew why no action was taken. The cops were being paid off, that's why.

"That's horseshit," said Gabe.

"But it's what they think. The honky cops don't protect black people because they're taking money instead."

Lt. Driscoll drummed his fingers on the desk, and took the abuse his friend dished out.

"Don't you realize how you cops look in the community? Don't you care about that either?"

Gabe's mind was on the pile of work he had to get through today. He wondered how he could move this priest out of his office.

Finally he suggested they go out and get a cup of coffee together. Quick cup of coffee and leave him there and come back. The trouble was, to find a coffee shop where you wouldn't get poisoned you had to go two precincts downtown, and Gabe didn't have time for that either. But it was a way to get rid of him.

Still in a rage, Frank refused. If Gabe wouldn't help him, he'd take care of the problem himself, he said, and he stormed out.

Take care of it himself? What did that mean?

Gabe soon learned, for now Frank came up with a scheme.

The scheme was simple, direct, and very, very dangerous.

What the priest did was to call in several of his older altar boys, average age about 15. He had taught them to serve mass, and in addition was teaching them to read and write, which the local public school, at this point, had failed to do. He held classes for them every afternoon in the church. He was trying to teach them to speak properly as well.

They adored him, would do anything for him.

He asked if they wanted to help him take the gun dealer off the street. "Yeah, Father," they said enthusiastically. Young teeth flashed with pleasure. They were kids, they didn't see any danger, and later on Gabe would wonder if Frank did either.

"You boys are going to be actors," Frank told them. He had invited them into the sacristy where the vestments for tomorrow's masses were laid out on a table. The chasuble lay in two dimensions. It was blood red because tomorrow was the feast of a martyr, St. Philip the Apostle — all the apostles had been martyred but one. The sacristy was both quiet and private. With money he would give them they were going to buy guns off that dealer, Frank told them. The priest himself would be on the roof across the street with a camera photographing every transaction. They would bring him the guns, which would serve as evidence, and the guy then could be arrested, and would go to jail.

"Can we keep them guns, Father?" the boys wanted to know.

"No, you can't."

"My brother had a piece, Father," one boy said. "You ain't a man around here, you don't have a piece."

"And where's your brother now?" asked the priest.

"He in jail, Father."

"Do you want to go to jail?"

"Everybody in Harlem go to jail, sooner or later."

This comment made Frank wince—it had made Gabe Driscoll wince often enough—because it was mostly true, one of the sad facts of ghetto life. Sooner or later most Harlem males got arrested for buying or selling or holding drugs, or for illegal guns, or just for standing nearby while someone else robbed a store. Jail, for ghetto youths, had become a rite of passage. Even for altar boys, like these 15-year-old babies now hanging on his every word.

It was part of the reason the gun dealer would see them as customers, not as children, and would sell them the guns.

"I don't need no gun," said the boy whose brother was in jail. "I got this," and he waved a sap in the air.

"Let me see that."

Frank studied it. Segments of lead wrapped in braided leather.

"Where'd you get this?"

"My bro, he keep it under the mattress, Father. When he go away, I take it. Now I got protection."

"You get caught with this thing, you'll go to jail too."

Frank put it in his pocket.

"You give it back, Father Frank."

"You want to be my friend? You want to be one of the boys in the plan to buy guns?"

Frank took out the sap. "My friends don't need weapons like this. You want it, you can have it, but then you can't be my friend, you can't be an altar boy anymore, and we'll get somebody else to help put that gun dealer in jail."

The boy stared at the sap in Frank's hand, but finally his head dropped and he nodded.

Now Frank began to rehearse them for the drama that was to come. "Okay, I'm the gun salesman. What do you say to me?"

The boys grinned. Five faces lit by brilliant white teeth. He rehearsed them for an hour that night, and another hour the next.

There were no secrets in Harlem, where most social life took place on the stoops and sidewalks, so he cautioned them each night as he sent them home. Not a word to anyone.

In between rehearsals Frank telephoned the district attorney's office and asked to be put through to Earl Finley, for he wanted to be sure that the buys he was planning would support a solid arrest, that the gun dealer would go to jail and stay there. He might have asked Gabe Driscoll, but was furious with him. In any case he had known Earl just as long, he was just as close a friend.

"Earl, I need to talk to you as soon as possible."

"Tonight," said the prosecutor decisively. "Come to dinner, and afterward we can talk."

For Frank, dinner at Earl's house constituted a problem.

"Rocky will be glad to see you," Earl said.

Rocky, to Frank, was the problem. He had not seen her in several years—or Earl either—and had avoided invitations to their house.

"I'll call her and tell her you're coming."

Lunch in a restaurant would have been better. Nonetheless, he agreed, telling himself as he did so that seeing Rocky again was nothing special.

Earl and Rocky lived in Yonkers, a mostly working-class suburb to the north, in a wooden Victorian house that was big but much in need of repair. Most of all it needed a coat of paint, Frank thought as he saw it again, parking his secondhand Ford out front. Well, Earl did not get paid very much. Compared to the rest of the rarefied world of lawyers, New York's assistant DAs were poorly paid, even supervisors like Earl. But because he loved trial work, loved putting bad guys in jail, loved, as he put it, being on the side of the angels, Earl had long ago come to terms with the low pay. At times he had talked about running for district attorney himself, if the incumbent ever died or stepped down. So that was his future — maybe.

Fine, Frank thought, as Rocky opened the door to him. But what about her? She wore blue jeans and a loose red blouse under an open cardigan. It pleased him to see her there, to look at her. He still thought her beautiful, but she did not look prosperous, or particularly happy either. She gave him a big smile, took both his hands, and kissed him — a very brief kiss on the cheek, but enough to stir him more than he was ready for. As he took his hands back he tried to get his focus on her, not himself. He tried to think of what her life must be like. How did she like living in this beat-up old house? As a girl, as a rich man's daughter, she had been used to much more.

"It's good to see you again, Frank," she said.

He was surprised at the strength of his reaction to her after so many years.

"Let me look at you," she said, taking half a step back. "You haven't changed. You're still the best-looking man I know."

This caused a momentary silence between them.

"You haven't put on weight, haven't gained an ounce."

"Neither have you," he said, for she was still as slim as when he first knew her. He had been careful to speak in a flat tone of voice, for he did not want her to see how she affected him. She was now a mature woman, not the girl he had known, and she seemed to exude a certain sexuality, even just standing there looking at him.

"Earl's not home yet, he phoned to say he'd be a bit late."

Frank had been afraid of this. He would rather not be alone with her.

Her children came downstairs, Earl Jr., who was about 15, and his sister three years older. Frank shook hands with them. "You're big kids now, aren't you. Last time I saw you, you were only this high."

Rocky led him into the living room and offered him a drink. "Is scotch okay?"

"Fine," he said. He liked scotch well enough, though he rarely drank. As he watched her fix the drink he wondered about her marriage to Earl. The former diving champion was not an introspective man, Frank knew, and he worked long hours. Was Rocky happy? He could imagine her trying to talk to her husband about happiness, but could not imagine a satisfactory response from Earl. Did they ever discuss their marriage at all? Was he looking at a dissatisfied wife?

He did not expect these questions to be answered tonight.

He had come to dinner here several times in the months immediately after his return from Africa, not since. What Rocky had liked to do was tease him, apparently, and if they happened to be alone, as they were at this moment, there were likely to be sexual overtones to the teasing so that sometimes at the end of the evening when he went back to the rectory he was tormented by thoughts of her, and could not sleep.

Once he had spoken to her sharply.

Earl had been late getting home that night too. When the teasing started Frank had got exasperated. "I mustn't come here anymore," he told her.

"Why not?"

"Do you have to ask me why not?"

"Say what you mean."

"Because you disturb me, that's why."

A big grin came on. "Why, Frank, that's the nicest thing you've ever said to me."

"And you do it on purpose," he said, still exasperated.

Her grin faded. "Do I?"

Immediately he regretted having spoken to her in this way. But the words were out, he could not call them back.

After that he had begun rejecting invitations like tonight's altogether.

Tonight, as he took the drink from her hand, what he regretted was not seeing her all this time. They sat down on a rather threadbare sofa, Rocky sitting a bit too close, he thought, but he couldn't move away because of the armrest. In any case, he liked having her there.

Though she wasn't wearing any perfume he could detect, he breathed in the scent of her.

"So did you miss me?" she asked. "Tell me you missed me."

"Of course I missed you," he said, adding: "I missed Earl too."

"Then why haven't you been around?"

"Well, one thing and another."

Her children had disappeared elsewhere in the house.

She said with a grin: "It isn't as if I intended to seduce you."

"No, of course not."

"Your virtue is safe with me."

He smiled, pretending this subject between them was a joke which, on both their parts, he thought it was not.

"So how are you getting on?"

"Fine."

"Does it get harder or easier?"

He knew what she meant, what she was asking. He sipped his drink. Finally he said: "What we did with each other shouldn't have happened."

"Going to bed together?"

"Yes."

"Making love?"

He looked away. I sound like a prig, he told himself. I don't want her to think me a prig.

"You can say it. Was it such an awful thing?"

He was silent.

"You do remember, don't you?"

He decided to make a joke of it. "If I try hard, I can remember."

"You like to think of me."

Again he did not answer.

"You do, don't you?   Admit it. You think of me all the time, don't you?"

He smiled. "Well, sometimes."

She made a movement forward as if she meant to kiss him, which caused another sudden unwelcome reaction inside him. Instead her eyes dropped, her smile faded, and she got up and went into the kitchen, where he heard her banging pots around.

After some minutes—he thought of it as a sufficient cooling off period—he took his drink into the kitchen and watched her work. It was a big, old-fashioned kitchen with counters on both sides, linoleum on the floor, and room for a breakfast table, against which he leaned his rump. At first he did not speak, and she ignored him altogether.

Then: "How's Earl?"

"Fine."

"How are his knees?"

"He may need an operation."

"I'm sorry to hear that." As boys it had never occurred to any of them that Earl's severely bowed legs would one day cause trouble.

"It's not sure yet. There's pain, but he puts up with it." Then she added: "He puts up with a lot of things. We have his mother on our hands now, for instance."

"Oh?"

"Her latest husband died and left her nothing. She's taken a small apartment that we're paying for." She carried a pot to the stove and turned the gas on under it. "I keep asking him to join a law firm that will pay him some money, but he won't."

Earl became more than an hour late, but did not call.

He was at that moment at a meeting at Democratic Party head-quarters on West 57th Street to which he had been summoned. He sat in an office with the four men who ran the party in New York, being quizzed about his availability in November if the incumbent district attorney, who was 70 and in poor health, should decide not to run for reelection. Earl had been waiting for this summons for a long time. He was unwilling to hurry these men now.

He could be available, he told them. Conditional tense. Of course he wanted to be selected to run for District Attorney, but this was the way politicians spoke. He could be available if—

He would have to move from Yonkers back inside the city limits, they told him.

He said perhaps this could be arranged, he wasn't sure. It all de-pended.

But in his head he was already selling the big old house in Yonkers that he hated. Would Rocky object, he asked himself. He didn't know and the question was beside the point. If he got elected they would move.

The other men began to talk about him as if he wasn't there. On the plus side he was the right age, middle forties, had the right experience, namely 20 years as a prosecutor. And he had handled some big cases. Remember when he put that Mafia capo in jail? What was his name, Amoroso. Mafia cases were notoriously diffi-cult, no other prosecutor had been successful in years. Yes, he had had some good publicity at the time. His name was better known than most of the other possible candidates. The incumbent liked him, and if they decided to run Earl as his successor, would prob-ably endorse him.

On the minus side was that business with former Congressman Rienzi, now in jail. Earl had prosecuted a Democrat who almost certainly would have been elected mayor. As a result the party had lost not only the mayoral race, but also Rienzi's "safe" seat in Congress when the candidate the party had chosen to replace him also lost.

"Rienzi was a thief and extortionist," Earl interrupted. "He had no business being a congressman, much less being mayor of New York. I did the city a service."

But the party had lost the mayoralty, they said, ignoring this outburst, and a sure congressional seat as well, Earl's doing.

"And when Rienzi gets out I'll prosecute him again," Earl added.

"On what?" one of the men said.

"Give him a couple of years back on the street, and he'll be into something, don't worry."

The men ignored this outburst too.

Finally they thanked him for coming in, and he left.

WHEN HE CAME INTO HIS HOUSE LATER, he whacked Frank with great affection on the shoulder while at the same time pumping his hand. His hair was still blond, Frank saw, but it had receded a good deal. Not as much as Gabe's, though.

Earl apologized for being late, more to Frank than to his wife, and explained what had held him up.

"Do you think you'll get the nomination?" Frank asked. Rocky had already gone back to the kitchen.

"Not this time," Earl said. "I think the boss will decide to run again. Next time, maybe. They're thinking about me. That's the important thing."

They sat down to dinner shortly after that, three adults and two children in an oak-paneled dining room that had once been handsome, until some previous owner had covered it over with white paint. Certain panels showed evidence of Earl and/or Rocky trying and failing to scrape off the paint.

Rocky served lamb cutlets, fresh string beans, and baked potatoes, followed by a green salad, and then an apple tart she had made earlier, simple enough fare, but very good, and a treat for Frank considering the rectory meals he was used to. Earl opened a bottle of California cabernet. There was never wine in the rectory in Harlem. He was not allowed to bring any in. The pastor had expressly forbidden it.

During dinner Earl talked to Frank with great animation, occasionally about the old days, mostly about cases he was working on, never about anything personal. When Frank asked about his knees, about his mother, he managed each time to change the subject.

From her end of the table near the door to the kitchen, Rocky contributed nothing. She moved the food around on her plate, but didn't eat much. Mostly she studied the tablecloth in silence. Her mood, Frank decided, could only be called surly, and he wondered if it was Earl she was unhappy with, or himself.

If Earl noticed anything, he did not remark on it.

The two children refused the salad, wolfed down the pie, and then asked to be excused, which their mother permitted. She excused herself a few moments later, and they heard her in the kitchen cleaning up.

Earl opened another bottle of wine, and filled the two glasses. "So what's on your mind, Frank?"

"Hypothetical case," Frank began. "Guy selling guns to kids from a stoop in Harlem. Fellow I know wants to send in some kids to buy some of those guns as evidence while he takes pictures from a rooftop across the street. He delivers the guns to the cops, and the cops arrest the dealer. Does that sound legal to you?"

Earl's mouth got tight. "Who are the kids involved, Frank?"

"Some altar boys, maybe."

"And who's the man on the roof across the street?"

"I thought maybe I'd handle that part of it myself."

"Are you crazy?" Earl had got very angry very quickly. "Possession of an unregistered gun is a class D felony. Once those altar boys of yours have the guns in their possession they are guilty of crimes. You also would be guilty of crimes. If some cop catches them or you with those guns you'll be facing three to five in the can."

But Frank only laughed at him. "The guns will be sealed in envelopes."

"Doesn't matter."

"I don't think anybody would prosecute me, or the kids, do you?"

"Don't count on it."

"I don't think a grand jury would indict, do you? Or that twelve good men and true would convict."

"You'll be risking the kids' lives as well. If the guy suspects anything he might shoot them."

"Oh, I don't think so. I've considered the risk factor. What's going to make him suspicious? They aren't old enough to be undercover cops. They're from the neighborhood like him. They have money. The guy will see them as customers and that's all he'll see."

"No, Frank, you can't do it. Absolutely not."

"The guy's a merchant, Earl. Merchants, last I heard, have to be nice to customers. They can't afford to rub them out."

"Even if it works, the risk isn't over, you idiot. There will be hearings, motions. It will go on for months. All that time the guy will be out on bail. The kids' names, your name, your addresses, will be in the court papers. He'll know where to find you. Those kids won't be customers anymore, they'll be witnesses. If something should happen to them before trial, the case goes out the window. Or if something should happen to you. If you get my meaning."

"I'm sure you're exaggerating."

"Maybe you think that cassock you wear is bulletproof."

But the priest only laughed. "We'll worry about all that later."

"If you have any brains you'll worry about it now."

"Suppose," Frank said, "just suppose it all works out as planned. What I want to know is, would you have a solid case against the gun dealer? Evidence to put him in jail for a long time?"

"An ironclad case, you mean? Maybe."

"I take that to mean yes."

"It's conceivable."

When Frank left a short time later, Earl walked him to the door where he said earnestly: "I beg you not to do anything stupid. Frank, Frank, promise me you'll reconsider."

"It was only an idea," Frank said.

"You'll think it over."

"Probably not a very good idea either, as you say."

Earl breathed what sounded like a sigh of relief.

The door opened. Frank looked out at the night and was more determined than ever to go through with his plan.

"I don't want you to worry about me," he said to Earl. "I'm not crazy, you know."

"Sometimes I'm not so sure."

Frank looked around for Rocky, who just then came out of the kitchen. As she walked toward him her eyes never left his, which made him forget Earl, forget his plan.

She said: "Good night, Frank. I hope I—we—won't have to wait so long to see you again."

This time she embraced him, kissed him on the lips.

The door closed behind him.

For Frank's altar boys there was one final rehearsal, but it was a long one. "You guys are the best young actors in the parish, in the city," he encouraged them. "You can't miss. But just to be sure, let's run through it again."

And again.

He kept them until satisfied that they knew their roles perfectly, could play them exactly as he wanted them to.

He mentioned Sidney Poitier, Bill Cosby, and other black actors they would be familiar with. "You're going to put them in the shade," he told the boys.

He gave them each a roll of marked bills.

They should haggle first, he told them, give the gun salesman time to reveal secrets any intelligent lawbreaker would know enough to keep to himself.

"He's proud of what he's doing," Frank said. "He'll talk to you. Ask him his name and address. Tell him you need to know how to reach him to buy more guns. Ask him where he gets his guns. If he's proud enough he'll tell you."

Frank's father, the Bronx beer salesman, had recently died, leaving him a few hundred dollars. This was the money that would pay for the guns, and also for an expensive camera and film that could take pictures almost in the dark.

The next night Frank went up onto the roof across the street from the stoop that served as the gun salesman's store, and by the light of the nearby street lamp he watched his altar boys—two in the first batch, and three others 15 minutes later—negotiate for guns.

He photographed both transactions. He was wearing his priestly black shoes and trousers, and an open-necked sports shirt. He was kneeling on the roof, his head barely above the parapet, his chin on the tile, the long lens balanced on it so he could shoot at low speed without the camera wobbling.

The first two boys had joined him on the roof by the time the second group approached the dealer. Frank had with him five manila envelopes. The first two guns, with Frank's initials scratched into them, went into two of the envelopes, which were then dated, sealed, and signed by himself and by the boys who had made the purchases.

A bit later there were five guns sealed into five envelopes. Looking over the parapet Frank saw that the salesman was gone.

"He say he come back tomorrow, Father," one of the boys said.

"His name be Malcolm Poindexter," another boy said. "He live over on Lenox and 136th, he say."

Father Redmond was slapping them on the back, shaking their hands. He was laughing happily. So were the boys.

The priest carried his five envelopes directly to the stationhouse where he dropped them on Lt. Driscoll's desk. "Guns," he announced. "And this is the film I shot on it. I think you're supposed to sign for this stuff, so as to maintain the chain of evidence." But as he explained what the boys had done, what he had done, a broad smile came on and he was almost chortling. "All you have to do now is go by tomorrow night and arrest him."

To Gabe Driscoll, Frank looked drunk with pleasure.

"You know something, Gabe," the priest told him, "I love playing cop."

The furious Driscoll began the same lecture Frank had already heard from Earl. The trial would not take place for months, the guy would be out on bail, Frank's name, the boys' names, and all their addresses would appear in the court papers, and their lives would be in danger. "You've put yourself and those kids at terrible risk."

"Yes," said Frank. "I realize that. I don't care about myself. I am worried for the kids, though."

"And I won't be able to protect any of you."

Frank nodded. "Maybe I can think of something."

In fact he had already thought of something.

"But you will make the arrests," Frank said. "You will, Gabe, won't you?"

"Yes, I'll make the arrests."

Gabe called in several detectives, including Cliff Spadia, and briefed them. Frank was allowed to listen. They would wait until ten thirty the following night, by which time the street should be free, or relatively free, of bystanders who might get caught in the crossfire, if there should be crossfire. Uniformed cops in radio cars would close off the street from either end, and the detectives would go in and make the arrest.

The following morning Frank said mass, served by two of what were now his favorite altar boys. The congregation was sparse, but he was scarcely aware of it. The two boys in their red cassocks had to be got out of the case, he realized, the other three boys as well, and although he thought he saw a way, he was not sure he could bring it off. The morning passed slowly, the afternoon even slower. He drank too much coffee which only made him more nervous.

He was on his rooftop more than an hour before the arrests were to be made. About nine thirty he keyed the hand radio Gabe Driscoll had loaned him, and reported that the dealer was on the stoop waiting for business.

Time passed, no buyers came by, and the dealer had begun tapping his feet and looking in all directions. In the manner of predators the world over, he seemed to sense that something was wrong. Each night so far he had arrived carrying his merchandise in a satchel, and then had stashed the satchel behind him in the well of the staircase leading to a basement apartment. He had done so this night also, but now he went down the steps and got it. After looking carefully around, he started off down the sidewalk.

Frank keyed the radio again. "Come quick, come quick, he's leaving."

There was time to hear Gabe Driscoll say: "Jesus," before Frank cut him off and started running.

He raced down from the roof. The dealer had almost reached the corner when Frank, this time wearing his clerical suit and roman collar, caught up with him.

"What's in that bag?" Frank demanded.

The dealer looked briefly puzzled. Then his expression changed and he merely looked dangerous. A revolver appeared in his hand so fast Frank never saw where it had come from, and he rammed it into Frank and said: "Priest, you gonna walk me to the subway, see I gets home safely." And he turned him around and started for the corner.

At this point, whenever he told the story later, Gabe Driscoll would interrupt his narrative with an aside. "This was exactly what Frank had planned. It was his way of getting the altar boys out of the case. He never intended to wait for the police to arrive. He intended to make the arrest himself.

"Now, you have to understand that Frank was a very athletic guy. He had expected the gun in his back, wished for it, and his reaction was virtually instantaneous, far faster than the dealer was ready for. In the coat pocket of that clerical suit he carried a leather-braided lead sap. Afterward, when I asked him where he got it he wouldn't tell me. Gave me this irritating smirk. He liked seeming mysterious. In many ways he was still a teenager. At heart that's what he was. Didn't believe anything could go wrong."

Whipping the sap out of his pocket the priest swung it into the dealer's face with the force of a backhand tennis shot, breaking the jaw in two places. The dealer went down, half stunned and in too much pain to cause further trouble to anyone. But the gun was still in his hand on the sidewalk, and Frank stomped on it, breaking nearly all the dealer's fingers.

And that's the way Gabe Driscoll found them when he and some detectives came running up about five minutes later, the gun dealer writhing and bleating on the sidewalk, Frank still standing on the gun and hand.

"I think his jaw's broken," Frank said. "His hand too. Sounded like it."

Lt. Driscoll on his knees was prying the gun out of the smashed fingers, which made the man scream.

Frank was breathing hard. He knew exactly how close he had come to getting a bullet in the back. "You've got a great job, Gabe," he said. "And to think you get paid for it." But this was only bravado. After the fact he was almost trembling. "You really can hear bones break, Gabe. It sounds — it sounds awful."

An ambulance came. The dazed perpetrator was pushed up the step and inside, Cliff Spadia and another detective jumping in behind him. At Harlem Hospital his jaw was wired together, his gun hand encased in plaster, and he was knocked out with morphine. Cliff and his partner guarded him there until much later when two uniformed men showed up to relieve them.

Gabe had brought Frank back to the squadroom, had sat him down, had brought coffee in a Styrofoam cup to which he added a dose of bourbon out of a bottle he kept, in defiance of regulations, in his desk drawer.

Thirty minutes had passed by then, but Frank was still shaken. "I don't think we have anything to fear from that guy, Gabe, do you? Not for a while, do you, Gabe?"

"Drink that," said Gabe.

As Frank drank from the cup, Gabe noted that his hand trembled.

"The altar boys are out of the case, right, Gabe? Their names don't need to come into it. I can be the only witness. We got the guy with a satchel full of illegal guns, and an illegal gun in his hand. The other charges can be that he attempted to kidnap me, attempted to murder me, right, Gabe? We don't need the kids anymore, Gabe, do we? My name is all we need."

"Maybe."

"In the court papers my name only. That's why I did it the way I did. To get the kids out of it."

"A stunt like that he could have shot you. He should have shot you."

"Call up Earl and run it by him. My name only. I need to know, Gabe. I need to know."

THE INVESTIGATION

8

ANDREW TROY IS ON THE TELEPHONE, HAS BEEN FOR DAYS. He is in his glass cubicle at the edge of the newsroom. With its rows of desks the newsroom resembles a schoolroom, but bigger, a full city block long. It contains a few cubicles like Troy's along one edge. The rest is the rows and rows of desks, most of them this late in the day occupied, for tomorrow's paper is now being brought into existence. Dozens of people are at work. Fingers flail. Terminals flicker. Phones ring.

Troy hears the bustle and buzz but his concentration is elsewhere. Spread out on his desk are copies of Frank Redmond's telephone bills sent over by Gabe Driscoll. The bills go back months. Dozens and dozens of phone numbers to which Telephone Company Security has attached names and addresses — names of people Frankie called up during those months, almost none of whom are known to Troy. He has had to study the names and make lists. Lists of numbers frequently dialed. Of numbers inside his parish, of numbers outside.

Then he started calling people up.

"This is Andrew Troy calling. I'm trying to put together a memorial on Father Redmond. I know you were a friend of his. What can you tell me about him?"

Often enough the response has been: "Who?"

Or dead silence, followed by: "I'm a druggist. If he was the guy I think you mean, he was a customer. I never spoke ten words to him."

Such connections he has broken off fast. But sometimes it is not so easy. The head of the ladies' sodality gushes for 20 minutes about what a nice man Frank was, and so good at arranging flowers on the altar. Troy can't get her off the phone.

A number of calls are to hospital switchboards: Harlem Hospital, St. Luke's, Sloan-Kettering. Sick parishioners, Troy supposes. He is having trouble getting the hospitals to attach the names of individual patients to these calls. Do they even keep such records?

Troy needs a picture of Frank's recent life. He is looking for Frank's intimates. Especially he is looking for fellow priests, who might have known him well. The telephone company has provided only names. It has not separated out the priests, if any. Or anyone else.

But surely, Andy Troy thinks, Frank must have been friends with one or more other priests. People in the same profession do tend to congregate. He himself doesn't. He meets rarely with other journalists, most of whom consider him, he believes, strange. But most people like to get together with their peers and talk shop.

Finally he finds a Father McIntyre from Our Lady Queen of Martyrs in upper Manhattan. He and Frank were in the same class in the seminary, McIntyre says over the phone.

"Can I talk to you about him?"

"Sure."

"Where can we meet?"

Troy goes down into the subway, and rides the A train uptown. He gets off at Dyckman Street, and finds the coffee shop on Broadway where Father McIntyre is waiting for him.

McIntyre's friendship with Frank was based on baseball, apparently. A parishioner would give McIntyre two tickets to Yankee games from time to time, and he would call up Frank. "It's not so easy to find people to go to ball games with," McIntyre says. "Except for kids. Grown-ups tend to be married. They tend to accept invitations as couples. Kids can be fun. But it's nice to talk to a grown-up once in a while."

McIntyre is a short fat man with thin hair and he answers questions willingly enough, but with a certain coldness that puts Troy off.

"So what did you discuss between innings?"

"Baseball, usually."

"Nothing personal?"

"No."

"Not the priesthood?"

"After so many years, what was there to say?"

McIntyre gives a brief laugh. "Sometimes we'd talk about his pastor. A real Neanderthal, from the sound of him. An empty rectory but he sticks Frank in the back in the smallest room in the house. A monastic cell."

"Yes," says Troy. "I've seen it."

"Gave him all the dirty jobs. The early mass and the late one on the same day, for instance. House calls in all kinds of weather. Had him doing hospital rounds in the middle of the night. Told him that submission to the will of the pastor would be good for his soul. I told Frank to complain to the Chancery, but he wouldn't. He said it didn't bother him. He thought it was all pretty funny."

The two men would go to ball games in civilian clothes, McIntyre says, for the roman collar usually attracted attention — too much attention. At the ball games they wanted to pretend to be normal human beings. Too often, according to McIntyre, the roman collar brought you favors you didn't want, or a recital of problems you could do nothing about. From non-Catholics it sometimes brought barely concealed contempt.

A baseball friendship only, Troy decides. No particular intimacy. For Troy this is a disappointment.

"Were you his confessor?"

McIntyre shakes his head. "Not at all. In fact I don't think we ever had a personal conversation."

In school Troy was taught that all priests, though living lives presumably without sin, were obliged to confess themselves regularly, at least once a week, and always to the same fellow priest, from whom they would withhold no secrets, would expose their souls totally.

"I'm not sure he had a confessor at all," McIntyre says. "Or needed one. You reach a certain age and some of that pious crap you have to throw overboard."

He paused. "One time a couple of years ago his pastor did something to him, accused him of stealing money from the collection baskets, I think. That did upset Frank. He was thinking of chucking the whole thing, he told me."

"Were you shocked?"

"Shocked? No. Which of us hasn't had thoughts like that from time to time?"

"So what else did you talk about?"

"Not much, I guess. There are various kinds of priests. The two principal ones are those who mouth pious platitudes all day—you want to stay away from that kind. They bore you silly. The second kind are those who don't tell you what they're thinking at all. Frank was the latter."

After a silence, McIntyre says: "At first we used to talk about guys we knew in the seminary."

"And?"

"He hadn't kept up with them. I had the feeling he didn't know many priests, had no close priest friends."

"What about sex?"

"That above all things we didn't talk about."

Troy was running out of questions. And McIntyre, he supposed, out of answers.

"So what happened on that rooftop?" asks McIntyre.

"We don't know."

"That was a tough neighborhood he lived in."

"Yes."

"He could have been surprised up there by someone he trusted."

"It's possible."

"He didn't strike me as the type of guy to jump."

"No, me neither."

"He was too much, well, if I had to select one word to describe Frank it would be levelheaded. He was too levelheaded."

"According to his phone records," Troy says, "he last called you some months ago. What was that all about?"

"I had tickets to a game. The Yanks against the Red Sox. He called to cancel. He didn't say why. And that's the last I ever heard from him."

Troy is obliged to leave it at that. The conversation has been unsatisfactory, and a few minutes later he is standing in a crowded subway car heading back downtown. People breathe on him. He clutches a pole, and as the train shudders and jerks, a heavyset woman rams a breast into his knuckles. The ride lasts 30 minutes during which he muses about the priest he has just left, and about Frank, and about priests in general, men who represented wisdom and authority to him once. No one wiser than priests, or more in command anywhere, even parents. He had been taught by them almost to worship them, but has come to see them as he does now. As ordinary men like himself, but with limited lives. It is hard to get through life in one piece whatever role one plays, but some roles are harder than others, and some, it seems to him, are impossible. The role of priest, it seems to him, is impossible. To live an entire adult lifetime without a home, without making a home. To watch years go by without, if they obey the rules, making physical contact with anyone. To wake up each day emotionally dependent on a so-called life of the spirit which may be no more than a dream man has dreamed up to satisfy himself. To depend on a creed no more real than a dream.

Impossible, Troy thinks, and he wonders about Frank, his child-hood friend, how to fit him in among thoughts like these.

The train is in a long tunnel, darkness all around Troy, who feels totally alone despite the crush of people. At his station the doors open and he is jostled out onto the platform where, finally, he is able to stand in an empty bit of space, and imagine he breathes freely again.

When he gets back to his office he gets out Frank's phone bills and continues down the list, dialing each number, making notes on whatever replies he gets. But he does not find Frank's confessor, if any. He finds no more priests at all.

What he does find, to his surprise, is Frank's psychiatrist. Who, however, refuses to talk to him over the phone. Troy can be persua-sive. It is what he does for a living. Half the people he interviews re-fuse, at first, to talk to him.

The psychiatrist, Dr. Greenberg, agrees to see him the following day after office hours.

TROY GETS OUT OF A CAB IN FRONT OF Greenberg's street-floor office which gives onto Fifth Avenue at 90th Street, opposite Central Park, whose bare trees hang out over the wall on that side of the street. He rings the bell. It is Greenberg himself who opens the door, leading Troy through the empty waiting room into his office. There are paintings on the walls of the waiting room, and more on his office walls as well.

Troy looks around at them, and then at the psychiatrist's couch. "So that's where the patients spill their guts," he remarks.

"As I hope I made plain on the phone, Mr. Troy, I can't discuss my patients with you or anyone."

"Your ex-patient, in this case."

"Nor my ex-patients. The only reason you are here is because I was curious to meet you. That was unfair of me, I know."

"Meet me?"

"You're quite famous."

Troy lets this pass. "There must be one or two things you can tell me."

"No, nothing."

After a pause, Greenberg says: "Also, I wanted to know more about how Father Redmond happened to go off that roof."

"I'll tell you how, you tell me why?"

Dr. Greenberg smiles. "Even if I knew why, I couldn't tell you. Whatever patients say in this room is privileged and must remain so."

"You knew Frank was dead before I called you?"

"Yes. Did he fall or jump? Was he pushed?"

"We don't know yet."

If Frank was murdered, Troy reflects, this man won't have any answers for me. But if it was suicide, perhaps he will. Troy says: "If it was suicide, would that surprise you?"

"Surprise me? Yes, I'll give you that much, it would surprise me."

"Because of the method?"

Dr. Greenberg shrugs. "Pills, guns, rooftops. It's all the same impulse."

"Do many of your patients kill themselves?"

"It happens."

"But you didn't think Father Redmond was that type of patient?"

Dr. Greenberg looks at him, but does not answer.

"Did he seem to you troubled?"

"You're at the edge of territory I can't go into."

"Why not? 'Troubled' is a vague enough word, or so I would have thought."

"Everybody is troubled. The ones I see are at least trying to do something about it."

"How troubled?"

Dr. Greenberg does not answer.

Troy tries another tack.

"Did he ever speak about having a confessor?"

"Did he have a confessor? I don't recall. But if he did you'd be wasting your time looking for him. He wouldn't tell you anything either."

Troy nods.

"If you were a detective with a subpoena, I still wouldn't tell you. And your subpoena wouldn't stand up in court. The law recognizes that conversations between a patient and his psychiatrist are privileged."

"How often did you see him?" Troy asks. "How long had he been coming to you? Can you tell me that much?"

Dr. Greenberg only shakes his head. "Let me offer you a drink?" he suggests. "It's the end of the day. I have a nice scotch. A pretty good chardonnay."

Troy decides to accept. "A scotch and soda might be nice," he says. In a social setting Dr. Greenberg may be less on guard. He might let slip something important. The drink might loosen his tongue.

This is a technique reporters often use. And often enough it works, though not this time.

As they sip their drinks Troy tries to drop in his pseudo-casual questions, but gets no answers. Instead the psychiatrist asks about columns he has written, politicians he knows. "You see," he remarks, "I'm a devoted reader."

Troy works hard but Dr. Greenberg remains tight-lipped to the end.

In the cab driving back to the paper Troy reflects on what he has learned—not much. That something was bothering Frankie. That he was troubled enough to see a psychiatrist, and try to talk it out. The Catholic Church has never believed in psychiatry. A little counseling from priests, or even nuns, was considered enough. Frankie may have been sure enough of himself to ignore such old-world, ill-informed taboos. Nonetheless, for such a man to seek out a psychiatrist was a major step. It meant that whatever bothered him seemed bigger than he thought he could handle. What was it? And was it enough to make him want to jump off that roof?

When he reaches his office Troy makes more calls. But none gets him any closer to the answers he is looking for.

CHAPTER EIGHT

ASSISTANT DISTRICT ATTORNEY EARL FINLEY died on the sidewalk in front of the Manhattan Criminal Courts building at 100 Centre Street, about ten feet from a rolling hot-dog stand from which he had just purchased two hot dogs. He was 51 years old.

It was precisely 12:36 P.M. on the last Tuesday in September. Earl had the half-eaten hot dog in his hand, and when he fell the mustard smeared his tie. Gabe Driscoll, who was with him, had been making jokes about hot dogs, about junk food in general, refusing to eat any himself, and the image of the mustard on Earl's tie seared his brain. It left the equivalent of the mark a tire makes when a car skids. It would not erase. It would stay with him for the rest of his life.

The day was unseasonably hot. The sidewalk was crowded. The umbrella over the cart was plastered with the logo of the hot-dog manufacturer. Steam rose from the vats and was caught under the umbrella. A bit farther on, a second cart was doing equally good business. People muscled their way to the front of the line and munched lunch standing up. Men in shirtsleeves, women in sleeveless dresses. Jurors, witnesses, lawyers, defendants, detectives. A judge or two, most likely; in their chambers upstairs their judicial robes hung from pegs. Probably a few passersby as well, men and women not even aware of where exactly they stood, which special world they had entered.

Gabe had been in court testifying before a grand jury in a police corruption case. Testifying against bent cops always depressed him, and he supposed it always would. He and Earl had got on the down elevator on different floors. Seeing Earl lifted Gabe's spirits, and after they had greeted each other he suggested they lunch in one of the restaurants in Little Italy, the edge of which was two blocks away.

But Earl didn't have time. "I've got meetings all afternoon," he said, "and two speeches tonight, first to black leaders in Harlem, and then to the bar association in Town Hall." He had time to buy a hot dog outside, but was not sure he had time to chew it, he said.

Gabe was aware that Earl, who had risen to the rank of chief assistant DA, was busy. In the absence of the district attorney, who was ill, it was Earl who now ran the office, eleven bureau chiefs reporting to him, over 400 assistant DAs to be moved in and out of courtrooms, thousands and thousands of new cases pouring in each month. In addition to this he was the Democratic candidate for district attorney, and the elections were six weeks away.

"You ever get home these days?"

"Not too often."

"How does Rocky like that?"

"I haven't had time to ask her."

They came out of the building.

"They know me here," said Earl, as they approached the rolling cart. "Mention my name, you'll be sure to get a good table."

There was a queue, and they got on it.

"Best restaurant in town," said Earl.

"I'm sure."

From where he stood, Gabe could see that the vendor was Chinese.

"Guy's name is Howard," said Earl.

"A Chinese guy named Howard?"

"They're not all named Woo Fung."

"I didn't know that."

"Woo Fung is in fact his name, actually, but he likes to be called Howard."

The vendor was forking hot dogs into rolls, thrusting money into a pocket in his apron.

"Howard is very unusual for a Chinese guy," Earl said. "He's a Harvard man, you know. Majored in Maître d'Hôtel. Graduated with honors. Maybe it was Michigan State. Some goddam place."

The vendor, serving fast, looked like he had three hands, a fork in each. The line shrank fast.

"After college Howard apprenticed in the best Paris restaurants."

"As you can tell from his technique," said Gabe, "his hand-to-eye coordination is extraordinary."

"If he speared himself with that fork he'd be out of business for a month."

Earl was on a high, and it showed. A *New York Times* poll showed him winning easily.

"I'm taking nothing for granted," Earl said.

The incumbent district attorney, after six terms in office, had suffered two heart attacks in the past eight months, had stopped coming to work, and had withdrawn his candidacy. The party's choice to succeed him had not been Earl Finley, though its leaders, before rejecting him, had sounded him out during a long interview. Gabe knew the story of this interview. Earl had listened to what he considered their asinine ideas about how the DA's office should work, and their other ideas about what the grateful candidate, himself, could do for the party once elected.

Finally they had asked him which crimes he would focus on as district attorney.

This question, to Earl, was as asinine as the rest of the interview. But because he wanted the nomination badly, he knew better than to say so. Instead he opted for a response which was far worse. His brow wrinkled, he seemed to grow more and more thoughtful, then said: "My No. 1 priority, as soon as I'm elected, will be to nail as many crooked politicians as I can."

The men interviewing him fell silent.

"That's a good idea, don't you think? Lot of crooked pols out there. Should be easy pickings."

The laughter came bubbling up inside him, but he held it in. "I hate crooked politicians," he said, "don't you?"

"What other ideas did you have?" one of them asked stiffly.

"Well," said Earl, "when I run out of politicians, I intend to go after the major political donors. Those guys are all crooks, or they wouldn't be trying to buy us public servants. I'd have my men dig a little, see what skeletons turn up."

One of his interrogators relaxed visibly, and a sudden smile creased his face. "You're putting us on," he said.

"No," said Earl. "So those are my priorities. First the politicians, then the donors. Indictment, trial, jail. The public will love it, don't you think?"

This was in a private room at the Princeton Club on West 43rd Street. Leather armchairs. A fireplace in which, later in the year, real logs would burn. Four men in a semicircle, Earl facing them. A servant in livery bringing drinks, serious drinks for the other four, tea for Earl.

Earl became bored, and began answering whenever possible with wisecracks.

After telling him they had no more questions, he could go, the other four put their heads together. Earl Finley harbored ideas far outside the accepted mainstream, they decided. He was not the man the party should choose to run for DA.

And they fixed on someone else.

Having more or less deliberately flunked the interview, Earl stood on the sidewalk outside the Princeton Club, and was not so much annoyed at himself, as furious at the party leaders inside. He was a man with a violent temper which manifested itself not in ranting or screaming but in a ferocious need to strike back, and he resolved on the spot to run for district attorney without them, or despite them. He watched the cars go past on 43rd Street. He was not going to let those idiots decide who was to be the next district attorney of New York County.

The next day he filed for the primary.

He had not raised a penny, and had no money with which to pay the expenses of campaigning, so at first he used his own money, of which he did not have much. When Rocky railed at him, he did not try to talk her around, but ignored her, turned away. He let her rail at his back.

There were four candidates in the primary, including the president of the city council, the city's second-highest elected official, though the office itself was without real power. This man was not a household name either, but he was better known than Earl, and he was the party's choice.

Earl began to stump. He stood on a box on busy sidewalks. He told those voters who chose to listen that he had more than 26 years' experience in the DA's office, the past four as chief assistant.

Each time the crowd thinned quickly.

The district attorney ought to be independent, and not linked to any political party, he told the ever-sparser crowds. He looked into faces as he spoke and saw that this was not a glamorous message either.

Now was not the time for jokes about locking up politicians and political donors. He had become a politician himself, and donors he needed. What other ideas did he have?

It happened that a political reporter from the *New York Times* invited him to dinner. The restaurant was Umberto's Steak House on the East Side, and as the two men sat down Earl recognized the man at the next table as Dominic Russo, the city's most powerful Mafioso,

the so called *capo di tutti capi*. Earl was surprised to note how short
the man was, about five feet eight. His shortness was evident even
sitting down. At the same time he was thick-necked and looked to
weigh over 200 pounds, little or none of it fat. Russo would have gorillas with him, Earl guessed — such a man would not dare move
about unescorted — and he glanced around the restaurant searching
for them. There they were, he saw, two men with narrow heads and
hooded eyes drinking Coca-Cola two tables away. Two others standing against the far wall as well.

Russo was wearing a silk suit with wide pinstripes, and brilliant
crocodile shoes. Seated with him was a woman who, since she was
middle-aged and overweight, Earl supposed must be his wife.

Earl decided to bait Russo. Was it because his campaign was not
going well? Was he only showing off for the reporter? Whatever, he
was in a mood to create trouble.

Without realizing it, he had found his campaign theme.

"That guy's Dominic 'The Fist' Russo," he whispered to the reporter, "the most famous Mafioso in the city." It was an exceedingly
loud whisper, audible many tables away. It stopped forks halfway to
mouths.

"Actually, I'm surprised to see him here," Earl whispered.

"Why is that?" said the reporter, already uneasy.

"Because restaurants are where these guys like to whack each
other," Earl whispered loudly. "You remember Masseria, don't you?
Facedown in the spaghetti. And Gugino shot through the chunk of
steak as he put it in his mouth. And Tartino, with two bullets in him,
who got up and tried to run, knocked over the hatcheck girl, tried
to push himself up, and died with a tit in each hand."

Conversation had stopped. Movement had stopped. Earl's whis-
pering seemed louder now than it had, for there was no other nearby
sound.

"You'd imagine the restaurant would think twice before letting him in. Blood in the soup is bad for business, I would think."

The reporter was squirming, saying nothing.

"And those bulky men there and there," Earl whispered, "body-guards." Heads turned in the directions he pointed. "Note the bulges under their arms." He nodded sagely. "Of course, maybe they're deodorant pads."

"You mean?"

"Be ready to dive under the table. More wine?"

He poured it.

"Do you like his shoes? I bet they cost money," Earl whispered loudly. "But if you want shoes that glow in the dark, you have to pay for it."

The reporter seemed to be trying to hide.

"Shoes like that used to be big in Harlem," Earl whispered. "Of course that was fifty years ago."

Despite the stares, the hovering forks, there was no reaction from Russo.

"Maybe he's trying to become an arbiter of fashion, bring the style back. Make it his own."

One of the bodyguards appeared between Earl's table and Russo's, his suit straining across the shoulders, wrists hanging below the sleeves.

"You want something, Boss?"

With a jerk of his head, still not acknowledging Earl, Russo sent the gorilla back to his table.

So Earl, in a manner of speaking, switched targets.

"Do you think she's his wife?" Earl whispered loudly.

No answer from the reporter.

"He usually has this blonde with him. Gigantic knockers. I thought the blonde was his wife, but maybe I was wrong.

"Must be his wife," Earl whispered.

"He certainly feeds her well," Earl whispered.

"I have a weight problem too," Earl whispered. "Maybe she'd like to hear about my diet."

Earl felt himself lifted out of his seat. When he looked he saw that the two nearest gorillas had him under both arms. Both were snarling.

"Your dinner just ended, Pal."

"It's over for you, Wiseass."

"Out you go."

Bumping between tables, upsetting glasses, the bodyguards half carried, half dragged Earl toward the door.

He had seen no sign to them from Russo.

"Would you call the police, please?" Earl cried out to the nearest waiter. "These men are trying to deprive me of my civil rights."

Not a sound elsewhere in the room. Only the Mafia capo, eyes on his plate, continued to eat.

"I'm Assistant District Attorney Earl Finley," Earl cried. He had his shield in his hand. As much as possible given the constraint he was under he waved it around. "And these two gorillas I intend to prosecute."

They dropped him at once, throwing frantic glances back at Russo as if for instructions.

"Dominic 'The Fist' Russo," Earl cried, pointing, "is one of the most vicious mobsters in the city. They call him 'The Fist' because he likes to slug people who are being held fast by two other people. After he's had his fun, he gives a nod and his men take the guy out and kill him."

Even Russo, though he did not look up, had stopped eating now.

"I'm running for Manhattan district attorney," Earl cried, pointing. "And if you elect me, within a year I will put that man in jail. The gorillas you see with him as well."

Russo got up, yanked his wife out of her chair by one arm, and

strode from the room. His men made a path for him, brushing waiters and other patrons aside. Nobody tried to make him pay his check.

Earl raised his voice to carry over the general din that had come
up. "Earl Finley, for district attorney of New York County. Vote for
me, I'll give you what you want."

Grinning broadly, he sat down beside the stupefied reporter, then
immediately stood up again. "And I hope you enjoy your dinner," he
called out. "Now where were we?" he said to the reporter, as he sat
down again.

From the restaurant the reporter hurried back to the *Times* office
and tapped out a detailed description of the incident. He described
Earl's baiting of Russo as high comedy against a deadly background.
The candidate's one-liners gave life to the piece, and when the reporter turned it in he watched his editors handing it page by page
one to the other, laughing. The *New York Times* played it on the
front page the next day.

Earl came to work, saw his picture two columns wide above the
fold, and knew, even before the phones began to ring — other reporters
clamoring for their share of the story — that he was on to something.
He appeared on television newscasts every night that week.

After that he ridiculed Russo regularly, constantly, and as his campaign attracted more publicity, more crowds, and more donors, Russo
became his theme song. In terms of publicity no district attorney candidate had ever cut such a swath, and the effect far exceeded his
wildest dreams. In his speeches, and in the ads he was soon able to
afford, he turned Russo into a clown, which he was not, continually
promising to put him in jail within the year. Him and others like him.

He knew that enraging such a man might be dangerous, and before long he had Gabe Driscoll, now a deputy chief working out of
Organized Crime Control, begging him to stop.

Gabe, uninvited, stood in his office doorway. "They'll put out a
contract on you," he warned.

"You're exaggerating."

"They'll whack you. For Christ's sake cut it out."

Seemingly complacent, Earl sat back, his hands behind his head. "They never kill cops, prosecutors, judges, or journalists. Never have. Not once in all the years they've been in business."

This was true.

"And they never will, either," said Earl.

"In Italy they do," Gabe said. "All the time."

"In Italy, not here. It's how they stay in business in America. They are careful never to get the populace mad enough to rise up against them."

"In your case, maybe they'll make an exception."

"How they enforce such discipline I do not know, but they do."

Gabe took two steps toward Earl's desk, but did not sit down. "Killing people like you is part of the tradition they come from. They could revert to it at any time."

"I don't think so," said Earl.

Chief Driscoll looked away for a moment, remembering the tough, tough competitor Earl had been as a boy as a diver. Willing himself to become calm, Gabe tried to adopt a tone of persuasion: "I don't think you understand these Mafia types as well as you think, Earl. In this job I deal with them every day. The one thing you can't do with them is make them look ridiculous, as you are doing with Russo. They can't afford that. None of them can. Russo can't. To his colleagues he begins to look impotent. He risks a struggle for power. He risks being whacked by one of the others. Suddenly you've made him vulnerable. He can't permit it."

"I've got an election to win."

"These guys kill people all the time. Killing is nothing to them."

"I have to do what I have to do."

"They don't have to put their name on the bullet. How about a little accident? Their hand doesn't show but you're dead."

"Maybe after the primary," said Earl.

"You don't even need to do it anymore. You've already got a big lead, according to the polls. Why keep after Russo when the polls—"

"The polls," Earl scoffed.

"Russo doesn't even need to order it himself. One of his dimwits might decide to do it for him as a favor. And to hell with discipline."

"See me after the primary."

"You should at least be armed."

Earl gave a mock shiver. "I have a horror of guns."

"You should go nowhere without a bodyguard."

"I have a car and driver assigned to me. The driver's a cop. He's armed."

"That's not what I mean. The dumbest guys in the department are the ones who get assigned as drivers."

Earl laughed. "Not my drivers."

Gabe went away and brooded. The next day he arranged for a detective to shadow Earl everywhere he went. And he phoned Earl's wife. "Make him stop," he told Rocky.

"When did anyone ever make Earl do anything he did not want to do?" she replied.

She's a cold woman, Gabe thought, hanging up. He had felt from the beginning that she didn't love Earl enough, or perhaps at all. He decided he didn't like her very much.

And after a few days Earl became aware of Gabe's detective following him, and he sent the man back to his command.

As the primary campaign wound down Assistant DA Earl Finley had half of New York laughing at Dominic "The Fist" Russo.

He carried the primary with 60 percent of the vote, and as the fall campaign got under way he decided not to change what seemed to him a winning game plan. He went on delivering much the same lines. He spoke them broadly, lightly, usually accompanied by an engaging boyish grin. "Some honest citizens," he liked to say during television interviews, "imagine these people to be really complete businessmen, when in fact they're really complete morons. Take Russo, for example. Poor fellow has a fifth-grade education. Does that sound like the makings of a businessman to you? In actual fact he couldn't run a shoe store without a baseball bat."

Gabe Driscoll had given up remonstrating with his childhood friend, and he supposed Rocky had never tried. Gabe did arrange to have two other detectives, alternating, to follow him at a more discreet distance. It was all he could do.

Now, the two friends, both approaching middle age, both wearing conservative business suits, waited on line at the hot-dog stand, An outsider would have thought them solid executives, never guessing that their clientele was different from most men's.

Gabe's eyes located the detective assigned to Earl this day. His name, Gabe remembered, was Detective Brough. He gave Brough a brief nod, got one in return, and turned back to Earl. How easy it would be to assassinate someone in a crowd like this, Gabe Driscoll thought. This was the first of the day's notions that tonight would haunt him.

There had been 20 people ahead of them in line, more or less, now there were about ten. Several times that many stood around dripping hot-dog juice and mustard onto the pavement, and the queue behind them extended back almost to the courthouse.

Gabe gave Earl's shoulder an affectionate squeeze. "Standing this close to you is proof of our friendship," he said. "The shooting starts, I'm right in the crossfire."

"Are you still worried about that?" said Earl. He laughed. "But you'd take one for me, wouldn't you?"

"I might not have any choice."

They were joking about it, another notion that would haunt Gabe later.

They reached the head of the line.

"Hello there, Howard," Earl said.

"Hey, Boss, I got special for you today."

He forked out a hot dog ten inches long, plunked it into a too-short roll, and handed it over.

"I'll take two like that," said Earl. "Hold these," he ordered Gabe, and he squeezed mustard on both. "And a big Coke," he said to Howard.

While Gabe stood to the side holding the overlong hot dogs, Earl took the Coke from Howard, then manipulated money out of his wallet with one hand.

At once Earl grabbed one of the hot dogs, wolfed down half, and swilled half the Coke.

"So this is lunch," Gabe said.

"Best restaurant in town."

"Yes, you said that."

Earl's lips were moist from the juice, his grin showed all his teeth. He really loves junk food, thought Gabe. It seemed to him that he had never seen Earl more alive, more enjoying the moment. Or perhaps this was another notion that came to him only much later.

Earl reached for the second hot dog, and Gabe gave it to him.

With both hands free, the detective chief glanced at his watch, thereby fixing, in his own mind at least, the time of death: 12:36.

"Keep eating that crap," said Gabe to Earl, "and you know what will happen, don't you?"

"What's that?"

"Your legs will bow out and you'll start losing your hair."

Earl laughed.

"And you won't be able to dive anymore. You'll try a one-and-a-half and land flat on your face."

Earl's mouth opened again, his teeth came down on that portion of the hot dog that extended beyond the roll.

"Hmm, succulent," Earl said, swallowing, grinning, his last words on this or any other subject.

He took another bite and a gulp of Coke, his face beginning to contort. Turned white. Gagged. Half-eaten hot dog spewed from his mouth, and then he fell, was racked by spasms, was still.

Gabe Driscoll, on his knees beside him, cried: "Earl, Earl. Speak to me, Earl." But part of him believed his childhood friend was already dead.

A crowd pressed around Earl. Gabe was aware of uniformed knees at eye level, civilian knees too that ought to be moved back, the detective assigned by Gabe kneeling beside him. Gabe had his shield case out, had hung his badge off his breast pocket, the first reflex of any cop, identifying himself to other cops, guaranteeing immediate assistance, 30,000 other men on his side, as much assistance as he might need. It established command as well. Most cops had never seen a deputy chief's shield, but would recognize it when they saw it. A shield that spoke loudly and must be obeyed.

Detective Brough cried: "I'll call an ambulance."

"There isn't time," Gabe told him. He looked around for his car which was here somewhere, but did not see it, no telling where his driver might have parked it, might have got to.

"You and you," he shouted at two of the uniforms, "where's your car?"

It was at the curb. They crouched to lift Earl, even as a hand and arm reached through the assembled legs for the hot dog Earl had never finished that lay on the pavement. Gabe stepped on this arm, came down hard on it, breaking bones for all he knew, not caring, seeing, as the hand and arm were hurriedly withdrawn, to whom they belonged: Howard, if that was his name, the hot-dog vendor. Gabe thrust the hot dog into his own jacket pocket. Until now he had supposed Earl was having a heart attack or stroke. Suddenly he was not so sure.

When he looked Gabe saw Howard already some distance off. Having lifted one end of his stand he had started down the street with it, was beginning to run, then running hard, Gabe already shouting to Detective Brough: "Arrest that man. Hold him until I get back. Grab the cart too."

Then he was in the back of the radio car, Earl's head on his lap. "Hold on, Earl," he pleaded, "hold on, we're almost there."

Every cop in the city knew the way to the nearest hospital. This car was from the 9th Precinct, so it headed to Bellevue. The siren was blaring, they were taking all the lights, driving of this kind being the most dangerous action that cops ever did, more dangerous than any shoot-out. They crossed Canal Street, which is six lanes wide, traffic in both directions, this traffic miraculously parting.

"Tell them we're coming," Gabe cried. "Tell them it's Chief Driscoll bringing in Assistant DA Finley. Maybe a heart attack, maybe something else." He heard the cop in the passenger seat relaying the information into the phone to Central. Gabe in the backseat could not distinguish the words over the siren, but knew what they were.

"Tell them we're five minutes out, Central," the cop shouted into the phone.

They went up the short driveway at 50 miles an hour, perhaps more, and skidded to a stop inches from the doorway. A gurney was waiting, and with it a man in a white coat with a stethoscope around his neck, and two nurses and a man rolling an oxygen mask attached to a stand. These people lifted Earl onto the gurney. It looked like 20 hands doing it. The mask was clapped onto his face, even as the intern tore the buttons off his shirt, ripped at the T-shirt underneath, exposing naked flesh. He applied the stethoscope to Earl's chest, and for a very short time listened for what, if anything, was going on inside.

The intern stood up and gave the assembled throng the same signal a football official gives when the ball sails out of bounds, and the play is over.

"The oxygen's not going to help," he said.

"Yes it will," said Gabe, "yes."

"He's dead."

"He can't be," said Gabe.

"My guess is he's been dead ten, fifteen minutes."

Gabe looked down at his friend. Earl's blond hair was mussed, his face twisted into a grimace. Gabe wished they would put a sheet over him, something. They shouldn't leave him like that. Somebody wheeled the gurney away, its unmoving burden with it. Toward the morgue, probably, which was next door.

The intern, who had Gabe by the arm, drew him into an office.

"I want an immediate autopsy," Gabe said. "Tell them it's urgent."

"I'll take care of it, Chief."

"Tell them."

The intern sat him down. A woman came in. There was a typewriter on the desk into which she rolled a form.

"Name of the deceased?" she said. "Address. Do you know his date of birth?" Gabe answered the questions as best he could. The typewriter clattered. "Next of kin to be notified?"

"No," said Gabe, "I'll do that."

When they left him he sat down on a bench, his head in his hands. He did not know how long he sat there. Presently they brought him the contents of Earl's pockets in a bag, which he stared at for a time, seeing nothing.

You've got to get moving, he told himself. As he stood up he became conscious of the wad of frankfurter in his pocket. Not knowing what it was, he reached in for it, and his hand came out covered with mustard, which he wiped off on his handkerchief. He went outside into the driveway where he thought he would find his car. But he had never called for it. His driver had no idea where he was. There was a radio car parked off to one side, however, either the one he had come in or another, he didn't know.

The same two cops came forward.

"You fellows still around?" he said.

"You asked us to wait, Chief."

"Did I?"

He got into the back and had himself driven to the Police Academy on 21st Street. The various labs were on the eighth floor. He rode the elevator up, found the detective he was looking for, and handed over Earl's hot dog.

"How soon can you tell me if there is something in this that isn't supposed to be there?"

"What am I looking for, Chief?"

"Some sort of quick-acting poison."

"There aren't too many of those."

"Do it as fast as you can."

"It may take a while, Chief."

"As fast as you can."

"A few hours."

"I'll wait."

While waiting, he phoned the St. Ambrose rectory, got Frank Redmond, and told him Earl was dead.

"Oh God, not Earl."

"It may have been a heart attack or stroke, or maybe it was something else. I don't know yet. I'll call you back when I know. In the meantime, go see Earl's widow. Tell her what's happened before she finds out some other way."

"Earl?" said Frank. "Earl?"

Frank had additional questions but Gabe cut him off. "That's all I know at present."

"Where is he?" said Frank. "She's going to want to see him."

"Negative," said Gabe. "With the election so close he's probably already being autopsied. He was a public figure. That's the way it has to be done." And he hung up.

Frank was good with widows, Gabe supposed, as he paced the lab. Or if he wasn't he should be. It was what priests were for. Gabe did not care for Roxanne Finley very much, but no woman deserved to learn of her husband's death on a news broadcast, and Frank would be a comfort to her until her children came.

He called his office. "Reach out for Detective Brough," he ordered. "Find out where he is, where his prisoner is, and have him call me forthwith."

Forthwith. The strongest command in the police lexicon.

He gave the lab's phone number, adding: "After that, call my driver on the radio, tell him to wait for me downstairs."

He went into the lab where he watched a detective in a white coat focus his lights, then photograph the partly eaten hot dog inside the untouched roll from all angles. Setting the roll to one side, this detective and another then examined the hot dog whole under the microscope, moving it this way and that while murmuring to each other, their voices so low Gabe couldn't hear.

"If there's something inside the hot dog besides meat," one said to him, "then how did it get in there? That's the big question, right, Chief?"

Gabe waited.

"Injected it—that's my guess," the detective said. "Take a look." Leaning back, giving Gabe room to peer through the lens, he pointed with the tip of a pencil to a spot in the middle of the sausage. "See that, Chief? Does that look like a possible puncture to you?"

After stepping away from the lens, Gabe nodded.

The detective, who was wearing latex gloves, picked up a scalpel and sliced the sausage lengthwise down the middle. It was as delicate as surgery. As the two sides fell apart a slight discoloration almost the length of them could be seen, together with some ooze that did not look normal.

"That's it, I imagine," the detective said, pointing with his scalpel.

The surgery continued, two more long dissections, making four precise lengths.

"All right," said Gabe. "Any idea what it is?"

"Let's see, shall we?" Gabe watched them mixing solutions, preparing slides.

The phone rang on the desk outside. Someone answered, called out Chief Driscoll's name, and when he emerged from the lab handed him the receiver.

It was Detective Brough. He had the prisoner and the rolling cart at the 5th Precinct stationhouse on Elizabeth Street in Chinatown, he said.

"What's happening there, Chief? Finley okay?"

"Finley's dead."

"Heart attack?"

"Probably," Gabe lied. "What's the condition of your prisoner?"

"We got a terrified Chinaman on our hands, Chief. He admits to being an illegal alien with a forged green card and an unlicensed food stand. Other than that, he's completely innocent, so he says. I've sent over to Intelligence to see what we have on him."

"The immigration stuff is enough to hold him on, so hold him."

"Completely innocent of what? What's he so scared about?"

"Did you make your notifications?"

"Not yet, Chief."

"Well don't."

"I didn't know who to start notifying. What do I have? There was no crime that I could see. I was waiting to hear from you first."

"Did you read the prisoner his rights?"

"Not yet, Chief. He's not under arrest."

"Tell him he risks deportation and read him his rights. Did he ask for a lawyer?"

"Not yet."

"Good. Don't question him again. I'll get there shortly."

Having hung up, he asked the lab detectives how much longer before they knew something. At least an hour, he was told.

It was at this point that he realized the Police Academy was another man's turf, and he should check in with Chief Cielo, the Academy commander, who was a deputy chief like himself. This was what protocol called for. Bad as he felt, he had best do it. The NYPD was a vast political organization. An officer got ahead by being careful. You made no enemies, even inadvertent ones. You snubbed no one, stepped on no toes, invaded no one's turf without permission. You remembered names, smiled a lot, asked about the health of wives and children. Everybody liked you, or at least didn't dislike you, and when a promotion vacancy opened up you might be considered.

It was by obeying rules like this that Gabe Driscoll had got as far as he had got, and would go further. He would get his second star later this year, and his third star the next.

He went into Chief Cielo's office and was lucky. Cielo was just leaving. The small talk lasted only a few minutes. When Cielo asked what Gabe was doing in the building, his answer was vague. He was having some tests done in the lab.

With an hour or more still to wait, Gabe went down to the shooting range in the basement. Like all cops he was obliged to move about armed at all times, even when off duty. He was obliged also to qualify with his revolver twice each year under the scrutiny of a range instructor, even though officers of his exalted rank did not normally make arrests anymore, nor normally go into dangerous situations either.

"Qualify" meant the shooting of 50 rounds at targets. Now the instructor moved Gabe into a firing lane, set up the first target, handed him sound barriers to put over his ears, and stepped back. Gabe was carrying his short barrel, five-shot Smith & Wesson detective special,

and he drew it out of its clip-on holster at his belt, and began firing
and reloading, firing and reloading. The target, which moved backward and forward on a slide, was overprinted with the image of a
gunman firing back. To Gabe the face of the gunman became
Howard the vendor's face, or else the face of whoever put him up to
poisoning two hot dogs, whoever had killed Earl. Over and over
Gabe blew this face to tatters.

But this did not bring Earl back.

FRANK TOOK THE TERRIBLE NEWS WITH HIM into the church and
knelt before the altar and tried to feel the presence of Earl and of
God, and of God's plan, because this was what, as an adult and as a
priest, he was in the habit of doing whenever troubled or baffled or
hurt. Today he was all three. But today also it was not working. He
could feel Earl well enough, could feel an aching sense of loss, but
God and God's plan were beyond him. This had become more and
more the norm in recent years. Somehow God had become dimmer
to him. God did not seem to be there to be conjured up when
needed. Frank did not know why this was so. Perhaps it was only increasing age. Or increasing maturity, which would be much worse.

Because he did not have time to indulge himself and these
thoughts any further he got up off his knees and went back into the
rectory and up the stairs toward his room, but on the landing he en-
countered Monsignor Malachy.

"I have to go out, Monsignor. I probably won't be back until midnight or later."

"Did I give you permission to go out?"

"Oh, come on."

"I'm the pastor here. You want to go out, you ask permission."

"There has been a death. I'm needed."

"In this parish?"

"No, in Yonkers."

"That's not your affair and you have Benediction tonight."

"You'll have to do it in my place."

"I'll permit you to leave, but only after the Benediction."

Frank stared at him a moment, then went into his room where he stepped out of his cassock, hung it in the closet, and put on his best black suit and a fresh collar. Then he made two phone calls, the first to Andy Troy's wife, Maureen, and the second to Gabe's wife, Barbara. Roxanne Finley must be told that her husband was dead, but he did not wish to be the sole bearer of such terrible news. With the two other women beside him it would be easier for everybody. He told both of them of Earl's sudden death, cut off their questions, and said he would pick them up in about 15 minutes.

When he came out of his room the pastor was lurking on the landing.

"Where do you think you're going?"

"As I told you, Monsignor, there's been a death and I have to go there now."

"I'm the pastor here. You'll do what I tell you."

"Sorry, Monsignor."

He went downstairs and out with the pastor sputtering behind him, found his nearly worn-out car parked at the curb farther down the street, and went and collected the two women.

He drove uptown with the Hudson River to his left, with Maureen in the passenger seat, and Barbara in the back beside her folded wheelchair. The river was turbulent, which meant a stiff wind was blowing. Across rose the Palisades, miles and miles of autumn color. They crossed the Henry Hudson Bridge, passed the statue of the great navigator beaming down on his river, and presently were in Yonkers. Frank found the big, increasingly shabby Victorian house, and pulled into the driveway behind Rocky's car, already there.

It had been a long, mostly silent drive. Frank and the two women got out, and went up the path to the stoop, Maureen pushing Barbara along. But there they hesitated, looking at each other. Then Frank rang the bell.

GABE WENT OUT TO A TAVERN ON 21ST STREET. It was full of cops from the Police Academy, or else from the 13th Precinct which operated out of the ground floor of the same building. He sat at the bar and ate a sandwich and drank a beer.

When he came up to the lab again the technicians were ready with a tentative identification of the poison within the hot dog that had killed Earl Finley.

"Tetramine," the lab detective told him. "At this point only an educated guess, you might say. It's a poison that attacks the central nervous system. It's odorless, tasteless. Used to be used in rat poisons, but it's been banned now for several years."

"Never heard of it," Gabe said.

"That's why your guy went down so fast. Took about three minutes, I would judge."

"Meaning it was the first hot dog that killed him," Gabe said, "not this one."

"Stopped his ability to breathe. It either asphyxiated him, or stopped his heart. The autopsy will tell you which. Overall, it probably took ten or fifteen minutes before he died."

Gabe was remembering the way Earl fell.

"There are one or two other possibilities we haven't ruled out yet," the detective said. "But tetramine is what we think at the moment."

He heard again the sharp crack when Earl's head struck the pavement.

"Tetramine is very big in China, Chief. Any Chinamen involved in the case?"

"I'll have to see," said Chief Driscoll.

"The Chinese use it in a rat poison called Dushuqiang. I looked it up. It used to be on sale in this country too, but it got banned."

The technician spoke in a tone of ordinary conversation. The use of a deadly poison, the murder of a prosecutor and political candidate was not enough to make him raise his voice. Cops saw entirely too much of this sort of thing, Gabe thought. They lost their ability to be outraged, or even surprised.

"How much tetramine would you say was in the hot dog?"

"The one I examined? Enough to stop a truck, is my guess. Must have been about the same amount in the first one, the one he actually ate, for him to go out of the picture so quickly. The autopsy should be able to tell you."

Gabe looked at him. "I don't want to read a thing about this in the papers."

"Sure, Chief."

"You get my meaning. Not a word."

"Yes sir."

He found his car downstairs and was driven to the Chinatown stationhouse where he had Brough call in the detectives he wanted. While waiting for them to arrive, he spent an hour in a small bare room talking—trying to talk—to Howard, the Chinese hot-dog vendor.

"Who paid you to serve those hot dogs to Mr. Finley, and how much?" he began.

The vendor said a man he didn't know paid him $100. He thought it was a joke. Would he be able to recognize the man again? Yes, he would. Would he testify in court if the man were arrested? Yes, he would do anything to be allowed to stay in America. He had a wife and four children. Who were probably illegal too, thought Gabe, who was having difficulty understanding him. He was so scared his English had become almost unintelligible.

When Gabe came out of the room, Detective Brough handed him a folder. "This just came over from Intelligence."

Howard, he read, had once been arrested in a raid on a Mott Street gambling den owned by the Nam Luong Tong.

Had Howard been a dealer or a customer? From the folder it wasn't clear. But if he was or had been a member of the Nam Luong Tong, maybe he was not as innocent as he claimed. The Nam Luongs, Chief Driscoll knew, were major importers of Far East heroin, but having no distribution network of their own, relied on Mafia partners to sell it. Their chief partner was the Luchese crime family. They did no known business with the Russo family.

Gabe could think of no conceivable reason why the Chinese might have wanted to murder Earl Finley. The Mafia, though, was another story. Not only had Earl insulted Russo over and over again, but he had promised to run all of them out of New York.

The second-floor squadroom had begun to fill up. More than 15 detectives, some of them Chinese, milled around.

Chief Driscoll called them together, called for silence.

He said: "Somebody laced a hot dog with poison, and ADA Finley is dead. A Chinese guy sold him the hot dog, and a Mafia guy may have ordered it. I know the Mafia never murders prosecutors, but this time they may have made an exception."

He paused. "We don't know who ordered it. Maybe no one ordered it. Maybe it was freelance. The idea looked good to one of those cretins, and he just did it."

He began giving out assignments.

There were only eight Chinese Americans in the department, two of whom worked out of this 5th Precinct on Community Relations only. The other six stood before him, and he ordered them to dig into the vendor's background. "Find out everything you can about him, about his associates and contacts. Anybody asks, he's being held on immigration violations. That's all you know." He named the poison used. "Anybody know anything about it?"

No one did.

"You get a chance, you hear anything about tetramine or Dushu-qiang you ask questions. Just casually, you might say. Whoever did this, we don't want to scare him off, understood?"

He sent the Chinese detectives out, and turned to the others, separating out several. They too were to try to find the source of the poison. "Start with the drug companies," he ordered. "Track it backward from there."

Most of the detectives left were specialists in one or the other of New York's five Mafia families. They were to go out into the city, talk to their Mafia contacts, find out what people were saying about the death by heart attack or perhaps stroke of Assistant DA Finley. They were to feel around for information without giving anything up.

"By now there should be talk," he said. "I want to know what it is."

He paused. "I can't tell you how delicate this case is," he said. "If the guy knows we're looking for him, we'll never find him. So as far as you're concerned, Assistant DA Finley died of a heart attack or stroke. Got that?"

Mafia types inhabited such a grotesque world, lived such grotesque lives that they could not keep their mouths shut. What they saw and what they did had to be talked about. Whenever a Mafia hit, or some other important crime occurred, the detectives almost always found out who did it and why within hours. Gabe could hope for the same information now. As evidence it would be mostly, probably entirely, hearsay, and therefore unusable in a court of law. But as information it was truer than most sworn statements, and could be relied on. Mafia hoodlums were the biggest gossips in the city, Gabe reflected now. And detectives were the second biggest, unfortunately.

The squadroom emptied out until only Detective Brough and a young detective named Lightner were left. "Get the photo books out, Brough. Show the Chinese guy every mug shot we have, see if he recognizes anybody."

"The Russo album you mean, right, Boss?"

"All of them," Chief Driscoll told him.

Brough looked surprised. "But Russo was the one Finley kept bad-mouthing these last few months, Chief. It was why I was guarding him. If anybody put out a contract on him, it would be Russo."

Not necessarily, thought Gabe, who had a funny feeling about this case. "Just do what I tell you." He had no intention of talking about hunches with this detective, or taking him into his confidence. "Lightner, you give him any help he needs."

He went downstairs. Head down, looking at nobody, he went out of the stationhouse and once outside was surprised to find that it was night. His car was there at the curb and he ordered himself driven to Earl's house in Yonkers.

He figured he had three days to find whoever it was who had killed Earl Finley. After that the guy would be in Sicily, or someplace. Perhaps it was too late already, the guy gone hours ago, out of reach forever.

At Yonkers every light in Earl's house was on, and Frank Redmond stood out on the stoop smoking.

He got out and walked up and shook hands with Frank. "How'd she take it?"

"Not well at first. She seems a bit better now. What happened to Earl?"

Gabe looked at him, considered telling him, then changed his mind. "He just collapsed in the street. By the time we got him to the hospital he was dead. When we have the autopsy we'll know more."

They went inside. His wife rolled forward and Gabe kissed her briefly. He shook hands with Earl's mother, who was sitting on a sofa. She looked to be in her eighties but seemed cheerful enough. Maureen Troy was there—Andy was coming in from an economic summit in Brazil and would arrive tomorrow, apparently—and Earl's son, who had come up on the shuttle from Washington where he was an intern at the Justice Department, but not his daughter, who had a husband and children, lived in Milwaukee, and was due any minute. A number of other assistant DAs from Earl's office were there — the mayor was due later, it was said — and some other people whom Gabe had not met before, or did not remember.

He found Rocky in the kitchen fixing still another pot of coffee, strands of damp hair hanging in her face, and he embraced her, and told her the same fairy story he had told Frank Redmond: They were awaiting the results of the autopsy. While he was answering her questions Frank came in and stood in the doorway.

Gabe left soon after and went back to the Chinatown station-house, and looked through the one-way glass at Brough slowly showing pages of photo albums to the prisoner.

Presently Brough came out and dropped a four-by-six photo onto the desk in front of Chief Driscoll.

"He thinks this might be the guy, Chief."

Gabe turned the photo over and read the name and affiliation on the other side: Bruno Catana, a soldier in the Luchese family.

"Not one of Russo's men then," Brough said.

Gabe nodded.

"So are you surprised, Chief?"

"No." He looked around for Lightner. "Get me the sheet on this guy, and whatever else we have." To Brough he said: "Prepare an album of six photos, this one and five others. Guys who look more or less like him. Show them to the prisoner. See if he picks out the same photo a second time."

Photo identifications were, some said, notoriously unreliable. In any case they were easily challenged in court. One took in advance what precautions one could.

Brough carried the new album back into the interrogation room. Gabe could see them talking through the window.

"The prisoner picked out the same photo as before," said Detective Brough when he came out.

"All right," Gabe said.

"Shall I book him, take him to court?"

"No," said Gabe. "Call up Immigration, have them come and get him."

"Those guys."

Gabe had no more respect for Immigration agents than Brough did — than any cop did. It was a corrupt, inefficient agency, but because it was obliged to file no formal charges under the law, it was ideal, in a case like this, for holding people incommunicado for indefinite periods.

"Go with them," Gabe ordered. "Make it clear we suspect him of other crimes. Make sure they hold him."

Chief Driscoll stayed in the squadroom until midnight, talking to the detectives as they came in, then sending them out again. From time to time he studied Bruno Catana's yellow sheet, or gazed at his photo. A high school dropout, 28 years old. Had been arrested eight times for extortion, assault, and other strong-arm crimes. Had spent a total of eight years in jail. The mug shot showed a young tough from 168th Street in Washington Heights. A Luchese man. A made man, meaning he had successfully proven himself, probably by killing someone. Having taken the oath, he had been inducted as a full-fledged Mafioso. From the Lucheses' point of view, a man absolutely disciplined and reliable. So it was impossible for Gabe to believe that Catana had decided to murder Earl on his own. Or that he would take orders to do so except from the very top.

A murder that went against all past Mafia tradition. A murder that would, however, seem to have been ordered by Russo.

A Mafia power struggle then.

Though baited by Earl for months, Russo had made no reaction.

In the Mafia world this made him seem weak, even tottering. And then, or so it was meant to appear, he commits the incredible stupidity of murdering a prosecutor. The Mafia Commission would meet, perhaps had already met, and would give permission that Russo be whacked. Whoever whacked him would get to take over most of his rackets. The other families would divide up the rest.

That night and for two more days and nights Gabe waited, while his men reported in. The detectives working the drug companies found nothing, but one of the Chinese detectives managed to track the poison to a defrocked Chinese druggist, who had been implicated in past poisonings in Chinatown. Though never convicted, he had been stripped of his license.

Chief Driscoll sent the same detective and two others out to arrest the druggist.

When he had been brought in they began showing him photos. He too identified Catana. Meanwhile other detectives staked out the building in which Catana lived, and tailed his girlfriend. They got a judge to sign a wiretap order, and wired his phone and also his mother's. But the tails and the wiretap accomplished nothing. The detectives visited all Catana's usual haunts, and talked to most of his contacts. No one admitted seeing him.

The city's chief medical examiner had signed the autopsy report, certifying poison as cause of death, but Chief Driscoll had impounded all copies of the report. Nominally at least, the investigation was still secret.

The detectives, and there were many of them out there every day, could not find Catana. Who must know by now they were looking for him.

Possibly his body would turn up, Detective Brough said hopefully. But, believing the Lucheses would protect him, Gabe told the detective not to count on it.

He took time out to go one night to Earl's wake. The pathologists had sliced and hacked the body to pieces, then sewed it up again, so the coffin was closed. Frank and Andy were both there, and many other people as well, as were some reporters fishing for information, for there had been rumors. Gabe smiled a lot, and put them off. He talked to Rocky, who seemed cheerful enough under the circumstances. But she was like the hostess at a cocktail party, moving rapidly from group to group. She could not keep still. Frank said he had talked to her at length about her future. She was like all new widows, he said, she was worried about money. She did not know how much Earl had left — not much apparently — nor how she was to survive. Like most widows it had been years since she had had to earn her own living. Frank seemed to be keeping an eye on her, and from time to time he backed her into a corner and put his hands on her shoulders, and talked softly to her and calmed her down.

Andy drew Gabe aside. "Frank and I are going to speak at the funeral. Do you want to say something as well?"

But Gabe hurriedly declined. "I'm no good at speeches."

Andy laughed. "The idea terrifies you, doesn't it?"

"Not at all," said Gabe. "Certainly not."

Andy was still chuckling.

"You and Frank do it."

The next morning was the funeral. Father Redmond said the Mass of the Resurrection, and then gave a homily that concentrated mostly on Earl as a boy, Earl in motion, Earl high above the diving board, spinning, flipping, the parentheses of his bowed legs, his blond hair flying. Before Frank was finished he had much of the church in tears.

Next came Andy Troy, who had written a touching tribute about Earl the dedicated prosecutor, his voice cracking as he read it. This same tribute appeared in his paper the next day on the Op-Ed page.

Rocky, it seemed to Gabe, was dry-eyed throughout, though her children, sitting to either side of her, looked teary enough. They all went on to the cemetery. After the graveside ceremony the widow invited the mourners to her house for sandwiches and coffee, but Chief Driscoll excused himself and went back to work.

The truth about Earl's death was about to break in all the papers, he sensed. For days he had smothered it. As far as the world knew, Earl Finley had been felled by a heart attack. But there had been leaks. Increasingly he had fielded calls from reporters who knew part of the story, and demanded more. And still no sign of Bruno Catana.

If Chief Driscoll was to make something happen, he had almost no time left.

He had himself driven home where he dismissed his driver, for there must be no police witnesses to what happened next. He stood on the sidewalk in front of his building and watched the department car drive off, watched the brake lights come on as it slowed at the corner, making sure it was gone. Next, figuring he had three or more hours to kill, he went upstairs and had a long dinner with his wife. They dawdled over it. Talking to her took his mind off what he meant to do.

When it was time to go he left his gun on top of the refrigerator, the five bullets upright beside it, told Barbara not to wait up for him, and went out. It was then about ten P.M. He walked around the corner to the garage where he kept his personal car. It took about ten minutes for the attendant to bring it out. While waiting Gabe started to question himself, and to fret.

He drove up to the north Bronx mostly through heavy traffic toward a roadhouse on Boston Road called Angelo's which was owned by Dominic "The Fist" Russo, or so it was believed, for someone else's name was on the deed. Russo was known to occupy a table there most nights. It was where he conducted much of his business.

Gabe had this information from detectives who had been tracking Russo's movements off and on for months. If you had business with Russo, this was where you found him.

But various federal agencies would be tracking Russo too. They would know all about this roadhouse. How close were the Feds to this guy? Were they taking down license plate numbers of the cars parked outside? Were they photographing everyone who entered or left? Did they have listening devices planted under the tables, in the toilets? If called before a grand jury to explain what he was doing there, Gabe would have no legitimate explanation.

When he had reached the door the risk to his career seemed so enormous that he almost turned back. Bad idea, he told himself. He had called off his own men for tonight. He had not, obviously, called off the Feds.

He hesitated only briefly, then went through the door into the din. The place was dimly lit, crowded, smoky, noisy, waiters moving through with trays above their heads. And there was Russo, just as described, sitting at a table in the back, a short chunky man with massive hands, his back to the wall, a plate of pasta in front of him, his thugs around him. Other men, even as Gabe watched, came by to offer the standard Mafia tribute, which was envelopes containing money.

Instead of approaching him, Gabe glanced around trying to spot any FBI agents present. He was alone, unarmed, with no backup. Worse, he was exposing himself to whatever federal surveillance was in place. He had been careful to park three blocks away and walk in. His plate number, he could be reasonably sure, would not turn up in some agent's report. He was wearing a raincoat with its collar turned up, the fedora on his head pulled down to keep his face dark. So photos of him, if any, would be difficult to identify. Or so he could hope.

It was the best he could do.

Finally he approached Russo's table. When he was about five paces away that entire part of the restaurant went silent, for in Russo's circle Chief Driscoll's face was as recognizable as a film star's. Every Mafioso in the room knew who he was, but not what he wanted. It was the conversation of Russo and his men that went silent first, but the silence spread slowly, then fast, until the noise level collapsed all over the restaurant. Even the legitimate patrons glanced nervously this way and that.

As Chief Driscoll continued to approach, Russo's men crowded around him, but the Mafia chieftain gave a jerk of his chin, and they faded back.

"Sit down," Russo said, "do you want to eat?"

Gabe looked at the big fleecy hands and knew why he was called "The Fist." Russo must have had bad acne as a teenager, for the scars showed through the stubble of his beard. Gabe said: "Where can we talk?"

"What do we have to talk about?"

Gabe continued to stare at him.

Russo said: "I got to take a piss."

Pushing back from the pasta, he stood up and, accompanied by three of his men, went out through a door at the side of the room. After a moment, Gabe followed. Beyond the door was a corridor leading to the toilets. When he came to the door marked UOMINI he found it blocked by one of the gorillas who stood with his back to it, barring entrance. But he stepped aside and let Gabe pass.

Gabe opened the door into the stale urine aroma. Russo stood at a urinal, his squat muscular form all but blotting it out. To all appearances he was intent on what he was doing. One of the two remaining gorillas leaned against the sink, the other against the far wall. The arms of both were folded across their chests, and they watched Gabe.

As he turned from the urinal, Russo zipped up.

Gabe said: "You should air this place out once in a while."

Russo went to the sink. The gorilla there stepped aside, and he washed his hands.

Gabe said: "A toilet pungent as this is bad for business. You might consider assigning someone to give it a good scrubbing. These two guys here look like they'd do a good job."

One of them started toward Gabe, but Russo stopped him with a look. After eyeing Gabe, the Mafioso gave another jerk of his chin. This caused one of the gorillas to grab Gabe's briefcase. Russo seemed able to communicate with his hirelings without speaking, Gabe noted, holding tight to the briefcase for a moment, before releasing it. It was handed to Russo, who glanced inside, then stood it by its corner in the sink.

Another nod, and one of the gorillas said to Gabe: "Legs spread. Put your hands on the stall door. You know how to do it, don't you? How does it feel, Cocksucker?"

Gabe had assumed the four-point stance to which cops habitually subjected prisoners. He felt the hands moving roughly over his body.

The gorilla said: "He's not carrying, Padrone."

"Where's your gun?" said Russo.

"I figured I wouldn't need it tonight. If anything happens, you'll protect me, won't you?"

"See if he's wired," Russo ordered.

Gabe was obliged to strip to the waist. Each article of clothing, as he removed it, was mauled and squeezed by Russo's men.

"What do you know," said Gabe, "I'm not wired."

"It could be hidden behind his balls," one of the men said. "Take your pants off."

"Since when do you employ fags?" Gabe said. "I'm not going to let these two fags go sniffing around my private parts."

Fists balled up, one of them started toward Gabe. A jerk of Russo's chin stopped him. A second jerk of chin sent both of them out of the men's room.

"What do you want?" said Russo.

Ignoring him, Gabe buttoned his shirt, then thrust the shirttails down into his pants. When fully dressed he reached into his briefcase and withdrew the photo of Bruno Catana.

"You know this guy?"

Russo studied the photo. "No."

Gabe glanced up at the ceiling, at the light fixtures. "Let's go for a walk."

"No need," Russo said. "My men are experts, we sweep this place twice a day."

"Let me tell you something, Pal. If the FBI decided to put a bug in here, the kind of men you hire wouldn't find it if they looked ten years. Let's go for a walk."

He strode out of the men's room, past the three thugs outside. Russo must have followed, for he heard him mutter: "Get me my coat."

Outside Gabe waited on the sidewalk under a tree. Presently Russo joined him.

"Sweet sound, traffic like that," Gabe said. "People who monitor listening devices hate it. Background noise, that's all they get. Assistant DA Finley didn't die of a heart attack. He was poisoned."

"Poisoned?"

"A very sophisticated poison. I've kept it quiet until now, but tomorrow or the next day you're going to read about it in the papers."

"Two in the head would have been easier."

"Papers will probably say you ordered it."

"Maybe I did."

"I don't think you're that stupid."

"Poison is for women."

"You're the one with the motive."

"Do I look like a woman to you?"

"Our information is the Lucheses are behind it. To embarrass you."

"Sounds like them. The Lucheses are women."

"You ask yourself why the Lucheses would want to embarrass you like that," Gabe said. "I can think of reasons. In your place, I'd watch my ass."

"The guy in the photo?"

"Name's Bruno Catana."

After a pause Russo said: "Why tell me this?"

"I want Catana. Our guys can't find him, and we've run out of time. If he isn't gone yet, he soon will be. I'm betting you can find him."

"You want to make a rat out of me."

"It's in your interest as much as ours."

Russo said nothing.

"You give him to us and I'll publicly exonerate you. I'll owe you one, as well."

Russo's head came up, and by the light of the street lamp they eyed each other.

"Cooperation," Gabe said. "If I don't get it I'll put every man I have on your operation. Your men won't be able to spit with without getting arrested. I'll cost you a fortune in legal bills."

"Don't threaten me, you fuck."

"I want him whole," Gabe said. "I don't want him killed."

But he was talking to the Mafia capo's back. The meeting was over.

Gabe watched him all the way to his roadhouse. The broad back and heavy shoulders. The short legs no tailoring could lengthen. The big fists.

Would Russo send out men to find Catana? Probably. Gabe did not see where he had any choice. Would they find him? Again, probably. Then what? The legal case against Catana was weak. It rested on photo identifications by the Chinese hot-dog vendor and the

Chinese pharmacist, both of whom were coconspirators an eventual jury might choose to disbelieve. Juries often—even usually—disbelieved such people. And probably the case could not be made stronger, because any additional witnesses would have to be Mafia types. Mafia types would go to jail for contempt rather than testify. This was part of their tradition. It was part of what made the prosecution of Mafiosi so incredibly difficult, almost impossible.

As he walked back to his car Gabe realized that he did not really want Earl's murderer brought in alive. Not only might Catana beat the case, but he himself dreaded having to face him, could not bear the thought of having to look at him. At the same time Catana must be made to pay the full penalty; otherwise the assassination of law enforcement personnel might look good to future Mafia capos, future Bruno Catanas.

No, he did not want him brought in alive, and had just assured that he would not be. His conversation with Russo was the equivalent of putting out a hit contract on Bruno Catana. That's how others would see it. It was how Russo had seen it. Was that what he had intended all along? The idea made him shiver. Mafia justice had no room for the police, or for courts. If Russo's men found Catana he would not be turned over to Chief Driscoll. Instead, his body, in a few days, would be found garroted, or riddled with bullets, having previously been mutilated in some disgusting way. This was standard Mafia practice. It was how punishment was distributed, discipline maintained, balance reestablished.

I'm no better than they are, Gabe told himself. He was in his car by that time, moving in lights and noise and heavy traffic along major avenues, but then a voice came into existence inside him, to which he listened, the voice of one of his Jesuit professors at Fordham, or perhaps of all of them. His conversation with Russo, this voice told him, the action he had just performed, was in itself neither moral nor immoral. His principal motive for this action had been to prevent future assassinations, which was morally good. His secondary motives need not be considered because they were collateral, and therefore morally neutral. His original action had been complete in itself, it did not extend into the future. Any future actions would be Russo's doing, not his own, he was in no way attached to them. His own action had ended just now at the moment when Russo had walked away from him.

The dichotomy—something Catholics like himself were so good at—was perfect. He was guilty of nothing.

He put the radio on and listened to music for a time, then turned it off. The above argument was no doubt flawless, but did not satisfy him. It seemed to him that he was guilty as charged.

THE NEXT DAY HE PHONED FRANK REDMOND, told him Earl had been murdered, and asked him to come with him to tell Rocky.

"How long have you known this?" Frank asked in the car driving up to Yonkers.

"From the start," said Gabe.

"You could have told me," the priest said.

"I hated to hold out on you, Frank."

Father Redmond was half amused. "You thought I'd tell Andy."

"I was going to tell you, and then I thought: If you want to keep a secret, you tell nobody."

"And Andy would put it in the paper."

"If he knew he might feel he had to."

Andy at that moment was on a plane back to the economic summit in Brazil.

They found Rocky and her daughter, both wearing shorts and T-shirts, cleaning the house.

"Stuff I've been begging Earl to throw out for years," Rocky explained, pointing to piles of refuse beside the front door. "Old magazines, old schoolbooks, old clothes. He can't stop me now, can he."

The girl was about 25, blond like her father, but with her mother's big eyes, full lips, and nice legs.

Gabe sat them all down at the kitchen table, waited while the daughter made and poured out coffee, then said what he had come to say.

"We have two of the guys who did this, and we'll find the other one," he concluded.

Rocky's face had got dark, her lips tight together. "Earl brought it on himself. You told him to stop baiting those people, I told him to stop. He wouldn't."

"Nobody is responsible for getting himself murdered," said Frank gently.

"Earl was." And she started to cry. Then she wiped her eyes and forced a rather ghastly smile.

"We'll break this case," said Gabe. "We'll get the guy."

"It's done," she said. "Who cares who did it."

Gabe knew better than to take this as a rebuke. A widow as recent as Rocky was liable to say anything.

Presently he rose to go, but Frank remained seated. "Coming, Frank?"

Frank said to the two women: "Why don't I take you both out to lunch?"

"Not me," the girl said. "Take Mom. She needs to get out."

"How will you get home?" Gabe said.

"Rocky can take me to the train."

They all trooped out to the front door. Good-byes were said. Gabe got into his car.

A WEEK LATER CATANA'S BODY WAS FOUND in Little Italy in a cellar on Mulberry Street after residents complained about the odor. His Luchese connections had not been able to save him, or perhaps had not wanted to. Catana's forearms and legs were broken, he had been hacked at with a hatchet, or some similar instrument, perhaps several of them, and had been allowed to bleed out, which must have taken a while. There was blood everywhere.

Looking down on him, Gabe again thought: I did this. I am as bad as they are. The dichotomy between action and reaction, the grand Catholic dichotomy he had so carefully worked out and counted on, did not help. He felt oppressed by guilt. Of being, if not a murderer, at least an accessory to murder. If still a practicing Catholic he would have taken this heaviness in his chest into the confessional and told the priest and been absolved. He would have come out feeling lighter, and perhaps purified. But there was no one to go to, had not been for years.

Afterward he never mentioned to anyone the guilt he had felt.

The deputy commissioner for Organized Crime Control, Gabe's boss, called a press conference at which he accused Catana of the murder of Assistant DA Earl Finley, revealed the evidence against him, and declared the case solved. The investigation into the murder of Catana himself was continuing, he said.

But as far as Gabe was concerned it was not continuing. There was nothing to go on. It was instead one of those Mafia hits on which no usable evidence would ever come to light.

THE INVESTIGATION

9

CHIEF DRISCOLL IS IN THE PRECINCT, WALKING THE STREETS, his department car trailing behind. For a week the investigation has not budged. He has read the DD-5s. They reach his desk via department mail at the rate of two or three a day. There seems to him a proper rhythm to them, a direction. The detectives have gone back over every lead, reexamined every dead end. They appear to be working conscientiously.

He has forced himself, until this afternoon, to stay out of the precinct.

He goes into the tenement and up the four flights. He has kept his key to the roof. Outside in the late afternoon cold, he stands peering about, a stocky man with narrow eyes wearing a fedora. There are patches of snow up here now. The sun is cold. There is a wind. He pulls his coat collar up, tugs the hat down over his mostly bald head. The parapet is still only knee-high. A man standing where he is standing, if unsuspecting, could be pushed over the edge with ease.

There are rooftops all about him, but they are vacant and, for New York, low. The skyscrapers start about two miles south, a wall of them, as if belonging to a different city. To the northwest, about the same distance off, rise the girders and stanchions of the George Washington Bridge, taller than all the houses in between. The bridge delimits the river of course. It delimits also that edge of the city, and of the state.

He glances at the parapet again, imagines his friend flying. Did Frankie go silently? Gabe blinks his eyes.

The roof has no answers for him, tells him nothing, never has.

He goes down to the street and, signaling his driver to follow, walks to Frankie's church. Inside, he sidles into a pew. The place is small, dim, and empty. Puffs of incense linger in the air, and he inhales them. There must have been a funeral here this morning, he thinks. He visualizes the smoking thuribles on their short chains, the altar boys swinging the smoke this way and that, as he himself once did, the smoke rising, the odor with it, for hours clinging to everything. He remembers his boyhood piety, remembers the odor of wax as well. Incense and exhausted candles, a blend. These are the odors of Catholicism, and they are as familiar to him as sun and sky.

What does he expect to find sitting here in this pew? The investigation has stalled. He is looking for an idea, even the hint of an idea, some new direction to send the detectives into. There has to be an explanation for Frankie's death. There has to be something, somewhere.

His driver comes in to get him. "A call just came over," he says. "Your office wants you to contact Lt. Begos on a landline."

The police radio is for code signals, orders, instructions, not conversation. He has no cell phone. The cell phone is not yet practical enough for widespread use. A landline means a phone booth, and in Harlem most booths have been vandalized, the receivers most often ripped, or half ripped, off the box.

Gabe gets into his car. "Take me there."

The Three-Two stationhouse is on West 135th Street, less than five minutes away. He will skip the intervening phone call.

He gets out of his car in front, goes in past the security cop, and up the stairs to the second-floor squadroom, and into Begos's office.

"You got something for me?" Gabe says. He takes the chair in front of the desk, and immediately feels diminished. He feels like a detective about to be dressed down by his superior, or a prisoner about to be booked. I shouldn't have come here, he tells himself at once. I've put myself in a position of weakness. I should have made him come to my office. In the Police Department such nuances are important. But Begos has news of the investigation—why else would he have called—and Driscoll wants to know as fast as possible what it is.

"It's about Poindexter," Begos says. "You know, the gun dealer that Father Redmond broke his jaw some years back."

"I seem to remember the name."

"You wanted us to find him."

"Don't string me along, please."

"We've put in a lot of hours looking for the mutt."

"Come on, I've got things to do."

"Well, the priest breaks the mutt's jaw, you remember. His hand too, I think. Mutt's in the hospital five or six days. Eats dinner through a straw. We can't handcuff him to the bedpost because of civil rights and all that horseshit. The press would roast us. We have to have guards on him around the clock."

"You got nothing." Driscoll rises as if to go.

"I'm coming to it."

"Speed it up."

"I talked to the guy who was precinct commander at the time. He was a captain then. He's a deputy chief now."

"Chief Burnside. He's chief of Support Services Division. He's got nothing to do with any of this."

"He's still burned up about losing all those cops to guard duty."

"You got something to tell me, or not?"

"Captain Sloane, the present precinct commander, is pretty burned up at all the hours we've put in investigating the priest's death. Same thing."

Driscoll turns toward the door. "I don't have time to listen to this."

"We did find Poindexter. Or find out about him. He got out of jail" — Begos consults his notes — "May the sixteenth, two and a half years back." He pauses, letting the suspense build, making Gabe wait. "He's back on the street less than a month and he's sticking up a store. Got in a shoot-out with two cops. Guess who won?"

Begos is 35, has been a lieutenant five months. Gabe has taken the trouble to look this up. What he does not know is where the young man's insolence comes from. Nor why he makes so little effort to hide it.

"So that particular mutt," Begos says, "had nothing to do with the priest's death."

"Took you long enough to find out."

Begos goes to the door and calls out for Detective Spadia.

"How many days you put in finding out about Poindexter, Cliff?"

"Six days, not to mention the overtime I probably won't get paid for." Spadia, who stands in the doorway, turns toward Chief Driscoll. "None of the records were where they were supposed to be, Chief. You know how it is."

Gabe does know how it is. Records relating to every case are out there somewhere, but some are held by the police, some by Corrections, some by the district attorneys, of which New York, being divided into five counties, has five. Not to mention those held by the various federal agencies. The law enforcement world is vast, its arms outspread in many directions, and there is no central system, much less a central collecting point. The police arrest someone, and a folder is begun. The perpetrator then goes on to the prosecutor, and what happens to him there the police may never know. That is, information as he proceeds through the system often enough does not come back. The perpetrator, if convicted, goes to prison — he is now in the hands of Corrections. Same thing — he's gone. The prosecutor may never learn what follows, much less the police. Detectives investigating a new case must go from agency to agency begging for information. It takes time. Most of the agencies most times are cooperative, though not always. Even within the police department, information is fragmented. Narcotics has some, Homicide. Intelligence, which is part of Gabe's command, is supposed to have it all, but doesn't. The number of crimes, the number of criminals, is overwhelming, and they are constantly being renewed. His files, Gabe knows, are inadequate. Not enough men, not even enough filing cabinets. He is trying to do something about it, but the going is slow.

Gabe has no quarrel with Detective Spadia. "I guess they ran you from office to office, eh, Cliff?"

"Right, Chief."

"If you'll excuse us, Cliff."

When Spadia has gone out, Chief Driscoll carefully closes the door, for he knows better than to humiliate a commander in front of his men. It makes you look small, and often it ruins the commander.

He turns to Lt. Begos. "Probably there's more you haven't even told me yet."

"Yes there is, Chief."

"Do you know what a 61 is?"

"Everybody knows what a 61 is."

"I'm asking if you know."

"Of course."

"Good. What you're going to do, you're going to send me a 61 on this case. Take your time. Write six pages, ten, twenty, whatever it takes. The entire case. When you've got it all done, you hand carry it to my office — you make an appointment with my secretary first — and you stand in front of my desk and you read it to me. Clear?"

Chief Driscoll steps to the door. "And in the meantime figure out what the investigation may have missed, and keep the men looking."

He goes out. Begos behind him watches him go.

CHAPTER NINE

ROCKY HAD LOOKED FROM FATHER REDMOND to her daughter and back again. Had looked doubtful.

"You need to get out of this house, Mom. Go with Father Redmond."

Finally: "All right, but I'll have to change first." And she disappeared up the stairs for a time.

In the hall Frank stood with her daughter, whose name was Sheila.

"You knew Mom before Dad did, I think."

"Yes, I introduced them to each other."

"And one of the results was me."

He smiled. "Yes."

"Did you know Dad's father, my grandfather?"

"No. I'm not sure your dad did either. He vanished just after your dad was born, I think, never to reappear. Your dad didn't have such an easy life."

"And then to end the way he did. Do you know anything more about—about what happened?"

"No. But we may find out more later."

"It won't bring him back, though."

"No."

"You look uncomfortable. Mom always takes a long time."

"I guess your father was used to waiting for his wife to change her clothes and get ready." The priest smiled again.

"If you're going to try to help Mom, you better get used to it."

They watched Rocky come down the stairs. She had put on a plaid skirt and a red sweater with the sleeves pushed up on her forearms just as she used to do in college. To her daughter, and to Frank as well, she looked clean and scrubbed, as if she had washed away most of the grief and some of the years as well. She rarely wore makeup, and wore none now, being one of those rare women — and she knew this about herself — who did not need to. Her full lips had enough of the rose in them already, her cheeks as well, and her eyes were exceedingly blue.

As they went out the door, Sheila called after them: "Have a nice time."

"Does the way I'm dressed shock you?" Rocky asked as they crossed the driveway. "I don't own much in black, and anyway I decided I didn't want to go out looking like a widow."

"You look lovely."

"Save your flattery, Frank. I've known you too long."

"How about: You look as good as the first day I ever saw you."

"You are nice at times."

They reached the car, and both got in.

"Where would you like to eat?" she asked him, settling herself behind the wheel. "Would the local greasy spoon suit you?"

"Let's go to a restaurant with tablecloths. I know one in Scarsdale, unless you think it's too far."

"Yes, you used to be stationed there."

"Stationed there. The military term. But that's about what it is, this business I'm in."

They drove there and went inside, where Frank glanced around at the other tables, as if worried about being recognized.

"Are you afraid someone will see you out with me?" asked Rocky with amusement.

"Someone who remembers me from my days as a curate here? No, and I don't care if anyone does."

Rocky looked at him over the menu and said: "I want to thank you for the way you told me of Earl's death. It could not have been easy for you. You were gentle and kind. You did it beautifully."

"He was my friend since we were thirteen years old."

"I didn't realize you could be so sensitive. I haven't seen much of your sensitive side these past few years."

"Have I been as bad as that?"

"And you've got a great shoulder to cry on."

"Hey, I was crying just as hard on yours."

She gave a wry laugh. "My eyes were pouring out tears. I was afraid I was going to melt that roman collar of yours."

When the waiter had come and taken their orders, he said: "How are you, really? How do you feel?"

"Okay," she said, and stopped.

"You have to talk about it, you know."

"I bet that's what you say to all the widows."

"It won't go away if you don't."

"I know."

After a pause, he said: "Well then, what's your strongest emotion at the moment?"

She smiled. "Anger at Earl for leaving me in this mess."

"Apart from your anger at Earl."

"Surprise, I think."

"Not grief?"

"I'm over the grief for the time being. But I'm not over the surprise of finding myself a widow. I wasn't ready. Eventually, yes. I think every woman expects her husband to die first. Look around you. Where are all the old men? All you see is old ladies."

She toyed with a knife. "I expected to be one of them one day, tottering around smelling stale and telling my great-grandchildren how beautiful I was once, and how fast I could run. But so soon?"

"Earl didn't leave you entirely alone. You have your children."

Rocky said firmly: "Sheila's going back where she came from tomorrow. And Billy's already gone back. I refuse to be a burden to my children."

"Is that such a good idea? You do need support. Every widow does, this soon after her husband's death. You mustn't imagine you can get by without it."

She grinned at him. "You'll be my support, won't you, Frank?"

"Sure."

"Thank you, but I refuse to be a burden to you, too."

He said: "And learning your husband was murdered couldn't have made it any easier for you. It's a brutal thing to hear and it must be hard to accept."

She shrugged. "This morning, hearing Gabe's voice on the phone, I knew exactly what he was coming up here to tell me. I never believed for a minute Earl died of a heart attack. I can't tell you the number of nights I've lain with my head on his chest hearing it beat."

She looked down at the table. "He had a very strong heart. There was nothing wrong with his heart."

To give her a moment to compose herself, Frank glanced around the restaurant. Most of the tables were occupied by women lunching together, and they looked rich. In a town where the men flowed out toward New York each morning, not to flow back again until dark, this was to be expected.

"It wasn't a particularly good marriage," Rocky said. "We slept in the same bed every night. Otherwise we didn't see each other very much. He'd come home late and leave early. He was always working. That's what he loved, not me."

"He was crazy about you," Frank lied. "He told me so many times."

"Did he? I don't think I believe you."

For a moment both were silent.

Rocky said: "Anyway, I miss him."

"Yes, me too."

This caused another silence, which lingered until Frank sought to end it with a comment that was not, perhaps, as lighthearted as he thought. Gesturing at the tables all around, he said: "I keep imagining I'm being stared at. People see the collar, see me having lunch with a beautiful woman, and start asking themselves questions."

"Wondering who we are, you mean."

"They must think I'm a Protestant minister having lunch with my wife."

"Or else that you're what you are, and having lunch with your mistress."

"Oh, no one would think that."

"Are you telling me priests never have mistresses?"

"Maybe it happens once in a great while. I've never heard of it, but maybe. If it does it's never spoken of."

"Really?"

"Really."

"You priests amaze me."

Had she hurt him by referring to him as a priest rather than just as a man? Probably he wanted everyone to see him as a man first, and as a priest only after. She knew enough about this man, and about the pride of men in general, to suppose priests no different from other men in that respect.

He said: "Do you ever dive anymore?"

"I haven't in years. Earl and I used to dive for the children sometimes. It made them giggle."

"Do you think you could still do it?"

"The easy stuff, maybe. I imagine it's like riding a bicycle. You never forget."

"You were fun to watch."

"The hard stuff I probably couldn't do, couldn't get around on them without a lot of practice, and maybe not even then."

"If you ever decide to dive again, let me know, I'll be there."

"Well, the weather doesn't lend itself to that right now. One day I'll dive for you. But you'll be disappointed, I'm sure."

She seemed to enjoy talking about diving. Was this because, as a subject, it was so neutral?

The waiter returned and they were served. During lunch the conversation became quite banal.

"The rolls are good, aren't they?"

"What would you like for dessert?"

"Nothing, thank you."

"Coffee?"

The waiter hovered.

"No coffee either," she said. "I haven't been sleeping well the past few days."

"That will pass," Frank said.

"You have coffee, if you like."

"Coffee doesn't bother me," said Frank, "I haven't slept well for years."

He sipped it slowly while looking across the table at her.

She had nice hands, one of them toying with a fork. He wanted to take up that hand or the other, and hold it a moment. He wished to make contact with her, and to comfort her. But she might get the wrong impression. As the luncheon progressed, the desire to touch her remained, but he stifled it, kept his hands in his lap.

"I should go back," she said.

"We could stay a little longer."

She shook her head. "I've left my daughter cleaning the house by herself, which isn't fair. And also—"

"Also what?"

"Also I've enjoyed so much having lunch with you, and if I stay I may bore you to the point that you won't ask me again."

"Bore me? Are you crazy?"

She drove him to the station and they sat in the car talking until the train came in. Then both got out.

"Thank you for lunch, Frank." She kissed him on the cheek.

He boarded. From the window he watched her back her car out of the slot, and turn toward home.

Six days went by before he called her again. Would she be interested in having lunch with him tomorrow?

He drove his old car up to Yonkers and turned into her street where leaves blew along the gutters. The sidewalks were dappled, multicolored, soaked with light.

She came out and got in beside him, smiling, looking happy, but squirming a bit as she tried to get comfortable.

"Something's sticking into me through the seat."

"There may be a broken spring."

"And it's trying to get through the upholstery, and also my dress. It just stabbed me in the you-know-what."

"I worked on it a week or so ago. I thought I had it fixed."

"How long have you had this car?"

"A fair amount of time."

"It's obvious you don't have a wife."

"How can you tell?"

"I think a wife would probably suggest you buy a new car."

He was amused. "I'll think about it."

"And keep suggesting it, too."

He pulled into the curb, where he said solicitously: "You drive and I'll sit on that side."

She laughed. "I'm exaggerating. It's not that bad."

So they were much easier with each other than they had been the week before.

Frank parked in front of the same restaurant and they got out. The difference this time was that Frank, instead of his clerical suit, wore jeans and a big sweater.

When they were seated Rocky said: "I think I like you better dressed this way."

"My pastor caught me going out and ordered me to go back and put on my suit and collar."

"Aren't you supposed to obey him?"

"I probably should obey him more than I do."

The waiter handed them menus.

"What do you do next?" he asked her.

"Look for a job first. After the kids left home I worked at one or two small jobs. As a volunteer mostly. I've got to find something better, if I can. Something that pays."

She gave him a smirk. "Failing that, I better start looking for a rich husband."

"Earl could have been rich, if he'd wanted."

"He wasn't interested in money. My next husband will be, believe me."

"How soon will you start looking for one?"

"Maybe I was joking. Marry some man I don't know, with whom I have no past in common? I'm not sure I really want to."

He nodded.

"But I may have to."

Frank said nothing.

"I have to find myself a social life as well. The first thing that happens when you're a widow is that everybody drops you. People move in couples. Nobody has room for a single woman."

"Yes, I've heard that."

"Being a widow is not so easy."

Her face brightened. "Maureen Troy called. We went to the movies together one night, and last Saturday we went to a Broadway matinee. Andy's never home, so Maureen is sort of a widow too. Maybe we can fill up a part of each other's lives."

He picked up the bottle of chardonnay he had ordered. "Would you like some wine?" When she nodded he half filled both glasses, and they raised them to each other.

Presently the waiter came, setting down their plates. For a time they ate in silence.

"How are you fixed for money?"

She grimaced. "Not good. I'll have to sell my house, I think. Do you know how much a house costs in taxes, heating, upkeep?"

She told him, adding: "It's too big for one woman anyway."

He was silent.

"And I'm never alone in there. Earl is in all the rooms. He's all around me."

"I should think that would make you feel more comfortable."

"No, less comfortable. That part of my life is over. I have to go on to something else."

"Leaving Earl behind."

"I don't mean to sound brutal, but Earl is dead."

He said: "I have money, if you need some to tide you over."

"Where would you get money?"

"I do get paid a salary, you know."

"It can't be a great deal."

"No, but it's more than I have much use for."

"And into the bank it goes."

"Usually."

"Where it grows and grows."

"I don't have anything to spend it on."

"Like a new car, for instance. Right."

"The one I have runs fine. And I'll get that spring fixed. The money's yours if you need it."

"Thank you, but no thanks. I'm a big girl. I'll get out of this on my own."

"I'd like to help you," Frank said. "If you want me to, that is."

"You're very sweet. Did anyone ever tell you that?"

They ordered dessert, and while waiting she said thoughtfully: "I notice you haven't been trying to convert me to Catholicism, the way you used to when we were—" She stopped.

"—courting," he said.

She laughed. "I think I was going to say 'when we were lovers.'"

As soon as the words were out she wondered why she had said them. If those incidents, now so far in the past, were ones he truly wished to forget, he might become angry.

But he only looked down at the table.

"Well, we were lovers," she said. "You might as well admit it to yourself."

Much to her relief he smiled. He also ducked further conversation in that vein. He said: "Somewhere along the line I got away from trying to convert everyone I meet."

"Why?"

"I came to the conclusion, contrary to what I was taught at Fordham and at the seminary, that there is more than one way to find God."

He fell silent.

"And that people ought to be allowed to take the road that suits them," she concluded.

"Something like that."

She thought over what this told her about him.

"What do you really believe these days, Frank?"

"I'm no longer quite so sure. I feel a bit lost, if you want to know the truth."

This admission so startled her that she found herself unable to meet his eyes. She thought he might say more, and was unwilling to prompt him. But when she looked up again he was gazing out the window. Whatever else he might have said he had decided, apparently, to keep to himself.

"People bare their souls to you, don't they?"

"Some do."

"But you can't bare your soul to anybody."

"I'm out of practice, I guess. There has been no one to bare it to. Until —"

"Until what?"

"Until perhaps you."

"Until me? Well, I'm listening."

"In Vietnam, in Africa, in Harlem — I've had to be stronger than anyone. If people knew how weak I was inside I would cease to be effective."

"Is that what life comes down to, being effective?"

"For me, I guess so."

"Do you really feel you can talk to me?"

"I don't know. Can I?"

"I wish you would."

He must have thought he had revealed as much of himself as he wished to. "I try not to get too introspective," he said, and again changed the conversation, asking her which show she had seen with Maureen Troy, and if she had liked it.

As the luncheon ended she tried to read what his feelings for her

might be. It seemed to her that he was careful to mask them, whatever they were. Obviously he felt a certain affection for her. She
hoped he did. It would be based on long acquaintance, and also on
his friendship for her late husband. Anything more than that? If so,
it was well hidden.

At the same time he treated her as if she were a vase with cracks
in it, who might at any moment and for no reason fall to pieces. This
annoyed her a bit.

AWAKENED BY THE TELEPHONE IN THE MIDDLE OF THE NIGHT, Father Redmond listened a moment, then said: "All right. Don't say a
word to anybody until I get there."

Now I'm talking like a lawyer, he thought as he hung up. But the
advice had to be given and, he hoped, obeyed.

He dressed, put on a fresh collar and rabat, his black topcoat, and
went into the office where he opened the safe, reached into a corner under a pile of papers, and pulled out his personal lockbox, from
which he withdrew money. He counted out $1,000, which he thrust
into his coat pocket, and put the rest back, covering the box with the
same papers. It was money he had held out of the collection baskets
over a period of time for purposes such as tonight's, its existence unknown to the pastor, or to the Chancery. Whenever the pastor had
come upon the lockbox and had railed against its existence, Frank
told him it contained only his personal papers, and money from his
salary. He had learned to ignore the repeated railing.

He went out and walked down sidewalks that were dark, empty,
that had a dangerous, expectant feel to them. As always, he listened
for footsteps. He was known to all in the neighborhood, but his safety
was not guaranteed.

The stationhouse came into view ahead, the globes lit up out
front. In an otherwise dark city the entire house was lit up, an oasis.
Several police cars were parked in front. Toed in against the curb op-

posite were the personal cars of the cops on duty tonight, a long row, perhaps 30 of them, perhaps more. He knew the names of many of these men, and was familiar with all of them, and with the house itself, which he thought of as the Three-Two, just as they did, for this was not the first time he had come here in the middle of the night, rousted from his bed, and doubtless it would not be the last. He went inside, nodding and greeting men he passed, and up the stairs to the second-floor squadroom.

Two detectives, one of them Jeff Barrett, sat at desks typing out forms.

"Evening, Father," said Barrett, looking up.

Frank had known this detective for some years. "How are you, Jeff?"

"I don't know if you've met my new partner," Jeff said. "George O'Hara, meet Father Redmond, who's a very good guy, you'll find."

"How do you do, Father?"

"Where's the master criminal?"

"I guess you were his one phone call," said Detective Barrett.

"In the cage," said Detective O'Hara.

"Am I right?" said Barrett.

"Who else was he going to call?" said Father Redmond. "The family law firm? His mother? She wouldn't know what to do, and in any case her phone has been cut off. I have an appointment with her tomorrow, as a matter of fact. I mean, later today. First the phone company, then her landlord. See if I can get her phone back on and get an extension on her rent."

"Being poor don't give her kid the right to stick up a store, Father."

"No, of course not. But that's probably why he did it. Get the money to keep the family from being evicted."

"How old is he, Father?"

"Fifteen, I think."

"That's what he said he was. But you can't tell with these mutts."

"He's not a mutt. He's a good kid."

"Until tonight."

"He didn't have no identification on him, Father. So we weren't sure."

"What were you looking for, a driver's license? He doesn't live in that world. What did he do?"

Barrett said: "I'm just finishing up the five on him." He tugged the form out of the typewriter and handed it over. "Read that. It tells it all."

The perpetrator, identified as Melvin Baxter, male, black, aged 15, was charged on the form with sticking up an all-night Chinese take-out joint. He had happened to be sticking it up just as these two detectives walked in looking for something to eat. The time given was about two hours earlier.

"Easiest collar I ever made," said Detective Barrett.

"He didn't put up no resistance, Father," said Detective O'Hara.

"Normally," Barrett said, "we have to go two precincts away to get something to eat that won't give us the galloping shits. But that Chinaman is not too bad, if you stick to the fried chicken wings. Anyway, there's not much else open at this hour. So we walk in there, and guess what we find?"

"He had the gun in his coat pocket," said Detective O'Hara.

"He was threatening the Chinaman with his pocket. He sees us, he tries to run. I grabbed him around the neck and he starts blubbering."

"Stupid kid was lucky he didn't get shot," said Father Redmond.

"No chance of that," said Detective Barrett with a grin, "inasmuch as we're not your usual trigger-happy detectives."

"Sorry, Jeff, I didn't mean to insinuate —"

"No offense taken, Father."

"Did he actually steal anything?"

"Didn't have time."

"Attempted robbery then."

"It's still felony weight."

"A little better, at least. That the gun there?"

The small, silver-plated revolver in its plastic evidence bag lay on top of the typewriter on the adjacent desk.

"Yeah. Saturday night special."

"Probably doesn't even shoot," said Detective O'Hara.

"If it doesn't you've got no gun charge either."

"You should have been a lawyer, Father."

"Well," said Frank, "I'm the only lawyer most of these people ever see."

"They didn't teach you that in the seminary."

"Can I see the kid?"

Mel Baxter, altar boy, sat disconsolately on the floor of the cage. Father Redmond looked in at him, and when the boy's eyes came up, gave him a disgusted shake of his head.

"I hope you're proud of yourself, Mel."

"I'm sorry, Father," the boy said, and started to cry.

To Detective Barrett, who stood at his elbow, Father Redmond said: "Can I talk to him alone? Could we use the lieutenant's office?"

"Sure, Father."

Barrett opened the cage, cuffed the prisoner's hands behind his back, and led him into the lieutenant's office.

After closing the door, Frank leaned his rump on the desk. The boy stood before him, eyes on the floor.

"You may go to jail. Is that what you want?"

"My mom, she can't pay the rent," the boy said. "They gonna put us in the street."

"Why didn't you come to me first? Sticking up a store is not the solution."

"That Chinaman, he rich."

"What am I supposed to tell your mother?"

"I was only gonna take enough for the rent."

"If you ever do anything like this again, you're finished with me, is that understood?"

"Yes, Father."

"I won't speak up for you, I won't help you in any way, understood?"

"Yes, Father."

"I don't know how much I can help you now, but I'll try." After a pause, Frank said: "They're going to take you downtown to arraignment court now. There'll be a lot of people there, and it will probably take a long time. Don't be afraid. I'll be with you. I'll be with you all the way, and I'll do all the talking. You're not to say a word to anybody. Is that agreed?"

"Yes, Father."

He opened the door and led the boy out of the office.

For the ride downtown Frank sat in the back beside the prisoner. There were no handles on the doors, and a grille separated them from the two detectives up front. The detectives chatted to each other most of the way. From time to time the police radio squawked, but there were no panicky calls from one cop to another, no crises that other cops were ordered to attend to. The city this late was mostly quiet.

At court Barrett got a docket number and in the hall outside the courtroom they commenced to wait. Hordes of uniformed cops, detectives, and prisoners also waited, one or two female cops among them. Most prisoners were in a holding cell, but many were out here handcuffed to benches, the arresting officers beside them dozing, caps and hats tipped down over their faces. Other cops paced and smoked. The floor was littered with cigarette butts. The cleaning women would not come to work for hours. Butts and crushed coffee containers made pyramids atop the cigarette urns beside the courtroom doors. Other containers, half empty, stood against the hallway walls. Legal aid lawyers interviewed prisoners, moving in and out fast, while harried assistant district attorneys, also moving fast, interviewed arresting officers, all these interviews lasting only minutes, sometimes only seconds. Too many cases for too few men. Seconds was all the time anyone had.

Father Redmond spoke separately to the legal aid lawyer assigned to Mel Baxter, and also to the ADA who would present the case to the arraignment judge. He drew them aside and spoke quietly. Much later, still waiting for their docket number to be called, he remembered that he was supposed to open the church in an hour, and then say the first mass. He wasn't going to make it in time so he found a phone booth and phoned the pastor, waking him up, earning himself still another dressing-down.

Later still the case was finally called. Frank knew some of the judges, for Mel Baxter was not the first parishioner to get in trouble, but he didn't know this one, and he asked permission to approach the bench, knowing there was no guarantee that this favor would be accorded. But the judge motioned him forward and he spoke to him, explaining who Mel Baxter was, and the circumstances, and asking for the boy to be released in his custody. The accused was underage, he pointed out, it was his first offense, and he had roots in the community. He, Father Redmond, would personally guarantee that the prisoner would be on time for all future court appearances.

"You're talking about maybe four, five court appearances," the judge said.

"Yes sir."

"You'll bring him to court each time?"

"Yes sir."

"See that you do. Five hundred dollars cash bail." The judge banged his gavel down. "Next case."

Father Redmond got the roll of money out of his coat pocket, and counted out five hundreds.

"I hope you didn't make a mistake, Father," said Detective Barrett, as they left the courtroom.

Out in the street it was broad daylight. People were going to work. Father Redmond bought Mel breakfast in a diner, then sent him home on the subway. He himself rode a different line up to Columbia where he swam his laps. He had had less than three hours' sleep, with much to do the rest of the day, and he hoped a good swim would wake him up.

When he got back to the rectory a woman waited for him in what Monsignor Malachy referred to as the parlor. She wanted him to read her lease "to make sure it's okay to sign." After that a woman came in who wanted him, on behalf of her son, to write a letter to the warden of the Attica Correctional Facility where the son was incarcerated.

After lunch, which was a ham sandwich and a piece of store-bought apple pie, the doorbell rang again and it was Mel Baxter's mother. After reassuring her about her son he took her to the telephone company building at 88 Pine Street, where they were received by a vice president named Carter whom Father Redmond had met during previous errands of this kind.

"Good to see you again, Father," Carter said.

"Yes," said Father Redmond, "though I hate to keep bringing you these problems," and he explained that Mrs. Baxter, who had four children at home and no husband, had always paid her bills until now, but her apartment had been burglarized about two months ago. She was in the habit of keeping her money in a jar in the kitchen which the burglars, unfortunately, had found. This was all her money, not just her phone bill money. There was not even money for food. She had been unable recently to pay any of her bills. She was regularly employed as a cleaning woman at Harlem Hospital, was hardworking, and she was trying to catch up, and hoped to be able to pay all her back bills soon. "And so, if I might ask the telephone company's forbearance —"

Carter sent them along to an assistant, where a repayment schedule was worked out and Mrs. Baxter's telephone service was restored.

Her landlord was a white man who worked out of an office on 125th Street, Harlem's principal avenue. He owned not only her building but a number of others, all of them rat holes, in Frank's opinion, for which he charged exorbitant rents. Most of the Harlem landlords, sometimes called slumlords, were also white, some were Jewish, and a virulent anti-white, anti-Jewish sentiment ran through the Harlem community.

This man made them wait an unconscionable length of time before admitting them to his inner office. There was no greeting, no preliminary conversation. He said: "Where's my money?"

Frank made his little speech, describing the burglary, a hardworking woman's attempts to catch up on her payments.

"Fairy tales," said the landlord. "I'm not interested. Hand over my money. You don't have the money, get out, we got nothing to talk about. Get out."

So Father Redmond was obliged to use muscle.

"I've been looking over some of your buildings," he said. "Not just hers, but others as well, and I noted some infractions that the Buildings Department might like to hear about. Rats, fire hazards, no extinguishers on the landings. Small things. Hardly worth mentioning."

The landlord fell silent, eyes darting about.

"Now, you seem like a kind and gracious sort of man," Father Redmond said. "So why don't we work out a payment schedule we can all live with? That would be the gracious thing to do, don't you think?"

"How do I know you won't go to the Buildings Department anyway?"

"Because then they'd condemn your building and Mrs. Baxter would have no place to live."

They eyed each other.

"You got a pen," said Frank. "Why don't I dictate a letter from you to her, agreeing to let her stay? You sign it, and we stop wasting each other's time."

In the street Mrs. Baxter, grinning happily, gave him a resounding kiss. He patted her shoulder, then stood on the sidewalk, people passing him in both directions, and watched her go off toward the subway.

During the interview with the landlord his tension was such that he had sweated through his shirt. Although he had permitted nothing to show, he believed, his back felt soaked. The roman collar was stuck to his neck, and he got his finger inside it and freed it all the way around.

Once back in the rectory he took a shower and changed his clothes, then went into the church and vested, stepped out onto the altar and, alone in front of 30 rows of empty pews, said his daily mass, the one he had expected to say just after opening the church this morning. There were no altar boys, no bells rang, and of course no congregation. By then it was dark outside. He raised the sacred host, recited the ritual prayers just as he had done nearly every day of his priesthood.

Normally he made his rounds of the two neighborhood hospitals, Harlem and St. Luke's, in the afternoon. Today he went out after dinner, bringing the blessed sacrament into the wards, and distributing it to those who wanted it. Sitting at bedsides, he tried to comfort those who sought comfort, to soothe those who were suffering, the patients and relatives alike. He listened to confidences. He tried to project cheerfulness in a cheerless place.

It took him three hours. Then he went home — to the rectory — and went to bed. Keeping busy cut off loneliness, though it sometimes left an emptiness in its place.

Not all his days were this charged, but many were. He had other duties as well. Saturday mornings there were usually funerals or weddings or both. Saturday afternoons he heard confessions for three hours. In former years practicing Catholics tried to confess themselves once a week. These days fewer came. During the long gaps, he would put the flexible light on, bending the neck to illuminate the breviary on his lap, or else the novel disguised to look like a breviary. Or else he would just sit there in the dark, waiting. Finally someone would kneel down on the other side of the thin wall, and he would slide the window back and listen to guilty secrets he had no desire to know. He would try to give advice to those who asked for it, hoping the advice was not specious, that he did not sound pompous or, worse, judgmental. Three hours in a coffin set on end, waiting, isolated from the world. But if he thought of it this way he never said so. After confessions it was his job to say the Saturday evening mass, then go up to his room and prepare his Sunday sermon. The next morning he would say two masses, preaching at both, then carry the sacks of money from the collections up into the office and count how much was in them. There was a machine for counting the coins. The bills and the few checks had to be counted by hand. Some Sundays the totals were substantial, for not all parishioners were poor. On 139th Street, in a row of buildings designed by Stanford White almost a hundred years ago, lived many of Harlem's politicians, judges, businessmen. The buildings were beautifully kept, as was the street itself, which was known as Striver's Way. On those Sundays when the take was above average, he would hold out some of the excess, putting it into his lockbox in the safe for emergency use, for he had learned early on that it was virtually impossible to get money out of Monsignor

Malachy, whatever the nature of the emergency that might have occurred.

But Wednesdays he tried to keep free so he could drive up to Yonkers, pick up Roxanne Finley outside her house, and take her to lunch. He always called her Tuesday night to make the date. In the restaurants they would sit talking, sometimes laughing for two hours or more. These meetings with her, he told her once, sometimes seemed to him the only sane time of the week.

"I look forward to them too," she said.

"Do you?" he said. "Do you really?"

ONE WEDNESDAY THEY VISITED ROOSEVELT'S HOUSE at Hyde Park. They walked through the president's rooms, examined his wheelchair, and stood before his tomb, which was also the tomb of Eleanor, his wife. Afterward they found a restaurant in Poughkeepsie. From their table they could look down on the great wide Hudson, the sun showering the river with coins. It was not a classy restaurant; it specialized in wedding parties, of which there were none that day. They giggled about this, deciding that the view more than made up for the mediocre food.

Another Wednesday they crossed the river and went north as far as West Point, driving onto the reservation and leaving the car in a parking lot — anybody could have done the same, for there were no guards, no security at that time. They dined in the Thayer Hotel where tens of thousands of cadets' girlfriends, and often the girls' mothers, had stayed over the years. When they came out they sat down on a bleacher and watched football practice. How young the players all looked, they decided. After practice they watched a parade. A visiting dignitary must have been present to merit such a display. What looked like the entire corps of cadets marched in review in front of a dais on which stood a handful of uniformed men, saluting. It was like watching the halftime show at the Army-Navy game, only this time from a few feet away. They were both enthralled. On the way home they drove through Ossining past Sing Sing, the famous prison where in the '30s and '40s so many mobsters had been strapped into what the criminal world called the hot seat, and electrocuted.

Another time, again crossing the river on the giant erector set that was the Tappan Zee Bridge, they drove through the narrow streets of Snedden's Landing, an address once favored by the New York art world, and looked over houses in which famous people had once lived, rating each house. They were like newly marrieds house hunting in a neighborhood they knew they could never afford. This house looked too dark, that one too big or too small. But that one there would be perfect to live in at this stage of their lives, if they had the money.

The day came when they drove to Larchmont. Rocky had not been back since her father died, she said. They drove into the club and parked and looked over the pool, covered now, where Frank had worked as a lifeguard that summer, while Rocky practiced to become, possibly, an Olympic diver. They went into the bar and the dining room but saw nobody either of them knew. Not being members, they could not sign for anything to eat or drink. They walked one or two holes of the golf course, but staying to the side so as not to disturb golfers playing through. Leaving the club, Rocky wanted to see her old house, so he drove into her street, remembering the way perfectly even after so many years. They got out and studied the house, looking it over carefully.

"They've painted the shutters green," Rocky said. "They used to be brown."

"I don't remember."

"I wonder what else they've done?"

"Would you like to go in?"

She looked at him.

"Whoever is in there now, if you rang the bell and said you grew up in this house, they'd almost surely invite you in."

"You think so?"

They started toward the front door, but then Rocky pulled back. "I'd feel funny," she said. "And I don't need to go in to remember what the inside looks like."

As they started back to the car Rocky pointed and said: "That's where we were parked the night the cop shined the light in on us. Do you remember?"

"Yes." He laughed. "We were both so scared."

"We weren't even doing anything."

"That cop terrified us."

"We were such children," she said.

"We were just kissing."

"It was nice kissing, though, wasn't it?"

"You had the most kissable lips I had ever known."

"Don't I still?"

He laughed. "Stop teasing me."

She gave him a smile, and took his hand. She held his hand all the way back to the car.

Tuesday nights on the telephone they might talk 30 minutes. Once Rocky mentioned that her gutters were full of leaves but she was having trouble finding someone to clean them.

"I'll do that for you," Frank said.

"Do you think you can?"

"Of course."

"All right. Then we won't go out this week, I'll fix something here."

But when he rang her bell she looked him up and down. "It's an awfully messy job, you know. Don't you have any old clothes?"

"I'll be fine."

"That nice sweater will get filthy. There are some overalls of Earl's in the cellar. I'll get them."

He stood in the entrance hall waiting.

"Here, put these on," she said when she came back. She led him into a downstairs bedroom. "You can change in here."

He did so. The overalls were much too short. His wrists and ankles showed. When he came out Rocky laughed at him.

"You look so silly in those overalls."

He dragged the ladder out of the garage, got it upright against the wall, and hauled on the rope until he had extended it to maximum length. He pulled it outward until it leaned at what seemed to him a safe angle.

"You look like a kid who has outgrown his clothes."

"If I fall off this thing, you won't be laughing."

"You're very much bigger than Earl was, aren't you? I hadn't realized how much."

He was about two and a half stories in the air, and the ladder shook a bit, and felt flimsy.

"There are times I really miss having a man around the house," Rocky called from below.

The gutter was half full of rotted leaves and rainwater. He combed the leaves toward himself from as far as he could reach in both directions, and dropped the muck on the flower bed below. Then he got down, moved the ladder, and repeated the process. The winter day was cold, clear, temperature not much above freezing. Below him, a coat over her shoulders, Rocky stood watching. The trapped water was cold, the muck was cold. Before long his sleeves were soaked and his hands felt frozen.

He collapsed the ladder, carried it around, and cleared the other gutters in the same way. By the time the job was finished his fingers felt frozen solid. He went into the house into the downstairs bedroom and changed back into his clothes, khaki pants, a shirt, and a sweater. His fingers were so cold he could barely button the buttons. In the kitchen he held his hands under the tap until some feeling came back. Apologetic, solicitous, Rocky took his fingers in hers and began kneading them under the water.

He had avoided being in the house with her alone. Now here he was in her kitchen, the water pouring down on their fingers. He was holding hands with her, he told himself. Of course he was, what else could you call it?

She fixed a quite nice lunch. He watched her fork pork chops onto each plate, sweep on potatoes, spill on peas. They sat down together.

"How are you on dripping faucets?"

"The best."

"This is my lucky day."

"How many are leaking?"

"One in each bathroom."

She put the dishes in the dishwasher, then led him into the garage, where they searched for Earl's cache of faucet washers. He disassembled the faucets, changed the ruined washers, put the faucets together again, then turned the water back on. Moving from one faucet to the other, he saw no further drips.

"My hero," said Rocky, patting him on the back.

"It was nothing," said Frank, as if bashful.

He drove back to the rectory.

The next week he helped her paint her dining room, the outer wall of which was discolored by water stains. When the job was not finished by nightfall he managed to clear part of the following day, Thursday, returning to finish what was left.

She had still not found a meaningful job, she told him as they painted. "I typed up a résumé. There isn't much on it, since I haven't worked in so long. I began calling up people, including contacts from when I did work. Most of them agree to see me, and then they brush me off. Send me down two floors or up two floors to see their third assistant personnel director who has me filling out forms for an hour. After which I go home."

"And that's the end of that."

She paused, the paint roller in her hand. "There must be lots of women my age trying to reenter the workforce. We're not old bags yet, but nobody wants us."

"You're not an old bag, anyway," he said fervently, after which both of them burst out laughing.

"Thank you. I seem to need a little praise these days."

Halfway up a stepladder he continued to roll on paint. "What will you do?" he said.

"Keep looking, and hope something will turn up."

The job was finished before noon. He had worn Earl's overalls again, and had got paint spatter on his nose and forehead. Rocky got it off using cotton balls soaked in turpentine, working tenderly, as if sponging off wounds.

Back in his room in the rectory he got on the phone. A number of the men he had gone through the seminary with were now pastors, and several were still running parish schools. One by one he called them, explaining who Rocky was, the widow of his oldest friend, children gone, sorely in need of a job. Were they by chance in need of someone, perhaps an administrator in their school?

A Monsignor Connolly, pastor of Sacred Heart in Mount Vernon, was interested. His school principal, an aged nun, was not well. He had been notified by the nun's order that she would not be able to finish out the term.

"A few more weeks, she goes into wherever they keep them — the old nuns' home." It was difficult to find a replacement on such short notice, Connolly said, so of course he'd like to interview Frank's friend. However, he couldn't pay much.

"How much?" asked Frank bluntly.

The pastor gave a figure.

"You can do better," said Frank.

"I didn't have to pay the nun."

"Whoever you get you are going to have to pay. The day of free nuns is over."

"Let me meet her."

Two days later Frank drove her there. They sat in the car outside, Rocky nervous.

"I'm not even Catholic. Supposing he asks me if I'm Catholic?"

"Tell him your husband was Catholic, your children are Catholic, and you're taking instruction."

Frank sat in on the interview, which went well. The monsignor said Rocky could start in two weeks' time. The aged nun would stay on for the first few days to show her the ropes, and after that Rocky would run the school, and would also help with the administration of the parish. The monsignor named a salary—the same figure he had given Frank earlier.

Rocky bit her lip.

"Can I speak to you alone, Monsignor?" said Frank.

Rocky waited outside.

"Leo," said Frank, "Leo. She can't live on what you're offering. You've got to do better. Her husband was murdered. She has very little money. She's hardworking, she needs the job. She'll be worth it, and if not you can fire her."

Rocky was invited back into the office, and a new salary offered.

"Your agent is a ferocious negotiator," Monsignor Connolly told her with a smile.

In the car outside Rocky was jubilant. "I've got a job, I've got a job."

He drove her home where he pulled into her driveway, but did not get out of the car.

"Do you want to come in?" she asked. "I'll make some coffee."

He was wearing his clerical suit that day, and he shook his head. "I have to get back. I have basketball practice tonight." He coached the parish team in the CYO league—the Catholic Youth Organization. Coaching too was among his duties, and he considered it one of the most important jobs he did, because it kept 20 or so teenage boys off the street and out of trouble five or six nights a week for as long as the season lasted.

With her hand on the doorknob, Rocky said: "Now that I have a job, I think I'll indulge myself and accept Maureen's invitation."

Frank knew about this invitation. The Troys owned the last two weeks of February in a time-share apartment at a beach resort in the Caribbean. Their turn came up beginning in a few days, just when Troy had to be with the president at a summit meeting in Moscow. Maureen was determined to use the time-share, even if she had to go alone. And she had invited Rocky.

Rocky laughed. "What she said we'll do is, we'll walk on the beach and see if we can pick up some men."

Earl by then had been dead five months.

"Does that idea interest you? Picking up men?"

She smirked at him. "Maybe."

"Now that you have a job waiting, by all means go."

"You don't want me to go, do you?"

"This is your chance to find a rich husband."

"You know what you sound like?" She laughed at him. "A jealous boyfriend."

"I don't have any right to be jealous."

"I think Maureen was joking."

"What do I have to offer you instead?"

"You'd be surprised."

She leaned over, kissed him on the cheek. "I'm terrifically fond of you," she said, and got out of the car, and swung the door shut.

————

ALONE IN HIS ROOM IN THE RECTORY AT NIGHT, Frank's telephone rang. He was reclining on his bed doing the crossword puzzle by the light of his bedside lamp, and the sound startled him.

Actually he had two telephones. One was connected through the rectory's switchboard. Calls at night came directly to him. In a parish where shootings and knifings were commonplace, phone calls were often of an emergency nature. Then it was his job to dress hurriedly, go out into the dark streets, and hurry to the scene, there to comfort the victim if he could, perhaps hear a deathbed confession, anoint with oils.

The second telephone was his personal line, and it was this phone that rang now. He picked up, and it was Rocky calling from the Caribbean.

The ostensible reason for her call was that she had met by chance a Dr. Goddet, who had known him in Africa. "He asked about your health. He asked to be remembered to you. He said you were a great man."

"Maybe he's the rich husband you're looking for?"

"You getting jealous again?"

"Not me."

"He's got his wife and kids with him."

She began to gush about the resort, its water so clear, its sand so clean, extravagant sunsets every night.

"It's so nice here. You should come down. There's plenty of room. All you have to bring is a bathing suit."

"What does Maureen say?"

"She's all for it."

He liked the idea, and in a moment decided. If he could get on a plane he would come, he told her.

"Good," she said.

In the morning he reserved his ticket, phoned the Franciscan monastery on 31st Street, and one of the priests there agreed to take over his duties for a week. He persuaded one of the parish men to replace him as basketball coach. At supper he informed Monsignor Malachy that he was taking a week in the Caribbean. This caused the usual row which he cut off by saying he hadn't had a vacation in six years, and he was, by God, taking a week now.

"Eat your dinner, Monsignor. I'll be back in a week. You won't even miss me."

The pastor stormed out of the dining room. Frank shrugged, and went on eating.

THROUGH THE PORTHOLE HE WATCHED THE ISLAND come up to meet the plane, the water transparent, greens and blues in ten different shades, depending on the depth. He stepped out the door into the hottest part of the day, came down the steps onto the tarmac and felt the heat through the soles of his shoes. In the customs shed he was asked to open his single carry-on bag, which surprised him. He changed money, then stood in the line of people waiting for taxis.

The drive took about 20 minutes. He watched the stunted trees go by, the poor villages, the women walking with bundles on their heads like in Africa. From time to time there was a view of the sea. Along the roads grew flamboyant bushes. He recognized jacaranda, bougainvillea. Giant poinsettias too, a Christmas plant back home but great red bushes here.

He got out at the beach club which looked rich to him, the opposite of poor in any case, and which appeared to be an all-white enclave except for a few workmen, and some women who probably cleaned the apartments.

He rang, and Rocky came to the door. "Oh, I'm so glad you could come," she said, almost jumping into his arms, kissing him lightly on the lips. "I'm so glad to see you." Her welcoming smile seemed a yard wide, but a bit forced as well. She had on a kind of multicolored muumuu, and was barefoot.

"You look hot. Do you want to go swimming? Let's go swimming right away."

She led him into a bedroom. "You can change in here. I'll be outside on the beach."

These commands seemed a bit frenetic to him too, but he did as told. He came out onto a small furnished terrace: a round table that had been run through by the spear of its umbrella, the four chairs distributed around it, and to one side a chaise longue. The umbrella was red, the chair cushions mostly red. Rocky's multicolored muumuu hung uninhabited over one of them. Two steps down, standing on the sand in a white one-piece swimsuit, still smiling broadly and perhaps inappropriately, she waited for him. She was well tanned, her nose beginning to peel a bit. Her figure looked to him unchanged from the first time he ever saw her, on the day he had got his lifeguard job from her father, and he had a sudden memory of the swimsuit she wore that day, a black one, and the lithe look of her body as she bounced up and down on the diving board. Oh, there was a little cellulite at the top of her legs now, not much. Perhaps her breasts had lost some of the firmness of those days, but this was something he did not expect ever to find out.

As he approached her his flesh felt very white to him.

She had a bottle of suntan oil. "Turn around," she said. "Let me rub this on you."

When he hesitated, she said: "The sun here will burn you to a crisp if you don't."

"I guess I look like I could use a little sun," he said.

He felt her liquid hand. "Now your front." Her hand patted and smoothed. It moistened his curls.

Finished, she handed him the bottle. "Now you do me."

He took the bottle. Her back was hot, her flesh smooth, her shoulders, her arms.

"I didn't even offer you a drink," she said, facing him again. "Would you like something? Would you like me to go inside and fix you something?" Again she sounded, for some reason, nervous, the words hasty, as if she had meant to say something else.

For an answer he grabbed her hand and ran her across the sand and into the water, the sand scalding their feet, the water when they reached it warm too. The water proved shallow until they were a good ways out and they ran high-stepping until finally the depth was too great and Rocky fell down, dragging him down with her.

They swam out a ways, and came back and sat on the bottom, the water up to their chests.

There was a wooded mountain behind them. It petered out into craggy headlands at either end of the beach.

The sun flashed into their eyes off every wavelet, and Frank said: "To loll here in the warm water with you, what luxury."

"You're nice, you know that?" she said, still sounding a bit nervous.

She found his hand under the water and squeezed it. Perhaps that was the moment he realized in which direction they were headed.

"Where's Maureen?"

"Oh, she's around."

A little later they walked along the beach as far as one of the distant crags, and then back again, the sun drying them, walking a yard apart, from time to time edging closer one to the other, her fragile wrist swinging close to his, then drawing apart again.

As the afternoon declined massive clouds assembled. They were blue-black on the edges. The wind rose. The other swimmers and sunbathers slowly vanished. The last of them began to run from the beach.

On the otherwise empty beach they sat with their knees pulled up, awed, while the wind went into a tantrum. The sea was waving white handkerchiefs. Rain first spat in their faces, then came down in spears hard enough to make indentations in the sand. The rain drove their hair down their faces, into their eyes. The wind was warm, the rain too. They sat there taking it, laughing.

The ponderous darkness moved off them, moved over some other island. The sun was brilliant again. The sand blotted up the pools that had formed, sucked on them till they were gone. Soaked, they went up the two steps onto the porch, where Rocky reached inside for towels, tossing one to Frank. Standing apart, they dried themselves off.

In the room he had been given Frank got dressed, combed his hair. When he came out Rocky was peering into the fridge. She was still barefoot, wearing her muumuu, her wet hair tied back in a ponytail. "Almost time for dinner," she said.

"Maureen's still not back," Frank noted, glancing around.

"I better start fixing it."

She took packages out of the fridge. "I have some local fish. It's called *vivaneau*. It's a kind of red snapper. Have you ever had it?"

"No."

"You'll like it."

He said: "Shouldn't we wait for Maureen?"

"There's a bottle of wine on the sideboard. Why don't you open it?"

"Where is Maureen?"

She came close to him. "She's not here."

"Where is she?"

"She got a call. Her mother had a heart attack. She had to go back."

"How long has she been gone?"

"So we—we have the place to ourselves."

"How long?"

She would not meet his eyes. "Four days, five days. I don't know."

Though Frank's hands were on her shoulders she would not look at him.

"Don't you think you should have told me?"

"I was afraid if I told you, you wouldn't come."

Frank said nothing, but he dropped his hands.

She said: "I know I should have told you, but I wanted you to come so badly."

Frank looked out the window in the direction of the sea.

"If you don't want to be here alone with me, there's a hotel down the street. It's not expensive — " Her voice faded out.

She put her forehead on his chest.

"For a week all I could think of was how much I missed you. How much I wanted to see you, wanted to be with you."

What could he say to this? The pressure of her head on his chest demanded a response, and none was possible except to put his arms around her.

"I'm in love with you, Frank. Can't you tell?"

"I didn't know." Though perhaps he did. Perhaps it was what he had hoped for, while at the same time trying to convince himself they were only friends and would never be more.

"I don't want to be a burden to you. I know you're not free. I know it's hopeless. I can't help myself. I'm sorry. I've tried. I've tried so hard."

His arms, almost of their own accord, had tightened around her.

"I've never loved anyone but you. When you went into the seminary it was like a kick in the stomach. I thought you'd come back to me. I thought you'd give me another chance."

He stroked her hair.

"Can't you love me a little?" Her face came up until she was looking up at him. "I'm not asking for much. Anything. Whatever you can give me."

"I've tried to love you only a little," he said. "It didn't work. People say you can't control love." He gave a broken laugh. "I always thought you could, if you were strong enough. That I could. Because I was strong. But I was wrong."

"Why, Frank, you're trembling."

"Once you start loving someone you can't stop. All those years in Vietnam, in Africa. I was trying to get as far away from you as possible so I wouldn't suffer so much."

"Frank."

"I fell in love with you the first day I ever saw you. I've been in love with you every day since, and I'm in love with you now. Love you a little?" he said.

But she was still not sure. "Do you want me to call the hotel?" She picked up the telephone, but he put his hand over hers, pushing the receiver back into its cradle.

"You used to like to kiss me," she said. "Would you like to kiss me now?"

And so they stepped into the weave of love.

He woke in the night with the moonlight coming in the window, and sat up and looked at her sleeping. Once he moved her hair away from her mouth. Otherwise he only looked, while the night unrolled around them.

In the morning when she awoke he was not there. In a panic she threw her muumuu on and rushed outside barefoot, muumuu swaying, peering up and down the beach, not seeing him. Then she saw a head far out swimming in, a nice smooth stroke, his stroke, and she relaxed.

When he reentered the apartment she had started the coffee, had put out orange juice, rolls, and butter.

"Go take a shower," she suggested. "Wash the salt off yourself."

He was in the shower, face and hair soapy, eyes closed, hair hanging down, when he realized she had climbed in behind him. She had a washcloth and a bar of soap, and she began to wash first his back, then his chest, his arms. Presently he did the same for her. Then they stepped out and dried each other off.

"Do you feel like going back to bed?"

"Sure," he said, "why not?"

"Yes, I thought you did."

"How could you tell?" he said.

They stayed a week on the island, then flew back to New York. On the plane they sat side by side, holding hands much of the way.

They had not discussed the future at all.

THE INVESTIGATION

10

AFTER WORK, AS ALWAYS, GABE WAITS FOR ANDY TROY in his car out-side the paper's offices, but when he sees him crossing the street he gets out and suggests they go into the nearest bar.

Once they are seated and have been served, Gabe tells him about Poindexter.

Andy's knobby face and thick glasses hang over his drink. He says: "What about those two Mafia guys who got sent away with him?"

Gabe shakes his head. "One of them got rubbed out several years ago. The other is in the can on something else."

"Could he have arranged something from jail?"

Again Gabe shakes his head. "He's not even a made guy. He's not high enough to arrange a hit."

They drink quietly for a time.

Gabe says: "You've got nothing either, I assume."

"Nothing from the only priest I've found who may or may not have been Frankie's friend, nothing from his psychiatrist. I'm still going through the phone and bank records, but they don't seem to go anywhere either."

"We're not doing too well, are we?"

"No, we're not."

"There must be something."

"Yes, but so far we haven't found it. I'm beginning to wonder if we ever will."

CHAPTER TEN

FROM THEN ON FATHER REDMOND LIVED A DOUBLE LIFE.

Neither he nor Rocky had the money for Broadway shows or fancy restaurants. When they went out they went to the movies, where sometimes they held hands in the dark like teenagers. They frequented pizza parlors, or sushi bars, as teenagers did. Usually they were the oldest people there. They sometimes made remarks about this teenage love affair they were having. The only thing they didn't do was double-date, they said, and both laughed.

One night, holding her close, he told her he was head over heels in love with her. He couldn't get enough of her. In that way he was like a teenager too. "Sorry," he said.

She looked pleased. "Hey, you don't have to apologize."

"In every other way, I'm completely normal, honest."

"I suppose you are a bit unusual. Most men your age are looking for younger women."

"And you?"

"Do you remember the first night we made love in that crummy motel on Lake Cayuga, and the room was so cold? There are emotions stirring inside me that I haven't felt since that night. Emotions I never thought I would feel again."

But it wasn't a teenage love affair, and there were times when Frank would go remote from her, and look off into the near distance, alone with whatever guilt he was experiencing, alone in a place she could not reach.

Once he said: "I went through a stage of feeling that Earl had left you in my care. Or perhaps that's just what I wanted to feel. I never expected it would come to this."

So she knew the guilt was there, though not what its extent might be, for this was the only allusion to it he ever made. And she herself was afraid to bring the subject up. A number of other subjects as well.

It was at this time that he began seeing Dr. Greenberg, the psychiatrist.

Most times he seemed to her lighthearted. When she would open her front door to him he was frequently standing there, looking a bit sheepish, holding a bouquet of flowers beside his ear.

She had never believed in the sanctity of eternal vows, especially a vow of celibacy made by a very young man who did not yet know what life was all about. Nonetheless, there was guilt on her side too — she worried about wrecking his life, which she didn't want to do, though perhaps she already had. Since he wasn't wrecking her life — there was nothing there to wreck as she saw it — his guilt on that score, assuming he felt any, was different.

Once, when Andy Troy was home for a week they were invited to dinner by Maureen Troy, not as a couple but separately, or so Frank thought.

"I used to hate these dinners," he told Rocky.

"Hate dinners with your best friends?"

"Seven people at the table, everybody married but me. I used to feel so lonely, such an odd man out." He paused: "And also — "

"Also what?"

"You were there, totally inaccessible, though I wanted you so much."

"You certainly never let on."

He laughed. "I used to have to keep myself in an iron grip the whole time."

"I could call Maureen, invent an excuse."

"No, I want to go. It will be different this time. No one will notice anything different. But this time I won't be alone."

On the appointed night they were six at table, not seven as in the past, Earl missing, though recalled again and again in splashes of memory.

The Troys lived in an apartment on Central Park West overlooking the park, and they had a woman to serve. Frank was vivacious throughout, talking, making jokes, charming the others, especially his two childhood pals, but ignoring Rocky as if she were a stranger, and afterward, on the sidewalk in front of the building, after Gabe had helped Barbara into his department car and they had been driven off, she turned on him.

"I can't stand it when people are there and you look at me as if you hardly knew me, didn't even like me."

"I'm sorry. I didn't realize."

"I can't stand it, and I won't."

"I was just trying to be careful."

"You did the same thing on the island the day we had lunch with your doctor friend."

"I didn't want him to think—"

"I don't care what he thinks. I don't care what anybody thinks."

"Well I do."

"Maybe you'd just rather call the whole thing off?"

"No, of course not. Rocky—"

"Maureen knows."

"Maureen knows?"

"I told her."

"You told her?"

"I had to tell somebody. I couldn't hold it in."

"She'll tell Andy, who'll tell Gabe."

"And maybe they'll both tell Earl beyond the grave. I don't care."

"I care."

"You don't have to worry. Andy and Maureen hardly talk to each other."

Frank looked away.

In silence they walked along. The sidewalk sounded loud under their shoes. They came to where Frank's car was parked. In silence they got into it, and drove to Yonkers, where they got out in her driveway, and in silence walked to her door.

Overhead rode an immense moon. There was no other light. "Good night," she said, and slid her key into the lock.

"You're not going to invite me in?"

"No."

"All right," he said.

Her mouth was a hard stretched line. "I'm not in the mood."

"I guess I have a lot to learn about women."

"I guess you do."

"During the years I should have been learning I was doing something else."

She said nothing.

"I'm trying to learn." He scratched his head, a gesture she had always found endearing. He said: "Do I even get a good-night kiss?"

She allowed him to kiss her lightly on the lips, then suddenly clung to him. "Please come in," she said. "I want you to come in. I don't mean to be awful to you. Please forgive me."

ON THE PLANE FLYING BACK FROM THE CARIBBEAN, holding his hand, Rocky had said to him: "Now that I have a job, maybe we won't be able to see as much of each other."

"It will be more difficult."

"Weekdays I'm working, and weekends are your busiest time."

"Maybe we can figure a way."

"I hope so."

He gave her an amused smile. "How often do you want to see me?"

"A lot."

"You'll get tired of me."

"No."

"I'll try to arrange something."

"See that you do." And then: "I don't want to lose you," and she had lifted his hand to her lips.

Once back in the rectory he had rescheduled his duties, crammed them in. By late afternoon of the second day he had had his life arranged, rearranged, his new life. He had guaranteed himself, he believed, three evenings a week free, perhaps Sunday nights as well. The pastor would just have to accept it. Three times a week he would be absent from dinner, absent from the rectory.

He went into the kitchen, cassock swirling, where he advised the cook not to set a place for him, then ran up to his room, pulled his cassock off, washed his face and hands, combed his hair, and put on brown corduroy trousers he had recently bought, a white shirt, and, over it, a brown sweater. Carrying his leather jacket and gloves in one hand, a bottle of wine in the other, he went down the stairs again hoping to slip out of the rectory without encountering the pastor, knowing in advance that this would be his hope every night that he went out. He knew too that some nights he would succeed, others not.

Tonight not. He was not to get a single free evening before the pastor's resistance began to harden. For there the old man stood, just inside the front door, shaking snow from his shoulders, stomping it off his shoes. The door itself was still ajar, and framed in the opening was the lamppost across the street with its tent of light, through which the snow drifted slowly down.

"Evening, Monsignor."

"Where do you think you're going?" The pastor closed the door, as if to close Frank in.

"I've been invited to dinner."

"In the parish?"

"Childhood friend."

Frank went past him. Out on the stoop, he looked up into the falling snow, let it wet his face. The streets were already white. He found his car and started for Rocky's house. Through the steering wheel, through his almost bald tires, he could feel the slippery road. He had to drive with extreme care, which made the relatively short drive overlong, which in turn caused his impatience to rise steeply.

"Are you sure you won't stay the night?" Rocky asked him later. They stood in her front hall, Frank zipping up his jacket, putting on his gloves.

"I better not."

"Do you have a curfew?"

He laughed. "Officially not, but I guess I do." He embraced her. "Another night," he said.

She gave him a key so that, if ever she were not there, he could let himself in.

He opened her door. The snow had stopped by then. They stood in the sudden cold. "You make me feel I have a home to go to," he said. "I've never had that."

"A home is important."

"I had my parents' at first. It was a place I could go. But they've been dead a while now."

"A life without a home," she said.

"I guess so, yes."

"All those jolly rectories instead."

He laughed. "Oh, it's not as bad as all that."

That was the start. From then on Monsignor Malachy seemed to post himself beside the front door every night that Father Redmond was scheduled to go out. Though sometimes his comments seemed affable, he probed always, as Frank saw it, for information.

"Where you off to tonight, my boy?"

"Seeing friends, Monsignor."

"Friends?" The pastor's eyebrows rose.

Each night the man's interrogation was delivered in what Frank always thought of as his fake Irish brogue.

"Friends, Monsignor."

"You'll wear out your welcome, my boy."

"You make a great sentinel, Monsignor."

He moved to go around him.

Other nights the comments were caustic.

"Catholics like to see their priests dressed as priests, I find, not as middle-aged hippies."

"A lot of my friends are Protestants, Monsignor," Frank said, going around him. "Even Jews, some of them."

One day, the snow began about three in the afternoon. Hour after hour it fell. The pastor was at the door as Frank came downstairs.

"Not going out in this mess, are you?"

"My car's good in snow."

"You'll get in an accident."

"I promise to drive carefully."

"She must have some appeal."

"She?"

"She, he, whoever."

"Hmm," said Frank.

Rocky had all the lights on when he got there, and a fire blazing in the hearth. "I thought you wouldn't come," she said. "I kept looking out the window for your car. Give me your jacket. Go sit in front of the fire and get warm." She brought him a glass of mulled wine.

It was almost a blizzard. At midnight the snow was still falling.

When Frank, preparing to return to the rectory, put his jacket on and opened the front door, he saw that his past footprints no longer showed. The snow on the roof of his car looked eight inches deep.

"You can't drive in this," Rocky said beside him.

"Perhaps not."

"The plows haven't even been by."

"It's very deep."

"Stay the night with me, Frank."

"I don't have a toothbrush."

"You can use mine."

"Or a razor."

"You can use mine."

"I don't have any pajamas."

"Well then, I won't wear any either."

It was his job to open the church at seven A.M., and say the first mass.

"You got an alarm clock?"

He woke in the night and heard the plows and knew the roads would be all right. The room was bright from the snow. Rocky slept with her nose against his chest, the length of her beside him, and she stirred, and he looked at her. He was content to have her there, he told her later, when they finally approached subjects like this, but at the same time he was amazed at himself at being in bed with her.

The pastor came into the sacristy as he was vesting.

"Surprised to see you back, my boy."

"It was a blizzard last night. I had to stay where I was."

"Where was that?"

"At a dinner party."

"The others bunk there too?"

"Monsignor, please stop quizzing me."

After that he stayed all night, some nights. He also seemed to Rocky more and more tense, as if approaching a decision. She herself had no confidence as to what this decision might be. He had lived a correct life all his life until then, but it was not correct now.

This they never talked of, though they sometimes came close.

"A man can't love without someone to love," he said once. "Whatever the Church teaches its priests, a man can't love everybody." He was still struggling, it seemed, with notions put into his head in the seminary or before.

And another time: "You go into it believing, then it becomes a job, and then you don't know what you believe."

"Do other priests have problems with" — she did not know exactly how to phrase what she wanted to say — "with faith?" she concluded.

"I don't know. We never talk about it. That's the Catholic way, isn't it? Smother passion, smother impulses, smother emotions. Smother thought."

"I would have thought priests could talk to each other."

"If another priest is having a crisis of faith, you don't want to know — it might shake your own. We're all aware of this, so we don't discuss crises of faith. If it's a crisis of sex we're tongue-tied as well. Sex is unmentionable in itself. Besides which, we're not supposed to know anything about it. The guys that do know about it, and I realize now there must be some, can't admit it, and so pretend they don't. So what's the point of trying to talk about it at all?"

Though they became more and more open with each other, more and more intimate, subjects arose that they could only talk around, as if their relationship itself was too fragile to support certain thoughts, even certain words.

They talked of sex often enough, sometimes jocularly, sometimes in the abstract.

"The night we first went to bed in the Caribbean," she said once, "I did wonder about something."

"What?"

"Just a stray idea."

"What idea?"

She laughed. "I wondered if you'd still know how to do it after so long."

He laughed too. "I think it's another of those things that's like riding a bicycle. If you've done it once—"

"Like riding a bicycle, yes." They were both laughing.

"Sex is not what I was taught in school and the seminary at all," he said another time. "It's not about lust, or slaking animal desires, is it? It's a manifestation of intimacy. We're two in one body. It's us against the world."

"My, my, you are thinking deep thoughts." But she wondered if he was trying to justify what they had together.

"My son seems to think my life is over," she said. "I should just accept it."

"He's how old, 22. At that age one doesn't know much. And I find you ravishing."

"Your opinion doesn't count."

They were in the bathroom. She stood in front of the mirror arranging her hair, primping this way and that. He stood behind her, watching her breasts move as she manipulated the comb.

"Monsignor Connolly asked if you were still giving me instruction."

"When was this?"

"Yesterday. I was just leaving work."

"What did you tell him?"

"I told him yes. Instruction in how to love being loved."

He put his arms around her, his hands over her abdomen. "You didn't."

"No, but I wanted to."

Her diaphragm in its plastic case lay on the shelf and he reached past her and picked it up.

He said: "You had this with you in the Caribbean too."

"Yes."

"Why?"

"I thought I might meet someone. I didn't think the one I would meet would be you."

"Why did you want to meet someone?"

"Perhaps to prove that I was still a woman, my sex life wasn't over just because my husband was dead. Don't look so surprised."

"I'm not surprised."

"Yes you are. I didn't invite you down for that," she said. "Perhaps it was what I hoped would happen, if I could get you to come down, I don't know. Women have urges too, you know. Less than men maybe, but they're there." She took the case from him, and studied it a moment. "If I had had one of these in college we might have got married after graduation. We might have been happy together all these years."

"We might have fought like cats and dogs."

"We might have twenty-five kids by now, too. You Catholics."

"You'd have banished me to the cellar long before. You'd have furnished me a room down there."

She put the case in the cabinet and closed the mirror on it.

"How many men have you been to bed with?"

"I don't think you should know."

"No, tell me."

"I don't think I will."

"Please."

"Most men would have got questions like that out of their systems long ago."

"Probably."

"Questions women only have to cope with on their honeymoons, if at all."

"Well, this is my honeymoon."

She laughed. "But not mine."

"I know," said Frank.

"Frank, don't be jealous."

"I'm not. At least I don't think I am." And then: "Do you think I'm a weirdo?"

She smiled at him. "No. A case of arrested development is all."

"So tell me."

"Why do you want to know?"

"I want to know everything about you."

"You want to know how far ahead of you I am."

"How much catching up I have to do."

"If you do any catching up at all, I'll scratch your eyes out."

"More than just Earl and me?"

She nodded. "More than just Earl and you."

"Please tell me."

"Five."

"Three others, then."

"Three others, yes."

"Who?"

"The first one was a year after you robbed me of my virginity. A year after what happened as a result. I didn't know him well. I didn't even like him particularly, but I felt I had to start again, sooner or later, and I wanted to prove to myself that I had got over you. I was scared of getting pregnant, obviously. I was tense, not ready, and he didn't bother, you know, to make me ready, and it hurt."

She fell silent.

"Another year went by before I tried again. Same thing, but it was a little better. Then came Earl."

"That's four. You missed one."

"You mean, did I cheat on Earl?"

"Did you?"

"Yes. Another crummy motel. I'm an expert on crummy motels, starting with you. Except that I loved it with you."

"Why did you do it?"

"Because I felt Earl didn't love me, and I wondered if it was my fault. If anybody could love me. Maybe I wasn't lovable." She paused. "I don't think Earl was capable of loving a woman. Not really. After the upbringing he had, it's not so surprising, I guess."

Frank was silent.

"What Earl loved was being a prosecutor. I don't mean he loved putting people in jail. There was no meanness in him. He was after truth. Truth was his goddess, not me. Gabe and Andy are truth seekers too. Not to mention you. You Fordham boys had a thing about truth, didn't you?"

"Not just truth."

"Earl wasn't religious at all. Didn't believe in any of that anymore, if he ever did. But he hung on to all the high principles. Justice, honor, duty."

"High principles of all kinds."

"Most of which don't work in the real world. Don't mock me. I'm serious."

"I don't mean to mock you."

"They brainwashed you there."

"Yes, perhaps they did." After a moment, watching her in the mirror, he said: "If you didn't love Earl, why did you stay married to him so long?"

"Because what I really wanted was you, whom I knew I couldn't have. And Earl was as good as anyone else. Better, in fact. With Earl you would still be in my life, a little. And I did love him in a way. He was a completely honorable man. Like certain of his friends."

She turned in his arms. "Your eyebrows are getting all tufty, do you know that?" She smoothed them with her finger.

He said: "You were unfaithful to him only the once?"

"No, twice. I felt awful after the first time. I felt like I'd been raped, and I thought, the guy deserved another chance, and I deserved another chance. Maybe it would be better the next time. It wasn't better, it was worse." She laughed. "After that I couldn't get rid of him. He kept calling me up while Earl was at work. I kept refusing him. It took forever before he stopped."

She put a bathrobe on, stepped into slippers. She smiled at Frank. "You must be a very good listener. I never thought I would talk to you about all this stuff." Then she said: "What about you? What's your sexual experience been besides me?"

"There's you — and you — and you."

"Aren't you curious about what another woman would be like?"

He embraced her, and for once was completely serious. "No. You're the only woman I've ever wanted to make love to, or ever will want to make love to."

"Don't say that. Life is long."

SHE PUT HER HOUSE ON THE MARKET. For two months people trooped through her rooms before she got any offer at all. And the one she finally got was low. It was for so much less than she had hoped that once she would have paid off her mortgage and her closing costs there would be almost nothing left. But because selling it would end the financial drain the house had come to represent, she was afraid to reject the offer. She had to get rid of the house. After a week in which no other offers came in, she accepted.

Frank helped her find a small apartment in the Inwood section of Manhattan, in the same building, as it happened, in which Andy Troy had grown up. This building was much older now, had been allowed to run down, and the neighborhood had been invaded by Hispanics and other poor immigrants, making the rent relatively low.

Her children came to the house in Yonkers to separate out what they wanted. They went through the attic, through trunks stored in the cellar, through the closets of their old rooms, and in so doing rediscovered their cribs and playpens, their baby clothes that Rocky had kept, old books, old toys. An entire evening was spent going through old photo albums. Frank sat on a sofa opposite, sipping tea while the three of them, heads together, commented on this photo or that, and remembered a time he had not been part of. Frank found himself wondering about the child he and Rocky had conceived. What would it have been like? At the same time he was filled with regret for all the years of family life that he had missed.

The two children were there for days. They seemed surprised to find Father Redmond hovering around their mother. Though they had known him for years, it was obvious that he was closer to her now than he had been. But they said nothing. They ran a tag sale on the lawn out front. It was autumn now, the trees had turned feverish. They sold off for derisory sums items that were in some cases valuable but that nobody much wanted and for which there would be no room when Rocky moved. Finally they went away. A day or two later shippers came for the piles they had put to one side, and the house, afterward, seemed bare.

Monsignor Malachy had taken to waiting up for Frank nights, the way his mother used to do when he was a boy. He would come in, bound up the stairs two at a time, and find the old man pacing the upstairs hallway.

Variations of the following dialogue then ensued:

"You're up late, Monsignor."

"Just wanted to make sure you got home safely, my boy."

"Well here I am, you can go to bed now."

Or, another night:

"Is it raining out, my boy?"

"No. Why?"

"Your hair is wet."

"Is it? I combed it a while ago. Wet it down first, and combed it. Good night, Monsignor."

He would go into his room. He was always careful to lock his door when he went out, but that particular night he found it unlocked.

Had he forgotten? He stood peering around. Did the pastor have a passkey? Had he been sneaking in here, snooping? Frank could see nothing out of place, unless perhaps his phone bill, which had arrived that day, and which had been on his desk, was not placed exactly as he remembered. He resented this invasion of his privacy, if there had been an invasion, but did not believe he had left anything compromising lying around.

He resolved to set a trap for the pastor. Before leaving his room two nights later, he left papers — bills mostly — positioned just so on his pillow, on a bookshelf, and on a chair. This time he was careful to lock his door behind him, even trying the handle several times to make sure.

When he returned some hours later Monsignor Malachy was again waiting on the upstairs hallway, still wearing the soiled cassock, the red piping of which denoted his rank. This time the pastor circled around him actually sniffing, the way a jealous wife might do, trying to find the scent of the other woman clinging to his clothes. Could he actually smell woman on him? Was it there? The scent of Rocky?

"You ought to stay home more often, my boy. We could play cards together." The pastor had never made such a suggestion before.

Puzzled by the offer, trying to ponder its meaning, if any, Frank said: "What card games do you know, Monsignor."

"Maybe some kind of rummy. You tell me, my boy."

"We probably don't know the same games."

"Think about it, my boy."

"I will. Good night, Monsignor."

Frank went into his room, locked the door behind him, and saw at once that the papers he had positioned had been moved.

It threw him into a rage. In a moment he was out on the landing again. "And stay out of my room," he shouted at the pastor's back.

"Who said I was in your room?"

"You were in there going through my things, and I won't have it."

"Let me tell you something, my boy. This is my rectory, and in it I'll do what I please."

"I'll have a locksmith in here tomorrow to change the lock."

"You do that, and I'll have it changed back again."

Standoff.

At breakfast the next morning, after the second of the two daily masses, the pastor, sounding much mollified, renewed his suggestion that they play cards together in the evenings.

"I'm not interested in playing cards with you," Frank said.

All of this Frank reported to Rocky two days later, telling it lightly, trying to make her laugh. And she told it, as she told almost everything, to Maureen Troy, who, from the beginning, had promised to tell no one else.

"I don't know what he's going to do," Rocky told Maureen.

"You should have a fair idea by now," said Maureen.

"To leave the priesthood he'd have to turn his back on more than half his life. That's what he's probably thinking. That's asking a lot of any man. I can't ask him to do that for me. And how would he support himself? What kind of job could he get? His résumé is as empty as mine."

Maureen said: "I feel sorry for both of you."

"He's a good man, a sweet man. He wants to give himself to people in need, to help people in need. There are no jobs like that out in the world."

"And so," said Maureen, "you wait."

"And so I wait."

A little later Rocky said: "If he leaves the priesthood the pastor of Sacred Heart will probably fire me, and I need this job."

In fact she was fired at the end of that very week. Monsignor Connolly called her in and told her that her services were no longer required.

"May I know why?" said Rocky, her voice almost inaudible.

"I've decided to go a different route."

"I could accept less money."

"It's not the money."

"I thought you were pleased with my work."

"Your work was fine."

"Then why—"

"I'm sorry."

IT BROUGHT FATHER REDMOND, WEARING HIS CLERICAL SUIT, to Sacred Heart in a rush. He found Monsignor Connolly in the sacristy and spun him around. "You fired Mrs. Finley."

"Yes."

"Why?"

"She didn't fit in here."

"Why?"

"That's my business."

"You owe me an explanation."

Monsignor Connolly looked him up and down, then said: "She's been having an affair with a priest."

"Who told you that?"

"Someone."

"Who?" Frank demanded.

"That person's identity is private."

"Monsignor Malachy."

"I see you don't deny it."

"I don't have to confirm or deny anything to you, Leo."

"No, I don't suppose you do."

"Whatever I do or don't do is no business of yours. Remember that, Leo. None whatever."

It was late afternoon, but the vestments for tomorrow's masses were already laid out on the vesting table.

"The Chancery doesn't know yet," Connolly said. "He hasn't told them."

"He's afraid he'd look bad."

"He's not the tyrant you suppose. He wants what's best for you, Frank. He wants to save your soul."

"Afraid they wouldn't believe him, too."

"That's what I want as well," Connolly said. "To save your soul."

"Why don't you let me save my own soul?"

"I may have to tell them downtown myself."

"Why?"

"Better for you, better for me," Connolly said. "Do you think they're not going to find out?"

Father Redmond shrugged.

"They find out, I'll be accused of the cover-up. That's what did President Nixon in, not the crime but the cover-up."

"Oh, for God's sake."

"You weren't very discreet, Frank. Some neighbor, a woman I think, saw your car there all night—several nights, apparently. Made an anonymous phone call. That's what put your pastor on to you. He doesn't know who the caller was, but he was able to confirm what she told him."

Frank's fingers drummed on the vesting table.

"Straighten yourself out, Frank. That's my advice to you." And then: "Do you want me to hear your confession?"

"No, I don't want you to hear my confession. I want you to hire her back."

"Can't."

"She needs the job."

"What about what the Church needs?"

"The Church doesn't need a thing," Frank said.

"I'll tell you what the Church doesn't need. Another scandal. That's what the Church doesn't need."

"She's innocent in all this," Frank said.

"Innocent? She seduced a priest."

"How do you know who seduced whom?"

"It doesn't really matter, does it."

"As an act of Christian charity, hire her back."

"No can do, Frank."

The sacristy windows were of stained glass. The light came through in many colors. Connolly's face was green, but when he moved his head it turned blue.

"Can I ask you this, Leo? Can you at least write her a letter of recommendation?"

Monsignor Connolly shook his head.

"A good strong letter of recommendation so she can at least get another job. Leo, please."

Again Monsignor Connolly shook his head.

"She managed your school well, didn't she? You were happy to have her there, weren't you?"

"Yes. She's very competent."

"Then why not?"

"I'd be severely criticized, that's why not. I'd be defending myself for months."

"Criticized? Criticized how?"

"They would come down on me," Connolly said.

"Who? The Chancery? For writing a letter? What do you care about the Chancery?"

"Be reasonable, Frank. We work for them. Those people down there can squeeze off our blood supply if they wish."

Frank glanced a bit frantically around the sacristy.

"So how about coming to your senses, Frank."

Father Redmond started for the door.

"Don't let it go too long, Frank."

THE INVESTIGATION

———

11

MAUREEN TROY, ALONE IN HER APARTMENT, is peering into her fridge when she hears the key turn in the lock. She looks toward the front door, which she cannot see, swings the fridge closed, dries her hands on a dish towel, and waits. In a moment her husband comes into the kitchen.

They stand looking at each other. Then Maureen says: "Well, well. Your name's Andrew Troy I believe. To what do I owe this honor?"

"Lay off, Maureen. It's been an extremely dispiriting day."

"And so you've come home so that I can have the privilege of cooking your dinner."

"I thought I'd take you out to a restaurant."

"For some reason you don't want to be alone."

"I don't want to be alone."

"It must be really bad, whatever it is."

"Please, Maureen."

"Give me a moment and I'll conjure up some tears."

"Gabe and I—our investigation seems to have hit a stone wall. Several stone walls."

"What investigation?"

"Frank Redmond."

"Frank?"

"Did he jump, was he pushed?"

"What happened was quite obvious, I would have thought."

But Troy ignores this statement. It is as if he didn't hear it. He never listens to me, Maureen tells herself. He never asks himself what I might be trying to say.

"There's another possibility we never really thought of until now," Troy says. "Maybe he stood too close to the edge of that roof and fell off. He wasn't afraid of heights. He proved that to me when he jumped off Victoria Falls. If he got dizzy and fell, there's no way to check that out. If that's what happened we'll never know."

Maureen studies her husband, this tall, gangling man who stands in her kitchen looking troubled. She watches Troy take off his raincoat, his hat.

"Cut-and-dried," she says.

"Gabe is investigating the possible criminal aspects. He's got nothing. There's no evidence of foul play whatever. I've been looking into Frank's personal life. I've got a few unexplained facts, but otherwise I've got nothing either. But I can't believe such a man, a priest, would do away with himself."

"You've been asking the wrong people—"

"The bishop wouldn't talk to Gabe. The pastor wouldn't talk to either of us. Both of them are hiding something, but we can't get at it, whatever it is."

"—and looking in the wrong place."

"There was something going on in his life. I'm not sure it's pertinent. In any case, we can't seem to find out what it was."

"If I'm being taken out to dinner, I should change my clothes."

"Sure."

"I'm glad you agree with me on something."

She goes into their bedroom and begins pulling dresses out of her closet. There is a full-length mirror on the back of the door, and she stands in front of it holding hangars against herself, one after the other.

Troy has followed her in. He sits down heavily on the bed. "Frankie was seeing a psychiatrist."

"I'm not surprised."

"Well I was. I found it extremely hard to believe."

"Perhaps you didn't know him as well as you thought you did."

"The psychiatrist wouldn't talk to me either."

"Would you have listened if he did? You certainly don't listen to me when I talk to you."

"The pastor even suggested that he had a woman or women on the side. Frank with a girlfriend? I find that preposterous."

"If you would listen to me sometime, you'd be surprised at the things you might learn."

"What are you trying to tell me?"

"Ah, now he's interested. The pastor was right. He did have a girl-friend."

"What are you saying?"

"That there was a woman in his life."

"You mean in a sexual way?"

"What other way is important?"

"How do you know?"

"Because I spent a lot of time with both of them these last few months."

"Why didn't you tell me?"

"I didn't know you were investigating anything."

"Even so, you should have told me. He was my best friend."

"I didn't think you needed to know. Also Frank didn't want you to know, or he'd have told you himself. Your continuing admiration was important to him for some reason."

Andy's voice has become heavy. "Do I know the woman?"

"Yes, quite well."

"Who?"

"Roxanne Finley."

"Earl's wife?"

"Earl's widow."

"Frank was a priest. He was the most dedicated priest I've ever known."

"Yes," Maureen says. "So?"

There is a phone on the beside table. Troy reaches for it, and dials a number.

"Gabe?" he says into the phone. "You better get over here right away."

CHAPTER ELEVEN

ROCKY REGISTERED AGAIN WITH EMPLOYMENT AGENCIES. She sat again in crowded anterooms waiting to be interviewed by assistant personnel directors. Every morning she went out early to buy the papers, swept them open on the kitchen table, and found and scanned the classifieds. Ignoring most of them, she circled others in Magic Marker, then got on the phone and began dialing numbers.

Nothing.

She called on the new district attorney. She had known him vaguely in the past. He had inherited the party nomination after Earl's death, and he pretended now to be glad to see her. But he could not hire her at this time much as he wished to, he said, because the city was running in the red and there was a job freeze. But he would keep her in mind if the job freeze ever ended.

She telephoned former colleagues of Earl, now in private practice. Most were cordial, and she went to see them. These were trial lawyers. They had been prosecutors, but now defended the same thieves, gangsters, wife beaters, murderers that, in a former life, they had put in jail. Most ran one-man offices. Behind them stood no part of the corporate establishment. For most of them their profession was less lucrative than people sometimes supposed. Hiring an extra body, Earl's widow or anyone else, was out of the question. They could not afford it.

While waiting—hoping—for something better to turn up she took a job in a bookstore for one dollar an hour above minimum wage. It was something. It was not much. It was not enough.

Frank borrowed a truck from a parishioner, prevailed on two strapping altar boys to help, and they moved her out of her house and into her new apartment, where Rocky served them all a picnic lunch using cardboard boxes for a table.

"What do I have to offer an employer?" she said to Frank when the boys had gone. She and Frank had taken a break. They were drinking lukewarm beer out of the bottles. At least half the boxes were still unopened. None of the pictures had been hung. "I've raised two children, and washed my husband's laundry for over twenty years. They don't give points for that."

On the sideboard behind her rested a pile of bills which Frank picked up.

"I'll pay those," she said with a wry smile. "One by one I'll pay them."

Frank put them in his pocket.

"Frank, you are not responsible for me."

He said: "But I want to be. Pay me back when you come into your fortune."

"You've got no money either."

"Well," he said, "I've got more than you." And then: "I'm leaving the priesthood."

This shocked her. "No, Frank, don't."

"I want to marry you."

"We're married already."

"I want us to be really married."

She put her beer down and walked to the window, then turned and, to his surprise, refused him. "I don't want to get married, Frank."

"You don't—"

"No."

"I don't understand."

"Not right now."

He looked away.

"I think we should wait."

"Wait how long?"

"Wait three months. In three months, if you still want to, I'll marry you."

"But why?" he said.

She gave no reasons, though she had some that so far she had disclosed to no one.

"Just tell me why."

"Because it's the right thing to do," she said.

"Three months?"

She nodded.

"It's going to be a long three months."

"And during those three months you won't quit the priesthood either."

He argued with her until his voice seemed to lose all force, but she was adamant. She was afraid she had crushed him. He certainly sounded crushed.

"Is it a deal?" she said at the end.

Glumly, he nodded.

THE INVESTIGATION

12

"ABOUT THREE MONTHS BEFORE THAT, MAYBE LONGER," Maureen continues, "Frank discovered a lump in her breast. Women themselves don't pay much attention to their breasts. I don't know if you know that. Left breast, I think it was. It's always the husbands who discover these things."

"He wasn't her husband," Gabe says.

She looks at him. Though he pretends to be such a tough, tough cop, Gabe is having trouble imagining a priest, particularly this priest, palping the breast of a naked or half-naked woman. Maureen sees this. Her husband says nothing, but from his face his reaction is the same. They are trying to reshape their image of this friend whom they have so admired over the years. No one likes to change idols, as they are being forced to do. Neither believes in the Catholic Church anymore, but old instincts die hard. Vows are vows. Frank's conduct, though normal in any other man, is to them an aberration. Stroking a female breast is a great sin. It is not allowed.

They are in Troy and Maureen's living room, whose windows look out over Central Park. The lights have come on in the streets, and in the park as well, but no one is admiring the view. Maureen leans against the windowsill, Gabe is pacing, and Andy mixes drinks at the bar hidden in the false bookcase in the corner.

Maureen says: "Frank didn't remember noticing this lump before, and suggested that perhaps she should have it looked at. She told him not to worry, women's breasts always have lumps in them. Which is pretty much true, by the way. And for a long time she did nothing. But the lump, at first the size of a pea, got bigger, harder. She realized she was often tired. She became worried about herself. This was one of the reasons she became anxious to sell her house. It cost too much to run, and she saw she might have medical bills to pay. If so, she would need whatever money the house would bring in. Earl's small insurance policy was nearly gone. His small pension wouldn't keep her. The house was pretty much all she had.

"Finally she went to someone. So now it was the doctor who felt her breast. She took off her sweater and bra and he looked at it, and then he felt it. Is that all right with you two?"

"Never mind the sarcasm, Maureen," says Andy. He hands her a drink, and she sips it.

"He didn't like what he felt. He made her come to the hospital where he had some scans made. She was there for hours, most of it waiting around while other patients came and went. At the end of the day he stuck Novocain in her breast, then made an incision and took out enough tissue for a biopsy. He also engaged her in the first of what were evidently some horrible conversations. He told her that just from the size and hardness of the tumor he suspected the worst. He explained the various prognoses, from not so bad to medium bad to very bad—leaning on the last, apparently. She would almost certainly lose her breast. She could be dead in six months."

"Nice doctor," says Andy.

"He told her he would call her up with the lab results the following day. She left him scared, but she was already in denial, and she got over being scared before she got home. She convinced herself the lump was not even malignant. And she told no one."

"Not even you, Maureen?"

"Now who's being sarcastic?"

Gabe says: "Go on, Maureen."

"So she's standing in the kitchen of her new apartment with a Band-Aid on the side of her breast that she has already shown Frank, saying she's sure it's nothing, no, don't touch, it's a bit sore. And now Frank asks her to marry him. Her answer is to make him agree to wait three months, and not to quit the priesthood in the meantime. She was cheerful, he suspected nothing, but she was also being realistic. She could die. If he quit the priesthood for her, and then she died, he'd be left with nothing. She couldn't do this to him. She was thinking of him not herself.

"So that's what the three months was about.

"She listened for the phone for a week. It didn't ring. Finally the doctor got around to calling her. Instead of giving the results of the biopsy he asked her to come in. He sounded very grave, so she knew the worst without being told. It made her truly scared, and she asked me to come with her to get the bad news.

"We sit in the waiting room a long time. At last we go in. The doctor tells me I have to wait outside. He was a tall man with rimless glasses and white hair, and he exuded superiority, as most of them do. He shows me to the door. He's got the door open, he's bowing me out, when Rocky says in this cold, hard voice: 'Let's get one thing clear, Doctor. I'm the boss here, not you. You work for me, I don't work for you. You're in my employ, and you will do what I say. My friend stays, or else we both go. You decide.'

"Well, I don't know when anyone last talked to him like that. There's a minute of stunned silence, and then he gives a slight nod, closes the door, goes back behind his desk, and begins reading the verdict—the lab report. Would he have been kinder if Rocky hadn't got so feisty with him? I don't know. The tumor in her breast measured almost two centimeters, he said, and under the microscope the cells were actively dividing. In fact he did not know when he had last seen such a virulent cancer. Furthermore, some of the cells had spread to the liver and the bones of her neck, according to the scans. Tests already performed on the cancer showed that certain drugs — he named them, but the names meant nothing to me — had had no effect on the cells whatever. Certain others might work for a time, we would have to see. She was in for a long bout of chemotherapy.

"Rocky was shocked and biting down on her lip, but all she said was: 'Will I lose my hair?'

"He answers: 'That's the least of your problems, Madam.'

"She might be able to function normally for a greater or lesser amount of time, he told her, but more than half the patients with her form of cancer were dead in under two years, some of them in under six months. There was no point in removing her breast, it was too late for that.

"He began asking her if she had a living will, did she want at the end to be on respirators and oxygen to not much purpose? I wanted to step up to the desk and punch him, but I glanced over at Rocky, whose face was ghastly, and I could not move.

"I got her away from there. We found a tearoom and ordered tea and sat opposite each other and didn't say a word, Rocky blinking back tears almost the whole time. We must have stayed there an hour, during which she only spoke twice. The first time, she said: 'I don't know how I'm going to pay for the treatment.' Because she had no health insurance — it ended when Earl was killed — and she had got very little for her house.

"Another twenty minutes passed. Then she said: 'Don't tell Frank. He'll be devastated, because he really likes me. Please don't tell Frank.'

"'You have to tell him sometime.'

"'I'll tell him. But every day that he doesn't know is a day he doesn't have to suffer.'

"And in fact she didn't tell him until her hair started to fall out."

Maureen looks at the three glasses, then goes into the kitchen. When she comes back she sets two bowls down on the coffee table. One contains pretzels, the other salted almonds.

"The first thing Frank did," she continues, "was get her out from under that doctor. Frank knew a lot of doctors, most of whom he had met when they were interns working the emergency rooms at Harlem Hospital or St. Luke's, cutting bullets out of his parishioners. One of them was now an oncologist at Sloan-Kettering, which is probably the best cancer hospital in New York. His name was Kessler. He and Frank had a personal relationship. They had had dinner together a few times. Kessler, who is Jewish, was curious to know why a normal man like Frank would become a priest.

"Frank went to him and persuaded him to send for Rocky's records, and take over the case. Kessler struck me as a kind, kind man. He was as kind as could be to Rocky, and as gentle. He told her he was obliged to confirm the other doctor's diagnosis, and the prognosis was not great, but that all was not hopeless. There were other kinds of drugs they would try. The cancer might go into remission. Some patients lasted years. In that time new drugs might be discovered that could actually cure her.

"Sometimes when she went for the chemotherapy I went with her. It was a big room with fifteen or twenty patients there, all with needles in their arms, and an IV stand beside the chair. The men wore hats, the women kerchiefs. You would have thought you were at a convention of Orthodox Jews. Some looked almost normal, although hairless, and they watched television while the drugs dripped into them. Some were as gaunt as Auschwitz survivors; they reclined in chairs and apparently were too weak to sit up, and it was clear they would die soon. And others were hidden behind curtains — you didn't want to look behind those curtains.

"Every two weeks Rocky went through this.

"At first she got a little better. She was able to work part-time in the bookstore, and she and Frank sometimes went to restaurants or the movies. He kept telling her that the three months were almost up, and he meant to hold her to her promise. But when he was alone with me and would talk about her, his eyes would fill up. He knew it was hopeless, and he kept saying, 'Why her and not me? I'm the one who sinned here, if anyone did, not her.'

"He said this and I heard him, and I didn't know what to answer, so I didn't say anything."

Gabe is still pacing. Each time he passes the coffee table he reaches down for a pretzel which he eats, almost certainly not tasting it. He is not drinking. His glass, barely touched, stands on the table.

"After about two months Dr. Kessler, who has been examining Rocky regularly, notices that one of her eyes is wandering, and she now carries her head tilted to one side, as if it is too heavy for her neck. He asks about her vision. Any trouble reading? 'My eyes seem to get tired easily,' answers Rocky with a smile, 'how did you know?'

"'Any double vision?' asks Dr. Kessler. Rocky answers yes, occasionally, especially coming down stairs.

"This probably meant that the cancer had spread to her brain, and was attacking the nerves at the base of the skull that control eye movement. Dr. Kessler ordered an MRI scan, but it showed nothing. Rocky was elated. You should have seen her. She was dancing around. She wanted to dance out the door, but Dr. Kessler said they should probably do a spinal tap, just to make sure. If the cancer had spread to the brain, the cells would show in the spinal fluid.

"So she lay on her side on a table and Kessler shoved an instrument, I think it's called a trocar, between two of her vertebrae. It made Rocky twitch, which was a scary thing to see. I stood to one side of the table, and Frank to the other holding her hand. Drops of fluid dripped out, and Kessler collected them in a test tube. He held the test tube up to the light and gave a grimace. The fluid was cloudy. Later I learned it was supposed to be clear. Rocky had to lie on the table for an hour so as not to get a headache. Before the hour was up Dr. Kessler was back. 'It's a major setback,' he told her.

"Rocky began to cry. 'I don't want to die,' she said.

"But by the time she sat in his office she had composed herself. She wanted to know how long she could live with the cancer having spread to her brain. Kessler said several weeks was the average, but some patients lived longer. He said that the essential thing was to preserve her quality of life as long as possible.

"She began new treatments with the chemo now being infused into her spinal fluid. After a few weeks she couldn't move her right eye, and she began wearing a patch over it. Then the muscles on that side of her face seemed to give way. All the flesh sagged downward. Kessler ran some more scans. They showed that the cancer had spread to the membranes lining the cortex and the spinal cord.

"By now Rocky was in the hospital. I went to see her nearly every day. What else did I have to do, my husband was never home." She glances at him across the room. He takes a sip of his drink, eyes her, and does not reply.

"She was very weak. She had an eye patch, a sagging face, and no hair, but she was always trying to smile and be cheerful, especially toward Frank, who sat beside the bed day after day, holding her hand. I don't know how he got out of whatever parish duties he had. He wore the clerical suit at all times because this gave him free run of the hospital even after visiting hours. I got chased out many days, but Frank never was.

"Rocky was very worried about money. Her treatment was costing thousands and thousands of dollars, and how was she ever going to pay for it? Frank would tell her, hush, he had found sources of money, he was paying the bills, she needn't worry about money anymore.

"She began to drift in and out of consciousness. She would come to and say something. 'Frank, you're crying,' I heard her say once. 'No I'm not,' he said.

"'What have they told you they haven't told me?'

"'Not a thing.'

"'I'm sure it's nothing I haven't figured out for myself.'

"Then she drifted off again.

"Another time she came out of it for a moment and said: 'See you in heaven.'

"'In heaven, yes.'

"She gave a kind of laugh. 'I don't believe in that heaven. I've already seen you in the heaven I believe in. I've seen you here. We had heaven right here. It didn't last too long, but we had it. Most people have never had it.'

"Sometimes when I would come into the room he would go out for fresh air. He would walk around the block. He was never gone more than ten minutes.

"The oxygen made her mouth swell up and soon she could hardly talk. She was now on regular infusions of morphine, but it didn't always help. Sometimes the pain got to her. She squirmed and moaned, she thrashed and bucked in the bed. Watching her suffer was agony, especially for Frank. One day it was so bad he went running out to the nurses' station demanding they give her more morphine. They said they could only do it on Dr. Kessler's orders, and he wasn't there at that time. Frank comes back into the room and begins examining the morphine drip. He was going to give her extra morphine himself, but by then she was unconscious, so he didn't.

"Her children came regularly and stayed a few days and went away again. She always rallied a bit to see them. The last time they were there she was pretty bad, but there was no telling when she would die. She might last days, even weeks, Dr. Kessler told them. He said he didn't think she was terminal, there should be plenty of time to call them back. So they left. The next day I couldn't bear to go to the hospital. Frank sat with her alone.

"That was the day she died. Frank called me and I went right over. Dr. Kessler and the nurses were in the room doing something to the body. Frank was in the hall outside. He stood in my arms crying. I've never seen a man so upset." Again she looked over at her husband. "Nobody ever loved me that much, I'll tell you that."

Andy made no reply.

"I stood out on York Avenue waiting for a cab, and here comes Frank out of the hospital, head down, walking fast. He goes down one side street and comes out the other one, and starts around the hospital a second time. It was raining. He was wearing a black hat with the water running off the brim. I kept waving at cabs but none stopped. Round and round the block Frank walks. He didn't see me. I don't think he saw anything. He was still walking when finally a cab pulled over, and I got into it."

She stops, and stares into her drink.

Gabe says: "There must have been a funeral. You didn't notify us."

"It was a small funeral, just her family and Frank and me. I didn't notify my husband because I didn't know where he was. I didn't even know what country he might be in."

"In Russia," Andy said. "You could have had the paper notify me."

"I did leave a message for you in your office," she said to Gabe. "When you didn't call back I figured you weren't interested. I know you never liked her. She knew it too."

"I never got the message. Believe me, I would have been there. When I finally heard it was too late."

There is silence for a time. Maureen's narrative is over.

Gabe's coat is draped across the back of an armchair, his hat on top. He puts them on, then goes to Maureen. "You're a good woman, Maureen," he says. "Thank you for what you did for Rocky, and for Frank." He hugs her. It is years since he has hugged her.

Andy Troy walks him down the long hall to the door. They are silent until they reach it.

"Is that it?" Troy asks with his hand on the knob. "Is our investigation over?"

"Plenty of guys," Gabe mutters, "lose their beloved wife or girlfriend and don't jump off rooftops."

"What are you saying?"

"There were three weeks between her death and his. He didn't do it the way cops do. In a moment of despair a cop puts his gun in his mouth and pulls the trigger and it's over. Frank had three weeks to think about it."

"You're not satisfied?"

"I sense there's more here than we know."

"Loose ends."

"Maybe not so loose."

"The money, for one," says Troy.

"I can think of a detail even more important. Maybe tomorrow I can tie these things up."

"I'll go with you," says Troy. "Call me when you leave the house, and I'll wait for you downstairs."

GABE'S DRIVER TURNS INTO CENTRAL PARK WHICH, during rush hour, is open to cars. Andy is in back. Gabe sits in front in the command position; the radio at his knees, the microphone clipped to the dashboard above it.

The radio is tuned to the Fourth Division band through which the car is passing. It is not Gabe's job to respond to precinct emergencies, but he will do so if one happens, and if necessary will take command until the superior officer in charge arrives to take over. He feels he owes this to cops on the scene, and to the city. He's seen too many crime scenes overrun by cops flailing around not knowing what to do.

The radio keeps squawking. He hears reports of bank alarms — tellers who forgot to disable the alarm first, most likely. A cop informs Central that a traffic light is out on Madison. Otherwise the city is quiet. Some days, even at this hour, the radio overflows.

After today Gabe will go back to being a cop on active duty, and will concentrate on his job. But today has to be got out of the way first.

The Park Drive winds north under the trees, separated from Fifth Avenue by very little, a few trees and bushes, a low wall. On the other side of the wall pass elegant hotels, and buildings with awnings with doormen out front. In the side streets stand ranks of town houses and art galleries. This is the most expensive, most chic part of New York. The city knows it as the Silk Stocking District, but to Gabe it is the One-Nine Precinct, the lowest of the low-crime precincts, though sometimes they have some ingenious burglaries in there.

The road loops around the Museum of Art. Is it the richest art museum in the world? Gabe is not immune to great art, but sees the building itself as a gigantic wart embedded in the flesh of the park. Additional display space is regularly added on in back. It grows backward like a tumor.

At 110th Street they come out of the park, and then they are in Harlem, moving up Lenox Avenue at first, and then turning into side streets, and the transition could not be more brutal. Graffiti, strewn garbage, derelict cars, run-down buildings, some of them boarded up and condemned, many, many churches of all denominations, some of them only storefronts, a number with Spanish names: Iglesia de la Salvación de Nuestro Señor.

They park in front of St. Ambrose, and get out and go inside into the gloom.

An aged man, shambling and humming, is pushing a padded broom up the nave toward the big doors. Gabe wants information, hopes he can get it without having to confront the pastor, and so identifies himself to this janitor, and shows his shield. This is a mistake, for the old man goes rigid with fear.

"I ain't done nuthin, Suh."

It takes Gabe a while to get him calmed down, but after that he proves talkative. He has been sacristan here—he gives his name and age—for over 16 years. He has white hair, a white stubble, and watery eyes. Yes, he has noticed the detectives being nosy in recent days. No, they never interviewed him.

"A case like this," mutters Gabe to Troy, "detectives are supposed to interview everybody." He gives a disgusted shake of his head.

Yes, Father Redmond was absent for some weeks, the sacristan says. "Looking after a dying relative, everybody say. When he come back, I see him many times."

"Did he seem normal to you?"

"What you mean normal? He seem same as always."

According to the old man, the Father said mass regularly after he came back, and officiated at weddings and funerals also, just like he used to.

A priest comes out of the sacristy, cassock swishing, turns up the center aisle and approaches them. He is tall, thin, and must be fresh out of the seminary for he looks about twelve years old.

"Something I can help you with?" His hand is outstretched. "Father Dan Quigley," he says.

Gabe identifies himself.

"Call me Father Dan."

Gabe says: "Andy and I are the executors of Father Redmond's will. It's the end of the month, so some fresh bills should have come in for him. I'd like to pick them up if I may."

As he leads the way out of the church and across to the rectory, Father Dan talks and talks. He was ordained in June, he says, and was immediately sent here to fill in for Father Redmond, who was at the bedside of a dying relative and was never in the rectory except at night when he would sleep four or five hours and then leave again. "His relative had cancer and she died," says Father Dan, "very sad." During the weeks after the death Father Redmond had resumed his duties: "You know what happened then."

"Yes," says Gabe, "I do."

Now Father Dan's assignment here has been made permanent. He knows nothing about the death of Father Redmond. "It's not my job to pass judgment on another priest," he says.

"I'm glad you see it that way," says Gabe.

As they go up the rectory stairs to the office, Gabe glances warily around, but the pastor is absent. "Won't be back till this afternoon," says Father Dan, adding: "He's a nice guy, isn't he? Gruff, but his bark is worse than his bite."

Gabe does not reply.

Father Dan hands over eight or ten envelopes containing bills, some opened, some not. "It was the pastor who opened them, not me," he apologizes.

Gabe eyes him.

"Father Redmond had a lockbox in the safe," the young priest adds. "It's there on the sideboard. Maybe you want to take that as well."

He presents the lockbox which has been jimmied open and is now useless.

"The monsignor did that," Father Dan apologizes. "Nothing in there but a paper." He shows it. "I don't see its significance, if any."

Gabe looks down at a list of dates and figures, then glances at Troy, who nods.

"I'll keep this too, if I may," Gabe says.

"Well—"

"One last question. Which banks does the parish do business with?"

The young priest names the Harlem branches of Citibank, and Chase Manhattan, and all three men troop down the stairs. "Are you happy to be assigned here?" Gabe asks him.

"Certainly am," Father Dan says. "This is the place to be a priest. The people need you. I expect to serve here for the next forty or fifty years. In Harlem a good priest preaching the gospel can make a real difference."

"You sound like a man of strong faith."

"Yes I am. My faith is solid."

"I hope nothing ever happens to shake it up," says Gabe.

"Oh, I don't see how that can happen."

"Good," says Gabe.

In the car he and Troy examine the papers they have come away with. "Credit card bills mostly," says Gabe. "And he hasn't been paying them. That's why we never knew about them till now. Look how much he owes."

"Seven cards," says Troy. "Every card maxed out. And that paper out of his lockbox. Are you thinking what I'm thinking?"

"Money he took from the Sunday collections."

They drive to the two banks. The parish, they learn, has a drawing account at both, to which Father Redmond had access, for it was he who signed the parish checks.

"So the bishop lied to me," mutters Gabe to himself.

"What's that?" the bank official says.

"Nothing."

Both accounts are limited to $25,000. Neither administrator will show them canceled checks signed by Frank. "You want more," one says, "you come back with a warrant."

"So how much is left in the church's drawing account?" Gabe asks.

The administrator does not answer.

"Never mind," says Gabe, "I can guess."

They drive to Sloan-Kettering where, after a considerable search, they are directed to a nurses' station on the fifth floor, and to a woman named Miss Anderson. She is a tall blond, about 45 years old. It is she who was on duty on Roxanne Finley's floor the day she died. She says she went into Mrs. Finley's room and found her dead, the priest sitting beside the bed. "Around his neck he had this purple thing they wear, and he was reading from a prayer book."

"It's a vestment called a stole," Gabe says. "Priests carry them in their pockets. Probably he was saying the prayers for the dead over her. You're not Catholic, I guess."

"Methodist. The Father had taken all the needles out of her arms, had arranged the kerchief on her head, had crossed her arms on her breast. He had removed her eye patch, even. He had arranged the pillow and the sheets. She looked real peaceful. He looked a wreck though. You would have thought she was his wife."

"No," said Gabe.

"I liked her a lot. She was always trying not to be a bother, even in the middle of the night when she was alone and sometimes in a lot of pain."

The machines in the patients' rooms—the respirators, oxygen, the different infusions—are monitored from the nurses' station. Miss Anderson shows them the monitors. If one of the machines breaks down, or goes empty, the monitors cause an alarm to sound, and the nurses go running. "What puzzles me," Miss Anderson says, "is how he got all those needles out of her arms without setting off the alarms."

"How should I know," says Gabe, and he asks her to page Dr. Kessler.

About ten minutes later, dressed in white and wearing rubber-soled shoes, Kessler approaches down the corridor, saying: "Is there someone here to see me?"

Gabe asks him a number of questions, which he answers. "I'm really very busy," he says, and starts to edge away.

"Just one or two more points, Doctor."

"All right, but please be quick."

"You told everybody she was not terminal, Doctor, yet the next day she was dead. How do you explain that?"

"We're not God, you know."

"Still, you must have asked yourself why."

"No."

"The morphine drip, what kind of setup was it? She could control it to some extent, I believe."

"She had a panel under her hand. The buttons did various things. She could call the nurse, for instance. Or if the pain got too much for her, she could call for an extra dose of morphine."

"Could she give herself an overdose?"

"Absolutely not. There is a control to prevent that. Otherwise patients would be killing themselves by accident all the time."

"Was there a way to override that control?"

"Not by the patient, certainly."

"But Father Redmond could have done it, couldn't he?"

Dr. Kessler does not answer.

"Did he do it, Doctor, override the safety mechanism and send an overdose into her veins?"

"That's outrageous. Outrageous."

"Did he kill her, Doctor?"

"If you had seen the way that man suffered you wouldn't even ask such a question." He turns and, shoes squeaking, strides away down the hallway.

Andy says: "He didn't answer you."

"I don't think he had to, do you?"

AN HOUR LATER GABE AND ANDY STAND ON THE ROOFTOP on 146th Street. It is a sunny, windy afternoon. The wind sometimes whistles in the TV antennas all around. The view is the same as it has always been, the low rooftops of Harlem, the skyscrapers far to the south, and to the north the city extending farther than the eye can see.

"Why are we up here, Gabe? I mean, it hasn't changed since the last time."

Gabe looks at him. "I'm trying to imagine Frankie during the last minutes of his life. How this rooftop looked to him. How he looked to himself."

"What his thoughts were."

"He had vowed as a priest to remain celibate his entire life. He had broken this vow, which had been sacred to him, sacred to the Church as well. Also he had stolen the Church's money."

"The fact that he kept track of what he took means that he intended to pay it back."

"And the credit cards. How much are we talking about here?"

"In all? Close to $100,000, it looked like. Chemo drugs are expensive. Hospitals are expensive."

"He had no way ever to pay it back."

"Perhaps not."

"Which he knew. That makes him a thief. He's also a murderer, because when he couldn't bear for Rocky to suffer any longer, he sent all that morphine into her veins, and killed her."

"We don't know that."

"No, but it's highly probable."

They stand on the roof looking more at their shoes than at each other, and for a time neither speaks.

"He was lost," says Gabe. "He was no longer playing a defined role."

"You have to say the words as written or the play falls apart."

Both of them are silent.

"What's the strongest force in nature?" asks Andy.

"You tell me."

"Grief is one of them."

"And love of course."

Again they are silent.

"He was only in the air about a second and a half," says Andy.

"Not a bad way to go, I suppose."

"Don't get cynical, Gabe. This is still Frankie you're talking about."

After a moment Gabe says: "The way I see it, he stood at the edge of this roof and looked at himself. Perhaps he remembered what all of us were taught growing up. He asked himself how he had got from there to here and it made him dizzy, it made him crazy, and he fell or jumped to his death."

"For the first time in his adult life," Andy says, "he had allowed himself to love and be loved, and it killed him."

"The strongest ones don't bend," says Gabe, "they break."

There is another long pause. "Good-bye, Frankie," Gabe says.

"Good-bye, Frankie," echoes Andy.

Gabe says: "I'll tell the detectives to close the case."